CHAOS REMAINS

GREENSTONE SECURITY #4

ANNE MALCOM

To my #sisterqueen, Jessica Gadziala. For everything you do. Everything you are. And for reading this book and not hating it.

Copyright © 2019 by Anne Malcom

All rights reserved.

No part of this book may be reproduced in any form or by any electronic or mechanical means, including information storage and retrieval systems, without written permission from the author, except for the use of brief quotations in a book review.

CHAPTER ONE

I'M NOT a person who panics.

Not when I found my father after he'd overdosed when I was seven years old. I calmly called 911 and followed their instructions until an ambulance arrived.

Not on my wedding day when a hurricane ruined our ceremony on the beach.

Not when my water broke in the middle of an important event for my father-in-law and I had to grit my teeth and wait for him to finish his speech before I was taken to the hospital.

Not even when my husband hit me for the first time.

Or the second.

And especially not when I finally found my backbone underneath fractured ribs and escaped the beautiful house that had become my prison, with my two-year-old and not much else.

But now, I was panicking.

I was speeding.

Veering in and out of traffic.

Scrolling frantically through my phone while simultaneously glancing up at the road.

Never would I be on my phone and drive. *Never*. Because I usually had my son in the car. His safety was everything to me and I wouldn't dream of risking it that way.

But my son wasn't in the car.

Which was why I was panicking.

Because my abusive, soon-to-be-ex-husband, also detective and son of a senator, kidnapped my son.

And I didn't know where he was.

I didn't know where my son was.

A fist fastened around my lungs, air coming strangled, in short, quick bursts.

At the same time, a location popped up on my phone and I veered across three lanes of traffic at the last minute to get to my exit.

I prayed that I didn't get pulled over as I sped through the streets of LA. Most people would have been happy to see the flashing blue and red lights behind them after their son was kidnapped by his abusive father. I was not most people in this situation.

And the police had proved to be worth less than nothing.

"So you don't have primary custody of your son, ma'am," the officer said, looking bored, and hardened to my distress.

The police in the precinct had originally been concerned and responsive when I rushed in there to inform them that my son had been kidnapped. That was until they found out he was kidnapped by his father. No, that was after they found out who his father was.

Their demeanor immediately changed then.

Much like the officers had in our old hometown when I went in to report the abuse.

Robert had power.

No, that wasn't quite right.

Robert's name *had power.*

Police generally protected their own. I already had that against me. But when one of their own was the son of a state senator who could end their careers with one phone call?

That was something entirely different.

With me, broken and brutalized, it sucked but I understood it. Because I'd had countless lessons of how hard, cruel, and unfair the world was. I didn't grow up with the illusion that life was full of justice for those who wronged others. I knew all about the ugly truths.

I had been frustrated but resigned when they turned me away after I finally found enough courage to report what had been then, years of abuse. I was resigned to the fact the police wouldn't help me, and, like always, I'd have to help myself. My son.

And I did.

But this was different.

This was a child.

My child.

Pure.

Beautiful.

Helpless.

And still, the officer was looking at me with that bored, hardened expression.

"I have full custody," I gritted out, my nails digging into my palms as I tried to stay calm. How does anyone stay calm when they didn't know where their baby was?

"Given to you by the courts?" he asked.

Tears prickled the backs of my eyes, I didn't let them fall. Not just because I wasn't sure I'd be able to stop them if I did, but because I wouldn't give this man that. This horrible man that was clutching onto a distorted version of brotherhood at the expense of a child.

"No," I said, my voice shaky but strong. "Up until today, his father had no interest in even fighting for custody. He has not been in his life in three years."

I wish I could say he had not been in my life for as long, but his visit yesterday made that impossible. I should have known that something would happen after. That he wouldn't just leave me alone.

The officer glanced at me without sympathy. "A father has a right to see his child, ma'am. And if he hasn't got a court document barring him from contact, he is within his rights to pick him up from school."

"He didn't *just* pick him up from school," I hissed. "He took him. Not because he is a father. Because he is a monster. He wanted to hurt me. He is a violent man. A dangerous one. I don't give a damn about the fact he has a badge just as shiny as yours, and you shouldn't either. Not when a little boy is in danger."

Something moved in his face at my tone. Something human, maybe. "You have evidence of this violence?"

I merely stared at him, the tightness of my eye speaking for itself.

He shifted uncomfortably. "Did you report any assaults?"

I gritted my teeth. "I tried. When we were married. Back in Virginia. I got all but laughed out of the precinct. I'm not here to report an assault. I'm here to report a kidnapping."

His face moved again. He glanced to his computer. "I can make some calls. Do a house call at his father's address. Check in on your son. But I cannot arrest your husband for taking his son when he was within his rights."

"Ex-husband," I corrected, hanging by a thread.

"You're divorced?"

I wanted to sink into my seat with defeat. With pain. But I couldn't admit defeat. If it were just me, I would have a long time ago. But I would never stop fighting for my son. "No. Not legally. He wouldn't sign the papers. We've been separated for three years."

"So you're still legally married?"

It was then, right then, that I realized that no one would help me get my son back. No one wearing a uniform at least.

So that's what had me in my car speeding toward the city, googling people without uniforms and with some kind of power.

Which had me landing on Greenstone Security's website and plugging their location into my GPS.

I DIDN'T TAKE note of my surroundings as I rushed into the building.

I wasn't even sure if I'd locked my car. My keys might have still been in the ignition.

I didn't care.

It was just a car.

A car that I couldn't afford despite it being a piece of junk and a car I needed to drive Nathan to school. But I wouldn't need to drive Nathan to school if this didn't work. That was what had me bypassing the thoughts of my car getting stolen, getting trapped in LA with only a handful of cash in my purse and a near destitute bank account.

I rushed into the cool foyer, it smelled pleasant, clean, calm. It might have been calm. If I wasn't on the verge of a mental breakdown.

But I couldn't break.

No.

Not now. Not when my son needed me.

"I need to talk to a private investigator, now," I said to the woman behind the desk.

Well, more like shouted at the woman across the desk.

I never shouted at people.

Especially strangers.

Especially strangers with kind eyes.

But this wasn't me.

This was mother without a child.

"Do you have an appointment?" the woman asked, face carefully blank and not reacting to the disheveled, sweaty woman shouting at her in her nice office.

"No, but it's urgent. I really need to see someone *now*," I said, my voice slightly less than a yell now, but still not an appropriate tone for this nice, calm office.

She gave me a kind look. "We are fully booked up right now, but I can refer you to a reputable office—"

I pushed the sunglasses atop my head that I forgot I was wearing just at the same time something moved in the corner of my eye. I didn't take notice.

"Please," I whispered. "I don't have time to drive somewhere else, find someone else. I need someone *now*." I paused, my hand shaking as I placed it on the clean black desk. "I need help." My voice cracked at the end and I was so ashamed at the weakness of it.

I was ashamed. But I wasn't above using that weakness, preying on other people's sympathy or pity in order to get them to help me. I wasn't above anything in trying to get my son back.

The woman gave me both pity and sympathy in seeing my bruised face now my sunglasses weren't covering it. There was something a lot more human on her face than on the police officer's earlier today. But there was also something else, a cold professionalism that I guessed someone who worked at a place like this might have to employ to insulate herself against the violence of the world.

I sighed and waited for the rejection.

It was then the shadow at the side of my vision that I hadn't been paying attention to became actualized.

"Boyfriend do that?" a gruff voice demanded with no warm

sympathy or pity, just hostility that sounded like it was permanent.

The voice did something to my already frayed nerves, exposed to the root. It flayed them. Turning fully to focus on the owner of the voice that did more than fray my nerves.

It shattered them.

Because the man in front of me had an aggression to his face, to his aura that was so much more violent and saturating that had been in his voice.

Robert had hated that. The fact I felt people's auras. That I believed in phases of the moon, in burning sage, in crystals bring positive energy, that I had a tarot deck and studied astronomy.

He hadn't let me display any of it at our old house. Forbidden me to talk about it in 'company' as if we were the type of people to have 'company'. That was his father, he threw the fancy dinner parties, benefits, galas. And I had to attend all of those in pre-approved outfits with conversation plans.

Small talk that did not involve auras.

Needless to say, the small house that we'd been living in for the past three years was full of crystals, dream catchers, astronomy charts, incense, books on the art of divination.

I didn't believe in magic, exactly, but I believed in auras, energies. I believed I was sensitive to some. Obtuse or blind to others, of course, otherwise I never would have married Robert.

But this man in front of me. I wasn't blind to him. I was blinded *by* him. Darkness, menace seemed to cover me just by proximity.

I stepped back slightly out of instinct. His eyes followed my retreat blankly then went back up to where the bruise on my face masked a lot of my features. I might have imagined the small change into a glint that wasn't just blank.

"No," I said, my voice a rasp. I cleared my throat. "My husband did it." I paused, thinking of the way the officer at the precinct told me that we were still married, legally. He still had rights as a husband and a father. "Ex-husband," I corrected. I didn't give a shit what the law said.

He had no rights.

He had no rights to come to our home, the shabby, but safe and cozy place I'd created for my son and I. The home that I'd made after leaving Robert with nothing but a small bag for me and Nathan and two hundred and fifty dollars in a secret checking account. I drove us as far away as I could, to the other side of the country, to be exact. I'd had to sell the fancy car I'd driven away with, and because the title wasn't in my name, I had to sell it at a less than reputable establishment for significantly less than what it was worth.

But it didn't matter.

It was enough to get me and Nathan the rest of the way to California, set us up in a house in a little town just outside LA.

I didn't have family to support me.

No friends.

I was alone.

And terrified.

But I'd made it.

For the first year, I'd lain awake at night, clutching my sleeping baby, staring at a watermarked ceiling, body taut, waiting for the sound. Waiting for the bang on the door, or the breaking of a window to signify that Robert had found us.

But he never did.

I didn't wonder if it was because he just didn't care to look or he was a really shitty detective.

The specifics of it all hadn't mattered. All that had mattered was that we were free. My son was safe. I was fed. I got a job at a café, found a decent daycare, made ends meet, barely, but I did it.

And last night, when I wasn't expecting it, when I was at

home cleaning, happy, enjoying rare free time while Nathan was at a playdate, he came.

As if he sensed that happiness.

That peace.

And he tore right through it.

I answered the door smiling because I thought it was Marie bringing Nathan home early.

"The spawn set something on fire or steal nuclear codes?" I joked, opening the door. My five-year-old was well mannered but not exactly well behaved. He liked mischief.

And he got away with all of it. Because he was cute. And I wasn't just saying that because he was my kid and I was supposed to think he was cute. He'd gotten the magical mix of Robert and me. A slight olive skin tone from my Cuban roots, but not as deep as mine because Robert didn't have 'ethnic'—his word—ancestry like I did. Just good old colonists. Nathan had midnight black hair, like mine, with a slight wave. He had piercing green eyes like his father, the thing that attracted me to him in the first place. Somehow looking into them, I never saw Robert. All I saw was Nathan. Because there was something about that kid. He was a fully realized human. Since he was born, he had a fullness to his eyes, a personality to them that transfixed you.

He was so unique for a five-year-old, so full of personality, charisma. People gravitated toward him, he was magnetic.

My little boy was special. Precious. The one thing I was indebted to his father for giving him to me. The father who I'd finally gotten comfortable with knowing I'd never see him again.

And now he was here.

On the doorstep of my little two-bedroom ranch in a working-class neighborhood outside LA.

I was so shocked, the smile stayed on my face. My heart paused in my chest. My breath caught.

He was the same. Hair a little bit longer so it curled around the collar of his black shirt. The sleeves were pulled up to show his corded forearms. He still worked out, ate chicken and rice, maintained his physique with a manic perfectionism. His jaw was clean-shaven, a couple of new lines underneath his eyes.

His shirt was tucked into dark jeans, badge pinned on his belt. It was polished, shining in the sun, the reflection from it seemed to burn me. It was a joke, that shield on his hip.

"Are you gonna invite your husband in or just stand there grinning at me like an idiot?" he asked, voice smooth, pleasing, on the outside at least. There was a threat slithering underneath it that I recognized.

My body moved robotically, outside of my own volition as I stepped aside and let him into my home. I let him into my sanctuary without hesitation, without a fight.

Shocked at myself, I was still holding the door handle as he walked past, his scent assaulting my nostrils. His cologne hadn't changed, of course. It was still too musky, too strong.

I stared at the beautiful garden across from me for a moment. Alice, my elderly neighbor, looked up from the flowers she was planting to raise her hand in greeting.

I robotically waved back.

I didn't make friends with my neighbors before. Robert didn't allow it. They were too close to us already, they could be a lifeline, a support system if I needed it. Which I did.

He made sure I had nothing I needed, and everything he wanted for me.

I was friends with my neighbors now.

Lucia and her husband Felipe had two kids, one that was twelve and another that was sixteen, who babysat for me now and again.

Eliza and Karen were on my other side, newly married and trying to start their own business. They moved in just after Nathan and I did and were my closest friends. Our family.

They were a support system.

I had them around me.

But I had Robert in my freaking house.

I turned, leaving the front door open. I needed it open, I needed the light from the outside world, from my current world, to seep in as my previous life dripped darkness all over my handmade rug.

Robert was looking around the living room in disgust.

It was an open plan, a patchwork sofa to the right of the front door, covered in pillows and throws. I usually fell asleep there with something stupid playing on the TV, which was pretty ancient, especially compared to Eliza and Karen's 'Smart TV' we watched Game of Thrones on. I didn't have cable. But I had a bulging shelf of books to the right of the TV. I had three different books on the giant oak chest I used as a coffee table. There was a rocking chair beside the sofa, covered with laundry that I used to rock Nathan in.

To the left of the door was a small round dining table that I'd found at a flea market, sanded down, restored and painted. Same with the chairs, and a few other bits of furniture around the house.

Karen told me I should start a business selling it because it was 'dope'. But I didn't have time for things. I had a kid and a job. And laundry.

There was a bowl of crystals in the middle of the dining room table. A salt lamp on a side table near the kitchen. A framed poster of the lunar cycle on the wall Robert was scowling at.

I wasn't sure if he was scowling at the poster or the chipped paint on the walls.

"You need to leave," I said, my voice small, but strong.

He snapped his eyes to me, running them over my body in a way that made me feel ill. It was a balmy day and we didn't have AC, only a laboring fan that was usually in Nathan's room.

I was wearing short yellow shorts with a rainbow on the right side and a matching yellow tank with an illustration of a sun. I wasn't wearing a bra. I didn't normally need to since I naturally had small boobs. They'd grown when I was pregnant and breastfeeding but somehow had reverted back to their small, perky state. Granted, they were a lot less perky than before, and covered in stretch marks, but still not bad.

The rest of my body had bounced back at first because Robert ensured I had an exercise schedule weeks after having Nathan and he monitored my diet because he didn't want a 'chubby wife'.

After we left, I didn't diet out of need, only necessity. At the start, I barely had enough money to feed both Nathan and myself. It went without saying that if it was a choice between us both, I'd go hungry. I'd never failed to feed my son, even when I'd done so for myself. Now we had a bit more money so our pantry was stocked with as much organic produce as I could afford—and we had a vegetable garden in our tiny back yard—and cupboards full of off-brand food, but I just didn't have time to eat.

So my natural curves were nonexistent.

I hated that Robert's eyes were on so much of my exposed skin.

"Robert," I snapped, finding the anger that should have been at the surface since I'd opened the door. "You need to leave. You cannot be here."

I didn't want to know why he was in California and not the state he'd been determined for us to live, and die in. It would be easier for him to run for office with his father's help and connections in the state.

Something moved in his face with my words. My tone. The strength in it. He despised it, I could tell. Robert only liked women weak, agreeable, beaten down.

The fury in his eyes sparked an old fear, and emotional flinch that was muscle memory.

I hated myself for the fact I did actually flinch as he moved toward me, the footfalls of his boots echoing in my ringing ears.

The hit that I was expecting didn't come.
Not until he slammed the door at least.
He didn't want an audience.
He made sure that no one saw the bruises, evidence of his abuse. Made sure that he seemed like the doting husband, father, and reputable detective on the surface.
Once the door was closed, he turned on me, got in my space, my entire body was held taut, shaking with his proximity. All the strength I thought I'd built up over the years tore like the flimsy film that it was.
"I cannot be here?" he whispered. He never yelled. In all the times he'd raised his fists to me, he'd never raised his voice. But those whispered threats, insults, warnings, they made my skin bleed. "I am your husband," he hissed, leaning in so I couldn't escape his face taking up my vision.
He was close.
Too close, taking up my space, my breathing room.
"I am allowed to be wherever I want to be. Where my wife is raising our child in fucking squalor," *he said, gazing around the room in distaste.*
I found my backbone with the mention of my son. I moved around him, away from him so I was standing in the middle of the room. I eyed my cell phone at the breakfast bar. I doubted I'd be able to dial for help if things went bad—and they always went bad when Robert had this look in his eye—but I could yell for help. I could fight. I would fight.
"Squalor?" I repeated, looking around my living room. Sure the paint was chipped, the furniture was second hand, the carpet was faded and the kitchen appliances were almost older than I was. But the pantry was stocked. Everything was wiped clean to the point of obsession—a takeaway from my marriage when I wasn't allowed to leave a speck of dust anywhere—the pile of laundry the only thing messy. It was cluttered, sure. With my

things and Nathan's toys. But it was so far from squalor it was laughable. I knew squalor. I grew up in it.

Squalor was cigarette burns in battered and filthy furniture. It was roaches crawling on the floor. It was an empty fridge. A rotting fruit bowl. A one-bedroom trailer housing three people.

It was beer bottles, empty and full within reaching distance of children. Along with a crack pipe.

It was filthy clothes that were two sizes too small.

My home was *not* that.

"This is a home," I said, forcing calm into my voice. "My home. Not one where I'm slapped for forgetting to vacuum a room. Or have my hair pulled for using the wrong fabric softener. Or being punched in the face for forgetting that you hate peas and putting them in your dinner. That isn't a home. That's a prison. Which you need to go back to. Right now."

I clenched my fists at my sides, my entire body shaking. I forced myself to maintain eye contact with Robert.

I enraged him. I could see that. It both terrified me and pleased me. Never had I stood up to him. Not even when I left, I'd stolen away in the night, when he was out drinking, or cheating on me.

He'd never seen this version of me.

It shocked him a little.

But only a little.

"You had everything," he snapped. "A home you never could've dreamed of when you were in the poverty I pulled you out of—"

"I'm not speaking about this," I cut him off, the memories too close. "I'm not speaking to you. Unless you're here to finally sign the divorce papers, I have nothing to say to you."

He laughed. It was unexpected and entirely unpleasant. It filled my beautiful, warm home and immediately turned it colder than any kind of AC.

"Divorce?" he said, still chuckling. "I didn't come to divorce you, despite the fact you've entirely let yourself go since we've been apart. That's easy to fix, though. No, I didn't come to sign anything. I've come to get my wife and son back."

I blacked out for a moment at his words. Pure, naked panic blinded me with the certainty and confidence at his words. Like Nathan and I were something he could just take. Own.

Hurt.

It was the thought of him laying a hand on my beautiful, kind, and special son that had me lucid.

"Never," I hissed, eyeing him, my eyes watering. "Never will you get back something that you threw away in the first place. With your violence. With your vile words. We were never yours. And we never will be again."

That fury came back as a muscle in his jaw ticked. Then he smiled, slowly as if he were realizing something.

Then he strode calmly over to me.

I stood my ground. I didn't flinch this time.

And this time he did hit me.

Hard.

I tumbled back into the breakfast bar that separated the kitchen and the living room.

White pain scored over my pain and my stomach lurched with the intensity. The memory of pain is a funny thing. Like childbirth, at the time it is so excruciating you're sure it'll be seared in your memory, into your bones, something you'll never forget. Something that will ensure you never do anything as stupid as deciding to grow human life ever again.

But pain fades. Even the worst kind. Especially when the worst kind is replaced by the most beautiful miracle in the world.

Even when it isn't replaced with anything, it fades away. Your body doesn't let you hold onto it. Not when you're moving on.

So I was shocked with the pain at being punched in the face. Even though it had happened many times before, I'd become used to it years ago, it felt like it was the first time. And maybe it was. Because I wasn't the same woman who used to be a punching bag.

I was a new woman.

But the same man was battering me.

Boots filled my blurred and tear-filled vision and more white pain exploded in my scalp as he grabbed a handful of my hair and yanked my head up to meet his eyes.

When I'd lived with him, I'd kept it short for this precise reason, less of it for him to yank. Now I was safe, I grew it long, past my bra strap. I liked it long. I liked to do all sorts of different styles, curl, straighten, braid. But I liked my thick, natural waves falling down my back too.

Now, I hated them.

"You don't talk to me like that, trailer trash," he whispered. "You've got some things to learn. To remember."

The promise was rancid in the air, and I almost vomited from the reality behind it. My worst fears come to life.

He continued to stare at me with a cruel and evil version of my son's eyes, taunting me with the power he thought he was entitled to over me.

My cheek was hot, the skin already tight and stretching from the swelling.

I was aware that Nathan could be coming home any minute. Coming home to see his mother on the floor with a black eye and the father he didn't recognize holding her by the hair.

A memory I promised myself he would never have.

A trauma that would never touch him.

I had to get him out of here.

I had to fight.

Right when I was about to, Robert let me go, I fell onto my hands.

My wrists buckled with the impact.

Robert didn't say a word, he didn't need to, violence always spoke louder than words. He just turned and walked out.

I'd lain on the floor for exactly five seconds.

That's all I let myself have.

Five seconds of pity. Fear. Tears.

Because five seconds was all I could spare.

Then I got up.

I tended to my face the best I could.

Looked up a reputable family lawyer.

Called to make an appointment for Friday, wincing at the initial cost.

Then I took a photo of my bruised face. I knew I needed it. The evidence. If it would come to that. I prayed it wouldn't. I really prayed that Robert had come here today to see if he could still control me, to see if I'd immediately go running back to him. And that I'd never see him again.

But I couldn't bet my life, my son's life on a prayer.

So I prepared to fight.

I considered running too.

It was an option. A tempting one. The smartest one.

But I had a home here. I had friends. A job that wasn't great, but bosses and co-workers that were. Nathan had just started school. Making friends. I was friends with a couple of moms who helped with the school run, playdates, and birthday parties.

I wouldn't run.

When Nathan came home, the bruise on my face was only beginning to form, and he was on a high from all the fun he had, so somehow I managed to get him in the bath and into bed without noticing.

I knew the next day would be a different story, when the skin swelled more, when bruising took over my face. There would be questions. From my kid. From Karen and Eliza. Everyone at work.

But that was tomorrow.

I'd figure it out then.

I went to bed sore, terrified, angry, but not without hope. I went to sleep thinking that whatever Robert threw at me, I'd fight. Because I had support. Because I was stronger now.

Or so I thought.

CHAPTER TWO

"YOU WANT SOME KIND OF REVENGE?" the man demanded, jerking me back into the violent present.

"Revenge?" I repeated.

The man nodded to my eye. Even his nod was violent.

"No, I don't care about revenge," I said. "I care about my son."

The man froze and this time the reaction was not small.

"Your son?" he repeated.

"Yes," I said, my voice strangely cold and calm much like this foyer. My yelling panic had receded in front of the man I knew it wouldn't affect. Plus, it wouldn't serve me right now. Wouldn't serve Nathan.

"My five-year-old son that my estranged, abusive husband kidnapped today from his school and that the police won't help me get back." I paused as utter and complete silence spread over the room. "The police won't help me because Robert, my ex, he's a detective. He comes from a powerful family. With money." I gritted my teeth. "I'm not powerful. I don't have money. But I am a mother. I'm not the best, because sometimes I forget that he has a dress-up day at school, or I do his homework for him because

I'm too tired from working ten hours to explain it to him, and sometimes I feed him boxed mac and cheese because he loves it and even though I know it's full of bad things, it makes him happy."

That memory of a smile in front of a bowl of mac and cheese almost brought me to my knees, but I kept speaking.

"I let him watch cartoons on Sundays and I probably let him stay up too late. But I'm a *good mother*. I don't have any of the things that Robert has, but I will do anything to get my son back. And anything includes asking for help. Because I don't know what else to do, except find someone who isn't the police, who isn't scared of my husband's badge and his name, someone who will help me." I sucked in a harsh breath and willed myself not to cry. "Will you help me?" I asked the menacing man.

I begged him.

He stared at me. Gaped might have been more of an apt description. Those harsh and cold features seemed frozen from my words.

I held my breath as he didn't speak. My heart was in my throat with the very real fear that the man in front of me had seen too much, done too much to be touched by my story, my desperation. That he would just be like the countless others I'd tried to look to for help. That would turn his back on me.

I vowed then that if that happens, I would knock on every door I could, offer up everything I had in order to find someone who had the means to get my son back. And if I couldn't find someone, I'd figure out any kind of way. I would figure out where he was staying, living now, and I'd go there if I needed to.

I'd have to physically fight him for my son. And I wasn't afraid of doing so. I wasn't afraid of any single blow. No amount of pain could reproduce what I was going through right now.

I couldn't be sure that he wouldn't kill me.

I would die for my son. In a second.

But I would not die knowing that my son would then be brought up by a monster pretending to be a man. A monster who would either lay his hands on my beautiful boy, or spew his toxic and violent morals onto my innocent and pure little human.

Neither of those options were acceptable.

I had to figure out a way to get my son back without dying.

I had a backup plan. If I had to.

I would go to wherever he was.

Not to fight.

To surrender.

I would go back there, back to the house of horrors, pretend I was going back to be the wife. I would abandon my home, my friends, all of it. I'd wear what he wanted, eat what he demanded, and take every hit he gave. If I could put my son to bed at night. Make him breakfast every morning. Listen to stories about his stuffed toy, Feebo, coming to life when I wasn't watching. I would do that for as long as it took to find a gap in the bars. Then, again, I would take Nathan and slip through those bars and disappear again.

I'd make sure that I did it for good this time.

But that was my last choice. Because in however long it took for Robert to get complacent and give me a chance to escape, Nathan would be exposed to a life that was so different than his own it was sickening. A house that couldn't be messy. That he couldn't draw on the walls of his bedroom in. That he'd be afraid of spilling in. He'd see his mother with bruises. Maybe even see his father inflicting them.

That was worse than death for me.

That was me failing him as a mother.

So I was standing here begging a stranger for his help.

"We'll help you," a different voice said from behind me.

It wasn't full of hostility. It was soft. Kind. Masculine still, but warm. The accent was slightly off, different. Pleasing.

The man in front of me jerked at the voice, but I turned to see the owner of it.

The man was standing at the entrance to the doors, having obviously entered at some point during my tirade and I hadn't noticed. He was tall. Muscled. Beautiful, with skin a similar shade than mine, but deeper. He was covered in tattoos, dressed in clothes that didn't suit the office at all, faded blue jeans, a plain white tee, and biker boots. He had kind eyes. He had eyes that wouldn't harden themselves from my pain. That wouldn't turn away.

And he didn't. He walked forward until he was standing right in front of me. His eyebrow twitched as his gaze focused on my bruise. Those eyes turned a little less kind, anger sparked them. Fury. This stranger was furious about someone hitting me and he didn't even know me.

"Keltan," he said, holding out his hand. "Brookes," he continued. "I own this place."

It surprised me, because he wasn't young, but he wasn't old either. He didn't really suit this fancy office or the fancy locale. But he also seemed like a powerful guy, not just with his muscles, but his whole aura. It felt light blue. Orange. Strong, loving, fearless.

I took his hand. It was dry. Warm. Huge. The grip was firm, but I had a feeling he was being extremely gentle with me, from his gaze to the softness of his voice. Looking at the man, I knew that he knew how to be hard and scary, like the other one that was watching the exchange. Who hadn't been gentle with me.

"It's nice to meet you, Keltan," I said, my voice shaky, unsure of what to say. "I'm Elena, Phoenix," I added, realizing I hadn't uttered my name when I came in here all but clinging to the scary guy's pant leg begging for help.

I'd changed mine and Nathan's last name once we'd been in California for a few months and Robert had come knocking at the door. I didn't want to go back to my maiden name, given to me by abusive, cruel parents. I didn't want to keep one given to me by an abusive, cruel husband.

So I chose one, one that represented my rebirth.

"Elena," Keltan repeated, voice firmer than his handshake. "We're going to get your son back."

Despite my knowledge of how cruel the world could be, despite wearing it on my face and feeling it in the hole in my heart, I chose to believe this kind man's words.

Because I had no other choice.

"I CAN PAY," I said, wiping my clammy palms on my bare legs.

I felt very conscious of the fact I was in a very fancy and expensive office wearing cutoffs and a black tank with a *Game of Thrones* quote on it. Luckily I was wearing a bra at least, because the room was blissfully cool and whatever dignity I had left would totally be squashed if my nipples started peeking out from my tank in front of Keltan—the owner of Greenstone Security—and Lance Knox—the aggressive man who hadn't spoken since I had spewed all my crap at him. I didn't blame him. He probably thought I was an absolute insane person. I didn't really care what people, even these hot guys—I noticed in a detached way that both of these men were incredibly attractive but I didn't focus on that because I wasn't focusing on anything that wasn't my getting my son back—thought of me right now. They could decide I was Susanna from *Girl Interrupted* for all I cared, as long as they got Nathan back.

Despite being detached from caring about what people thought of me, my outfit was decidedly inappropriate in this atmosphere, it was what I had been in to pick Nathan up from school. As little as possible, as my AC in my junker of a car had just crapped out and I still had two more paychecks to go before I could complete my car fund and buy a new one.

I'd been scrimping for a year, not so I could look good in front of the moms at school—even though almost all of them apart from the ones I was friends with, drove cars that were worth my yearly salary—or so I could drive with AC. No, because my child was in the car. And I needed something safer.

Currently, my child was in more danger than being in a shitty car with no AC. So I'd use the new car fund as a deposit, or retainer, or whatever they needed to get started. If it wasn't enough, I'd find somewhere to sell plasma.

"I don't have much but I promise I'm good for it, I can do weekly installments, anything," I continued, hot flush of shame blooming on my cheeks. I'd never been ashamed of how tight things were with money over these few years. I had left an abusive relationship with barely anything to my name, barely anything on my resume, and managed to make a home for my son and myself. I was not ashamed of that. I was proud of that.

As long as I had enough money to feed, clothe, and house Nathan, plus keep him safe, I was proud of myself.

But I imagined that the money it would cost him to get him safe would be more than I made in a year, judging by these offices and the fact I'd sneaked a look at their previous clients as Keltan had shown me to his office and excused himself for a second. Lexie Decesare, the frickin' *rock star*. Numerous famous actresses, big names in the entertainment industry.

I was way out of my depth here, with my crappy Corolla parked down the street, with a twenty-dollar purse with little to no cash in it.

But I'd make it work.

"Money is not a conversation we need to have right now," Keltan said, interrupting my thought processes. "Our main and only focus is getting your son back to you safely." His voice was gentle, kind, calming. Not exactly things I would expect to come from a man who looked like this. I glanced to the ring on his left hand. I was happy whoever the faceless wife was had a man like that.

Lance, who wasn't sitting, was just standing there rigid, dripping testosterone and menace all over the place. But it wasn't directed at me, I had a healthy amount of experience of what it felt like to have menace directed at me. I wasn't sure if it was the situation in general, the bruise on my face or just that was his default. I suspected it was the latter, but I didn't have time or headspace to focus on this man. Instead, I focused on Keltan, who seemed like he could help me. Who seemed the kind of man who had the ability to take care of people.

I did not have a healthy amount of experience with men like that, but I recognized it just the same.

He leaned forward, clasping his hands together on his desk.

It was very orderly, I noticed. If Nathan was here, he'd be wandering around, picking things up, asking what they were and putting them back in the wrong places.

But Nathan wasn't here.

The cold reminder was so sickening I had to hold my breath so I didn't throw up the Pop-Tart I'd eaten on the way to Nathan's school all over Keltan's tidy and expensive looking desk.

"I'm gonna be honest with you, this isn't usually our kind of thing," Keltan said. "We usually pass things onto the police if we feel like they can take care of it or if it gets dicey for our client to circumvent the law. But from what you've told me, this isn't something the police can take care of." Again his words were even, but there was something in his eyes, frustration, anger.

I understood that, any decent man, decent human being would be appropriately horrified at the fact the police turned a blind eye to abuse and frickin' kidnapping if the perpetrator had the right job title, right family name.

"I'm doing this because it's what any decent person would do," he continued. "I apologize that you haven't met any of them in what seems like a long time. I'm doing this because I'm a father. I cannot even fathom what you must be going through right now." The man actually grimaced, his face graying slightly.

I was happy that this child had a father like that.

I was happy that my child had a father like that who was going to be looking for him.

"Now, I heard something on the tail end of what you were telling Lance that I need to comment on," Keltan continued. "You are a good mother. I don't want you to question that. I may not know you, but I've seen more than enough to see that you're a wonderful parent. A good parent is one that is willing to fight, pray, beg and do everything in their power for their kid. That's you. And I promise you that we're gonna get your boy back."

Tears bit the backs of my eyes. I gritted my teeth against them. I was not allowed to cry now. I could cry after I had Nathan in my arms. After I smelled his hair. After he smiled at me. After I cataloged every inch of his body to make sure it was the same as it was before. After I fed him as much boxed macaroni and cheese as his little body could handle. Then, when I put him to bed, watched him fall asleep into a slumber without nightmares, then I could cry. I could sob.

But only then.

For now, and until then, I had to hold it the hell together.

"Now, we have alternate methods of doin' things, want to make sure that you're—"

"I'm okay with it," I interrupted Keltan. "Any and all ways to get my boy back unharmed, you do whatever you have to do. Whatever you're willing to do."

Keltan nodded, the corner of his mouth turning up only slightly. Not a full smile. Because there was no place for smiles right now. I didn't feel like I'd ever smile again. I was empty, hollow. At the same time, I was full, bursting with fear, despair, rage, worry.

"The piece of shit, you want us to take care of him?" Lance spoke finally.

I jerked at his voice, so different than Keltan's. Rougher. More violent. He wasn't softening himself for me as I suspected Keltan was. Wasn't trying to make himself less threatening, make me more comfortable.

Then again, all the soft-spoken men in the world in sleek offices couldn't make me feel calm, so I weirdly appreciated it. The honesty of it.

"Excuse me?" I said, blinking.

"The husband," he elaborated, or his version of elaborating. I suspected he wasn't as articulate as Keltan. Keltan had explained he was the owner of the business and therefore had all the people skills. With a business like this, I knew there was a call for a different kind of people skills. A violent, dark kind.

This man excelled in the dark. You need only look at him to know that.

"Take care of him?" I repeated.

I thought I got what he was saying, but surely I must have been mistaken, my thoughts clouded by my own panic and feelings toward Robert.

Though the fact that Lance referred to him as a 'piece of shit' had me thinking he didn't exactly have warm feelings toward him either.

But still, this was a reputable security company that had nice offices, celebrity clients, a location in a respectable neighborhood in a seriously nice part of LA. Surely he couldn't be offering what I thought of it.

"You mean, like..." I trailed off, not sure if I was actually meant to speak about such things out loud. I didn't know the etiquette.

If you'd told me this morning as I was chopping up bananas for Nathan's oatmeal with him singing about giraffes in the background that I'd be sitting in a fancy office in LA with two attractive badasses potentially talking about putting a hit out on my husband I would have laughed my butt off.

But that was life.

So instead of verbalizing what I was going to say, I brought my thumb across my throat in an unmistakable gesture.

Keltan raised his brows, looking almost amused, but Lance merely nodded once.

I gaped and waited for Keltan, the more reasonable and kind of the men to correct him. He didn't. He just stared at me in expectation.

Were these two men really waiting for me to confirm that I wanted Robert dead? Was this some kind of trap? I didn't see how it could be, so it really seemed like if I responded in the way my evil heart wanted me to, they would do it.

"No," I said finally.

Keltan raised his brow again, not in amusement. I wasn't sure if it was disappointment or respect.

"A very big and dark part of me wants him to never breathe air again. Wants to make sure he does not walk on the same earth as my son. Wants to make sure that we never have to worry about him again," I said, even as I verbalized it, I was tempted to change my answer. "But that would be letting his vile and deplorable actions change who I am as a person. Change my beliefs. I've given him a lot of power over me in the past. I will no longer give him permission to take anything else from me."

Now I was sure I saw some kind of respect on Keltan's face.

The other man's, I wasn't sure, because there was still that blank menace that masked any kind of human emotion.

But I noticed the veins in his arms protruding from his

muscular arms and saw his fists were clenched at his sides. I couldn't be sure that they weren't like that the whole time.

I darted my gaze back to Keltan. "It's not my choice to take Robert from this world, I don't *want* that choice on my shoulders. That's for someone different to decide. God, Buddha, Shiva, Isis, or whoever takes care of that kind of stuff. But I know that he's obviously got a plan here. Robert is a meticulous man. He will have decided, for whatever reason I don't even know, that he needs Nathan. Not *wants*." I swallowed glass but forced myself to keep going. Information was power, all the power I had right now.

"I know he doesn't *want* his son," I said, voice even. "He doesn't want people. He needs them. For image, personal gain, for punching bags." I paused as a fresh wave of nausea rushed over me. He could not be hitting Nathan. No. He couldn't be laying his hands on him. He hadn't, not before. Because he was a monster, that was for sure. But even monsters recognized things that they couldn't touch. Couldn't hurt. That was the lie I needed to tell myself in order to get through all of this.

The thought of my little boy being hurt almost had me catatonic.

I needed to continue speaking. Keltan needed all the information on Robert so he could understand this man.

"I know that when we get Nathan back, he won't give up," I continued. "He doesn't like being bested. He'll try to retaliate. And he knows where I live now, obviously we'll have to move. I'm okay with that. But if he knows your company's involvement and tries to—"

"He's not gonna touch us," Keltan interrupted. "And we don't give a shit if he tries. That's not something that's gonna make us hesitate at getting your boy back to you. Don't worry about that."

My heart felt heavy, so heavy I wouldn't be surprised to find it sitting between my feet, bleeding. "You're going to get my son back?" I whispered, all strength gone from my voice.

His gaze didn't falter. "We will get your son back. I promise."

Lance

"You shouldn't have promised," he said, closing the door behind him.

Keltan looked up from where he'd been staring at his desk, head in his hands. Lance guessed this was hitting him. Keltan was a tough motherfucker. A hard one. Not much could land on him, because he'd seen it all, death, torture, pain. They'd all seen that too much recently, with what happened with the Sons of Templar. They saw more of it with what happened to Polly. And that shit scarred all of them. Even him, who didn't think there were any places left on him that were free to scar.

Didn't even know her well, but you didn't need to. You just *knew*. There were people so dark that you felt sick just being around them. Lance knew that because that was all he knew. It was all he was. Then there was another kind of people. The light kind. The kind that made you feel good.

Polly was that.

So yeah, that hit him, hit Keltan, because he and the rest of the men had pretty fucking strong thoughts toward men that put their hands on women.

But this was different. This was hitting him square in the chest.

It was a fucking *child*.

Lance had dealt with everything. Even shit with children, shit that sickened his fucking soul, but he'd seen it. Considered himself immune to it. To brutality. Emotion.

But seeing that woman in the fucking foyer, it awakened something in him.

Fury.

"What?" Keltan said as he walked into the room, he went to sit across from him, but he paused. This was the chair that *she* sat in.

He could already smell her in the room. She smelled of coconut and sweat. He liked it.

Too fucking much.

So he stayed standing, as far away from the chair as he could.

Keltan noted it as the fucker noted everything.

"You shouldn't have promised her that we'll get her son back," he continued, folding his arms. "That's not something you can promise. You know as well as I do, we don't find that kid within twenty-four hours, we've got slim chances. Knowing what we know already about this fuck, chances are already slim. Promising that woman her son is gonna get back to her in one piece is a mistake."

Lance felt sick even uttering it, which was foreign. He wasn't usually affected by the uglier truths in situations like this. He lived in the ugly truth. He liked it.

Until now.

Until the woman who smelled like coconuts hit his gut with her bruises and her stupid fuckin' tank top and her visceral fear and love for her son walked into these offices.

Keltan's face changed. His whole body. He was out of his chair in a blink, and across the room right in Lance's face in another one.

He didn't move. He never was one to back down from a fight, even with a man he respected and liked.

"We are going to find that kid," Keltan hissed. "He's gonna be in one piece. And that woman is gonna fuckin' hold her son again."

"Not for you to say," Lance replied, even though he wanted to believe it.

Keltan's eyes hardened. "Yes, it fuckin' *is*. Because we've got intel on the guy. Recently transferred here, working as a detective. Wire has already told me he's got plans on runnin' for office like his dad. Most likely scenario is that he wants the pretty wife and son back to help boost votes. He's not gonna lay his hand on that kid. He's a piece of shit of the worst kind, but from what I understand, he's not stupid enough to hurt him."

"He was stupid enough to hurt *her*," Lance replied, thinking of the bruise on her beautiful and delicate face and having to withhold his wince. That was odd. It wasn't even that serious of an injury. He'd seen much worse. On plenty of people who didn't deserve it. But with her it was different.

"Men stupid enough to lay their hands on women don't have any smarts," he continued. "They don't have anything left to make them a man. They're lowest of the low. They've got no limits. Morals. So that kid is in trouble."

Keltan chose this moment to grab him by the shirt. He was surprised he didn't hit him, he could tell he wanted to. It didn't faze him, he was used to people wanting to hit him for telling them a truth they didn't want to hear.

He wanted to tear the flesh from his own skin hearing that truth echoing in his brain.

"You need to stop, now," Keltan commanded, voice cold. "You need to do your job, focus on that. And make sure you stay the fuck away from Elena. I don't want you spewing any of your shit anywhere near her. She's gone through enough."

After a beat, he let him go and stormed from the office.

Keltan didn't have to worry about him going near Elena. He planned on keeping as far away from her as he could.

He also planned on getting her kid back for her.

"FUCK," Luke breathed after Keltan had briefed them all.

He'd gotten the whole team together.

Usually each of them was competent enough to handle shit on their own, most of them specialized in certain fields. Duke was good at the celebrity babysitting crap, Luke did a lot of the security installations, had law enforcement connections, Heath with roughing people up when needed, Rosie, being all-around fucking insane, and him with the dirty work. And cleaning up after the dirty work was done.

This shit was all hands on deck.

They were gonna go and get the kid as soon as possible. But there were logistics to take care of. Safeguards to make sure that piece of shit knew he could never go near Elena or the kid again if he wanted to keep breathing.

And they had to keep the fucker breathing.

She didn't want him dead.

It angered him unlike anything had.

He didn't think he had the ability to be angry again. Anger was an emotion, wasn't it? And he didn't have emotions.

Until today.

Now he had too many, it was hard to think straight. It was because he knew she was in here, somewhere.

He needed to get out of here. He was crawling out of his fucking skin. But Keltan had called the meeting.

"Yeah," Keltan agreed.

Rosie's eyes were hard and her small hands fisted on the table. "Where is she? Elena?"

"In the rooms upstairs. Got Stella getting her something to eat 'cause she honestly looks like she's about to pass out."

Lance thought about that. The fact that her body was lean to the point of gaunt and she was a woman who was meant to have curves. You could tell that by just looking at her. Full lips, all that fuckin' hair. Beautiful caramel skin.

He was a piece of shit for even thinking that in this situation, but he was a piece of shit.

And he'd never had a reaction to a woman before. He didn't have much of a reaction. He fucked them because he knew it was a necessary release of pressure, but it wasn't something that drove him. There was no animal need.

But he had it with the bruised, battered single mother pleading for help to get her son back.

Yeah, he was a piece of shit.

"She won't pass out," he spoke, even without meaning to. All eyes went on him because he never usually spoke at these things. He kept words to a minimum. He didn't like the sound of his own voice in his head. "Woman like that, only time she'll fall over looking for her son is if her heart stops beating."

Keltan's eyes focused on him, too fucking intensely. They were still hardened from the exchange earlier. He nodded, before looking to the rest of the room. "Lance's right. She's strong. Tough. A good woman. But she's holding on by a fucking thread."

"Of course she is," Rosie snapped. "Her abusive, spineless, piece of camel shit husband kidnapped her son. Please tell me I'm the one that's allowed to kill him."

Keltan focused on her.

Luke rolled his eyes at his wife, then reached over to squeeze her hand because he was in tune with that woman and could hear the underlying emotion in her bloodthirsty tone.

"We're not killing him."

Rosie glared at him. "Is this some more of this weird New Zealand humor than I don't get because I don't get it and it's *not funny.*"

Lance was happy that he was not the only one who thought that this was bullshit. And of course it would be Rosie, out of all of the men at this table that would have the strongest feelings about killing this roach. Because the men at this table were among some of the toughest he'd spent time with, but Rosie was in another ballpark.

You wouldn't know the small, beautiful woman with all sorts of crazy hairstyles and outfits would spend her nights killing drug dealers and rapists, but that was kind of the point.

She was also a mother.

And there were fathers at this table, but Lance had learned that there was something different, something ferocious about a mother's love.

"It's not a joke," Keltan replied, voice hard. As much as the man needed to stay professional, Lance knew he wasn't happy about it either. They were not hitman for hire, not officially at least. But there were circumstances in which they agreed that death was part of their invisible service list. In cases of rape and anything to do with children.

"Of course it's not," Rosie hissed. "Because it's not fucking funny."

"Elena doesn't want him dead. You meet her, you'll understand," Keltan explained. "She's... different. Soft. Kind. She's not a person that can have death on her conscience, not even when that someone has done all that to her. I'm gonna respect that. I'm gonna protect that. Because it's rare in this world to find someone who doesn't want revenge. Who doesn't want to meet ugliness with worse." He looked around the table, taking extra time on him and Rosie. "We're *all* going to respect that."

Lance gritted his teeth.

Rosie let out an impressive string of curse words, some even Lance hadn't heard of.

Duke nodded.

"We got you, got her on this, brother," Heath said, something moving in his eyes. The man had more experience with the kind of women who didn't live in a world of blood and vengeance, who were thrust in there anyway. "You want me to get Polly in? Have her sit with her?"

Keltan nodded. "Yeah, that's a good idea."

And it was.

Elena was all kinds of dark right now, she needed some light. Some peace in this chaos.

Polly was that.

She would give the woman as much peace as she could. Though Lance knew the only true peace she'd have was her son in her arms. Which was why he knew chaos so well.

CHAPTER THREE

Elena

"TELL ME ABOUT HIM," Polly said, her voice soft and kind.

Her entire presence was soft and kind. She'd come in about an hour after Stella, the receptionist showed me to the room above the Greenstone offices. It was a small apartment, clean, modern, like the rest of the place.

There was a small lounge area with a dusky gray couch, only slightly lighter than the color on the walls. It looked comfortable, not cheap like a lot of sofas in places like this. It looked like it might swallow you up, and your troubles too. Right now, nothing could swallow my troubles.

There was a big TV mounted on the wall across from the couch. It was sleek. New. On the coffee table, there was a neat stack of books, a candle burning, and coasters.

Framed artwork scattered the walls, it was all beautiful landscapes, some seascapes too. I'd wandered over to gaze at them because they were so beautiful, so full. The artist was someone named Lauren Mathers. Someone very talented, and someone I likely couldn't afford.

Off the living area was a small kitchenette with a nice coffeemaker, a stocked fridge, and a small dining table. There were bedrooms down the hall, "if I felt like napping," Stella had said.

No way could I close my eyes and do something like sleep when I wasn't under the same roof as my son.

The bathroom had a big tiled shower and bath, nicer than a fancy hotel. Even though I'd only been to a fancy hotel once in my life, on my honeymoon, and we'd only stayed one night because we had to cut it short for a case.

It was all much nicer and trendier than my home. But it didn't feel cold. Professional. The artwork, the books, the candles, throw pillows, all told me that someone had put thought into this.

It was nice for any other situation.

But it didn't mean anything in this situation.

Until Polly came in. She carried around more calm than this room. She was beautiful, but that was not the first thing I noticed. She seemed bright, full of color, and that had nothing to do with her clothes. But it was her. I could feel a pureness to her energy.

She had focused on me. "I'm Polly," she said in greeting. "I'm Heath's wife. He works here. He's one of the people who won't rest until we get your son back."

I blinked. There was something about the way she said it that shook what was already rattling inside me. There was a hurt, a personal kind of loss inside of it. Like I wasn't some stranger, like my child was not just some job for her husband. Like it was her blood, her family, like my hurt was hers. It was an impossible thing for a stranger to do, but she didn't feel like a stranger.

If this were another circumstance, I guessed we might have been firm friends. I would have been *excited* to meet such a person.

But I felt like I'd never be excited about anything ever again.

I realized that I'd just silently been staring at her after she spoke. But she didn't seem impatient or irritated at my lack of response. She just stood there, warm and sad half smile on her beautiful face.

"I'm Elena," I said, my voice a whisper.

Once I spoke, she nodded, moving to the small kitchenette to boil the kettle. "I'm going to make us tea," she decided.

She wasn't asking me if I wanted it, she was taking the decision from me as if she sensed there was no way I could even make a choice as to whether I wanted tea or not right now. All my willpower was going to the decision to inhale and exhale, the effort to hold myself together.

"You go sit on the sofa," she called gently. "It's more comfortable there. I know nothing is comfortable right now, but we'll sit there anyway."

I obeyed her because her voice was calm, decisive and something else. A little bit haunted. Some shadow of a past knowing of hurt. Of trauma.

So I sat.

She boiled the kettle.

Made us tea.

And then came to sit beside me and immediately asked about Nathan.

I clutched the warm mug, wishing the heat would seep into my bones, but it didn't, they were ice cold.

Her words filtered through me and I paused, preparing to launch into all the things I spouted about my son whenever someone asked.

But I couldn't.

My mind cleared.

Blanked.

I blinked rapidly, panicking. "I," I choked out the single word, trying to call up my memories. It was like trying to scrape the bottom of a dried-up well for a glass of water.

Nothing.

"I can't remember him," I choked out. "I can't even remember anything." Never in my life did I think I'd forget a single detail about my son, not a strand of hair. But here I was trying to call up what frickin' *color* it was.

"What's happening to me?" I whispered. "*I can't remember my son*. What is my body doing? Does it know I'm never going to see him again? Is it trying to prepare me for something?" My voice was shaking now. Rattling with panic. With horror.

Polly gently took the mug from my hands and placed both of them on the coffee table. She squeezed my palm. "No, your mind is in immense pain right now," she said. "It is helpless right now. And people deal with pain and trauma in all different ways."

"I'm a terrible mother," I whispered not taking in her words. "I can't remember my son."

Polly squeezed my hand, harder this time. "You are not a terrible mother. I can tell you that for certain. And you know what? You don't *need* to remember him. You're going to see him soon."

There was something in her words, some kind of strength, different, completely separate from Keltan's strength.

And, for some reason, I believed her.

Most likely because my survival and sanity depended on it.

Lance

"I'm taking point on this," Keltan told him as he grabbed the handle on the door before the car had come to a complete stop.

Lance clutched the handle. "Like fuck," he snapped.

He couldn't explain or understand the anger in his voice. He was sure it confused Keltan since it wasn't characteristic of him.

That was his specialty, handling any situation without the burden of emotional reactions.

"It wasn't a request," Keltan said. "I'm taking point on it. Can't trust you not to go off on this, and we already discussed that isn't how we're doing this."

Yes, they had discussed it. Despite him and Rosie having big misgivings about it. Rosie had been most vocal, of course. He communicated his hatred for this course of action silently. But they all were unhappy with it, even Keltan, who was the one to have the final say on it.

They all wanted to punish this motherfucker. Lance didn't just want to punish him, he wanted to bury him.

But with the information they'd collected over the past eight hours, it became apparent, the way they wanted to handle it—with a bullet to the temple after a painful beating—would not be smart, nor would it get the kid out clean. And there wasn't a guarantee that it wouldn't blowback on Elena or the kid.

That was the only reason that Lance hadn't gone rogue and did what needed to be done. Not because he cared overly about his job, or even because he respected Keltan—though he did. Because whatever small chance existed of this affecting the two innocents in this situation, he couldn't risk it.

That was foreign to him, along with all of this emotion. Risks were inevitable in situations like this. Innocents usually got caught in the crossfire. It was an inescapable and ugly truth you had to figure out how to live with if you wanted to live a life like Lance.

He didn't want to live this life how he did, there was just no other choice. So he turned his emotions off and became resigned to the fact that the wrong people got hurt a lot more often than the right people.

But there was no risking this. He was willing to forgo his animal need for blood and justice.

But he wasn't willing to give up complete control as Keltan was forcing him to do.

He clenched his teeth. "I won't go off," he said.

Keltan regarded him with a raised brow. "Callin' bullshit on you there, brother." He clapped him on the shoulder, even though his boss likely knew how dangerous human contact was with Lance right now. "We're gonna get that boy back."

It seemed like they were. Because inside that shitty McMansion, inside a gated community, was Robert Hudson's official place of residence as of two months ago, when he relocated from Virginia to California, with a promotion and a shot at running for office.

Rosie was going in first.

Because a man like Robert would think with his dick first seeing a woman like Rosie. He definitely wouldn't consider her a threat.

Which would be a big fucking mistake.

Then they'd go in.

Retrieve the boy, deliver their instructions to Robert. Those being never to contact, see or touch Elena or the kid ever again. And show him just what would happen if he did.

They were using information instead of fists in order to deliver this message. Lance would rather use knives. But sometimes, to people who already spoke with their fists, information was more powerful and damaging.

Especially a fuck like Hudson who was trying to get votes and relied on the shiny image below the rotten exterior.

He ultimately cared only about himself, not his wife or kid, so he would protect himself in all the ways he didn't protect them.

It was deeply fucked up, but it was going to work to their advantage.

Elena's advantage.

He'd heeded Keltan's orders and stayed away from her the

entire time that they were at the offices, waiting for intel, making plans. Not because his boss had commanded it, but because he knew he couldn't be around her. That didn't stop him from watching her on the monitors. She hadn't eaten, from what he'd seen, and that also had almost him breaking all promises to himself and Keltan and storming up there to force feed her.

But he didn't.

Because Polly, Rosie, and Lucy were all in and out of the room.

Each of the wives had dropped everything the second they heard what was going on. Because they were good mothers. Good women. And they would provide Elena with something she needed that Lance couldn't.

But he still watched her, whenever he could, which wasn't often. She hadn't slept. And neither had he. The rest of the team had snatched a few hours in shifts, but no one was comfortable sleeping on this shit.

Everyone knew the stats on missing children.

Even when they were taken by someone known. Especially when it was known that person was violent.

So they barely took breaks.

And it paid off.

Because it brought them here.

"Okay," he hissed out through his teeth, his mind on the last image he'd glimpsed of Elena in the monitor. Time spent trying to argue with Keltan was more time that fucking look would be painted on her face. More time when she wasn't giving her body nutrients.

Keltan looked surprised, as if he'd been preparing for more of a verbal battle, his body was taut, like he'd been expecting a physical one.

Not that Lance had given him reason to expect such things.

Sure, his job description meant he handled the most violent

parts of the Greenstone Security business, it didn't make him an aggressive man. He was violent by nature, but it was controlled, ironclad. He didn't get in fights with people at bars, with men who said stupid shit, didn't let himself be controlled by such things. Mainly because that shit didn't even puncture the surface. But because if he unleashed in those environments, where a black eye and maybe a couple of broken ribs were what was expected, he'd be covered in blood and the other person wouldn't be breathing.

So he had to keep control, otherwise he'd keep a trail of bodies in his wake.

Keltan knew to an extent about this, Lance was sure. He wasn't an idiot, he knew what he was hiring.

But Keltan was also perceptive as fuck. The man obviously saw that this case was different for Lance. Fuck, he couldn't hide it.

That was something to rectify after.

"Okay," Keltan said after a beat. His hand left his shoulder. "Let's go and get this kid."

Elena

I wasn't pacing.

Or crying.

Screaming.

Pulling the wallpaper off the walls with my bare hands.

Upending the coffee table and smashing every single glass in this place.

I felt like doing all of those things.

My body and soul were crying out for some kind of outlet, some kind of destruction, pain to distract me from just sitting here, waiting.

The second I realized Robert had taken Nathan, after I

threw up in the school's parking lot, I knew a lot of horror lay ahead of me. Because it is every parent's worst fear realized. And parents spend too much time thinking about situations like this. Because after giving birth, tired, in pain and feeling like the lower half of your body now resembles the Grand Canyon, you are given the whole world to balance on your chest. To take care of.

You are given the most beautiful thing in the world and entrusted to keep it safe. You are introduced to a love that you didn't know was possible for a body to contain. And fear. Fear goes along with that, because it is impossible to love without fear. Loving someone is giving away a part of your sanity to something vulnerable. Something fragile. My child had all of me.

I thought of every possible scenario, nightly, I tortured myself with it at the start. SIDS, choking, meningitis, dropping him, him being allergic to something. And someone taking him from me.

I thought I'd explored those scenarios in my brain.

But I hadn't.

The most horrible part of it all was something I hadn't even considered. It was the waiting. The torturous spread of seconds against the hour, dragging over my skin like sandpaper. I felt older. Empty. Sucked dry of all that made me human.

It had almost been twenty-four hours. One day.

One day didn't used to mean much.

One day was a blink of an eye in my world, Nathan waking me up at five in the morning for a dance party. It was getting him ready for school, and telling him, no he couldn't just wear his underwear even though "all the important things were covered," it was dropping him at school, hurrying to the diner for the breakfast rush. It was the blur of full plates, empty plates, the smell of grease, sore feet. It was picking Nathan up from Karen's, a friend's or taking him back to the diner with me, and then making dinner. Playing with him, arguing over bath time, putting him to bed, cleaning the house and passing out forgetting about dinner or changing out of my uniform.

Every second of my day was filled, busy.

Now, the lack of anything was bursting from my skin, it felt stretched, bloated, ready to explode.

The power of the utter helplessness in this situation was intoxicating, drugging me with feelings of inferiority and self-hatred. I was relying on *strangers* for the safety of my son. Strangers with pretty, kind and kick-ass wives to be sure. Strangers with kind eyes and calm voices. Strangers with a glint in their eyes that told me they were more dangerous than anyone I'd come across in my life.

But strangers nonetheless.

Somewhere, right now, they were getting Nathan back. That's what Keltan told me, at least when he'd come here a couple of hours ago. Was it two? Or three? You think that for someone who was focusing on nothing but the time dragging on, I'd have a grasp on the specifics. But it was all melting into one, just a collection of seconds where I hadn't seen my son.

Keltan said they found him. That they were going to get him. That everything was going to be okay. He reached out and squeezed my shoulder. The touch was kind, human, something else telling me that this was not just another job to the owner of Greenstone Security.

I had somewhat of an inkling that of all the people I could have stumbled onto, I'd hit gold. So somewhere in the midst of my son's kidnapping, I'd been given some kind of luck or fortune to walk in here.

It wasn't comforting.

Polly was sitting next to me, silently.

Where most other people would be trying to speak, reassure me, keep my mind busy. Lucy and Rosie had definitely done that.

But Polly seemed to understand at this point, there was nothing left.

"I should've left," I whispered, still staring at the beautiful painting on the wall, wanting to dive into it. "After Robert came, I shouldn't have had all those stupid thoughts about trying to fight, trying to beat him. I shouldn't have been so naïve. I should've taken Nathan, gotten out of there. If I did, none of this—"

"Stop," Polly said gently.

I met her eyes.

They were hard and soft at the same time. "The first thing we do when something so horrible we can't comprehend happens is try to find someone to blame," she said. "I don't know why, it's human nature. It's also human nature to figure out a way to blame ourselves for other people's actions. Good people that do that. People that want to believe the best in others who have done the worst to them. But I'm telling you right now, that your son being taken *is not on you*. Not even a little bit. I know me saying that isn't going to mean shit until he's here, but it's the truth. You don't have to believe it right now, but I just want you to hear it anyway."

She squeezed my hand. Took a breath.

"I promise that this horror will stop being this bad," she said. "I can't promise it will ever be truly over, because when people like us, those deep feeling good people, experience something that punctures to our bones, the horror kind of stays. Even when it's covered in joy and happiness in love, it's always there. Like a root we're unable to pull out. I'm not going to lie to you and say you'll forget this time. It will haunt you forever. But I can promise you that flowers grow and bloom even over the most rotten of roots."

I blinked rapidly at her. The poetry of her words. The pain in them. It was that pain I held onto. It was incredibly selfish of me, to be happy to see some of her hurt exposed so I didn't feel so alone in mine, but it was a life raft. And I was clutching it.

Because I'd drown otherwise.

So I held onto this kind woman's hands and the evidence of her suffering and pain.

I SNAPPED up the second I heard footsteps coming up the stairs. I wanted to run to the door and thrust it open but my legs were frozen in place. Terror stuck me to the spot. Fear that it would be someone opening that door with news I would not survive.

So I stayed, frozen, listening to those footsteps, straining to hear smaller ones, the sound of a familiar voice.

I couldn't hear over the dull roar in my ears.

Then the handle turned.

I held my breath.

"Momma!" my little boy screamed, grinning with a beam that speared into my soul. "Captain America came to get me."

My vision blurred and I struggled to stay up with the weight of my relief. My utter joy. Nathan was here, standing in front of me, wearing strange pressed and beige clothes but he was clean. Safe.

He was frickin' *smiling*.

I'd been so certain I wouldn't be able to handle the bad news I didn't consider that the good news—the best news that could ever exist—would hit me just as heavily.

Nathan's small hand was engulfed in a much larger one, clinging to it.

I followed the hand, the muscled arm upward to dead eyes.

Not dead, no, something else.

The aggressive, violent man who I'd been so sure ate puppies for protein was holding my son's hand.

It was jarring.

For about half a second.

Because there was only one thing important to me at this moment.

It was the little human being grinning at me like there was no reason in the world to be unhappy.

He ran at me at the same time I sank to my knees.

Nathan's little body hit mine, and I wrapped my arms around him, inhaling strongly.

"I missed you, sugarbear," he said into my chest.

"I missed you too, honeybun," I choked into his hair, willing myself to keep the promise I'd made to not break down in tears.

I inhaled deeply, pressing my face to his head.

"Are you smelling my hair?" his little voice asked, muffled from how tightly I was holding him. I couldn't physically loosen my grip. I wasn't sure if I'd ever be able to loosen my grip again.

"Only because it smells so good," I replied, my voice still thick and choked with unshed tears.

There was a pause. "Well, Mommy, I'm sorry to say that you don't smell good. Did you forget to shower again?"

There was a choked giggle from behind me.

When I'd thought—in this very room, mere hours ago—that I'd never smile again, my little boy made me smile.

Keltan had kept his promise.

I had my son back.

CHAPTER FOUR

Lance

HE SHOULD'VE LEFT THEM.

The second the tiny hand released his, he should've walked out of the room. Then he should've kept walking, out of the office, down to the parking lot and onto his bike. Then he should've driven. A long fucking way away from here. To the ocean. Where he could smell the salt and nothing else.

But he didn't.

He just stood there, watched Elena sink to her knees as she lost the ability to keep herself upright. Watched as the kid ran full force into his mom.

The way she clutched him hit his gut. She held him like his little body was the only thing tethering her to this earth. He could fucking *taste* the emotion in this room. Him. And instead of it bouncing off the hard shell he'd grown over himself, it got in. Sank under his skin.

Just like the way the kid had.

He hadn't intended on having any real contact with him, or

her ever again. He intended on making sure they were back together, safe, and never laying eyes on them again.

No, that was a lie. He had already planned on watching her house, the kid's school—once he talked to the dipshit teachers—and her work. For how long, he didn't know. Until he was satisfied.

But he didn't plan on *her* seeing *him*. On those golden eyes touching his, searing into him. No fucking way.

But then they got in the house. Somehow, the kid found his way to him. Walked right up to him, in the middle of the chaos around him.

"Hi sir," the little boy with caramel skin and green eyes greeted him. He was holding a battered rabbit by the ear. "You're very tall," he commented. "And muscly." There was a pause as the kid inspected him. "Are you Captain America?"

At this point, Lance almost fucking laughed. Him. He hadn't even cracked a smile in a decade, hadn't laughed in recent memory, but this kid, who'd been essentially held captive by a stranger claiming to be his father, was seemingly unrattled by strangers around him.

"No, kid," he replied. "No way am I any kind of superhero."

The kid furrowed his brows, focusing with an intensity that a five-year-old definitely shouldn't have.

It was cute.

Lance didn't think *anything* was cute. He'd never used the word in his life, never fucking *thought* it. But now here he was, thinking it when he'd been sure he'd be in here restraining his urge to kill, not to fucking *laugh*.

"You're here to take me back to my mommy, aren't you?" the kid asked after a beat.

Lance was shocked. Another thing that never happened to him. People were reasonably predictable, the shit they said was rarely shocking—Rosie was not included in this—he was bored and detached from most useless babble.

But fuck. This kid.

Lance nodded once.

The kid smiled. Big. Wide. It hit Lance in the gut. Just like those green eyes had. "Well, then, you are a superhero," he decided. Then, he held out his hand.

Lance stared at it for a second, not quite sure what the kid wanted from him. Candy? He didn't carry around loose Werther's Originals in his fucking pockets.

But then he realized. The kid wanted to take his fucking hand.

And he didn't even hesitate to take it.

Him. Who abhorred and avoided all human contact, *especially* with children.

But he did that.

And he took the kid's hand, then, and when he held it out to him once they'd gotten out of the SUV they drove here in, Lance led him up the stairs of the offices while he chattered on about how he "didn't know superheroes had offices, but it made sense." The kid had cracked up every member of the team. Charmed them all.

Everyone was on a high.

They'd hoped for the best. But they were trained, they'd seen some horrible shit, some of the most horrible shit humans could do to each other, they'd seen it happen to people they loved. So they were hopeful, as hopeful as people could be knowing that the worst-case scenario was more common and horrifying than anyone thought.

But they got something rare.

They got the absolute best-case scenario.

The kid didn't have a bruise on him. He was clean. Seemed to be well-fed, didn't show any signs of emotional trauma, not one fucking tear. Lance wouldn't have believed it if he hadn't seen it with his own two eyes.

And the kid was something.

Not that that was surprising given his mother.

Everyone recognized it.

Everyone wanted to protect this kid and this woman because they dealt with so much shit, they knew when something real, good and rare came along.

Hudson had caved like any bully would when confronted with someone tougher and more powerful. It wasn't surprising, given what a fucking coward he was. The footage of him with multiple prostitutes getting fucked up the ass with a dildo also helped. Plus the evidence they had against his father helped if he decided to get Daddy involved.

It seemed the senator had been a naughty fucking boy himself, with embezzlement and money laundering among the list of crimes that would put him away if they took it public.

Why was it that all these people that thought they were better than everyone were usually doing worse shit than the criminals?

Lance didn't care. The bloodlust that he'd been so sure he'd be choking on dissipated with the small hand in his.

So maybe that's why he stood there, watching the mother and child embrace, because of that lack of constant fury that he was so sure would be permanent. It was gone around them.

And when he heard the kid's muffled comment about Elena's smell, it happened again, he wanted to laugh. Or at least smile.

The need was almost as strong as the one to kill.

But he overcame it.

Polly, who was standing behind the mother and son, let out a giggle as tears poured down her face.

Lance didn't tear his gaze away from the small dark head and the larger one with thick hair for long.

He watched until Elena finally let the kid go, framing his face with her hands, eyes roving over it as if she were needing to commit it to memory. Lance had expected her eyes to be wet, tears streaming down her face.

But nothing.

He knew how deep she was feeling. It was painted all over her. In every part of her body, the way she held herself, the way she fucking breathed. It was painful to watch. She was experiencing it, without shedding a fucking tear.

Even Rosie had leaked from her eyes when they got the kid back.

Rosie.

But Elena's eyes stayed dry.

"How come I had to stay with that guy?" the kid asked. "He said he was my daddy. Is that true, Mom? Because it sounded real true. And he even had the same eyes as me, and a badge, just like you said my dad had. He promised me that it was okay. Did I do wrong by going with him? Is that why Captain America came to get me?"

Something in him clenched.

Something in his chest area.

No matter how often he'd tried to correct the kid when he'd referred to him as 'Captain,' he hadn't let up, not even when he tried to snap it at him.

He seemed immune to the demeanor that had ensured most of the population avoided him at all costs.

The way he liked it.

Elena paused with the question. "No, honeybun, you did absolutely nothing wrong. And yes, that was your daddy. He just didn't tell me that he was taking you for a sleepover. And I got so worried I had my friends come to pick you up."

"I didn't know you were friends with superheroes, Mom! That's so cool."

Elena grinned, it was sad, tight, full of exhaustion and sorrow. But it was beautiful. She was. Even in the same, wrinkled clothes she'd been wearing since the previous day, her hair knotted and tangled, her eyes bloodshot and paleness to her face that wasn't natural. She was stunning. It attracted him even more, all that pain changing her. He liked it when ugly things brushed beautiful things.

Except that bruise. That fucking bruise that had only gotten worse since the previous day. It was shades of black and purple, the skin raised and it covered almost half her face.

The fucker must have put all his strength behind that punch. Everything he could give.

He didn't give a fuck what Keltan said, about Elena's wishes, he was going to end that piece of shit. Not today, or even tomorrow. But one day, when all of this had blown over, when he was least expecting it. He'd nurture this feeling, this toxicity in his bones looking at her beautifully bruised face, looking at the years shaved off her life worrying about her son.

It would happen.

"What happened to your face, Mom?" the kid asked, moving his small hand to gingerly brush it over the violence his father had wrecked on his mother.

She smiled. Tight still. "I was silly and forgot about being careful," she replied.

Lance noted that she didn't feed her son a lie about falling over or walking into something. She didn't tell him the specifics, but she didn't lie.

That was important to him somehow, and he wasn't even sure how.

"Do you want me to butterfly kiss it better?" the kid asked.

Elena's eyes lit up.

It was a gut punch.

"I thought you'd never ask," she said, tickling her son.

He let out a giggle that seemed so separate from this whole environment. Kids were really resilient as fuck.

Though he should have walked out a thousand times before this, and despite the fact he knew he was making a huge fucking mistake, he got to watch the small boy press his face up against his mother's and brush her angry bruise with his eyelashes.

It was then, and only then that he turned and walked out.

Elena

Nathan grinned as he pulled back, eyes lit with happiness that was so simple and so precious because it had meant someone survived these past hours.

"Better?" he asked.

I nodded, choking on my happiness. "Better," I croaked out.

Better was not a word for what I was. I knew that these hours had broken something in me, and I would have to deal with it for life. I was worse in that respect. Knowing that Robert was obviously intent on getting back into our lives. That terrified me. It also strengthened me. The little boy who'd just used his eyelashes to fix the bruise on my face his father created had fixed a little part of my soul. Solidified it. Turned it into armor, ready for a battle.

I remembered in that moment, someone who had fought in this battle for us. Someone, by the looks of it, had fought in countless battles, someone who seemed like a human who was war.

Who had walked in holding my son's hand and been dubbed 'Captain America.'

My eyes were loath to leave my son, but I managed to move them to the doorway.

But it was empty.

He was gone.

"I HAVE no words for how grateful I am to all of you," I said, addressing the table.

At the table sat five men, all different forms of hot as balls. All muscled. All manly in every sense of the word. My friend Marie would be drooling right now. And then trying to hit on them, though not the three out of the five wearing wedding rings.

And not the one who had once held my son's hand.

No. She would not hit on him because the thought of it made my fingers curl. I didn't know why. He wasn't my property. I didn't *know* him. I was pretty sure he hated me, because he'd been glaring at me since I'd sat down at the table with the whole Greenstone Security team.

It was a meeting I'd requested, despite the thought of leaving Nathan so soon made me sick. But it had to be done.

Polly had promised not to let him out of her sight. I trusted her.

I'd also showered, because my son was right, I was ripe—but Nathan had been sitting on the toilet seat beside the shower, swinging his legs and chattering on about how weird the food had been at his 'dad's.'

"There was nothing colorful," he said. "And it was cold. They made me wear different clothes. And there was a room that he said was my bedroom but I didn't like it one bit and he yelled at me when I drew on the walls."

I had paused, shampoo bottle poised above my palm.

My hand shook.

He had yelled.

Yelled at my son.

I squeezed the bottle tight, fury coursing through my veins. Had I made the wrong choice in telling Lance not to kill him?

Because the thought of Nathan having to breathe his air ever again had me wishing I'd killed him myself.

But the thought washed away with the shampoo I'd squirted everywhere.

"Do I have to go back there, Mom?" Nathan asked. "Because he said it was my house, I told him I already had a house with you that I liked much better." A pause. "I don't think I liked him. Is that bad? All my other friends love their daddies but..."

He trailed off and the hurt and confusion in his voice speared me.

I yanked the shower curtain aside.

Nathan didn't blink at my nakedness, he'd seen it all before, since living with a child meant your time, your privacy and your body was never your own. He was pounding on the door if I took longer than two seconds in the bathroom.

"You are not meant to love anyone you don't want to love," I told him over the trickle of the shower. Well, not trickle, but amazing pressure that was like nirvana compared to the either scorching hot or freezing cold dribble at our place. It was a waterfall shower. I wanted to live in there. Also because you didn't have to face reality in showers.

"Your daddy is a complicated man who is not ready to be a daddy," I said, striving to be as honest as I could be with a kid who couldn't comprehend the truth. "He has troubles that he needs to fix. And maybe he won't ever fix them. Some people aren't born to be daddies and that's not your fault. So maybe you might not ever see him again." I paused, trying to read my son's face. "Is that okay with you? Are you happy for it just to be you and your momma?"

He considered the question, as he always did. My boy was a thinker, he never responded straight away on instinct. "I'm okay with that. Sugarbear and Honeybun forever."

I smiled, glad the shower could mask my tears. "Forever and ever, kiddo."

Polly had provided me with some clothes from a closet that they had for clients. I'd expected a scratchy tracksuit... not a pair of cashmere sweatpants, the thinnest and softest fabric I'd ever touched or put on my body, and a crisp white tee.

I'd never understood people paying hundreds of dollars for clothing, didn't get how something as simple as a tee shirt could be worth hundreds. It was a *tee* for goodness sakes.

But this. I got it. It *felt* like hundreds of dollars on my skin.

I'd braided my damp hair and then asked Keltan if it was possible to speak to everyone involved in getting Nathan back to me.

He'd smiled, squeezed my arm and said he'd take care of it.

I got the idea that when Keltan said he'd 'take care' of something, it would happen, immediately and in some kind of magical badass type way.

Like somehow getting my son back to me unscathed and unhurt, still smiling.

Yeah, that was some badass magic right there.

I knew that it wasn't just him.

Hence me sitting at the table with five badass men and one arguably more badass woman.

Rosie was pretty much who I wanted to be when I grew up. When I had a different life. She was beautiful, swore like a sailor and gave me a hug when she first met me that did the same as Keltan's *"I'll take care of it"*—it gave me faith.

"I can't express in words what you've done for me," I continued, addressing the table and everyone sitting in it apart from one person. One person who I physically couldn't make eye contact with.

I wasn't sure if it was because I was afraid of him or... something else.

I couldn't think about either of those things right now.

"Thank you seems hollow, but thank you," I continued, my voice breaking.

Rosie's hand found mine under the table. "Babe, you're the one we should be thanking," she said, eyes shimmering. "I got to spend time with your kick-ass little dude and it's given me faith that not all small children are simmering wusses, there's hope for mine yet." She paused. "He cries too much."

Her husband, Luke, an ex-police officer and a serious hot guy scowled at her. "He's a *baby*, Rosie."

She rolled her eyes. "He's *our baby*, honey. Therefore both of our awesome badass genes should've meshed and made a superbaby who didn't wail just because he was *hungry*. You don't see me doing that, do you?"

"You cried yesterday over a taco," Luke shot back.

She narrowed her beautifully sculpted brows at him. "It was a fucking great taco and you're a traitor, outing me like that. I'm gonna have to divorce you."

Luke smiled at her in a way that made my whole heart hurt.

There was so much in that simple smile, in their bickering, in their energy with one another. With the obvious love and respect for one another. I longed for something like that, someone like that.

I mentally shook myself.

Who was I longing for something when I had already been given the greatest gift? My child, safe, unharmed, smiling.

It was selfish of me to want more.

I met Keltan's eyes. "This is a debt that cannot ever be repaid, but I promise you I'll pay everything I have."

Keltan's eyes hardened. "We don't have to think about that now. You just need to think about your boy."

I nodded once, already mentally doing the numbers in my

head, feeling vaguely nauseous about the prospect of how I was going to afford this.

It would be okay.

I'd take extra shifts.

Maybe even work at a bar a couple of nights a week. Karen and Eliza would have Nathan.

I'd work it out, I always did.

"We need to talk about Hudson," Keltan continued.

My blood ran cold. I'd almost forgotten about Robert. As if that were possible, to forget about the husband that abused me, that tortured me, and who kidnapped my child. But I had, with the joy and the emotions surrounding me, with Nathan surrounding me, I momentarily forgot the man that gave him his eyes and almost took him from me.

My hands were clammy and suddenly my butt felt hot and sweaty in these damn cashmere pants.

I steeled myself to be strong, straighten my back and deal with this.

"I'll move first, I guess," I said, thinking about how sad it would be to pack up our home, to leave our neighbors who had become family. I wouldn't leave town, but it would just be too risky to be somewhere Robert knew about. Though I was sure he'd be able to find any new place I rented in a couple of clicks.

I suddenly felt hopeless.

"You're not movin'." This did not come from Keltan. It was not spoken in a kind and gentle tone.

It was almost a snarl.

I steeled myself to look in his eyes, and the eye contact was akin to stepping my bare feet into snow. A chill shocked me, traveled upward, turned me numb and electrified at the same time.

He didn't say anything else.

Neither did I.

I was struck dumb. And I looked pretty frickin' dumb, sitting there staring at Hades himself while a table full of badasses watched.

"What Lance means," Keltan said after a beat, amusement in his voice. "Is that we're not gonna let him drive you from your home or Nathan from his school." He paused. "We feel like we've shown Robert it's in his best interests to stay away from you and Nathan indefinitely, and men like this are driven by what's in their best interests. I am fairly confident you won't see or hear from him ever again. But I'm not going to stake your or your son's safety on 'fairly confident.' We're going to put a security detail on you, for a few weeks at least, check in on Hudson and install a state of the art security system in your house."

He looked to Luke, who I assumed was the security system guy.

He nodded once. "Already on it."

"Wait," I interrupted when it looked like Keltan was going to keep speaking. "I can't—" I cut myself off from saying I couldn't afford the security system, even though it was blatantly true. "I don't need a security system, or the security. I've already taken up enough of your time. You've already done enough."

Keltan's eyes were hard and soft at the same time. "All due respect, sweetheart, I'm gonna be the judge of when enough is enough. Enough for me is you and that kid livin' a life where you're not looking over your shoulder constantly, expecting a threat from a weak man trying to be strong by hurting you. I won't be able to sleep at night if I don't make sure that doesn't happen. And not just because I'll be sleeping on my couch after my wife kicks me out of bed for not helping you in every way I can. Because that's just who I am." He looked around the table. "That's just who we are. And I know I don't know you, but you seem to be the woman who doesn't ask for help ever, mostly 'cause the world hasn't given it to her. And for the most part, you haven't needed it. Now, Elena, you need our help. It doesn't make you weak for accepting it or needing it."

I will not cry.

I opened my mouth to protest some more.

"If you don't say yes now, I'll just come to your house at two in the morning blasting Miley Cyrus—Hannah Montana era—every single night until you agree," Rosie cut in.

I glanced at her, and I didn't doubt the woman was serious. I was pretty sure she was like a tiny bit unhinged.

She was grinning.

I sighed, my muscles were taut and mind wired against doing such a thing, putting my troubles on all these strangers. All these good people with better things to do than get me out of the mess I have gotten myself into by choosing the wrong man.

But no. I could never regret that choice, because I got Nathan.

No matter what I had been through or would have to go through, nothing could make me regret him.

It was Nathan that had me conceding, because Keltan was right, even the slightest chance that my son was still at risk was a chance I was willing to forgo my dignity for. Well, and the fact that I needed my sleep and I knew Hannah Montana Miley would make sure that didn't happen.

"Okay," I whispered.

Lance

"First things first, I need to let you all know that this case is gonna be unpaid," Keltan said after Elena had left.

The fucking room smelled of her again.

She had come fresh-faced, hair wet in a long braid and all he could fucking think about was yanking onto that braid and taking her.

What the fuck was wrong with him?

Thinking *that* while they were discussing keeping her son safe?

Well, he knew what was wrong with him, everything that could be wrong with someone.

He hated her. For making him hate himself.

Because all the things he'd done, the man he was, he didn't hate himself for it. He accepted that it was what it was.

But she made him hate everything about what he was, all that hardness, violence, all that inability to handle a proper human conversation.

Because he couldn't do that, which meant he couldn't be near her and the kid and he wanted to be.

"Anyone who has a problem with that, no hard feelings, you don't have to be in on it," Keltan continued.

Obviously no one left the table.

No one here gave a fuck about the money. Each of them had plenty of it.

"We overcharge rich assholes especially so we can do shit like that," Duke said, vocalizing what they already knew. "This is the part of the job that actually means shit."

Nods around the table.

"I also want to bring Rogue around for playdates with Nathan, make him a little more badass like him," Rosie interjected.

Of course Rosie had named her fucking kid Rogue.

Luke pinched the bridge of his nose.

Heath grinned. "I'm sure Andrew could do with another little buddy too."

Andrew was the kid him and Polly had recently adopted. The kid who had almost made Lance feel something. Because the world had battered him. At ten years old, he'd seen more hurt than most people would see in a lifetime. Now he was with Polly and Heath, they'd make it their mission to make sure he saw only beauty.

"Keltan chuckled. "Right, glad we're all on the same page." He glanced to Luke. "You set to install the system tomorrow?"

Luke nodded. "Apparently I'm bringing *my child* to the installation."

Rosie grinned.

"She lives outside the city, so I've got us a rental down at the end of her street," Keltan continued. "Friend of a friend happens to own it and is willing to let us use it as a base."

Lance was not surprised at this. Despite the fact that Keltan wasn't even from this country, and he'd only been based in LA for a handful of years, fucker seemed to have contacts and friends everywhere.

Lance only had enemies and ghosts.

Keltan looked to Duke. "You good to follow them home? Take the first shift?"

Duke's eyes lit up too much at that. Lance saw the way that fucker had looked at Elena. He knew that look.

"I got it," Lance all but growled.

When Keltan focused on him with a glint in his eye, he knew the fucker had purposefully played him.

"You sure?" he continued. "I know the people part of the job isn't exactly your favorite."

"I don't have to talk to them to keep them safe," Lance snapped, intending to make sure he didn't speak with either of them at all if he could help it.

Keltan's mouth twitched. The fucker was having a great time with this, and Rosie seemed to be enjoying herself too. Of course she was, she loved to torture monsters, and that's what he was.

He clenched his fists.

Keltan seemed to sense enough was enough. "You good to monitor Hudson then?" he asked Duke.

The man nodded once, eyes taking on a glint. "Wish I could monitor him as he suffocates on his own fucking blood after I'm done with him," he muttered.

Everyone at the table agreed with the sentiment of Duke's words.

But everyone was also going to accept the fact that sometimes even assholes got to keep breathing when they shouldn't.

Except him.

And Rosie. That bitch spent her evenings making sure that rapists and child molesters didn't keep breathing, she was a wild card. Especially since the Sons of Templar war. That had shaken them all. Only now were they getting over the aftershocks.

Lance didn't know the club well, but he knew it would be a long time before those wounds scabbed over.

He wasn't sure Elena's would.

Which was why he'd be burying Hudson.

"Okay, so we're good on what we've got to do?" Keltan asked the table.

Nods.

"Right, get back to your families, get to your jobs. I need to hug my fuckin' kids after this," he announced.

Everyone got up.

"Lance."

He knew it was coming even as he turned.

Rosie winked at him.

He sighed and sat down in his previous seat and the door closed behind the rest of the team.

He waited for Keltan to speak.

"This case, it's different for you."

Not a question.

Therefore Lance wasn't socially obligated to respond.

So he didn't.

Keltan wasn't put off. "The woman, she's different for you."

Again, not a question.

Again, no answer.

Keltan grinned, shaking his head with a knowing glint to his eye. "Fuck, it seems the men here never get it boring when it comes to this shit," he muttered. Then he turned serious. "She's got a kid."

Lance made a sound at the back of his throat. "Think I missed that part?"

Keltan didn't acknowledge this. "She's got a kid, a good one. She's a good woman that's gone through a lot of shit, and even though I'm hoping it's over, I'm thinking it's not if you're in the mix." He narrowed his eyes. "You don't fuck her around. Not a single mom who still has fresh bruises from the husband that beat her and kidnapped her kid."

Lance bristled, his blood simmered uncomfortably. He wasn't used to the sensation. Everything he did was in cold blood. Therefore controlled.

But since yesterday everything in him was reactive, the control he'd considered second nature was more difficult than anything.

"I'm not fucking with shit," he gritted out. "I'm doin' my job."

Keltan raised his eyebrow, challenging him, as if he knew something Lance didn't. As if he knew what this woman was doing to him.

He guessed he had an idea since he was perceptive as shit and it was obvious as fuck that Lance was not acting normal.

He gritted his teeth but didn't speak.

Keltan waited a beat, eyes still hard with his warning, but Lance could tell the fucker seemed amused at this whole situation.

He clenched his fists and reminded himself that he was not prone to random acts of violence. Especially against his boss. And friend.

"You gotta promise me you won't touch Hudson," Keltan said finally, all amusement wiped.

Fuck.

He pursed his lips. Lance never lied, and he never made promises he knew he couldn't keep.

Keltan sighed. "I'm serious, brother. I know you. And I know the look you get when you're plannin' on digging another grave. I get it. Fuck, thinking about my kids, thinking about that woman, seeing her face all bruised up." Keltan clenched his fists. "It's not comin' easy to me to stay out of this guy's life. It really fucking isn't. And I know Rosie is the same. I can't guarantee she isn't planning on planting a fucking bomb in his house. But we made a promise to the client. She has her wishes. Beyond that, he's the son of a fucking senator. A shady one, but that's not surprising. So we need to tread carefully. Not because I'm afraid of the blowback on the business, we can handle anything. We've had worse people gunning for us. But Elena, she can't handle that shit. I've got a feeling that senator even gets a whiff that she's had any connection with his son's death, he'll ruin her fucking life. In ways we can't protect her from."

Lance wouldn't let that happen. "We kill him too then."

The solution was simple.

Keltan leaned back in his chair, eyes wide. "Jesus Christ, Lance. He's a fucking *senator*."

Lance didn't reply. He was aware of his position and that meant exactly shit to him.

"We're not goin' round killing people. We gotta do this smart. If not for our sakes, then for Elena's."

Keltan hit his mark and he knew it.

"Now go see her and that kid home," Keltan said.

CHAPTER FIVE

Elena

LANCE HAD SEEN us to my car, stared at it with a stiff jaw as we got in and then informed me that he'd be following us home and taking the first watch.

His sentence had not been as articulate as that, but I figured the rest out.

I wanted to ask a lot of questions about this. About the logistics of such a thing, but my five-year-old was tired and hungry and needed to go home.

I needed to go home, I was dead on my feet.

Which Lance obviously noticed because he put his hand to the driver's door to stop me opening it after I'd strapped Nathan in his seat in the back.

I stared at the corded and muscled arm, it was one of the most attractive arms I'd ever seen up close. Sure, Robert worked out, but it was hard to appreciate muscles used to beat the shit out of you.

I didn't doubt that Lance beat the shit out of someone, but I had the distorted certainty that it was people who deserved it and certainly not women.

I had a sense about the man.

Beyond that, Keltan would not employ a man who hurt women.

"You good to drive?" he clipped.

I blinked, looking up at his empty eyes. I wished that one day someone would fill them. It was a strange wish to have for a practical stranger—albeit a hot one—but it was sincere to my bones. I guessed it wasn't strange to wish the man who helped bring my son back to me be rewarded with something to light up his life.

I got the feeling it was pretty dark.

"Good to drive?" I repeated.

He nodded once. "You haven't got shit for sleep in twenty-four hours. Barely eaten." He looked to the back seat. "You even *think* you're not good, you tell me now. Not havin' you take risks."

It was the most words I'd heard him say since I'd met him.

And from what I understood, they were words of concern for the safety of my son and myself. Not spoken kindly, but the meaning behind them was.

I swallowed the lump in my throat.

"I'm good to drive," I said with confidence. "I think I'm still on adrenaline or something, because I feel tired emotionally, but not physically." I narrowed my eyes at him. "I wouldn't just say this to be independent or whatever. If I wasn't good to drive, I'd frickin' say so. I wouldn't drive in the first place."

He inspected me. Like he was rooting around inside my head, throwing out junk he didn't find useful and looking for the good stuff. It was violating. That stare. Uncomfortable. Addictive.

His eyes cleared and he nodded again, seeming to find what he wanted.

He opened the door for me.

Robotically, I got in, throwing my purse on the passenger

seat. It was then I realized that a pair of panties were hanging off the edge. I'd stuffed my dirty clothes in there earlier, complete with the panties because Polly had made sure to include them.

And now, my bright red donut panties that were not a lace G-string were poking out the top of the bag that had been on my shoulder the entire time Lance was standing right in front of me.

Heat bloomed in my cheeks and I gripped the steering wheel, willing him to walk away so I could comfortably die of mortification.

He didn't.

He stayed, keeping the door open with his arm. No way could I fight him trying to get it closed.

I didn't speak.

Neither did he.

His eyes did not move to the passenger seat. Maybe he didn't see the panties. No, this was not a man who missed anything. I was pretty sure his job required him to notice everything. Not just his job. Something inside him, the intensity of his presence told me that he needed to control his environment and in order to do that he had to know everything that existed in his environment. Including my dirty, totally unsexy granny panties hanging outside of my cheap and worn purse.

Nathan was having a conversation with Feebo in the back. He had no idea what kind of emotional and physical mortification his mother was going through.

What did I do here? Did I swallow the shame and act like I *mean*t to have my panties hanging out for the world to see? Ignore it all completely? Slyly move over and tuck them back in? But that option wouldn't work with Lance's glare gluing me to my frickin' seat.

"I like donuts, okay? And the cotton is more comfortable than lace. Practical too," I blurted out, unsure of what kind of sickness I had but pretty sure that I needed to be medicated for just saying what I said to possibly one of the hottest men to walk the earth.

I wanted to sink into my car seat and never emerge.

"Are we getting donuts for dinner?" Nathan said from the back. "Because I want one with sprinkles. Like that one."

I didn't need to turn in my seat to know his chubby little hand was pointing at the large donut with sprinkles that took up the ass of my panties.

Someone fucking save me.

"Can I get a sprinkles donut and a chocolate one, Mom?" Nathan continued, unaware that he was contributing to possibly one of the most mortifying moments in my life.

I made a mental note to punish him for it later in life, kiss him straight on the mouth on his first day of high school or something like that.

I didn't dare look at Lance. "Sure, we can have donuts for dinner," I said, deciding to roll with it and give my five-year-old all that refined sugar before bed. Partly because I was willing to forgo my strict no sugar on weekdays routine to get the fuck out of this situation but mostly because at this point, I was ready to say yes to anything my little boy asked me.

"Do you want to have donuts with us for dinner, Captain?" Nathan asked Lance.

I still didn't look at him. "Lance does not get muscles like that eating donuts, honeybun," I said, not even knowing what it meant until after I'd vomited the words out.

Oh my god, now he knew I noticed his muscles.

But that wasn't bad, it's not really something you missed about the man.

"Okay, well, I don't want donuts either," Nathan decided.

I turned and gaped at my son, because him deciding, on his own, that he didn't want sugary treats for dinner on a Thursday was enough to shock me out of whatever shame-filled paralysis I'd been experiencing.

"Just like that, you don't want donuts?" I said.

He nodded very seriously. His eyes went behind me. "Because I want to be big and muscly like a superhero and donuts are just stupid if they aren't what superheroes eat."

Oh sweet Lord.

"What do you eat for dinner, Captain?" Nathan asked.

I turned back in my seat. There was silence for a beat, and Nathan was waiting expectantly for Lance to give him a detailed rundown of his nutrition. I didn't think this inarticulate hot guy was going to do so and I didn't want to let my son down. I also saw this as my chance.

"He likely eats a lot of vegetables, green ones, like broccoli, spinach, carrots and yummy things like lentils, chickpeas and things full of protein and nutrients," I answered for Lance to help my efforts at dinnertime and to save my son from being hurt when his new hero treated him with the same loaded silence I was.

For my son's sake, I braved a lot at Lance, giving him a look. "Right?"

He waited a beat, holding my gaze hostage before moving his eyes to Nathan. "Right."

The single word was enough for Nathan, and he beamed. "Let's go to the pro-teen and nutree-ant store then, Mom," Nathan decided, stumbling on the words he hadn't heard before.

I grinned.

"Okay, buddy, we're going," I replied, then I looked back to Lance pointedly trying to communicate with my face he was the one stopping me from leaving due to his entire muscled form in my door.

"Seatbelt," he grunted.

I jerked in surprise.

I was always one to wear a seatbelt, of course. If we crashed, no way did I want to go flying through the window, leaving Nathan. And kids learned by example, always.

I had planned on putting it on, once Lance had left my presence and I regained normal brain function.

But it seemed that Lance was not going to leave the vicinity until I buckled up.

I did so, fumbling with the buckle three times.

Because of course I had to finish this encounter with more mortification and awkwardness.

Once I was buckled, Lance was satisfied. "Wait here 'til I get my bike. I'll follow you."

I raised my brow. "Bike?" I repeated.

He nodded once.

My ovaries were toast. The man rode a *motorcycle*.

I hated the things because of the horror stories I'd heard about crashes, I'd already told Nathan that motorcycles secretly made your pee pee fall off and that was why he could never own one or ride on one.

But the thought of Lance's thighs straddling a motorcycle, watching the man ride it... yeah that was hot as balls.

Luckily, I managed to keep those thoughts to myself and just waited for him to close the door.

Still, he didn't. This was torture. Was I being punished for something? And my child, who was usually the best way out of a boring situation, was annoyingly patient right now.

"Need your affirmative," Lance clipped.

"My affirmative?" I repeated.

Great, I'd gone from talking about my underwear and his muscles to just repeating everything he said.

Granted, I wasn't fluent in badass speak. Pig Latin, yes. My son's imaginary language he created before he spoke real words, totally. But hot guy speak? Nope.

"That you'll sit your ass in this car, doors locked, wait for me, then leave," he expanded, sounding seriously pissed at my lack of fluency in his language.

"Oh, ten four rubber ducky," I replied, doing a little salute.

Kill. Me. Now.

Something ticked in his jaw, probably utter annoyance that he was stuck with a woman who seemed like she was experiencing some kind of brain injury that made her act like a total dork.

He held onto my eyes and my sanity for a moment longer before he stepped back and closed the door.

I exhaled.

But he was still standing there, waiting for something.

Oh, the locks.

Only when I did lock them did he walk away.

"I GOT HIM," a voice said from behind me.

I jumped because although I'd heard, seen and drooled over him pulling up behind me in my driveway, illuminated by the streetlights, I didn't expect him to be right behind me, close enough for his breath to tickle my neck.

I hadn't expected him to move from the bike. He didn't seem like he enjoyed my company and since my son was unconscious, it was just me.

He was meant to be 'surveillance'. I didn't know what the heck that meant, I'd watched cop shows. Wasn't that just sitting in an Escalade eating snacks?

But he didn't have an Escalade, he had a Harley and no way a man who looked like that binged on any kind of processed snacks.

Or maybe he did, he could just have a monster metabolism.

So that's what I did, sat in my driveway thinking about what

Lance snacked on while staring at him sitting on the bike. That was until I realized exactly what I was doing and the fact that Lance was watching me and likely wondering what in the fresh hell I was doing sitting here staring while my son was in the back, head in that unnatural and uncomfortable looking position all kids adopted when they fell asleep in cars.

That's when I jumped out of the car, scolding myself for making my son sleep with his chin touching his chest, possibly damaging his little neck and sitting in a cheap car seat while I perved at a man I had no chance with and no business perving at.

And somewhere in my journey around the car where I forced myself not to look in his direction, he'd managed to get off his bike, walk up my driveway and stand behind me just before I was about to lift Nathan and take him inside.

I turned, taking in Lance covered in shadows. He was wearing a leather jacket.

I was not allowed to notice or think about how frickin' hot he looked in that leather jacket.

"You don't have to," I said, my voice lowered only slightly because Nathan could sleep through a small pipe bomb going off. "I'm used to it."

"Didn't ask if you were used to it, said I got him."

The words were harsh, just like his profile. His presence.

Was I really gonna let a guy that spoke with that harshness, embody that harshness, carry my son in his arms into my frickin' house?

I stepped aside.

Apparently I was.

I was officially a terrible fucking mother.

But my heart melted at the tender and gentle way he picked up my son, somehow natural.

With a tight throat, I closed the door for him, starting to dig for my house keys from my purse and walked toward the house.

"DO YOU WANT COFFEE? Tea? Water? Grape Kool-Aid? I'm sorry, I don't have beer, or bourbon, or whisky, or any kind of tough guy drink. Or any alcohol at all, really," I babbled, not quite sure to do with myself standing awkwardly in the middle of my living room with the hottest guy to ever exist standing right in front of me.

I *wished* I had alcohol in the house. I needed it. But I couldn't even afford the cheap wine for another two days. Whoever said that they didn't drink being a single mother was a liar or a frickin' saint.

I needed something to dull the edges, and the cheapest red at the supermarket didn't exactly go down smooth but it worked well enough.

Karen and Eliza were always 'accidentally' buying my favorite red when they only drank white.

It embarrassed me, but I also accepted it. Because I wasn't going to let the wine go to waste and I knew that Karen and Eliza had good hearts and wanted to help.

Lance just shook his head to my offer.

Shit.

"What about a snack?" I offered, immediately regretting it thinking of the lack of anything that would be acceptable in my pantry to serve to an Adonis. "I mean, I mostly have kid stuff, but I can make you peanut butter crackers. Nathan loves them. His friends do too. Not that I'm saying that you're anything like a bunch of five-year-old boys but everyone likes peanut butter, right? It's protein."

Shut up! I screamed at myself.

I was not a babbler. Sure, I liked to talk a lot, you kind of had to when you had a kid that never shut up and when you were a waitress who relied almost entirely on tips.

But I considered myself reasonably articulate for someone without a college education, and I managed not to sound like a blithering idiot for almost my entire life.

And here I was.

Blithering. Idiot.

I was still riding off the adrenaline that the past day had pumped into my system. I felt wired. Manic almost, my body unsure of what to do with the undiluted cocktail of emotions that was coursing through my cells at the moment.

Lance shook his head.

Okay, so I was lost for words. I took a breath. "Um, okay, then. I'm not really sure how this works, do we meet up tomorrow? Do I call you every hour to tell you all is quiet on the Eastern Front?"

I really needed him out of my house. But then, I really didn't. Because I was rather terrified at what would happen when I forced to decompress everything that happened. When I finally allowed myself to feel what I'd gone through.

I'd promised myself that I could cry, and I was scared I might never stop.

Lance was working as a distraction. A dam to the onslaught of saltwater that I'd be expelling through my tear ducts.

"I'm stayin' here."

It wasn't a question. A request. It was a statement.

"Here? As in, in this house?" I clarified.

He nodded once.

I digested this. I hadn't even become accustomed to him *existing* in this house, or on planet earth at all—because he had to be otherworldly for all his aura and power he seemed to have—and now he was trying to say he was going to be staying at the house? No freaking way.

Not because I worried about a strange man sleeping in the same house as my five-year-old son. I had a weird kind of feeling knowing that he would never hurt him. He'd just fricking *saved* him. Nathan was attached to him in a different way than I was of course, but that kid was a special judge of character.

It wasn't Nathan I was worried about, he'd be thrilled to hear about this sleepover.

I could not handle this male energy in the house.

I wouldn't sleep a wink.

But I'd feel safe.

And that couldn't be. Just like I promised myself I'd never let a man make me feel unsafe again, I didn't want my safety to be defined by a man. My *anything* to be defined.

"We don't have a guest bedroom," I said, though it was obvious since he'd already done a 'walk through' of the house that took about thirty seconds.

"You've got a sofa," he said in way of reply.

I bit my lip. And looked from the sofa to him. "That sofa is too short for you. You'd be uncomfortable. Kink your neck. Then you couldn't do your job, which I'm sure requires a fully mobile neck."

What in the fresh hell was I even saying right now?

He watched me, or more accurately, it seemed like he was watching my mouth, and me capturing the lip between my teeth.

An unexpected and not entirely unpleasant heat shot in between my legs.

I ignored it. And stopped biting my lip.

"Slept on worse," he said after a beat.

Seriously, did this man only speak in three syllables?

"I get up to pee a lot at night," I blurted, desperate to find a reason he couldn't stay. And it seemed I wasn't above informing him of my bladder habits. My mouth kept moving. "I drink a lot of water, because no one ever drinks enough water and it's super good for you. But I have a really small bladder and I pee a lot."

Oh my god, why am I still talking about pee?

"It's only gotten worse after Nathan," I continued, seemingly possessed by someone with no social boundaries. "You know, childbirth kind of wreaks havoc... *down there.*"

Stop. Stop right now. You just referred to childbirth and the fact your vagina is effectively ruined to possibly the hottest man you've ever seen up close.

"I mean, it all still works, I don't pee myself or anything," I said quickly.

For the love of God. You're done now. Just done.

Nothing in his face moved. No amusement, he didn't find me endearing in a dorky way. No, that much was apparent.

I sucked in a breath. What else could I do? I think talking about my pee and my vagina after the birth of my son was a good moment to tap out and hide in my room for the rest of time.

"Right," I whispered. "I'll just go and get you some blankets and..." I didn't finish my sentence. I escaped the room.

I definitely took my sweet ass time retrieving the blankets from our linen cupboard. I was trying to calm myself down until I focused on the blankets I'd buried my face in and let out a little scream into.

It was a worn Barney comforter that Nathan had banished away because he decided purple dinosaurs were too 'common.' I shit you not, he said that.

I kept it because I didn't throw anything away, especially in case Nathan had an accident in the middle of the night and I had to change his sheets.

But now I was going to have to walk back into the room I'd talked about my bathroom habits in and give the baddest of all badasses a fucking *Barney blanket.*

"Well, it is what it is," I muttered to myself.

I walked back into the living room, Lance was standing in the exact same spot, eyes moving from his inspection of the room to focus on me.

I wanted to shrink under his gaze.

Instead, I placed the folded blanket on the sofa.

"Thank you," I whispered, straightening, all my mortification and shame melting and I stared at that Barney blanket.

It was very possible that I could have been in an empty house surrounded by memories of my son right now if it weren't for this man. Or I could have been in a very different house, getting the shit beaten out of me.

"For getting my son back to me, for holding his hand, for taking time out of your life to come all the way out here to sleep on a shitty couch and use a Barney blanket," I continued when he was silent.

One single tear landed on the fabric.

"Don't have to thank me," he said, voice hard and not affected by the emotion in my own. "Doin' my job. Nothing more."

I swallowed roughly. Looked up at him. "Well, to me, it's a lot more. It's everything." I weathered his stare for a few beats longer. "I'll leave you to it," I said, unable to stand here for a second longer, I felt the tears pressing at the backs of my eyes and I couldn't cry in front of this man.

He nodded. Didn't say anything.

What did I expect, 'sweet dreams?'

I turned on my heel and walked out.

Lance

He watched her disappear with his fists clenched to his sides. His entire body was shaking with the effort it took him to stand in that exact spot. To keep his face a mask as she spoke in that gentle, tortured voice. As one tear dropped from her face onto that blanket. That stupid fucking blanket he was glad as hell would be covering his body because it had her tear on it.

He was a sick motherfucker.

But she was fucking with him. Making him want to want to laugh as she spoke shit about peeing and childbirth like she had no cares in the world, to staring at a kid's blanket with every single emotion a human being was capable of possessing. All of the ones that were foreign to him.

He had to stay still and silent because he didn't trust himself.

Not to move.

Not to take advantage of her fragility. To utilize the moments of her weakness and selfishly take parts of her for himself.

He told her it was a job because he was trying to convince himself that's exactly what this was.

So why the fuck was he here? In this warm, shitty house that didn't seem at all shitty the second you stepped foot inside. With all the colors, patterns, photos, hippy shit on the walls. It was a home, it was something that Elena had put effort into making it more than what it was.

He shouldn't know what the inside of her house felt like. He should have only known the possible security weak points. He should not be sleeping here. That's the whole reason why Keltan got the house down the street, so they didn't invade on the privacy of a single mother who had just gone through major trauma.

It would have been right of him to leave her and the kid to have some kind of normalcy. For her to have a moment alone to deal with this.

He didn't do the right thing.

Because he didn't want her alone in the house, even if he was just down the street and they had eyes on Hudson. He would have sat outside on the bike if it weren't so fucking visible. They weren't meant to be drawing attention. He didn't want Elena to have to answer questions about shit when he didn't even know what she was gonna tell people about this.

If she would.

He didn't want to take that choice from her. A man had already taken a lot from this woman. She shouldn't have anything stolen from her again. Lance was trying to remind himself of that as he lay down on a sofa he shouldn't have and covered himself in a Barney blanket.

CHAPTER SIX

Elena

I WOKE up suddenly and with something wrapped around my throat, strangling me.

Panic rushed through me as I opened my eyes, until I realized that it was a tiny arm of a tiny human who I was all tangled up in. For a small boy, with small limbs, he sure managed to position one of them just perfectly so it laid across my throat, obstructing my airway.

I moved it, gulping air in as Nathan continued to sleep as if he hadn't just tried to kill his mother in his sleep.

The early morning light was peeking through his blinds. I reached across the bed to snatch my phone from his bedside table, squinting at it.

It was just after six.

We had time to get showered, fed and dressed for school and work. I'd have to put some extra effort into my makeup to try and cover the angry bruise on my face. It throbbed dully after sleeping with it pressed against a pillow in Nathan's small bed.

I'd snuck in here after tossing and turning in my own bed, my pillow soaked in tears that had swallowed my fractured sobs.

After I'd drained myself dry, I decided I couldn't sleep in that bed, even with Nathan only next door, not with the memories of the day before still so close.

I snuck into his room, not before I chanced a peek into the living room, where I saw a large shape on our sofa. The urge to move closer to get a good look at a sleeping Lance was squashed when the shape moved, as if sensing me—I wouldn't put it past him to sense being stared at in his sleep—and I darted into Nathan's room.

As it was, I didn't get much sleep even with my warm, safe and healthy little boy beside me. Not just because he hogged the bed. And not just because I was torturing myself with all the other ways this could have gone wrong, or worrying about how in the heck I was even going to start a payment plan to Keltan. Money was the main thing that had me staring at the ceiling with a pounding heart and overarching sense of panic routinely. Despite my strict budget that accounted for every cent of my earnings and expenses, I still went over it all, terrified I was missing some expense, worrying about the future, figuring out how the heck I was going to keep going like this.

In the morning, it all seemed manageable. It all seemed okay. Nighttime was the worst, that's when the darkness coaxed all your worst fears out and tortured you with them.

That took up a good chunk of the hours creeping toward midnight.

Then there was Robert. The fear of him coming back, but for some reason, I didn't hold onto that fear as I should have. Keltan had taken that from me. Though it was terrible of me to dump that on a stranger, to rely on one to protect me from things I should have been taking care of myself, I couldn't bring myself to dwell on it.

The thing that had me moving past midnight, no closer to sleep was not a thing at all.

It was a man under my roof, on my sofa, sleeping under a Barney blanket.

How could I sleep knowing how close he was?

I troubled myself with his stare, with his flat voice for far too long. They were thoughts that I wasn't entitled to, since Lance had given me no reason to dwell on him. No signs to show me that he even thought of me beyond anything other than a job.

No, he'd explicitly said that's exactly what I was to him.

Still, he kept me up.

Until there was nothing, not even money troubles, an abusive husband, and a really hot dude could do to keep my tired eyes awake.

I'd probably got about three hours of sleep all together.

Not ideal, considering the fact I got none the night before. But I was a mom, sleep wasn't something considered essential to our productivity. It didn't matter how little you had, if you had a hungry kid up at five, there was no one else to feed him, you figured it out.

I'd operated off less.

No amount of sleep could prepare me for what awaited me after I'd snuggled with Nathan for a little longer then dragged myself toward the kitchen in the direction of caffeine.

Lance.

Shirtless.

Naked, actually.

Well, apart from the towel wrapped around his waist.

His hair was dripping.

Droplets of water trailed down his abs.

His six-pack.

No, I counted. Eight.

Eight abs. I didn't even know people actually had the ability to acquire eight abs.

But here it was, evidence. And the 'V'. I could see it all, because the towel was slung low. *Way low.*

Then I realized what I was doing.

Staring at Lance's junk at six in the morning, likely with a mess of hair, wearing an old Ramones tee that only just covered my ass.

Fuck.

My eyes snapped up.

Met his.

Red bloomed in my cheeks and suddenly I didn't need coffee right now. Or ever again. I was pretty sure that I was alert enough to go the whole day. And the next three hundred and sixty-five after this.

"I-um-the coffee..." I pointed down the hall. "I was going to get the coffee. I didn't mean to... ah." I cleared my throat. "Well, I'll let you get naked... I mean dressed. I'm going to go to my room. And close the door. I'll count to two hundred. Then I'll go and get coffee and I will pretend this never happened."

On that, I darted to the room, closed the door and started banging my head against the wall.

What a start to the day.

I did as I promised, I counted to two hundred, well, I got to about eighty-nine, because after that, I heard the front door open and close, and in a handful of seconds, the roar of a bike starting then driving off.

Shit.

I scared him off.

My eyes went to the mirror.

I flinched.

Of course I scared him off. I resembled some kind of swamp

creature, and I stared at his junk, babbled about who knew what, and then scampered off into my room.

We'd probably never see him again.

IT WAS as I was emerging from the shower that I realized I shouldn't have used the word never.

I also should have brought my clothes into the bathroom with me, and I certainly shouldn't have left all of my clean underwear in the laundry basket in the living room.

That became apparent when I entered the living room that was no longer empty.

Some time between shaving my legs and deciding that I was no longer allowed to talk to hot men without an adult present, Lance had arrived back, entered the house with the water of my shower somehow drowning out the noise.

And he was sitting on my sofa.

And I was standing in the middle of the living room.

Naked.

Except for a towel.

But that was just details, because in order to get dressed, I had to walk toward him, to snatch a pair of underwear from the hamper almost directly in front of him. Not only would he see that, but there was no way to hide the fact I was planning on grabbing a pair of boy shorts with prints of hamburgers on them.

How in the holy hell had I managed to show him my entire underwear collection in the space of twelve hours?

And why did all of my underwear have to be so frickin' *embarrassing*?

"Oh, so we've both seen each other almost naked, so we're even now I guess," I said as a greeting, blinking at him, clutching the towel to my body and dripping water all over the place.

What the heck was wrong with me?

His gaze was blank, and he seemed unaffected by the fact that I was standing in front of him naked. His fists were clenched on top of his knees but I couldn't tell if that was his resting posture, rigid, taut, as if he were ready for an attack from an inappropriately horny, naked single mother.

He obviously didn't respond to my idiotic opening sentence.

"I didn't think you were coming back. I thought the lumpy sofa, the Barney blanket and the whole me seeing you naked thing kind of scared you the heck off," I continued, realizing that a man like this had likely been through a lot scarier shit than this and I was thinking a lot of myself if I thought I was puncturing through whatever his badass professional shield.

Again, no answer, he just moved his eyes from where they were locked to mine—they did not stray any lower than my small towel, in a strangely chivalrous gesture—to my coffee table.

I followed his gaze.

Amongst my books, a couple of Nathan's coloring books and crystals, was a box of donuts.

The good kind too. From the best bakery in town, owned by a woman who seemed totally trendy, awesome and all-around nice. And from what I heard, she could bake. I'd tried her stuff once or twice when we had brunch at my or Karen and Eliza's and they bought pastries and muffins that seemed to be the baked goods version of crack.

I actually dreamed about them for the week after.

As good as they were, they were out of my price range. I baked for Nathan and myself mostly because it was cheapest and also made sure I knew what I was putting in the food.

But I did fantasize about one day being able to wake up early, drive to the bakery, get coffee and a plethora of baked goods, sit outside and just *enjoy* them.

That was not in my budget or my schedule.

But here was Lance, at seven in the morning, bringing the good donuts. My eyes moved to the tray of four coffees.

I opened my mouth, to do what, I wasn't sure, maybe propose marriage, but he beat me to it.

"The door was unlocked," he said, voice flat. Something moved in his eyes, though. I knew that because despite the fact I was staring at the bakery box with something akin to love and longing, his voice was a magnet, pulling all of my attention.

"What?" I replied.

"The door. When I left, figured you'd hear, you'd lock it behind me... considerin'." He paused, his fists stayed clenched and they seemed to tighten as if he were trying to control something. Everything else about him stayed even. "Yet I come back, you in the fuckin' *shower*, kid still *asleep* and the door is fucking *unlocked*."

I blinked, digesting his words. Despite being distracted by the donuts, his gaze and the fact we were having this conversation while I was standing in front of him wearing only a towel, I got where he was coming from.

He didn't need to spell out his meaning. The accusation. It was threaded through his words. Anyone could enter the house while I was in the shower, while Nathan was vulnerable.

Not that this was a neighborhood was one where strangers waltzed into other people's houses at seven in the morning with nefarious intentions, but that wasn't the point.

And we were more at risk than most people.

"Captain! You stayed over!" Nathan yelled, bounding into the room with the energy that he had naturally without any kind of stimulant, just youth. Unlike me he noticed the box on the coffee table immediately. "And you brought donuts from the good place. Mom said we can only go there on special occasions, is this a special occasion?"

Despite everything happening right now, the only thing

important in this second was the kid in the Avengers PJs, grinning at a box of donuts, waking up in his own home.

"Yes," I said, cupping his face. "It's a very special occasion."

He didn't blink at my attire, considering he'd seen me walking around the house in only a towel while I waited for our laundry to dry multiple times. He always had fresh clothes, but I didn't have a huge selection and put off washing my own.

"Can I eat them right now, Mom?" he asked, eyes wide and hopeful.

I grinned. "You will first have to thank Mr. Lance, he was the one who got them."

Nathan turned, and that meant I had to let go of him. "Captain, *you* got donuts? But I thought you only ate spinach and lentils?"

"For dinner," he said. "For breakfast, I eat donuts."

My heart melted at my feet. It didn't matter what he was like to me, the fact this man was good with my son was all that mattered.

Nathan's beam lit up the room and he dove right into the donuts. My eyes widened at the sheer volume and variety.

My mouth watered as I stared at them too.

I moved my eyes to the coffee, arguably just as important as the sugar. "I know that Nathan is smart for his age, but I don't have him caffeinated yet," I said in reference to the multiple coffee cups. "Or are we expecting visitors? I guess that explains the volume of donuts that this kid couldn't get through without lapsing into a coma," I said, nodding to the boy with chocolate all over his face.

"*One*, buddy," I told him as he reached in for another with a half-eaten one still in his hand.

"Didn't know how you took your coffee," Lance said. "Know you're a single mom with a full-time job, so know you drink coffee. There's one with milk, one without, and one with that almond milk crap that all woman seem to drink."

I didn't say anything, I just stared. He couldn't be real.

"You should get dressed so you can eat," Lance continued.

"Mommy doesn't need to get dressed, this is her eating outfit," Nathan contributed with a mouth full of donut.

I closed my eyes.

"Mommy does need to get dressed," Lance answered.

My eyes snapped open. Was I imagining the heat in his voice. Upon inspection, his gaze hadn't changed.

It was lack of caffeine, sleep and the trauma of the past days. I was hallucinating. Or whatever the hearing version of hallucinating was.

In a smooth move—that I was certain wasn't smooth-like at all—I leaned forward, snagged a pair of panties and rushed from the room to get dressed.

And to have a lobotomy.

"DO YOU HAVE A PEE PEE?" Nathan asked Lance, looking from his bike to him.

I gaped at my son.

He did *not* just say that.

He was a five-year-old. Of course he frickin' said that. I wanted to be angry at the little human with no filter, but the twenty-four hours without him was too fresh, therefore he was going to get away with a lot for today and the near future.

Like eating two donuts for breakfast when he was never allowed that much sugar in such a condensed amount of time, definitely not before school. I penciled in a call with his teacher about two hours from now when he tried to lasso a squirrel or something at recess.

"Nathan," I hissed. "You cannot just go asking questions like that."

He looked to me, eyes wide, innocent and too beautiful for their own good. He was going to break some hearts, first of all, my own. "Why not?"

"Because it's rude, and when you're older, grounds for a sexual harassment suit," I snapped, my voice not having much of a bite to it.

He folded his arms. "I don't want to wear a suit," he decided. "Captain doesn't wear one and he's still a superhero. Even if he doesn't have a pee pee," he added, looking back to the bike.

Someone save me. What did I do here? Especially with Lance just standing there, not saying a frickin' thing, not walking away to save me any further embarrassment, seemingly not worried about the kid in front of him talking about his junk.

"He has a pee pee," I whispered at him, though even my yelled whisper was loud enough for Lance to hear.

Nathan's gaze moved to me. "You told me that boy's pee pees fall off when they ride motorcycles. Why does Captain still have his?"

Were we seriously talking about Lance's dick, right in front of him, at seven-thirty in the morning? Yes, yes we were.

I took a long breath, wishing that Lance hadn't had to be such a hot guy with his motorcycle and muscles and his donuts. "Because he's a *man*, not a boy. And we are no longer having this conversation, you are getting your butt in that seat and possibly into some kind of therapy," I replied, really hoping this was the end of it.

I didn't dare look at Lance.

"But Mom—"

"In the car, this instant," I said through clenched teeth, the universal, 'mom is about to lose her shit' tone.

Nathan scowled but did as he was asked because he was the

best kid in the world. Ah, I loved that little fucker, even when he made me talk about the private parts of the man I was a little bit obsessed with and the man was completely and utterly indifferent to me.

I wanted to scuttle to the car and escape having to clean up my kid's mess, but I was an adult, and I had to some time, in the immediate future, stop staring at Nathan getting himself into the car and look at those eyes that had seen me pretty much only at my worst. First, when I'd been sweaty and out of my mind at the offices. Then, when I was trying to hold on to my emotions getting my son back.

Then, running on empty handing him Barney sheets and word vomiting all over the place. This morning, staring at his stomach and then standing in the living room in my towel and unable to speak like a human. Now wasn't much better, the lack of having to make breakfast or coffee gave me extra time, but I needed that extra time in order to cover my angry black eye. And even my most practiced hand wasn't great, because I'd had to scrape at my concealer. I didn't usually wear makeup, and my stash was pretty much nonexistent. I hadn't needed to be constantly stocked up in the heavy-duty stuff as I had when I was still living with Robert.

He liked me with more makeup, to cover my freckles, my imperfections, the bruises he gave me.

I guess it was my rebellion to go fresh-faced now, well, that and I couldn't afford luxuries like makeup. I survived off skincare samples, cheap cleansers, and really fancy creams that Karen and Eliza got me for my birthday.

So the concealer only kind of worked at hiding the huge bruise on my eye, it was definitely noticeable when you looked up close, and the dark circles under my eyes didn't fare much better. Though I did dab some almost expired red lipstick underneath them to color correct.

I put on a swipe of mascara, telling myself it wasn't for the man in my living room I could hear Nathan chattering away to as I got ready.

I only had time to half blow dry my hair, so I quickly braided it and put on my work uniform. I thanked Esther and Logan—the owners of the diner, and mine and Nathan's family—daily for not having some ugly, polyester, pastel uniform that was unflattering and embarrassing.

It was just simple black pants, high-waisted, good quality, and did things to make my legs look long and my butt look good. Despite most of my curves disappearing, my butt stayed large enough to fill out the pants. The top was a fitted tee with a small logo on the breast. I could get away with wearing it to and from work, even to the grocery store. Heck, it was nicer than most of my clothes.

Today, I knew shitty concealer and black pants that made my ass look good would not save me.

I did not want to make eye contact with Lance right now.

But my life was just a series of doing things I didn't want to do. So I held my breath and did it anyway.

His expression was exactly the same as it had been when I'd walked into the living room after dressing and trying to give my bruised and exhausted self a pep talk in the mirror. Well, I wasn't as exhausted as I thought I would be considering that the coffee from Alice's was even better than my shitty coffee machine stuff. Of course it was. It was coffee for people that had enough disposable income to grab it on their way to work without a thought.

I would be one of those people.

One day.

For now, I'd tried to make my coffee last for as long as possible, and had still been holding onto it when I walked into the living room, dressed, purse on my shoulder ready to go.

I'd already braced for the impact of Lance in my living room, but his presence still hit me, even if he barely glanced at me.

I pretended that didn't bother me and I focused on my kid, preparing myself for a face full of chocolate icing, a stained t-shirt, sticky fingers. I was pleasantly surprised seeing only the tiniest smudge on his forehead—who knows how it got that far away from his mouth—and nothing on his shirt, or hands, by the looks of it. He even had his backpack on his back, which I, of course, had to check before he left the house. He once somehow fit our entire toaster in it so he could make toast for all his friends.

"Alright, I'm ready to go, have you got everything you need in there, bud?" I asked Nathan, sipping the last of my coffee with a broken heart.

Nathan nodded.

"No toasters?" I probed.

He shook his head looking very serious and sincere, but you could never tell, five-year-olds were the best at deception. Well, about toasters in backpacks at least, everything else he sucked at lying about. A habit I was going to make sure followed him into adulthood.

After checking his backpack and finding the remote control for the TV in there, I was happy to see that he had everything else.

I straightened. "Right, we're going."

Lance chose this moment to stand and give me his full attention, something I could not avoid even if I wanted to—and I wasn't sure if I wanted to or not.

"You haven't eaten," he said.

I glanced down at the box of donuts, realizing that I hadn't managed to get one. Who was I? I definitely didn't think I'd be the person who forgets about a delicious stack of refined sugar and beautiful carbs sitting on my coffee table, but motherhood does that to you.

I also realized how incredibly rude it was of me to not eat one when Lance had got up early, been accosted by me, driven across town, got all the donuts and all the coffee and I didn't even say thank you.

I snatched one from the pile. "I didn't even thank you for these," I said, holding it up and staring at the glaze glistening off it like diamonds. This was totally better than diamonds. "Just tell me how much I owe you, please," I continued, taking a bite, even though I couldn't really afford to pay Lance for all the donuts and coffee.

I wasn't a charity case either.

When I got the full flavor explosion in my mouth, I realized that I would pay whatever he wanted for these things. Shit, I'd almost give away Nathan, if I wasn't so attached to him and the mere thought of him being out of my sight again was enough for me to make this beautiful donut turn to ash in my mouth.

I swallowed roughly.

Lance was glaring at me.

"You're not payin' for shit," he said by reply, obviously not classing shit as a curse word inappropriate to say in front of Nathan.

I braced for him to echo the word, but he didn't. I utilized that silence. "Right, we need to go, like now." I closed the box and handed it to Lance. "Do you want to take this to work and feed everyone there? Change their lives while you're at it, because those are some damn good donuts." I smiled at him, even though he was staring down at the box like I was offering him a severed head.

No, wait, I doubted a severed head would make him even blink.

"Didn't buy them for anyone else. They're for you." He looked to Nathan. "Both of you. And we're not leaving this house until you finish that one, and eat another."

I gaped at him. Surely I couldn't have heard him right.

But my five-year-old helped.

"Mom! There's enough there to even have them for breakfast tomorrow. And they're *all for us*," Nathan shouted.

I focused on Lance. And the fact he just ordered me to eat something. "I don't need more than one," I said, a slight bite to my voice, my spine straightening. The command reminded me of the way that Robert used to control what I ate. But then again, he was more about limiting my food intake, not buying me donuts and all but shoving them down my throat.

Lance's eyes went up and down my body, there was nothing sexual about the look. No, it was assessing something, and when his gaze returned to mine, it seemed he found me lacking. "You need more than one," he said. And apparently, his word was law, he splayed his legs and folded his arms.

I gritted my teeth. "Nathan will be late for school."

"I don't mind being late," he piped in. "Especially if you get to eat donuts, Mom. You never eat enough of them, and they're really good."

Bless his soul.

The little traitor.

I gripped the box, hating that I actually really wanted another one, especially the one that looked like it was peanut butter custard. Peanut butter was my ultimate weakness.

And my son.

And it turned out, the steely glare from a stranger.

I sighed, shoving the rest of the donut in my mouth, snatching the peanut butter one from the box and stomping into the kitchen to place the box on the counter.

It was in there that I finished the two donuts, to calm myself down and so Lance didn't see the fact I was almost as messy as my kid when it came to eating donuts.

I also did not want to admit how good they were and how much my stomach and soul needed them.

After cleaning myself up, I walked into the living room and studiously avoided Lance's eyes, focusing on Nathan and the charade that was leaving the house.

But now, Nathan was not able to be used as a distraction.

"I'm sorry about the... pee pee comment," I said, face flaming. "It was just something I told him about motorcycles because I don't want him to be anywhere near one, so I thought that it might be a good motivation for him to stay off it," I blurted. "Not that there's anything wrong with motorcycles," I said quickly. "It suits you."

Lance didn't say anything.

I decided I needed to stop talking about motorcycles and dicks.

"I'm not sure how this works," I said, moving to the more practical version of having him in the broad daylight, when panic wasn't running through my bloodstream. "The whole security thing," I expanded.

In broad daylight, with Nathan back and talking about pee pees, the need for it seemed a little obsessive. I didn't need to reach far back into my memories to realize that any extra protection I could get for Nathan I would take.

"I'll take him to school, have a discussion with his teachers, of course, and then I've got work. I do the breakfast rush, and then the afternoon, usually I pick up Nathan and he comes to hang out with me at the diner. Or my friend Karen takes him." I glanced over to the house next door. I'd already fielded countless texts from both women as they noticed that I was absent, we were supposed to have dinner. I knew they were worried, and I was selfishly happy that neither of them were morning people so I didn't have to face them just yet.

I also didn't think I could have Nathan away from me for that long, even though I knew that both of those women would protect him with their lives. They'd come to love him like he was blood over the past three years we'd been neighbors. I also had a sneaking suspicion that they now had enough money to move to a much nicer neighborhood but stayed mostly because of Nathan and me. Also because Karen hated packing.

I was selfishly happy about that too.

No matter how much I loved and trusted the both of them, I couldn't have Nathan away from me. I had been trying to stave off anxiety all morning, Lance and donuts were a good distraction, but it was going to be hard as all hell to drive away from that school.

"I'll be at the school all day," Lance said as if the terror had leaked into the voice I was so sure sounded calm and collected.

Although accepting help from anyone was hard for me, my shoulders sagged with that knowledge. It was unexplainable, I barely knew this man and I was trusting him with the most precious thing on this planet. But he had proved himself in regards to Nathan. And despite the darkness surrounding him and his aura, there was something else too, a strength, a comfort, something I couldn't explain and definitely not verbalize without sounding certifiable.

So instead of protesting or talking about his aura, I just nodded, glancing to the bike. "As much as it suits you, I think the school is gonna notice a man sitting on a motorcycle watching outside. And I really don't want to be the reason you get arrested."

"Luke's meeting us at the school," he replied, voice tight as if he was pissed at having to explain himself to me. I guessed someone who looked like him rarely had to explain himself, he just had to flex a bicep, narrow his eyes and all of the world would likely do his bidding. "He'll keep watch while I follow you to work, then we'll switch out when I get back to school."

"You don't need to follow me to work," I protested. "I'm not the one that needs to be protected here."

Lance's gaze changed. Only slightly, enough to be called a trick of the light, but I felt the change. On my skin. "That wasn't a question," he clipped. "You need what I say you need."

I gaped at him, old wounds opening at the command in his words. But I knew that this was different, though my body didn't know that, my traumas.

A honking of a horn got my attention.

I snapped my gaze over to where Nathan had climbed into the front seat, obviously having had enough of being an agreeable and patient kid for the day. For once, I was glad of it.

I turned, ready to stomp off to the car, even though it was childish. I got myself. Paused. Then I turned. Lance was still standing in the same place, as if he hadn't planned on moving until I was in the car.

"Thank you," I said, my voice a little harsher than it should have been when thanking someone. "For the donuts, the coffee, for the protection."

And before he could answer about it only being his 'job' or whatever, I turned and walked to the car.

CHAPTER SEVEN

I THOUGHT I was prepared for walking into work and the inevitable questions.
    Firstly, because I'd called in sick yesterday.
    I never called in sick.
    People like me couldn't afford sick days. Moms certainly didn't get sick days, so I had perfected the art of being able to do pretty much anything while suffering from the flu. I also filled myself full of every natural remedy I could, partly because they were way cheaper than medicine from the drugstore, and mostly because they did the same job and were much better for you. I didn't want Nathan growing up with antibiotic resistance and dependence on over-the-counter painkillers.
    I did that where I could, made homemade cleaner with vinegar and baking soda, made soap with lye and essential oils, toothpaste, anything else I found online.
    People at work knew me and knew this. They would have been worried about me being on my deathbed, because almost everyone had text me asking if I needed anything throughout the day.

I replied to everyone, despite not feeling like it, because I knew that it worried them more if I didn't reply.

Walking in, I expected everyone to be concerned. Esther had even texted me telling me I didn't have to come in today if I was still sick. She never did that with people, she would never make someone work if they were sick, but she was kind of a hardass. Well, to everyone but me and Nathan. I replied quickly telling her I was better.

No way could I afford another day off, even if I wanted to do exactly what Lance was doing, and sit outside Nathan's school watching him and eating the rest of the donuts he got.

We needed the cash.

I saw Bobby, our cook, first, and he greeted me with a smile. "Ah, she's alive!" he declared, throwing his hands up in the air, one of them holding a huge cleaver.

I grinned, despite the fact I was thinking about Nathan. Worrying about Robert. Obsessing over Lance. He'd done as promised and followed me all the way to work, and I hadn't heard his bike roar off until I was walking in the back doors to the diner.

"Yes, I'm alive and ready for a fun-filled day," I replied, forcing cheer into my voice.

But Bobby was no longer smiling, he was rounding the stainless-steel counter in the kitchen, his attractive features morphing as he focused on my face.

Shit, so my concealer really wasn't working.

Bobby clutched my face in his hand, moving it so my bruised eye was tilted to the light.

"Who did this?" he demanded. "I need a name, address, social security number."

His words were steel, his entire body radiating with fury.

Bobby was usually a mild man, soft-spoken, shy until you got to know him. But that was because he'd had a really frickin' rough and dark history. He was brought up in a bad situation, and he looked for solace in a worse situation—a street gang in East LA—he had ink on his arms as evidence. He refused to cover it up because he wanted the reminder of who he used to be and who he wasn't now.

He'd been to jail, I knew that, Esther and Logan knew that. A criminal conviction made it impossible for him to get a job in the city, especially since he was trying to get as far away from his old life as he could.

But Esther and Logan had a way of reading people, not by their pasts, or their resumes. Just like they took a chance on a single mother with no waitressing experience, they took a chance on Bobby.

And it paid off, he was one of the hardest workers, best damn cooks around and kindest people I knew. I'd almost forgotten his violent past, because even with his muscles and tattoos, he wasn't that to me, or anyone who knew him.

But right now, with him standing in front of me, shaking from rage wearing a foreign expression on his face.

Before I opened my mouth, Logan walked into the room. "Elena, you're back. We're so glad, I was about to..." He trailed off as he walked fully into the kitchen and saw Bobby's face and likely felt the energy in the room.

"Bobby, what are you doing?" he demanded, but then he must have gotten a look at my face because I heard his harsh intake of breath.

"You need to tell me who did this, right now, baby doll," Bobby gritted through his teeth.

"How about you step back, take a second, Bobby," Logan said, always the peacekeeper, but even though I couldn't see his face, there was an anger in his voice that was as foreign as Bobby's expression.

Bobby didn't move.

"How about you give *Elena* a second?" Logan added, enunciating my name. "She's likely been through a lot."

That had Bobby immediately letting me go. But he didn't take a step back. His face did soften slightly, and he lifted his hand to gently stroke my bruised skin.

"I'll kill them," he whispered.

My eyes were brimming from Bobby's reaction, and from Logan's voice. Because of the emotion in them. The concern.

"We're not talking about killing with you still holding a meat cleaver," Logan said. "We'll do it over coffee."

I looked to my boss and father figure for the past few years. Nathan called him Pops, to his great delight. He and Esther had lost their daughter when she was fifteen to an overdose. I felt that pain in them every single day, and as a mother, I considered them saints for still finding the ability to go on, to smile, to love each other like they did after something as soul-destroying as that.

Logan was wearing a different kind of pain right now.

I flinched that it was because of me.

"I've got to get to work," I told him. "It's the breakfast rush, and I'm not going to put you out."

"Fuck the breakfast rush," Logan said, shocking me more than Bobby had.

Logan never cursed. No matter what disasters happened at the dinner, and all sorts of crap happened. Waitresses stealing, customers complaining, toilets flooding, food deliveries getting lost, small kitchen fires. All through it, he kept his calm while Esther did all the swearing and stressing. He was a pond on a summer's day, no ripples. His wife was the Atlantic Ocean, stormy and unpredictable. It worked.

But there were ripples today.

"I can't right now," I whispered, a plea to the two men. "I just need to wait tables, deliver food and pretend that things are normal, just for a couple of hours. After that, I can do it."

Both men regarded me, both gazes softening as I knew they

would. Though Bobby was still gripping that cleaver pretty darn hard.

Logan nodded, understanding on his face. He moved across the room to pull me into his arms. He smelled of peppermint and Old Spice. I sank into the embrace and bit my lip so I didn't cry.

I didn't want to let go of the safety in his arms, the love, but I had to.

I pulled back, took a breath, put on my 'customer service smile' and readied myself for the day.

"Two hours," Bobby barked. "Then we're hearing about this. You're not dealing with this alone."

I bit my lip even harder to make myself not cry at that one.

"Two hours," I promised.

"OH HONEY," Esther whispered, reaching across the table to squeeze my hand. Tears swam in the woman's eyes.

Never had I seen that.

Or heard the softening in her voice, apart from with Nathan, and even then, she was still stern. And he loved her for that. Everyone cooed and fussed over him, because he was the cutest kid ever and also the coolest to be around. He adored the fact that Esther spoke to him like an adult and didn't take shit.

As promised, Logan had come and got me after the breakfast rush was over, and exhaustion was catching up with me. A couple of the other waitresses noticed my face and either ignored it, sensing I couldn't talk about it or gave me soft smiles.

Apart from Kaitlyn, of course. The newest girl who inexplicably hated me when she first started.

She scowled at me and then ignored me.

She definitely wasn't happy about Logan pulling me from the floor, muttering about having to cover my tables.

I hadn't planned on telling them everything when Bobby, Logan, and Esther sat me down in the back office with a plate of peanut butter pie and a large pot of coffee.

You'd think I would be sick of peanut butter baked goods with the sheer amount of sugar I'd consumed this morning, but you'd be wrong.

I dove into it and somehow ended up diving into my entire story, starting with meeting Robert and finishing with one of the top security firms in the city currently staking out my son's school to make sure he wasn't kidnapped again.

"Why didn't you call us?" Esther demanded, her voice sharper than before but eyes still glassy.

"I..." I trailed off, looking for a reason why I didn't ask for help from any of the numerous people that hadn't hesitated to give it to me over the years. I tried to think of why I went to strangers before my new family. "I don't know," I whispered.

Even though I did know. I was ashamed. Of what my choices had done to my son. "I think I was scared of showing you what I'd gone through for so long, how weak I'd been. How stupid. How stupid I was to not do something sooner, and put Nathan in danger. And then, after the police did nothing, I kind of blacked out."

Logan's jaw hardened. "I'm gonna be having a stiff word with Martin about this," he hissed.

Martin was the chief of police, and Logan was good friends with him, he came in for breakfast a handful of times a week. I thought he was nice enough, a decent tipper, didn't stare at my ass or try to ask me out like the rest of the single—and married—male regulars. I was a single mom, young at that, working at a diner and I had a decent face and a round ass, it was hard to get through a meal rush without being hit on.

"He wasn't even there," I said, trying to sift through the

memories of rushing into the police station. "I didn't recognize the officer who took my statement."

"Doesn't matter if he was there or not," Logan said. "This is his team, and if he's got people on his force who don't help mothers find their children, he needs to know about it, then do something about it. Otherwise he can eat his pancakes somewhere else."

"Or I'll put something special in them," Bobby muttered. His fists were clenched on top of the table.

"No, I don't need any of that," I pleaded. "I know how it works with the cops. Robert's one of them. His father is a big deal. And I'm... no one."

"You shut that mouth right now if that nonsense is gonna keep leaking out of it," Esther snapped, her tone more familiar and sharp. But she was still holding my hand. "You are a lot of things, all of them good, even without knowing your past. A single mom whose little boy has better manners than most fully grown men I know. A kid that is always happy, never throws a tantrum and adores his mother. You're a hard worker, you always smile at customers, you never turn up late, always happy to work more than you should. You're kind to everyone you come across, even that little witch Kaitlyn." Esther scowled at the mention of her name. "You never complain about how hard you've got it, and sweetie, I know it's tough. You brought light into Logan's and my life with you and your boy. You're our family. You're a fighter. You are not no one. *He* is no one. He doesn't deserve a name or a set of balls."

"I'll happily relieve him of those," Bobby bit out.

"I don't want to give him the satisfaction of any kind of attention," I said. "I just want him out of our life. I want to know he can't get to us."

"He's not getting to you, I'll make sure of that," Bobby declared, the soft, kind cook no longer on the surface. No, this was definitely the Bobby of the past. "I'll stay at your house every night if you need, I've got friends who don't mind burying a cop."

"Bobby!" I snapped. "You can't go talking about killing someone in *front of our bosses*." I paused. "Wait, you can't go talking about it, full stop."

Scarily, Esther and Logan didn't seem ready to back me up.

"I promise, this security company is really legit. Like fancy." I bit my lip, thinking about the fancy meaning money.

"I'll need to meet them," Logan said, in a tone that was what I imagined a worried father would have. Not that I really knew what that sounded like.

Bobby nodded.

"And you need to tell me if you need any help with anything," Esther demanded. "Paid leave, somewhere to stay, you need help with what I know is a hefty bill, we won't hesitate."

"I'm not asking you to do that," I said, jutting my chin up slightly and clenching my hands on my pants so I wouldn't cry.

"I know, I'm offering," Esther said, eyes narrowed. "You're not alone in this. We all love you and that kid to death. And you've got some fancy security team, that's all well and good, but you've also got us. Don't forget that."

I nodded, because I couldn't speak.

"Now get back to work," Esther commanded, voice hard but eyes soft.

I didn't hesitate to obey, but the words echoed through my head the rest of the day.

"You are not alone in this."

NATHAN WAS WAITING for me at the gates to the school when I pulled up.

And he was not alone.

I'd gone in with him this morning, first to make sure that they never released him to Robert again, and I'd been in the middle of politely telling them how important this was to his teacher, Hannah, when her eyes widened and the skin on the back of my neck prickled.

The moms around us were all slack-jawed.

So Lance had decided to follow us into the school.

And he had not been as polite to Nathan's teacher.

But I didn't even think she noticed.

I definitely noticed when he demanded to be put on the pick-up list.

My eyes widened at the same time as Hannah.

I didn't even have time to argue him on it, Hannah was already nodding and looking between us, likely trying to figure out the connection. Because no way could this guy be my boyfriend, I knew what it looked to the outsider.

And there were a lot of outsiders watching, making assumptions, judgments.

Frankly, I didn't care. I cared that my son was being taken care of. Plus, I was a single mother who was dressed either in a diner uniform or a boho getup that erred on the side of slutty when I picked Nathan up. Judgment was part in parcel of my day.

I had worried for the rest of the day at work, because that was a mother's job, but I didn't freak out, because I knew Lance was there.

It wasn't healthy, that feeling, I couldn't welcome it, invite it to stay. Because Lance was temporary, as was the protection. And I worried about that more for Nathan's sake than my own. I didn't date because I didn't want to bring men in and out of his life, I didn't need him having all sorts of issues with abandonment and father figures.

He had Logan and Bobby, both of whom were solid. Both of whom adored Nathan.

He worshipped them, of course. But it was different, the way he looked at Lance—he was his superhero. And he was going to have to say goodbye to him at some point.

I pulled up at school with Lance standing right beside Nathan at the curb, my son's little hand in his larger one. Nathan's head was craned up as he babbled on about who knew what.

"Keep it together, Elena," I whispered to myself as I pulled up, pretending not to notice every single mom on pickup duty needlessly exit their cars in order to gaze at Lance.

None of them tried to talk to him, though. They weren't that brave. He pretty much had a giant 'fuck off' painted on his forehead, despite the fact he was holding hands with my little boy. It took an extreme amount of badass to hold hands with a five-year-old, with what looked like a gentle and natural grip, at the same time as letting everyone else around you know you could kill a man with those same hands.

Given my history, that should've given me pause.

Like *a lot* of it.

It certainly shouldn't have had a warmth settling in the bottom of my stomach and a straight-up heat even lower.

"You're at a frickin' elementary school, Elena," I hissed under my breath as I put the car into park.

I left the keys in my car and got out.

"Mom!" Nathan screamed, running to me and jumping into my arms. I caught him, exhaling properly for the first time today. Nathan hadn't reacted like this to me picking him up in months, not since he'd gotten adjusted to school. Since then, he'd been more likely to be sprinting away from me with a grin on his face, excited to see his teachers, his friends and to learn—the little nerd.

My little boy was strong, but he was not completely unaffected by what happened. That simple fact speared agony through all of my nerve endings and fury into my blood. I hadn't even felt such an anger when Robert used me as his punching bag. But even a scratch on Nathan, emotional or physical, was enough to strip me down to my baser instincts. I squeezed him extra hard before letting him go.

"Captain came to meet me outside of class," he said, grinning while I smoothed his hair. It was a constant battle, thick and shiny like mine and always messy. It would have been easier to shave it close-cropped to his head, but I didn't have the heart.

"I see that, bud," I said, doing my level best not to glance upward at the man whose shadow blocked out the frickin' sun.

"Are we going back to your work?" Nathan asked.

I straightened. "Yeah, but Momma isn't working. Pop and Esther just want to see you and Bobby has some leftover pie that was gonna go in the garbage..."

Nathan's eyes widened in panic. "We need to get there before the pie gets throwed out," he said.

I grinned. "*Thrown out*, sweetheart and don't worry, Bobby would never do that to you." I ruffled his hair. "Get in your seat and I'll buckle you up in a sec."

Nathan paused, looked up to Lance. "Do superheroes eat pie, Captain?" he asked. "Because I will share mine with you. It's even better than donuts today."

My heart clenched at my kid willing to share his pie. He barely even did that with me. My child liked his baked goods, especially since they were a big treat. This was kind of pivotal.

Lance glanced to me then back at Nathan. "I don't say no to pie."

Nathan's eyes lit up.

"Go get into the car, kid," I instructed. "I just need chat to Lance for a second."

Nathan didn't need to be told twice.

I braved his gaze. "I hope you don't mind. My bosses, and my friend Bobby kind of want to meet you." I paused. "Well, they don't *want* to meet you, they've *demanded* to meet you. I couldn't exactly hide this from them." I pointed to my sunglass clad face that did the job from hiding the bruise from the moms and teachers. "And then they all ganged up on me and the whole story came out," I explained. "They'll just turn up at the house if we don't go there now. And they want to see Nathan with their own eyes. They're worried. That's why they want to meet you. I know that it's not in the job description but there will be pie, and it's good pie." I smiled at him.

He did not smile back.

"I'll come," he replied.

I waited for more.

That was it.

"Okey dokey," I replied, grinning wider.

Did I just say okey dokey?

This was trouble.

BOTH KAREN and Eliza were waiting on their porch when I pulled up. Lance was meeting up with Luke, who was apparently installing our security system. I couldn't argue with him about this because he'd turned and walked away as soon as he'd informed me of this.

This was after meeting everyone at the diner, being taken into the kitchen by Logan and Bobby for what I assumed was 'man talk'. Everyone came out with all their digits, so I assumed it went okay.

Everyone seemed satisfied, most especially Nathan, since he was spoiled by the entire diner. Not just pie, but his favorite meatloaf and mac and cheese being brought home for dinner. Bobby 'accidentally' made it when it wasn't on the specials menu until Monday.

I didn't argue because I knew they wanted to do what they could to help.

I mentally told myself to have them all over for dinner when I could afford it. Esther had forced me to have the afternoon off, paid, to be with Nathan. I weakly argued, but she steamrolled me because I was dead on my feet and dying to hang out with my kid.

I did reevaluate that when Karen crossed her lawn and had my car door open before I'd even properly parked in the driveway. The fury, panic, and sadness in her eyes told me that Bobby had called her. Or Logan. They hung out at the diner a lot and we had Christmas, Thanksgiving, and birthdays together.

Somehow, I'd managed to create some kind of patchwork family for myself and my son, when I'd come here with an almost empty bank account and wounds that will never quite heal right.

"Aunty Karen!" Nathan yelled, oblivious to the look I was being treated to and the tension in the air. "We have meatloaf, pie, mac and cheese! And donuts in the kitchen. Wanna have dinner?"

Karen's eyes immediately softened. "Sure, monkey. As soon as I crucify your mother." She looked over her shoulder at the woman rounding the car. "Aunty Eliza is gonna take you inside, 'kay?"

Eliza opened Nathan's door, eyes kind on mine and unbuckled Nathan, yanking him into her chest in a hug that wasn't just because she hadn't seen him in a day. She squeezed him too hard for that. Held him for too long. And her eyes were glassy and kind when they settled on mine.

So they both knew.

Crap.

"Karen—"

"Nope," she cut me off. She stepped back, considering I couldn't get myself out of the car without her moving. She was built, as Logan would say, like a brick shithouse. She had broad shoulders, wide hips and was almost as tall as all the Greenstone Security men. She had her hair piled on top of her head, she changed the color monthly, it was red today.

She was wearing a ripped tee and cutoff shorts. Tattoos covered her arms and legs. I guessed she looked intimidating to some people, especially glaring at me like she was right now, but she was one of the most generous and kind-hearted people I'd ever met in my life.

Though she didn't look to be feeling kind right now.

I didn't really blame her. Eliza and Karen pretty much helped raised Nathan over the past three years, ever since Eliza had come to the door with cookies and seen him clinging to my leg, my house in shambles, something burning in the kitchen and my hair unwashed for who knew how long. She'd immediately thrust the cookies at me, yanked Nathan into her arms and barged into my house, demanding I take a shower while she took care of the kid and cleaned the house.

I had done so, mostly because of sheer surprise, lack of sleep, and desperation for a break. And because I saw her aura, felt it. I was comfortable around her from the start. The same with Karen. They were my sisters, my mothers, my aunts, my best friends.

And they had to hear, second-hand, what happened to Nathan.

I got out of the car, bracing for Karen's wrath.

The past three years had been filled with mostly kindness, laughter, food, wine and happiness. But now and again, mostly when I hid how bad things had gotten a while back and didn't accept help from her, Karen showed me she was a woman you did not want to fuck with.

She was very slow to anger, but when it came, hurricane sirens needed to be sounded.

I braced for it.

But she yanked me into her arms instead.

I sank into her embrace, though it threatened to break some of my ribs.

When she let me go, she was still scowling and her eyes shimmered with tears I'd never seen her let fall. "I can't believe that you went through all of that and I was stressing over fucking website coding and *Instagram algorithms*," she hissed.

I blinked away tears of my own, knowing full well I wouldn't be able to stop them if I started. "I'm sorry," I whispered.

Her eyes only narrowed more. "Why are *you* sorry? This is *my* fault, I should've been a better friend. Should've checked on you. Should've..."

"Been clairvoyant and known that my estranged husband who we haven't seen in three years would come here, punch me in the face and then kidnap Nathan the next day?" I finished for her, my voice dry. I reached out to squeeze her hand. "You are one of the best friends I've ever had. I've never had anyone like you and Eliza. You're my family. And I'm sorry that I didn't tell you earlier, that you had to find out from Bobby. I just..." I trailed off. How could I tell her that I was ashamed? Ashamed that I let myself get in this position in the first place. Ashamed that I couldn't protect my child. And terrified that if I called her and Eliza, if I called anyone who loved Nathan, that it would make it all real, permanent.

"I know, kid," she said, hearing what I was saying without me having to speak. Her anger fizzled out of her, with only compassion left.

It was then Eliza walked up to us. She was night to Karen's day. Tiny, shorter than even me, pure white-blonde hair, and always in a fifties-style dress. One of her arms was a full sleeve, in pastels and a true work of art. She was delicate, beautiful, soft-spoken but could totally be scary when she needed to be.

Karen let go of my hand so Eliza could hug me. I inhaled her sweet perfume. My body was starting to relax from this morning when I felt like all my muscles were going to snap from tension. It was really true that important people helped shoulder heavy weights.

I just needed to stop being so resistant to it.

"Nathan seems great," she said when she released me, her eyes pausing over my face, her pink painted lips thinning.

I nodded. "He is taking this better than anyone," I replied honestly. Definitely better than I was.

"'Course he is," Karen contributed, grinning, though it didn't reach her eyes. "He's a badass."

I smiled back, thinking about what Rosie said about him. Neither of them were wrong. My kid was a badass. I needed to follow his lead. Well, in some respects, not in the wetting my bed and picking my nose type situations.

"He says he wants to show you the donuts," Eliza said to Karen with a wink. "And they're the really good ones… from Alice's Bakery."

Karen's eyes lit up. She was a bigger sweet tooth than my five-year-old son. She looked to me. "We're coming over for dinner tonight. With wine." It was not a question.

I nodded, I was relieved, not sure if I could be alone in my house. Lance had informed me that the 'team' managed to get a house down the street. I didn't get time to question how they did this in such a short amount of time or what this was costing. I was being completely and utterly immature about all things pertaining to him and Greenstone Security, burying my head in the sand until I was strong enough to deal with the reality of it.

Karen kissed Eliza, reached over and squeezed my hand and walked toward the house.

"I'm sure Karen's already done the whole angry lesbian thing," Eliza said, watching her wife's back. "But I just want you to know, you tell me where he lives, they'll never find his body."

See? Totally scary.

"The number of people that have offered to kill my estranged husband for me lately is quite worrying," I replied, smiling.

Eliza smiled back, sadness in her irises. "That's the number of people that love you and would do anything for you and Nathan."

I nodded, heart heavy, with both joy and sadness. I could use this whole event to lapse into a depression full of fear, self-pity, pain. Surely it was tempting and I had enough material to work off. Violent husband deciding to make our lives hell, money problems only made worse by the huge bill I was going to get lumped with, a car with a broken AC and likely ready to break down at any moment. No career prospects beyond being a waitress at a diner.

Sure, I could let that all turn me into a sad and bitter person who aged prematurely thanks to all the frowning and such.

But this had shown me other things. Other people willing to do everything and anything to help me. Like give me food that I didn't need but made my son feel better, like offer to commit homicide. And other people, for some reason, bought donuts in the morning and held my son's hand after school.

It was then that Eliza's attention moved from our conversation of murder and to the curb. Or more likely, who was pulling up to the curb.

"Who is *that*?" Eliza breathed.

I already knew who my neighbor was talking about with a slack jaw. I didn't need to turn. But I did anyway, because I never missed a chance to stare at Lance and torture myself with his complete and utter lack of interest in me.

And yes, as my eyes locked with his shades—totally kick-ass

black Ray-Bans—I was tortured with his utter hotness and utter lack of interest in me.

"That's Lance," I said by explanation, watching him walk from the SUV he'd emerged from. His muscles moved, glinted in the afternoon sun underneath the fabric of his tee. If I squinted really hard, I might have been able to see the outline of his abs.

What is wrong with me?

"I would like to climb him like a tree," Eliza breathed, eyes following Lance like mine were.

I moved my head and pushed my glasses to the top of my head so she could see my raised brow. "You're gay," I reminded her.

"Honey, something like that transcends all sexual affiliation," she said without looking at me. Her eyes widened as the sound of another door echoed through our yards. "Dear God there's two of them," she muttered.

I moved my eyes again.

Luke was moving around the truck, aviators on his face, wearing worn jeans and a plain white tee.

I felt weird even staring at him for too long because I wouldn't be surprised if Rosie had some perceptive powers to know if I'd checked out her husband and I was kind of scared of that woman.

I was actually sure that the women who surrounded me could probably do a lot more damage than the men, and that was saying something. But I was also proud to be around such strong, badass women. That wasn't exactly me, I wasn't born to be a badass, for a start, I was a punching bag, a doormat. I just wanted to be half as strong as them.

"*This* is Captain America?" she asked as Luke bent into the passenger's seat. "Because *that* is America's ass."

She and Karen were huge Marvel fans. It's where Nathan got it from.

Though you didn't have to be a Marvel fan to agree that was America's ass.

"No, though I'm not disagreeing with you on the ass," I said, whispering, just in case Rosie was hiding in the bushes. "It's him."

Lance was walking toward us with a box in his hands, so I could only kind of nod my head toward the man-god who may or may not be Hades reincarnated.

"Yeah, I can see that too," Eliza said out the side of her mouth as he approached hearing distance. I wouldn't have been surprised if he had some kind of badass powers that enabled him to hear us from the frickin' curb.

As long as his powers didn't extend to him being able to read my mind, I would still be able to walk away from this with a small amount of dignity.

Lance stopped in front of us, not taking his sunglasses off, not saying a word, just staring at me.

"Eliza, this is Lance," I said after a prolonged awkward silence. I'd been too busy looking at how his biceps were defined holding the box full of electrical stuff.

"Pleasure to meet you," she said, her voice a little breathy. I was happy that even a woman who was well and truly into women was having trouble sounding normal or not drooling when confronted with Lance.

He nodded in response.

Apparently, badasses didn't actually verbally greet people anymore, they just nodded. And it worked for him in a big way, somehow he pulled it off without looking like a rude asshole.

I couldn't decide whether he actually was a rude asshole or just super mysterious and damaged.

The hotness was distracting.

Maybe that was the point.

"And thank you," Eliza said, not at all perturbed by the lack of response. She threaded her hand in mine, which was all clammy because of my body reacting to Lance. "For doing this for Elena, Nathan," she clarified. "We can't tell you how much we appreciate you getting our nephew back to us."

There was never a point when we spoke about Nathan being their 'nephew,' but he just started calling them his 'aunts' at some point within the first month of meeting them and they acted like family from the start.

It was natural.

Lance nodded again. "We're gonna start installing security shit," he said by answer.

Again, that response to my friend's heartfelt thank you should have cemented his place in the asshole hall of fame. Somehow it didn't.

Another awkward silence.

"Um, yeah, okay, do you need help or anything?" I asked, looking from the wires and things in his muscled arms and back to his face.

Eliza snorted. I glared at her.

"You don't even know how to use your TV remote," she teased.

"I didn't mean helping them hook up the system," I snapped, forgetting all fond feelings toward her. "I meant like help with the boxes."

"We're good," Lance barked, some kind of emotion in his previously flat voice. My eyes went to him immediately, and my stomach dipped at the hardness of his jaw.

Apparently badasses didn't appreciate women questioning their badass ability to carry boxes.

"I'll take that help," Luke's voice sounded from behind us, smooth, warm, nothing like Lance's. "Here's somethin' you can hold onto."

He came into view holding possibly the cutest baby I'd ever

seen. Mine included. I was not blinded by motherly love when Nathan was born. Of course I adored the absolute heck out of him since I locked eyes with him, but I was also able to admit that he wasn't adorable. Nathan was kind of weird looking as a baby. He grew into his features once he was about two. Robert was happy about that, about Nathan finally inheriting 'his genes,' and I couldn't decide whether that meant his features or his whiteness.

The kid in Luke's arms was beyond beautiful. And not really a baby, I guessed he was about two, with a full head of hair, wearing a white tee, ripped blue jeans, and frickin' *Timberlands*. I'd never seen a grown-up male look like cool—present company excluded—let alone a kid. And there was not a stain on that shirt. Or the beautiful kid.

Of course, looking at his mother and father who may or may not be vampires, for all their flawless beauty, it did make sense.

"Yes, I can definitely help with that," I said immediately, smiling and holding my hands out to the baby. "What's his name?"

"Rogue," Luke said as he gave him to me, grinning with warm eyes.

Rogue. Of fucking course.

He immediately cuddled into me, seemingly not upset about being handed to a stranger. He was heavier than he looked and didn't realize how much I missed that heaviness from when Nathan was little. He never let me carry him anymore, which was probably good since he was getting big and my upper body strength left a lot to be desired. I leaned in and inhaled the baby scent that attached itself to every child that left them when they turned about four. It was rare, pure and beautiful.

Calming.

Maybe because I associated it with a kind of safeness. Whenever things got bad with Robert—which was often after I gave birth—I would sneak into Nathan's nursery, pick him up, hold him into my chest and inhale. He was the thing that saved me and made me strong enough to leave Robert.

"I'm Luke," the man himself said, holding out a hand to Eliza, jerking me out of my baby scented coma.

She took it, blinking rapidly. "*You're* security guys?" she clarified, looking between him and Lance.

Luke nodded.

"Wow," she replied.

I laughed, now able to do things like that knowing Nathan was inside the house most likely on a sugar high with Karen and that I was holding a baby, in front of a man who only glared and grunted words but somehow made me feel immensely safe.

Luke laughed too seemingly not offended by Eliza's response, then again, being that hot I was sure he was used to it. "I'm gonna get this system hooked up, might be a bit noisy, but Rosie is comin' out with Polly in a couple of hours with all sorts of food, drinks, and shit. Just thought I'd give you some time to prepare, make sure all furniture is bolted to the wall," he joked.

Luke's smile was easy, as were his words. He couldn't be more different than the man beside him. But then again, he had a beautiful kid, a scary but hot as shit wife. He seemed like he had a lot of reasons to smile easy and tease people.

Lance had shadows behind his eyes, a naked ring finger—of course I checked—and never spoke a word about any kind of family.

I guessed there were a lot of reasons why he was the way he was.

I wanted to know those reasons. I had the strangest urge to be the reason he smiled with his eyes.

But that was insane.

What was also insane—in a slightly better way—was the fact

that Rosie and Polly were driving all the way out here with drinks and food.

"We can make it a party!" Eliza decided while I was staring at Lance without even realizing it.

He was staring right back, blankly.

Luckily the toddler pulling my hair demanded my attention. I held his chubby hand.

"I'll get Karen to bring our picnic table and grill over," Eliza continued, starting to speak faster as she got more and more excited. She loved a party. "We'll set up the back yard. We've got wine and chips. You can make guac." She winked at me then looked to the men in front of us. "Seriously, Elena's guac will make you want to propose marriage. Karen already tried, no matter the fact she's married to me and Elena isn't gay. But I wasn't even mad, I was too busy eating the guac."

Luke chuckled. Lance didn't even crack a grin.

I didn't argue with her. My guac was really good.

"Feel free to invite the whole team," I offered, thinking about what they'd done for me. The least I could do was make them some frickin' guac. "If it's not too late notice and they feel like making the drive," I added, thinking of the hour—in good traffic, which was rare—each way they'd have to travel.

"Well, I'll tell you Heath will come 'cause Polly's comin'. That means Skye and Ziggy—their two kids are coming, if that's good with you to have more little monsters around?"

I nodded enthusiastically. Because Nathan would love having kids around. I loved it too. I'd always wanted a big family, a house full of kids. Happiness. It had been the plan with Robert. But he'd started beating me when Nathan was born and I'd started secretly taking the pill so I didn't bring another child into the mix.

Luke grinned and continued speaking. "Keltan will likely come when he hears about the guac, he likes to eat. That means that Lucy and their daughter, Amelia, will be comin' too. That good?"

I thought about what I had in the pantry, which wasn't much. "Sure," I said, smiling brightly. "I'll run to the store and get supplies." I looked to Eliza. "If you guys don't mind watching my spawn and this angel?" I squeezed the baby in my arms again.

I thought about taking Nathan with me, but I knew he wouldn't want to be taken away from the men and the excitement of what they were doing. Plus, the sugar that he'd probably already overdosed on.

"I got it," a voice clipped.

We all looked to Lance.

Eliza blinked rapidly at him, I was unsure if this was because of the unexpected bite to his voice, him speaking at all or because she was still drooling over him. Maybe a combination of the three.

Luke only grinned knowingly. Knowing what, I had no clue.

"Got it?" I repeated, focusing my eyes on Lance's shades.

"Shit from the store," he clipped, seemingly annoyed that I was asking him to expand on his three-word grunt. "I'll get this shit done, then go to the store."

My eyes widened. The offer itself was unexpected but hearing it come out like it was causing Lance pain was even more shocking. I tried to imagine him with a cart, walking down the aisles of a grocery store, grabbing party items, scowling at every shopper that gawked at him. Couldn't see it. Surely he ordered his groceries online.

"It's okay," I said quickly. "You've done enough for me already, and that's going too far out of your way." Plus it felt like charity, as if his intense stare could see into my rapidly emptying bank account and empty pantry.

"It wasn't a question," Lance said, voice tighter than his ass, and that was a tight ass. "You got your kid." He nodded his head to Eliza. "Friends. Plus the preparation for Rosie and Lucy. Got it covered."

The last three words of his sentence were structured like a decision made. No argument. A dismissal.

He even started to turn away from me.

Something heated in my blood.

And not in a good way.

"Ah, it's my house, my guests, so I'll cover it," I snapped at him.

Luke somehow grinned even wider at the prissiness in my voice.

Lance paused, his jaw stiffened, eyes moved back to me. They were cold, challenging, kind of scary and also kind of hot. I could see that through my annoyance.

He didn't speak. The stare likely worked on its own most of the time. I was tempted to give in, let him do whatever he wished. But I had my pride. What was left of it at least.

"Thank you for the kind offer," I said through gritted teeth. "But as I said, you've done enough and I want to do this as a thank you."

And before he could say anything more, with his words or his frickin' smoldering eyes, I turned and walked away.

CHAPTER EIGHT

I'D GONE into the house feeling all triumphant over facing off with a badass who looked like he could melt paint with his eyes, I'd had another donut, my third for the day. I'd hugged my kid again. Then I'd gotten ready to leave for the store, mental list in hand and ready to spend money I didn't really have on people who went out of their way to help me and my son when they had no need to.

I got as far as the driver's door of my car.

A hand fastened around my wrist as I was going to open it. The grip wasn't painful, but it was firm, intended to get me to stop what I was doing.

It did that.

And more.

I couldn't think about the more since I had to make eye contact with the man holding my wrist without turning into a puddle at his feet. So I sucked in an uneven breath and looked up.

"Keys," he ordered the second my eyes touched his sunglasses.

His hand stayed on my wrist. I tried not to focus on that. But when a man like Lance was touching you, even if it was only to restrain you while he tried to get your car keys, you focused.

"What?" my voice was far too breathy for my liking.

The grip tightened only slightly, still not enough to be painful, but enough to be forceful. To show me how easy it would be for him to make this painful. As a survivor of abuse, this should have sent me into a panic, triggered something in me. It had happened enough times at the diner, when a customer grabbed me to ask a question, or even Bobby coming up behind me in the kitchen. I got flashbacks, I flinched for a hit, my breathing got shallow and I'd come close to passing out a few times. All from contact not intended to be violent, and none of that contact originating from violent people.

Lance was a violent person.

I knew that the second I laid eyes on him.

It served me well.

It served my son well.

But I should have left it at that, been more forceful about his presence in my life. In Nathan's life. Not because of that violence. Because of my reaction to it. To him.

"Your keys," Lance said, jaw hard. "I'm drivin'."

My spine stiffened at yet another sentence where my bending to his will seemed like a forgone conclusion.

"If you need to drive anywhere, you've got a perfectly good SUV parked right on the curb," I informed him, jerking my head.

He stared at me, annoyance radiated off him, coated me.

The silence stretched long.

The pressure on my wrist remained.

For once in my life, I hoped for a bruise, a mark, something physical as a reminder of this contact.

And with that thought, I realized I really needed to get my

head examined, or at the very least my ovaries, they were taking control.

"Figured it would take me carrying you across your front yard to get you into the SUV," he said finally. "And figured that wouldn't go down too well. So I'm drivin'."

"No, you're not," I said, trying not to imagine what it would be like to have Lance carry me across the yard. "*I'm driving. And I'm going to the store. Alone.*"

"Think you've forgotten why I'm here," Lance replied, his jaw ticking, obviously this conversation was too long and too tedious for his liking.

"No, I'm not soon to forget my son being kidnapped," I snapped, my voice sharp. "I know exactly why you're here, to make sure that doesn't happen again. And considering my son is inside the house and not in this car, definitely not in the store, you're not needed here."

He stared at me for a long time. Long enough to make me uncomfortable, make me want to squirm under his gaze like ants underneath a cruel kid's microscope.

"I'm exactly where I'm needed," he decided. "You're wearin' a bruise as evidence of that."

I flinched, even though the words weren't flung with force. His presence was violent, his touch was coated with it, it radiated from his stare, from his very aura, but the words themselves were not meant to harm, not meant to rub anything in my face. Just a simple statement of fact, spoken as gently as the truth could ever be spoken. And truths like this were a proverbial wrecking ball to the soul.

I swallowed roughly and straightened my spine. "I'm aware of the evidence of my estranged husband punching me in the face," I said flatly. "Unfortunately, I'm also used to wearing such things."

It was his turn to flinch now. As much as I wanted to be indifferent to the man who practiced his own indifference like breathing, I couldn't. The simple flinch affected me. It told me things too. That he was not wholly devoid of emotion and not some sexy man-shaped robot.

But I had to keep going.

"My husband is a lot of things," I said. "He is a sadist, a narcissist, a cruel human being, a bad father, even worse spouse. But he is not stupid. So I do not see him walking up to me in a grocery store and trying anything."

Lance's lips were a hard line. "This isn't a discussion."

And then, he did the unthinkable. The unforgivable. He snatched a handle of my purse, which was hitched on my arm, and he rifled through it for about one second and located my keys. A feat that *I* wasn't capable of. It took at least five minutes of rifling through spare snacks for Nathan, wet wipes, old Chapsticks, coupons and whatever Nathan decided to put in my purse that week to find my keys.

I was battling between being super impressed and incredibly pissed at the invasion of my privacy. A woman's purse was sacred.

Everyone knew that.

I didn't have time to decide which emotion I was going to land on because my purse was hitched back on my shoulder, my body moved swiftly, firmly and somehow gently out of the way so Lance could slide into the driver's seat and close the door.

I stared at the door for a long time, gaping at it and trying to figure out what the heck was happening.

The window rolled down.

"Get in the car, Elena," Lance said, dipping his head down slightly so I saw his irises over the top of his sunglasses.

I gulped.

Really tried to muster up the courage to be decisive, sassy, say something like Karen might say to put an alpha male in his proper place.

But I did none of that.

I turned on my heel and got in the car.

The entire ride to the grocery store was silent.

Lance obviously liked it that way.

I did not.

I had a five-year-old. I hadn't had a silent car ride since he was born.

It wasn't uncomfortable for me, that silence. No, what was uncomfortable was being in such an enclosed space with Lance, alone, close to him, his hand moving back and forward to the gear shift, so close to my thigh that the air kissed it with his movements.

Or maybe I was imagining it.

Then there was the heat.

Partly due to the fact it was nearing a hundred-degree day and the car had no air conditioning. But that was not the reason why sweat was beading on my upper lip, temples, inner thighs, and my butt. Yeah, my frickin' *butt*. Not enough publicity was given to this phenomenon that seemed to only affect women. In fact, not enough women even talked about this, because it was embarrassing as hell, but it happened.

Mostly on the very rare—read, two times—occasion I found the time to work out. But also in really hot restaurants, or if I was wearing cheap fabric—which was always—on a really hot day and forced to sit on leather seats.

Also, when I was really nervous.

As a rule, I didn't really get nervous about things. Namely because in order to get nervous, you had to be going really far out of your comfort zone, going on a first date, in a job interview, starting your own business, public speaking, cooking dinner for the husband who beat the shit out of you if you didn't do it right.

I stayed well within my comfort zone since arriving here.

I'd reckoned I'd ventured far enough out of it just by finding the courage to leave my cage cleverly disguised as just another McMansion in the suburbs.

Sitting in a car with Lance was so far out of my comfort zone I forgot what comfort even felt like.

Therefore my butt was sweating.

So in addition to worrying about Lance driving my crappy car without air conditioning, about being in this crappy car *alone* with Lance, I was worrying about having a stain of butt sweat on my white shorts when I got out of the car.

I'd chosen the shorts because it was hot, they were clean and because they made my legs look good.

Now I cursed myself.

What was I thinking? I *never* wore these. Because wearing white around a child was a recipe for disaster.

Also wearing them around a hot guy that made your butt sweat was also a recipe for disaster.

So that's pretty much what I was thinking about the entire, stifling, panic-inducing ride to the grocery store.

It wasn't until we actually pulled up that I realized I was going to be grocery shopping with Lance. Not just that, I was grocery shopping for a large number of people who deserved some great food for being great people and I really could not afford to do that.

This thought, of course, only made my butt sweat more.

Lance, hopefully oblivious to the sweat situation, didn't even look at me as he got out of the car.

I took a deep breath, tried to subtly wipe the dampness from my forehead with the back of my hand and got out of the car.

There was no real way to check for wet patches on my ass without looking like a maniac, so I just had to hope for the best.

Luckily, Lance didn't seem too bothered about waiting on me after he'd locked the car, he just strode toward the entrance.

I watched him for a beat, his purposeful, lithe strides, his shirt and jeans free of any sweat and looking sinfully delicious.

I gulped in a swallow of humid air and followed him to the grocery store.

Which was where the problems continued.

He'd already gotten a cart by the time I made it into the foyer. The big kind, not the small ones I usually used with Nathan. I'd always looked enviously at the moms with the designer bags and leggings, pushing around the overflowing large cart full of name brand food. They didn't even glance at prices when they threw things into their cart, didn't consider whether they really needed it, didn't look at the shelves with an eagle eye for the things that would go the furthest and last the longest.

No, they shopped for what they *wanted*, what their kids wanted.

Whereas I was pushing around a sparsely and strategically full small cart of off brand products, whatever fruit and veggies were on sale that week, clutching coupons and doing mental calculations in my head as every new item landed in the small cart.

Nathan, the angel that he was, sensed my quiet panic about going grocery shopping. So, unlike other children, he didn't run up and down the aisles, picking up things he wanted, or begging me for all sorts of treats.

He walked in step with me, chattering about whatever he'd learned in school that day, a cool cloud he'd seen, or his new goal of farming ants.

I loved that little dude for so many, infinite reasons, but the supermarket thing nearly broke my heart. So, usually, I'd find a way to sneak a candy bar or something into the basket and slip it into his lunchbox the next day.

I was not in charge of this grocery trip, as Lance made clear by wheeling the large cart right into the fruit and vegetable section.

I pursed my lips to stop myself from saying anything about the cart, though the gesture was not needed, my pride shut me up plenty.

"Get the shit you need for the guac," Lance said, snatching pre-made salads from the chiller.

Again, I had to purse my lips to stop myself from saying that the pre-made salads were grossly overpriced and the ingredients for salads were cheaper and would go further.

I went and got the *shit* I needed for the guac, looking for the cheapest variety of tomatoes, onions, and avocados.

By the time I made it back to the cart with my careful selections, the cart was already a quarter full. My eyes went wide with everything Lance had dumped into it while I was trying to find the best avocado.

Meats of varying kinds, more salad ingredients, some pastries from the bakery section. Huge bottles of iced tea, both sweetened and unsweetened. Sodas. Fresh bread. Pretty much the makings of an epic barbeque.

And bankruptcy for me.

I opened my mouth to say something, but Lance beat me to it.

"You're not a vegan or some shit, are you?"

I snapped my head up from the cart to focus on him. He'd hooked his sunglasses in the front of his tee, in a way that looked both effortless and incredibly sexy. His expression was blank, hard, if anything, a little impatient.

He pretty much looked like a man who would rather be anywhere but here, not a man who had all but accosted me—at the very least, accosted my purse—in order to get here.

I tried to think of all the places a man like Lance would like to be than grocery shopping with the single mother who had a crappy car, butt sweat, a violent ex, and an adorable kid.

A gym, by the looks of his body.

Likely some trendy, edgy, masculine loft in downtown LA with sparse furniture and some weights in the corner—where I imagined he lived.

Or some in between some slim and tanned twenty-year-old legs. Beautiful, big hair, an easy smile, no baggage, able to do things like buy groceries without having a panic attack and emptying her bank account.

"Elena," he said my name with more of that impatience that edged his eyes and yet my stomach dipped at the way my name sounded coming out of his mouth.

I jerked when I realized I hadn't answered his question, instead I'd just stared at him, likely with a blank gaze and a slack jaw.

"No, I eat meat. I love meat of all kinds," I said quickly, my mind taking three whole seconds to catch up to my mouth and realize what I'd just said.

My cheeks went hotter than the ones inside my white shorts.

Lance didn't even blink. Obviously he was laughing on the inside. At me. The grown-ass woman who had no control over her sweat glands or her words.

"Allergic to gluten, dairy? On some crazy diet you pretend you're allergic to it?" he continued.

I shook my head, not trusting myself to speak this time.

I wasn't allergic to anything, especially not gluten or dairy, thankfully. My diet consisted of mostly those things, considering they were some of the cheapest. Also, bread was happiness. Anyone who didn't eat it for reasons that weren't medical was insane.

"Good," was all he said before he moved the cart forward.

I followed him, rather helplessly, as he heaped various name brand foodstuffs into the cart, much like those Lululemon housewives, but with a lot more manly force and sex appeal.

The housewives were all but banging into each other as we passed them, everyone gaping, staring at Lance. Then at me. Likely they were trying to figure out what happened in the universe to make a man like that go grocery shopping with a woman like me.

I had given up on even trying to say something about the sheer amount of expensive food that now filled the cart. I was already planning on using the 'in case of super-duper emergency' credit card that I never used. As desperate as times sometimes got, I didn't want to get myself into a hole of debt I couldn't get out of. I also didn't want to find myself in a position where I had no backup apart from asking Eliza and Karen for money.

Which they would give to me in a heartbeat.

Which was why I'd never ask.

I figured this credit card was probably going to be seeing a lot more use considering I'd be swiping it at the Greenstone Security office and be spending the rest of my life paying it off. But it was payments I'd be making gladly with my son at home with me.

"You drink?" Lance asked me after he'd put a box of beer into the cart, somehow finding room amongst the decidedly awesome foods he'd chosen for tonight. Most of which I'd only coveted in other people's carts and never brought home with me.

Nathan would be so excited.

And that was worth it.

"I have a five-year-old, an abusive ex-husband and a shitty job," I told him with a raised brow. "Of course I drink."

Something moved, slightly, almost imperceptibly in his face, something that might have been amusement, but it disappeared too quickly to tell.

"Wine or beer?" he asked.

"Wine," I replied. "I'm not really fussy with what kind, as

long as it has an alcohol content and doesn't taste like vinegar if it's red." My secret weapon was the 'Two Buck Chuck' from Trader Joe's that was $2.99 a bottle and tasted excellent to my unrefined palate. But Trader Joe's was a thirty-minute drive away, so it made the wine decidedly more expensive when you factored in gas prices.

Lance looked at me for a second longer than was regular with him, and regular was already plenty long, then he directed the cart to the wine.

I followed him, but because my gait was dreamy and stilted, I made it to him just as he was putting three bottles of wine into the cart.

Three, beautiful bottles of Cab Sav I'd stared at on the top shelf before I'd reached down and got my five buck bottles.

The bottle that cost thirty bucks a pop.

And there was three of them.

"Wait, as much as my life is somewhat of a mess right now, even *I* can't drink that much wine," I said, picking up one of the bottles and intending to put it back on the shelf, ready for a woman in expensive leggings to pick up.

"I'm not refined enough to appreciate such an expensive bottle. I'm good with the cheap stuff it—"

I was cut off by a hand on my wrist. The hand that was reaching toward the shelf, intending on putting the wine back.

The very same hand that had been on my wrist not thirty minutes ago, but somehow the effect was just as jarring. I reasoned Lance's touch was something that no one could get used to.

I moved my eyes to his.

They were hard, stormy.

"Bottle's thirty bucks, Elena," he said.

I nodded slowly. "I'm aware, which is why I'm putting it back."

"Thirty bucks, it's not expensive."

I gritted my teeth, shame embodied in the heat and I was sure the redness in my cheeks. Again, like his comment about my face, there was no malice or judgment in the words, but it sparked malice and judgement that I harbored for myself.

"Yes," I said through my gritted teeth. "Thirty bucks, three times is *ninety*. Considering I'll personally only drink about two glasses because I'm a lightweight and because I don't feel comfortable having anything more when I'm taking care of my son, and that Eliza and Karen will likely bring their own because they're wine snobs. Rosie has already informed me—by text, even though I never gave her my number—that she's bringing the makings for margaritas, which I don't drink, so unless any of you big badasses prefer a full-bodied red then two and a third of these thirty-dollar bottles are going to waste," I said, expelling a breath after I spoke, because I'd all but spewed those words out while forgetting to breathe. And I still wasn't done.

"Furthermore, I'm a single mom on a waitress's salary with a hefty bill to a fancy security company on my horizon," I continued. "I'm not spending a hundred bucks on something that is completely unnecessary and selfish."

Lance didn't speak after my little monologue, nor did he let go of my wrist, the grip only tightened as I got more steam to continue ranting.

I bit the inside of my lip in order to keep staring at him without looking away or blinking, he was obviously trying to have some sort of stare contest with me to establish his dominance.

For whatever reason, I was going to fight.

I didn't fight when my husband yelled at me, called me a whore for wearing cutoffs to a Fourth of July barbeque, when he hit me after we got home from that barbeque or when he forced himself on me later that night.

But I was fighting a relative—albeit one I had a totally inappropriate crush on— stranger in the middle of a grocery store over *wine*, of all things.

It seemed that Lance awakened something inside of me, other than word vomit and butt sweat.

So I didn't back down.

In no world did I think I would win a staring contest with anyone. I lost against Nathan on an almost daily basis. But something in me broke, right there in the wine aisle, I'm not quite sure what. The events of the past few days, the exhaustion of the past few years got to me in a way that gave me strength enough to win a staring contest with a badass who looked like he waterboarded infidels for a living.

His grip left my hand and like last time, I felt an emptiness without his touch that made no sense and that definitely wasn't sane.

I was about to do an inward victory dance when the bottle of wine was snatched out of my loosened grip and placed not at all gently back into the cart.

"You're not spendin' a hundred bucks on the wine," he said, all but barking at me. "I am."

And before I could argue about how this was *so not going to happen*, he turned on his heel and pushed the cart away from me and the wine and toward the cash register.

Again, I lagged because I was kind of stunned, tired from everything I'd just said, angry, confused and turned on.

This meant by the time I found him, half of the cart was already unloaded and he was standing in front of the card machine like some kind of Greek statue.

I glared at him and pushed my way forward to the screen, schooling my reaction so my shock didn't show at the total of only half of the items.

"I'm paying," I said through gritted teeth, rifling through my purse for my wallet.

"You're not," he replied, not looking at me, his voice frustratingly even.

I took a breath, smiled fakely at the cashier who was staring between us with ill-concealed interest.

"This is food that will feed *my* guests," I said, still rifling. How did he find my keys, which were comparatively tiny, when I couldn't seem to locate my frickin' wallet?

He had some kind of magical power over women and their purses.

It was the only logical solution.

"This food is for my guests, as a thank you for doing everything that they've done for me and Nathan," I continued, glaring at him. "*You* are a guest. So let me thank you and stop being such an asshole."

He raised his brow. "You're thankin' me and calling me an asshole in the same sentence?" he asked with an annoyingly even cadence to his voice.

I glared at him, finally finding my wallet in time for the cashier to scan the last of the items. "Yes, that's exactly what I'm doing. Now move out of the way."

He did not move out of the way, in fact, he only crowded the card machine more, so it was impossible for me to put my own card in the slot. Unless I got physical with him in a grocery store, in broad daylight, seemingly unprovoked.

It was tempting to do so, really freaking tempting.

Pretty much the only thing that stopped me was the fact I didn't really trust my own strength and I deduced that trying to move him would result in me making an idiot of myself instead of achieving my goal.

Because of this, he was able to swipe his own card without hassle.

He barely even blinked at the total that took my breath away.

Then again, I was sure his hazel eyes had seen a lot more disturbing things than a huge grocery bill.

I guess I should have been relieved at the fact someone else had paid for something I couldn't afford. That I wouldn't have to put myself in debt when I had plenty of debt on the horizon.

But I wasn't.

I felt humiliated and ashamed at the fact he'd deemed me a charity case and had felt enough pity for me—somewhere deep down in the dark recesses of his soul—to pay for food that he would only eat a small portion of and wine he wouldn't even be drinking.

Tears prickled the backs of my eyes as the bagger finished with the food and Lance grasped the cart and wheeled it off without comment. Because of all the things the seemingly kind gesture made me feel, it mostly made me feel like my parents. It reminded me of the many, many times at the supermarket when their card was declined and they put on the right expressions, shoved the hungry daughter in the faces of a cashier or fellow shopper and somehow guilted someone enough into helping them out.

It was a skill that they perfected and excelled at.

One that disgusted me on so many levels. Mainly because my parents had the money, thanks to them figuring out ways to cheat the system in order to get all sorts of benefits they weren't entitled to.

But all that money went to booze, drugs, and in my father's case, hookers.

Something I learned about early in life and that was sworn to secrecy with my father's harsh words, threat and a purplish bruise on my upper arm that took almost two weeks to heal.

That memory and the thousands of others I had of my childhood were reasons why I never accepted things from others, even those who loved me and only wanted to help. I always found my own way. I did it honestly. Because I wanted to teach my son. I wanted to give him memories that wouldn't cut him every time something reminded him of them.

And as I was following the brutal, beautiful man through the parking lot, back to my shitty car with no AC, him pushing hundreds of dollars of charity, pain, and memories, I was being cut. The knife sliced through layers of flesh, scar tissue, right to the core of me.

Every step I took I bit the inside of my cheek harder in order to stop myself from crying. From leaking out all my trauma and issues onto the hot concrete of the parking lot, to stop myself from exposing myself to Lance.

The ride back was silent again.

This time it was a thicker silence. Darker.

I wasn't worrying about vanity, or the fact that Lance's hand almost brushed my bare skin. I was torturing myself with memories. I was emotionally flagellating myself with the bitter and ugly truth of what I was.

Who I was.

My parents.

I couldn't even provide for my son.

Worse, I couldn't even keep him, or myself safe.

The man with the grim, devastatingly handsome face and terrifying disposition was doing that.

But I didn't think he'd keep me safe in the end.

CHAPTER NINE

I WAS HAPPY.

It was that simple.

Anyone who'd lived a hard life would know that of all the complicated things in the world, happiness had the top spot.

Especially after the events of this afternoon, I would have told anyone that simple happiness was about as likely as me summiting Everest.

I underestimated the people around me. What good food, better company and a balmy evening could do.

Everyone from the diner had filtered in throughout the evening, after I'd texted them and informed them of the impromptu party.

The back yard had somehow been transformed only an hour after Polly and Rosie had arrived. Candles were lit, despite the fire hazard in California. I reasoned we had enough badasses around us to stop a fire before it began.

Fairy lights I'd never plugged in were strewn over the fence and turned on when the sun began kissing the horizon. Scents of beautifully charred meat filtered through the air, with Luke and

Heath taking turns at manning the grill, with Bobby gleefully giving up the position. As good of a cook as he was—and he really frickin' was—he existed on heat and eat meals and processed junk when he wasn't working.

The Greenstone Security gang and their wives had begun to trickle in with the most perfect of timing, interrupting me having to tell Eliza what exactly was going on with Lance. Which was nothing, obviously.

Rosie, Lucy, and Polly brightened up the night, their energies warm and comforting. I felt as if I'd known them for years, and that I'd met them under different, happier circumstances. I had been so certain that everything attached to those twenty-four hours without Nathan would carry a horrifying reminder of what happened, even people. Especially people, because I would never have come into contact with these beautiful, glossy, foul-mouthed and kick-ass women in my regular life.

I'd braced when they'd arrived, not in the way Luke had suggested. More emotionally. Readied myself for flashbacks, something I was used to and still got when I smelled something, saw something or felt something that reminded me of my marriage.

PTSD was most likely what it was. I didn't have the money for a therapist to tell me that, but I didn't really need an overpaid professional to tell me my husband's continual and brutal abuse left emotional wounds.

I did not get a single flashback when Rosie bowled through the door without knocking, grinning and a bottle of tequila in each hand. Her eyes went around my living room, with none of the distaste or judgment I might expect a woman with a three-thousand-dollar purse hanging from the crook of her arm to have at my shabby chic—and that was being generous—living room.

"Oh, you are a spiritual queen," she deduced, without saying hello. She dumped the alcohol and the crazy expensive, beautiful purse on the coffee table and her eyes zeroed in on my Tarot cards. "You are so doing me later," she decided.

Luke emerged from the hall where he'd been wiring up something, grinning at his wife. "Who is doing you later?" he asked, voice warm and teasing and sexy enough to make my knees weak.

Rosie's eyes turned mischievous. "Well you, much, *much* later." She winked before she moved her eyes around the room. "Is my child around here somewhere?"

I gestured to the back yard. "Playing with my neighbors and my kid."

To say Nathan had taken to Rogue was an understatement. He was in love with a beautiful little boy to entertain and teach all sorts of things.

Her eyes lit up. "Great, I'll leave them to it." She picked up the tequila. "Where's your blender?"

And that was Rosie's entrance.

Polly's was a little more subdued and she did greet me. She also presented me with a small wrapped box. I took it, surprised. A lump formed in my throat when I opened it.

"Agate—grounding and strengthening," she whispered. "I was worried it was a risky thing to give someone, considering that people have some strong opinions about crystals." She looked around the room. "Now I see it was the right choice."

I nodded, unable to say anything more.

She smiled warmly, obviously understanding that I couldn't speak.

I didn't have to, because of Heath emerging from behind her, a beautiful little girl in his arms and an equally beautiful little boy at his side.

He was older. Had to be about eleven. Tall, gangly, but in a way you'd know he'd grow into it. He had deep caramel skin and piercing blue eyes that radiated with a deepness no child could have. Because a deepness like that was carved out from pain.

Suffering. None of which lay behind those eyes right at that moment, but it had been there.

"This is Ziggy," Heath said, ruffling the boy's already messy hair. "He's our son."

Ziggy had a reaction to this. A palpable glow went over him, his aura. A happiness that could only come from people who had experienced true suffering.

He was theirs. Completely. But not by blood. Birth. By heart. Soul. It was something anyone could see, feel. It was beautiful.

"Hey Ziggy," I said, smiling. "I've got a little boy named Nathan who is quite a bit younger than you but is sufficiently mischievous to provide you with entertainment. He's out back."

Ziggy's eyes lit up even more and he tipped his head upward to Heath in a silent question. Heath smiled down at him in a way that hit my heart. Pure adoration. Dedication. The exact way a father should look at a son. Robert had never looked at Nathan that way.

"Of course. Go and raise hell, Zig," Heath said.

The quiet boy rewarded his father, and everyone around him with the widest and most beautiful smile I'd ever seen.

He held out his arms. "I'll take my buddy," he said, voice quiet but clear and strong.

Heath smiled even wider and handed the little girl to his skinny awaiting arms. She immediately made a little sound of happiness and curled into Ziggy's chest.

I bit my lip to stop from crying at this as Ziggy moved through the living room, slowly, carefully, purposefully.

"His sister is his best friend," Polly explained, eyes shining with happiness. "He's only just become ours." She paused. "Well, he's been ours since the second we saw him, but we've been having a tough time with adopting him. He's been legally our son for just under a month." Her voice was low, happy. No, happy was too light a word for it. Because her eyes were deep too. Carved out with pain, filled up with happiness.

Heath put his arms around his wife and kissed her head. "He's only just started getting comfortable talking around people," he explained.

"Well, I'm sure Nathan will do enough talking for the both of them and the rest of the people at the party," I said.

Lucy and Keltan arrived then with their beautiful little girl, Amelia.

Everyone made themselves at home, and I loved it. It felt like home.

Lance and I hadn't spoken.

Not one single word since I'd called him an asshole in front of a supermarket cashier.

I knew I wasn't angry with *him*. I knew that it was my own issues that made me angry and ashamed enough to project onto him.

That didn't make him any less of an asshole.

I was sure he knew his fair share about male pride. About the human race. The way he looked at people told me he was collecting information, making all sorts of deductions, learning everything about someone by the way they tied their shoelaces.

He worked as a private investigator, or security guard or whatever. I was sure knowing and reading people was part of his job.

Therefore he was likely to know about female pride. About a mother's pride. How powerful that was. How penetrating. Whatever he'd deduced about me, about my situation, should have told him to know better than to do what he did.

Therefore I was mad at him.

In between smiling at my kid, at the people who surrounded me and filled me with joy, I glared at the man in question.

He didn't seem at all affected by my glare, or me at all. But every time I happened to look in his general direction, my stare locked with his empty and hard one.

I tried to tell myself he hadn't spent the *entire night* staring at me. And if he did, it was likely because he was watching for me to do something insane as I'd acted like a total crazy person every time I was in his presence.

That and it was his job.

Obviously neither Nathan or myself needed protection tonight since the entire Greenstone Security team was in my back yard, but he had made it clear how seriously he took his job. And without humor. Or emotion.

I was totally talking myself into thinking it was anything more than a job to him.

Luckily, I was distracted by the happiness, the warmth, the company and the laughter of the evening. My friends blended in seamlessly with everyone from Greenstone Security. Nathan lapped up the fact there were other kids around, and the males who taught him how to grill a hot dog. I was right, he hit it off with Ziggy, who wasn't as outgoing or outwardly as nuts as my little boy, but it worked. My kid was kind. Sensitive. He saw that Ziggy was different in beautifully painful ways, so he made sure to treat him exactly how he'd treat any other kid.

My heart hurt a little seeing Keltan hand him the tongs and stand beside him while he grilled.

I'd always promised myself I'd do everything with my son, I'd play catch with him, I'd go to any sports game he decided he liked. He would know how to change a tire and the oil in his car before he was allowed to drive it. I'd teach him the things that a father would teach him. I'd make him into a good man. Nothing like his father.

But there was a gaping hole in any young kid's life when they didn't have a father. Different for girls and boys, but with Nathan, it was that male role model to look up to.

I couldn't let myself dwell on it because I wasn't allowed to. My happiness didn't let me. The women around me didn't let me.

It was in the midst of my pure happiness that my cell phone rang. It was a surprise I even heard it since we had music playing, laughter, and chatter drowned out the low vibration. But I'd just happened to walk into the house and heard it on the kitchen counter.

I snatched it up and answered without looking, heading back into the back yard.

"You made a mistake, pumpkin."

I stopped in my tracks, the smile that had been almost constant for the entire night frozen on my face.

"Which of them are you fucking?" Robert continued, his voice cold, even.

My body responded to that tone, erupting in shakes, bracing for the hit that would always accompany the faux calm.

"Or are you fucking them all?" Robert spat. "I shouldn't be surprised. You always were a whore. I snatched you from the gutter and you act like trash when you don't have me to discipline you. You're using that pussy of yours to get men to come into my home and take away my son? Big mistake, Elena. I'm gonna show you just how big. When I get my hands on you, I'll—"

I didn't hear anymore.

Because my phone was snatched out of my shaking hand by a large and strong hand that most definitely wasn't shaking. A hand attached to a muscled arm, an iron jaw and hard eyes.

Lance held the phone to his ear for exactly seven seconds.

I counted.

He didn't say a word.

Didn't move a muscle, which was a feat considering all the muscles he had.

After those seven seconds, he moved the phone from his ear. To smash it right against the concrete at our feet.

I watched it shatter.

Then I watched Lance's boots move away from me. I had to lift my head to watch him tear through the back yard, then disappear from sight as he rounded the house.

Lance

Keltan was waiting for him after he emerged from the gates, wiping the blood off his knuckles with the back of his shirt.

Lance expected him to be.

He was sure Heath or Duke would be down the street, waiting in case he needed backup.

Lance never needed backup.

That was kind of the point.

But Keltan was here, leaning against the SUV, arms folded, expression clear.

Lance wondered how long he'd stayed at Elena's. Long enough to get her to talk to him, tell him what happened in order for him to know to come here. Long enough to likely calm her down, get her to stop fucking shaking, wipe some of that cold, vacant terror from her eyes.

Lance clenched his bloodied fists with the mere memory of that expression. That faraway expression that was miles from the beautiful, full smile that had spread to her whole body, fuck it'd spread to the whole back yard, crept through all the layers of his skin, his scar tissue, snaked through until it found something inside him still able to feel.

Yeah, that happiness had affected him.

Warmed him.

And the loss of it, the absence of it had chilled him. He'd watched it drain from her just like he'd watched her fill up with it since everyone had started arriving. Though she didn't have those smiles, that warmth for him. It intrigued him, that anger that he'd not seen her direct toward anyone else. He treasured it, that menace. It was obviously rare, precious. Because she gave everyone her smiles, the warmth dancing in her eyes. But he was the only one that got that cold fury that had begun in the wine aisle at the supermarket.

It had come from a place of pride. A place of hurt.

He'd seen it all mixed in her eyes like the most potent, delicious and dangerous cocktail on the planet.

He was already fucking drunk on her when he'd made sure not to even sip that shit. Because she shoved it down his throat. With her stupid fucking awkward words that made his cock hard and his mind intrigued. With her thinking that thirty bucks on wine was expensive, with her trying to stand up to him when she was wearing the bruise as evidence of another man's violence.

He knew she couldn't afford to feed everyone that would be at her place. He didn't want her paying for that shit. Lance lived simple, his main expenses being weapons that were scattered throughout his shitty apartment. Money did little more than pile up in his accounts since he had nothing, and no one to spend it on.

It gave him a rush, spending it on shit for this party.

Shit for Elena.

It gave him more of a rush that she was so against him doing that shit. She was independent. Fiercely so. It was clear she did not want to exist on handouts, or help from the people around her who obviously adored her and her son and wanted to help her.

Life hadn't been kind to Elena Phoenix, previously Hudson, originally Pérez.

Lance had looked her up and saw that shit. Saw the doctor's records. Looked into her parents. They had a long list of priors.

Of offenses. Her father was currently serving time for beating the shit out of a hooker. Mother was still living in the trailer park that Elena grew up in. Surprised the fuck out of him. She did not look like a woman that came from that. Did not speak or act like a woman that came from shit.

Life had been hard to her, it should have calcified around her, carved sharp edges, jaded her.

It hadn't.

By some miracle, she was all soft and round, even when her body was all skin and bone. She was soft everywhere she should be and everywhere she shouldn't.

So watching that happiness leak from her eyes with the single phone call, hearing that fuck's threats to come into her life and try and make it even dirtier than he had, Lance was not having that.

He did not give a fuck about Keltan's orders to leave that fuck alone.

He didn't give a fuck about anything but that deadness in Elena's eyes. The way she *shook*.

He couldn't comfort her, he wasn't physically able to do that. So he did what he could. The only thing he could. He made that fucker *bleed*.

He didn't greet Keltan as he approached the SUV, he just waited.

"He still alive?" Keltan asked casually.

Lance nodded curtly once.

Keltan raised his brow in surprise. Lance wasn't known for losing his temper. And when he did, he wasn't known for leaving anyone alive when they made him lose it.

"Elena didn't want that," he said by answer.

Keltan's look of surprise only intensified. "And that's what stopped you? A client's wishes?"

Lance gritted his teeth at the knowledge behind the fucker's words, his eyes. He didn't know shit.

So he didn't reply.

"This is gonna make it more complicated," Keltan continued. "Leaving him alive."

Lance nodded. He knew that it would. Leaving rats alive just meant they could continue being vermin. Better to exterminate.

But he couldn't.

Him.

The firm's resident grim reaper.

Because of a client.

A *woman*.

A *kid*.

He clenched his fists, relishing in the burn from his bleeding and bruised knuckles.

"Could blow back on Elena and Nathan," Keltan said.

"I won't let it," Lance hissed, the very thought of fresh bruises on Elena's face making his trigger finger itch.

Keltan nodded. "I know, brother." He clapped him on the shoulder and Lance stiffened with the contact. Keltan didn't move his hand. "She's good. Recovered well after you left. Got her people there with her. Duke's down the street at the house." Keltan paused. "Assume you're gonna relieve him of that duty?"

Lance only nodded once.

Keltan grinned, more knowledge in that fucker's face. "Welcome to the club, brother."

Elena

Lance didn't come back.

I pretended I didn't notice.

Surely there was enough to distract me.

Like the fact him smashing my phone and storming off garnered quite a bit of attention.

Keltan had been calm, collected and totally on his game at getting me to tell him what happened without having a panic attack. Then he'd seamlessly passed me off to a calm and smiling Lucy when he and a couple of the other guys left, presumably to follow Lance.

I didn't get to wonder exactly where they were going because I had to focus on my son, who was perceptive as shit and even if he wasn't, his favorite grown-up smashing a phone inches away from his mother caught his attention.

It was the superpower of a parent to mask all kinds of pain and panic so their child wasn't faced with it. Burdened with it. Children were little sponges, so yes, they parroted curse words they'd heard at home at school or in church. But they also soaked up the emotions of a parent. I tried to make sure Nathan always soaked up smiles, jokes, stories, lessons. None of my pain, my worries, my sadness. The world would inject enough of that into him as he grew into himself. He would inherit my skin tone, my hair, my obsession with peanut butter, but he would not inherit my sorrows.

So his little face, asking what was wrong was the cold splash of water I needed to jerk myself out of whatever Robert's phone call had triggered within me.

Luckily it took a smile, a hug and letting him have more pie to distract Nathan from the shift in the evening.

While he was distracted, Karen ordered me to repeat everything Robert had said, cheeks getting redder and redder as I did so.

Bobby got that scary look on his face again.

As did Logan.

And Esther.

"I'm fine," I told everyone.

They did not believe me.

But they pretended to, because they knew calling bullshit on me when I was this fragile would break me.

And the people around me, worried for me, angry for me, murderous for me, they would do everything that it took for me not to break.

Everyone trickled out at different times, but everyone staying long enough to help me clean something, wrap up leftover food or drain leftover wine. It irritated me that two bottles of the wine I'd convinced Lance I wouldn't drink were gone.

Of course I hadn't drunk two bottles by myself, no matter how tempting it became after Robert's phone call. Eliza and Karen had helped, eyes widening when they saw the label, even though it was red.

My five-dollar bottles personally offended them.

Rosie and the rest drank margaritas. An impressive amount for women their sizes, and none of them seemed even the least bit tipsy as they left with their husbands and children.

I was definitely a lot tipsy, having gone over my two-glass limit. Nathan had stayed up well past his bedtime, but I managed to get him to bed at a time that would hopefully afford him enough sleep.

The refrigerator was stocked with plenty of leftovers, even though I'd sent a lot home with everyone I could. I knew that Nathan and I physically couldn't eat that much food before it went bad and I had a bit of a weird thing with throwing food out.

I had all but had to kick Eliza and Karen out of the house, them being the last to leave because they had the shortest distance to go. Eliza had tried to insist on staying the night, but I had managed to lie convincingly and tell her I was okay. I doubted she believed the lie, but she knew that the Greenstone Security guys had installed the fancy new security system—that

Luke taught me how to use before my second glass of wine—and that I had Duke down the street.

I hadn't thought about Lance, not properly at least, until Eliza and Karen had left, making me promise to shout out my window if anything went down.

Because of course I didn't have a phone now.

I couldn't afford to buy a new one, but I needed one since we didn't have a landline. Fury ran through my veins at the fact Lance had smashed my crappy, third-hand phone because he heard the tail end of something that shouldn't have even meant anything to him.

Sure, decent guys—if that's what Lance was—hearing the horrible stuff men like Robert could spurt at women likely were going to have a reaction. But a reaction like smashing my phone and storming off without a word?

Not cool.

Infuriating.

And really frickin' confusing.

Lance didn't strike me as someone who lost his temper and smashed things. Everything about him was controlled, cold. I had only seen glimpses of what might be emotion from the man. *Might*.

He definitely made it clear that I was nothing but a job to him. He made it clear he was a man who controlled every situation and that he wasn't shaken by anything.

If the pieces of my phone on my back step were anything to go by, he was shaken by that phone call.

Which was what made all this confusing.

He had to feel *something* about me in order to lose it like that. He had to feel something beyond the indifference that leaked from his pores.

I tortured myself with that truth. I tortured myself with that remaining bottle of fancy wine, with the food that filled up my fridge, with the lack of cell phone.

While I tortured myself, I waited. Because surely he was coming back. He couldn't just smash my phone and walk off, never to be seen again. There had to be an explanation, or at the very least his cold presence informing me he was back to do his job.

Or that he'd killed my husband and the father of my child.

The look I'd glimpsed on his face just before he'd disappeared from sight had punctured the numb state I'd been in. At the time, I didn't process it. But with all my crazy replaying, I realized what that expression was.

It was death.

He was capable of killing someone, I knew that deep down. I'd known it all along. Heck, he'd offered to kill Robert the first frickin' day I met him. And I'd let him around my child. I'd berate myself for that bad parenting a lot later, when this was all a memory. When Lance was a memory.

I ignored the stab that came with that thought and focused on a particular memory. A fresher one.

That look on Lance's face.

The one that had me pacing the house, half expecting someone to knock on my door and tell me Robert was dead. I was half hoping for that. What was wrong with me? That wasn't who I was, wishing people dead because of how they'd wronged me. But that wasn't it. I didn't care how Robert had hit me, abused me, defiled me. I cared that he posed a threat to my son. And it was the mother in me that called for the blood of anyone who harmed my child.

So I waited for news.

For Lance.

Neither one came.

CHAPTER TEN

WHEN MY ALARM BUZZED, I was awake.

Luckily, I still had an actual alarm clock unlike many people that relied purely on their phones. I bought it at a garage sale because it was kitschy and a faded gold that went with the rest of the décor in my room. My purple velvet comforter, the mishmash of throw pillows I'd collected over the years. Photos in gold frames all over my restored nightstands that I'd painted white and put gold accents on. There was an old armchair in the corner which had a furry ottoman in front of it, I'd sit there sometimes, just looking at the moon when it was full.

I'd sat at that chair for most of the night before I moved to my bed and tried to sleep.

It wasn't my lack of phone that kept me up all night. Though that was a contributing factor.

It wasn't even Robert's phone call, as it should have been. It was Lance.

He was haunting me, torturing me and he'd never even spoken more than a handful of sentences to me.

My lack of sleep was a punishment I deserved for letting two different men penetrate my consciousness, my sanity.

I resolved as I sucked down the strongest coffee I could possibly make, that I would have a new strength when it came to Lance. That I would be professional with him as he was with me. I'd have a meeting with Keltan and inform him as much as I appreciated their services, I wouldn't need Greenstone Security anymore. Though I didn't know how effective that was going to sound since last night's phone call kind of showed everyone that Robert wasn't going to back away quietly.

I hadn't expected him to.

I was still waiting for his father to get involved somehow, as he always had throughout our marriage, reminding me how powerful he was and how weak I was.

It was surprising to me that he hadn't tried to use that power when I ran, taking his grandson with him. Jeffery Hudson was a lot of things, much like his son. Robert's mother had died before I met him, breast cancer, so I never knew if she suffered like I had. I'd seen photos of her, beautiful, regal, always put together in a way suiting who she was. It was impossible to discern whether years of abuse hidden behind the picture-perfect smile.

But the fact that Jeffery knew what his son was doing to me, saw the bruises, and did nothing, told me all I needed to know. The way he treated me, looked at me and dismissed me told me more.

But he was different with Nathan. Almost warm. But not quite. It was clear he loved his grandson, and that scared me too. Because he loved Robert. And his love had nurtured a monster.

My son wouldn't get that kind of love.

Not ever.

Jeffery had never tried to find us, with the tools at his disposal, he could have, showed me he loved his grandson in all the wrong kind of ways.

It was that wrong love that terrified me as I got Nathan breakfast, packed his lunch, making sure to put the last piece of pie in it.

Would he make an effort now? Now that his prized son had lost his battle to take Nathan from me?

I knew that Jeffery would use a lot more civilized means to steal my son from me. He was smarter than Robert. He'd use the law. He'd use his money and power to try and get me painted us an unfit mother, snatch my boy away from me in every way he could.

I wasn't sure which one scared me more.

But I made sure none of that fear leaked onto my face the entire morning Nathan chatted to me through his oatmeal about what a great night he'd had last night and how he was going to tell all his friends and they'd be jealous.

I let my son's simple happiness chase away the surface fear. It worked better than coffee to wake me up, strengthen my resolve.

Robert might have brute strength and a badge. Jeffery might have money, power, influence. But there was nothing stronger than a mother's love. Her determination.

Getting out of the house was somewhat of a production, making sure that Nathan had everything he needed, that he hadn't decided to get changed into his Superman costume at the last minute, or gotten into my lipstick or any food item. Making sure I turned off all appliances—I was paranoid about setting the house on fire, we had renter's insurance but still, it would destroy me—making sure that I didn't have toothpaste on my mouth, that my clothes weren't on inside out—that had happened multiple times—I had my keys, my purse, some semblance of sanity.

It wasn't until we were out the door did I start looking for my keys to unlock my car. My keys weren't there.

"Shit," I hissed, pissed at myself for letting Lance's presence, lingering or not, distract me to make me have to go back into the house and find them. For the hundredth time, I cursed myself for not taking the two seconds it would take to attach my house keys to my car keys.

When I looked up, I saw that my car wasn't there.

"Fuck," I said louder this time.

"I thought you said we weren't allowed to say fuck, Mommy. Because our teeth will fall out if we do." Nathan said. He squinted at me. "Your teeth aren't falling out."

I tried to focus on my kid and not the fact that someone had stolen my shitty car right out of the driveway. Who even does that? If you were going to put yourself at risk of going to prison for stealing a car, wouldn't you make it worth it?

"Because adults are allowed to say it three times a year, if something really annoying happens," I said, staring at the empty space where my car used to be, trying to figure out what the heck to do here. I had insurance, but I was sure that would take an age to come through and we needed a car like yesterday. I still had my new car fund, but that was allotted to going toward paying Keltan back.

"Annoying like our car driving away without us in it?" Nathan asked, following my stare.

"Yeah, just like that, buddy," I said.

It was then that a black SUV pulled up at the curb.

Lance emerged.

I watched his entire journey from the curb to us, the troubles attached to my stolen car a memory. I was too busy thinking about how good his walk was. Like really great. Did he practice it? Or was it just a natural thing?

"Hey Captain! Our car drove off and we're allowed to say fuck without our teeth falling out because it's annoying," my little bundle of joy greeted.

I pinched the bridge of my nose. "*We* are not allowed to say it, only Mommy is, and you say it again then you'll be having your hamburgers through straws because you won't be able to chew with your bare gums."

Nathan's eyes widened. "I can eat my hamburgers with a straw?"

Okay, that didn't work.

"Can you make sure he doesn't like run into traffic or something while I call the police?" I asked Lance.

"Why you calling the police?" he asked, entire body wired.

"Um, if you hadn't noticed, there's an empty space where the car used to be. I didn't figure out how to make it invisible like Ron did in *Harry Potter*. Someone decided to put a cherry on top of my sundae by stealing it."

"Can I eat a sundae through a straw too?" Nathan piped in.

"No one stole it," Lance said.

I stilled. "What?"

"The AC is broken," he said as if that was an answer.

I put my hand on my hip and pushed my glasses to the top of my head so he could see my narrowed eyes. Something in me told me what was coming next.

"I took it into the shop."

"You took it into the shop," I repeated, this time not sounding all dreamy and idiotic repeating his words. My voice was sharp holding warning. "And you didn't think that this was something to consult me, *the owner of the car?*"

A muscle in his jaw ticked. He seemed irritated. Good for him. I was pissed. "You can't be drivin' in a car with broken AC in the middle of summer," was his response.

I took a breath. Another one. And then I looked to my kid who was standing there patiently eavesdropping like the little sponge he was.

"Nathan, please go sit in Mr. Lance's car. That's what we'll be taking to school for today."

Nathan's eyes lit up with happiness that I was so not frickin' feeling. "Groovy!" he declared. I had no clue where he learned that word, but he was Nathan so it made sense. He turned and ran across the yard to the car.

"Don't touch anything," I yelled after him.

Lance and I both watched Nathan until he'd safely climbed into the car.

I snapped my gaze back to his. "You cannot just take my frickin' car from me without saying anything," I hissed.

"The AC was broken," he said as if repeating it made it something that worked as an excuse.

"I get that you're a big badass who gets more badass points for the fewer words he speaks but that is not gonna fly right at this moment, dude. I know the AC is broken, considering I'm the one sweating her ass off driving in it."

"It needs to be fixed."

I told myself not to stomp my foot or scream or anything that would prove as setting a bad example to my son. "I know that," I said through gritted teeth. "But I also need it to drive my son to school, drive myself to work and I also need the money to get it fixed. Which I won't have for a long time because I've got more important shit to cover."

Namely the service he was currently providing.

I think the pissing me off came free.

"You're not paying for it," he said by answer.

"Considering it's my car, yes I am," I snapped.

"Nathan is gonna be late to school," Lance said by response.

I wanted to keep arguing with him until I was blue in the face our until he understood how out of line he was, I had the feeling it would be the former. But the dick was right, Nathan would be late if I kept doing that.

I hated that he was using my son against me like that.

"This isn't over," I said, pointing him and stomping to the SUV.

I was right.

It wasn't over.

Because sitting in the passenger seat of the SUV was a small rectangular box.

"What is this?" I demanded as Lance situated himself in the driver's seat.

"New phone," he answered, though it was obvious what it was.

I clenched the box. "Whose?"

He regarded me. "Yours."

"You are not buying me a new phone," I said through gritted teeth.

"Already did," he commented.

"Well take it back," I demanded.

"Get in the car," he countered.

I tried to take some long, cleansing breaths so my son, watching raptly from the back seat, did not see his mother lose her shit right before he went to school.

It was that thought that had me getting in the car. Not because Lance told me to in that cold, authoritative sexy voice, but because my son needed to get to school.

That's what I told myself anyway.

Lance didn't pull the car from the curb until I had checked Nathan's seatbelt inside his car seat—which had been put in at an earlier date—and buckled my own.

I pretended that didn't affect me in the slightest.

"I'm not accepting this," I said, shaking the phone at him while he drove.

"You are."

"I can buy my own phone," I lied through gritted teeth.

He looked sideways at me as he pulled up to a stop sign. He waited the full three seconds before he went, even though the coast was clear. He didn't strike me as a three-second man—in any sense of the expression—so I reasoned it was because me and Nathan were in the car.

I pretended that didn't affect me either.

"I smashed your phone," he said by answer.

"He did, Mom," Nathan chimed in, making sure that we both knew he was following the conversation. "Why did you do that, Captain?" he asked, curiously. He hadn't asked me that question last night or this morning. I'd honestly thought he'd forgotten about it.

But no, my kid didn't forget about anything. He just held onto things and waited for the perfect moment.

Lance glanced in the rearview mirror to make fleeting eye contact with Nathan before his eyes went back to the road. "I did it because I lost control of my temper."

I did not expect Lance to answer honestly, but then again, I didn't expect him to lie to my son either.

"What does temper mean?" Nathan asked.

Lance glanced back again. "It means you get angry in front of people you shouldn't and do things you shouldn't. Good men never lose control of their temper. Especially not in front of women."

I blinked rapidly as he spoke, my stomach swirling. Because he was talking to Nathan, but the words were for me.

Was this some kind of distorted apology?

"Momma, I'll never lose my temper with you," Nathan said. "I promise I'll always remember where I put it."

I choked out a laugh and turned in my seat to regard my little boy.

"I could never be angry with you anyway," he continued. "You're the best mom ever. You play games with me outside, you let me watch movies and never yell at me like my friend's moms do. Plus, you're gonna let me eat my hamburgers through strawers."

I tried to swallow both my laughter and tears at this. "You're the best son ever," I responded, my voice kind of thick.

He grinned wide. "Duh."

I turned back in my seat so Nathan didn't see the single tear that escaped from the corner of my eye.

Lance saw, of course.

Because he saw everything.

Even things I didn't even know I was showing him.

NEITHER OF US spoke after we'd dropped Nathan off. Not until we'd almost made it to the diner.

Me, because I was totally pissed off and couldn't trust myself not to yell at Lance and say things that I might regret later.

I didn't get angry often, and when I did, I made a concerted effort not to speak to people from a place of anger. Because anger was only temporary, but words born from it were not. I was well versed in how words could cut, carve, and destroy parts of people that even fists couldn't do.

Though I doubted that whatever I could say to Lance would really affect him.

Then again, I hadn't thought that *I'd* affected him at all until my phone was smashed at my feet.

"Where were you last night?" I asked as we stopped at the last set of traffic lights before we'd pull into the diner's parking lot.

"Your ex's place," he answered, looking straight ahead.

I turned so I could gape at him. It wasn't like I'd half expected him to have gone there, I just didn't expect him to offer up the information so readily.

"Why?"

He still didn't look at me. Nor did he answer.

"What did you do to him?" I asked, glancing up at the light, knowing this conversation had a time limit.

"Educated him on how it would be in the best interests of his health if he stayed away from you and Nathan. Showed him the consequences of what would happen if he didn't."

I swallowed as the light turned and we started moving. My eyes focused on his hands, and they widened when I saw the reddish bruising and scabs covering his knuckles. I didn't know how I hadn't noticed them before. Well, I did know. I'd been distracted first being pissed off about the car thing and then the phone thing. Then my kid being super cute, then staring out the window at anywhere but Lance while trying to get a hold of my anger.

"You hurt yourself," I whispered as he pulled into the parking lot. I had to clench my fists on my knees to stop myself from reaching over to touch the skin.

This time he did look over at me. "You're concerned over a couple of scrapes when I know you're smart enough to read between the lines of what they mean?"

He still had his sunglasses on so I couldn't read his expression. No doubt it would be blank, as always.

I nodded. "Robert's had those scrapes plenty on his fists," I replied. "I'm not concerned about him experiencing just how hard someone has to be hit for that to happen."

This time I didn't need to see his eyes in order to see his reaction. Lance's entire body stiffened, the cords in his neck pulsated with my words. Another violent, confusing and kind of hot reaction.

"I'm more concerned about you hurting yourself for me," I continued, my voice raspier than before. "I don't want you doing that."

His entire energy focused on me, and the force of it hit my lungs, constricting them, making it difficult to breathe.

Lance lifted his hands, turned them, regarded them so I could see their large span, the bruises and marks. So I could imagine them on me.

Wait, no, that wasn't what this was supposed to be.

"This isn't pain," he said, gaze now directed at his hands. "If anything, this is a remedy to the pain I live with every day." He paused, lowering his hands and focusing his shades back on me. "I don't hurt myself for you. I don't hurt with you. And that's the problem."

On that, he opened the door and slammed it in my face once he got out, leaving me blinking, struggling for breath, confused and turned on all at the same time.

If I had wondered whether I affected him at all before, I didn't need to know.

CHAPTER ELEVEN

THREE DAYS HAVE PASSED since the exchange with Lance in the SUV. Since something cracked in his steely façade and I saw something. Something ugly. Something beautiful. Something that showed me I was more than a job to him.

We were more than a job to him.

I held onto those bruises on his knuckles, the bruises on my soul from the words he'd spoken for the three days he went back to cold, detached, almost cruel. I held on tightly. As he drove Nathan and me to school for the next three days, as he responded to everything Nathan asked him with less coldness, and even when he didn't speak to me at all in the car.

I don't know why I was holding onto it. No. I knew exactly why. Because it was a distraction. From the silence I'd heard from Robert since the phone call. From the growing dread at the bottom of my stomach, that this wasn't done. Wasn't over.

I couldn't do anything about that dread. Or even Lance. There was no use pushing, trying to get him to talk, to open up to me. I knew that. So I controlled what I could control. Working. My son. Our routine.

Which was why I was in a demure—for me—dress and cork wedges with my hair delicately curled and makeup covering up the angry bruise on my face. My dress had long sleeves, which were wide and loose, it was tight at the chest and the flowed down to just past my knees.

Nathan was in his little navy button-up and tan shorts. Tennis shoes I'd scrubbed so they weren't covered in whatever dirt a five-year-old managed to discover.

I knew Lance was inside because I heard the door open and close and the security system disable. He did that. Let himself in. To bring coffee for me in the mornings. Not donuts, not every morning. Just on weekends now. But he ensured our interactions were brisk, silent if possible. Silent interactions with Nathan were impossible, but he humored my son, making him fall even more in love with him.

I braced, hearing that beeping, the air in the room changing. But I didn't stop what I was doing, I was determined not to show Lance just how much he affected me.

The low thump of boots against the carpet told me he was moving closer.

As did my son's scream of "Captain!!"

I assumed he greeted my son with his usual forehead lift and lack of verbal response, which Nathan inexplicably loved.

The boots stopped thumping against the carpet.

The air smelled of him.

Still, I didn't look up.

"Where are you going?" he demanded. And that's what it was. He didn't ask questions, he demanded answers.

I brushed crumbs off Nathan's shirt. Somehow, even though I'd cleaned his hands immediately after his breakfast, he had managed to get oatmeal on his shorts. I didn't worry about it, you could barely notice, we didn't have time to change, and he was a kid, they were always gonna get dirty. Messy. Trying to get his clothes clean was a losing battle.

His hair was combed, his teeth were brushed, he didn't have anything sticky on his face. That was winning.

"To church," I replied, squeezing Nathan's cheek and winking at him.

He grinned back and my heart skipped. My child was grinning with no shadows behind his eyes. Maybe those twenty-four hours wouldn't haunt him.

They would haunt me. For every day of my life.

But I could be okay with haunting memories if my child was unscathed from them. Gladly I'd take them.

Granted, he was holding his stuffed bunny, Feebo, in his right hand, by the ear so he dangled almost to the floor. I couldn't separate him from it. I'd explained to Hannah, who was kind and understanding. Perhaps because she felt bad about giving him to his father in the first place.

But it wasn't her fault.

I hadn't told her to watch out for him, hadn't thought I'd needed to. He had proof, a badge, a friendly face. They were fooled, just like the rest of the world.

I wondered how long the friendly face had stayed with my son, the lack of shadows told me most of the time, but the clutching of the bunny worried me.

I didn't let the worry show—no parent did—and I let him take the bunny wherever he wanted.

It was his way of dealing with complex emotions and situations that no child should have to process.

"Church?" Lance repeated.

I focused on him. He was standing in the middle of the living room, still looking absolutely comical amongst all of my things.

"Yes," I replied, snatching my purse from the coffee table and putting it over my shoulder. "You're most welcome to come."

His eyes widened only slightly on his granite face, communicating a nonverbal 'no way in hell' response to me without cursing in front of Nathan.

I noticed that he was very careful with his words in front of my son. He still didn't speak much, I was sure he had some kind of daily quota of words he couldn't go past or something, but the words he did speak were at least seventy percent curse words.

When you had a kid, and slammed your finger in the door and let out one muttered "shit, bastard, motherfucker," under your breath and then had to deal with your three-year-old singing it like his new favorite tune for the next week straight, you learned to curse only in your head. Most of the time.

That and my parents had cursed and spewed vile, bigoted views out, regardless of whether I was in the room or not. Granted, they barely actually noticed when I was in the room.

But my son would never be exposed to *that*.

He could curse when he was old enough to know what the words meant and didn't do it in unacceptable places.

I did not expect Lance, the big, bad, scary man who seemed to command violence just by breathing to watch his Ps and Qs around my son, but he did.

He didn't change much else about himself but I got the idea that this was not a man to bend or even flex a little for anyone, so what he was doing for Nathan was big.

I appreciated it in a way I couldn't explain.

"You should come with us, Captain," Nathan piped in. "It's pretty boring but we always go out for pancakes afterward. I am even allowed chocolate chips in mine," he whispered as if it were the secret to a great treasure. "And maple syrup," he added with a wink.

My face stretched from smiling so wide. Nathan had taken to winking at people when he communicated important things. He had a way of soaking up little gestures and expressions adults did that usually went unnoticed by children. Not only that, he used them correctly.

And it was some of the most adorable and heartwarming things to watch.

I was surely biased.

But Lance's reaction told me that even though he seemed to be hardened to most things, he was not immune to a wink about pancakes from an adorable five-year-old. His hard edges softened, only slightly, but a slight change in such a granite face seemed huge.

The corners of his eyes crinkled slightly in what I was learning was his version of a smile. They only did that when they were focused on my son.

I was darkly jealous that only Nathan got that. But that was insane and terrible, being jealous of the way a hot guy looked at *my child*.

"Pancakes are pretty good," he conceded.

Nathan's eyes lit up and his grin spread across his face, across the room. My kid's smile always had a way of leaking into the air around him. "So you'll come?"

There was no way to say no to that, to him. I wasn't sure about going to church with Lance, about having to share an enclosed space with him, having eyes stare at us, assume things. I'd been going to the same church since we moved here and it was well known I was the 'single mother.' I wasn't treated differently because of that in this church, which was why I picked it. They were good people. The priest was younger, his sermons a little more interesting and new age than others I'd experienced.

But without fail, I was always approached by older ladies, trying to match me up with their sons, nephews, grandsons.

They all meant well, of course, but no matter how many times I told them I wasn't interested in dating and only wanted to focus on my son, the matchmaking continued.

Lance being with us would provide them with month's worth of gossip. And having to explain what he was, or more precisely, what he *wasn't*, would not be a fun time.

Especially because the thought of vocalizing such things filled me with an inexplicable sadness, hurt.

So, no, I did not want Lance to come with us. But I would not be the one to burst my son's bubble. Not with that smile. No one with a heart could do that.

"I think I'd burst into flames if I walked into a church, buddy," Lance said as response in his attempt to burst Nathan's bubble.

I wouldn't be convinced the man didn't have a heart.

Nathan's bubble would not burst that easily. His brows furrowed. "Burst into flames?" he repeated. "Why would you do that? It's not *that* hot outside."

I smirked.

Lance stared at Nathan, probably trying to figure out how to respond. "I don't really go to church, kid."

"Yes, but it's not about church, it's about *pancakes*," Nathan said as if such a thing should have been glaringly obvious.

I rolled my eyes. There went my attempt to teach my son about a higher power. To him, a higher power was IHOP.

"Kid, we're gonna be late," I cut in, saving Lance. "You know how I explained how everyone in this world is so beautifully different and that means all their versions of church are different?"

Nathan nodded dutifully.

I ruffled his hair, pointedly not looking upward to the man I was talking about. "Well, Lance doesn't have the same version of church as us. And that's okay. Remember that?"

Nathan nodded again, though he was frowning still. He moved to look at Lance. "What's your version of church?"

Oh shit.

I didn't know Lance's version of church, or even if he had one, but if he did, it would not be appropriate for five-year-olds.

Something moved in Lance's face.

Please let him not say tying up his enemies and waterboarding them.

"Fishing," he said, eyes not leaving Nathan's.

My own eyes widened, not that Lance noticed, his focus was on my son.

"A calm lake, a cold beer, radio on," Lance continued, expanding when I knew he didn't need to. When I didn't expect him to.

"Fishing?" Nathan replied on a low whisper.

Lance nodded once, jerky, almost dismissive, but there was a slight softness to his face that I was coming to understand he only had with Nathan.

I liked it.

I was also jealous as all hell I didn't get my own soft look.

Good thing I was going to church, coveting the look my security guard gave my son was definitely some kind of sin.

"Will you take me with you?" Nathan asked. He looked over to me before Lance could answer. "Mom, can we go fishing today instead of church?"

"No, sweetie, we can't. We're dressed for church, we're already late and I think the whole point of Lance going fishing is for solitude," I said. I cupped his face. "You, my darling boy, are a lot of wonderful and amazing things. And you can give people many wonderful and amazing things just by being you. But you cannot give Lance solitude. Sometimes people just have to do things on their own, 'kay?"

Nathan frowned at me, I wasn't sure if it was because he didn't understand what the heck I was saying, or if it was because, despite my best efforts, I'd hurt his feelings.

"Like go potty on their own?" he asked after a beat.

Okay, so the frown was not due to either of those things.

I sighed. "We've got to go, dude."

"But you'll come for pancakes after?" Nathan asked Lance, his face all cute and eyes all wide in the expression that got him pretty much anything he wanted with me.

Though the expression was ridiculously cute and would have worked on most of the human race, I didn't think it would work on a man who was almost certainly made of stone.

Lance's expression surely communicated that.

"Sure, bud," he said.

I would have gaped in utter and complete shock and my boy being able to put some cracks in Lance's façade, but we were really frickin' late.

"Okay, cool, so you can meet us at IHOP in like an hour?" I said, glancing at my shitty watch. I swear I was one of the last people my age who actually wore them. Everyone used the phones that were attached to their hands as a timekeeper as well as a life raft. I was constantly running late, thanks to the crumb ridden cutie and my crappy phone was usually somewhere in my purse, underneath baby wipes and tampons. Watches were easier.

Even if the leather on mine wasn't real and the face was kind of scratched.

One day I would buy myself a nice watch, when I had a house, land, a life that seemed so far away and too tauntingly close at the same time.

"I'll drive," Lance said by answer.

I paused all of my hustling out the door. "You said you don't go to church."

"I don't. You do."

It took everything I had in me not to gape at the simple yet infinitely complicated answer. "Lance, you don't have to come with us, everything will be—"

"Didn't you say you were late?" he interrupted. "Better get in the car."

I gritted my teeth, took a breath and hated that he was frickin' right.

So we got in the car.

Lance drove us to church.

Sat next to us on the pews, ignoring all the looks and whispers.

Then, he went to IHOP and had pancakes. Blueberry pancakes to be specific.

And it was probably one of the best Sundays I'd had in a while.

Maybe ever.

One Week Later

"Mom?" Nathan asked, not looking up from his coloring.

I knew it was a question because every mother knew there were thousands of different kinds of 'moms' uttered by children who wanted different things. There was the high-pitched whine when they were told no and weren't ready to take it for an answer —luckily I didn't have much experience in that. There was the low whisper that told you your kid was sad and needed a hug but didn't want to ask for it outright because he was a 'big boy.' There was the shout when your kid was doing something he decided was awesome and needed a cheerful and encouraging audience to show off to.

And a lot more.

This one was spoken in a rather regular tone but with an inflection at the end and a question on its way.

With Nathan, it could be "what's for dinner?" just as easily as it could be "why aren't there gas stations in the sky for planes that run out of gas?"

I stopped frowning down at the bills in front of me and put on a smile for my kid. "Yeah, baby?"

"Why is Captain hanging out with us so much? Is it so my daddy doesn't come and take me for a sleepover again?"

Shit.

How did I not know this was coming?

We'd had the talk about his dad, and why he picked Nathan up, why he acted weird, why Mommy was really upset when she saw him. Why he probably wouldn't ever be seeing him again.

But I had avoided the whole reason for the strange men around the house because I wasn't quite sure how I was going to explain it to him. So far, he'd been acting like they were new friends and took in their presence without blinking. Probably because there was usually almost always someone for him to play with, he and Ziggy were fast friends, despite the age gap. But there were significant changes in our lives. The security systems. Lance doing a 'walk through' before we were allowed in the door.

I wanted to tell Nathan as much of the truth as I could. At the same time, he was five years old and telling him that these men were here to protect him from his violent father was not a truth he could handle and not one I wanted him to.

He had taken them all in his stride, as if it were normal to have beautiful badasses around all the time. As if Lance was just a new friend that lurked around the house, speaking mostly in grunts and smoldering looks.

Well, there weren't as many grunts for Nathan, and definitely not smoldering looks, which was maybe why he had waited until now to bring it up.

I stood up from where I was sitting to move to the sofa and bring Nathan into my arms. I pushed his hair from his face so I could give him a forehead kiss, breathe him in for a second and also think of what the heck I was gonna say.

You'd think, as a mother, I'd have something prepared for this, knowing that the question would arise. But I didn't. Because I'd been putting my head in the sand for most things, like paying the bills on the table along with the hefty one from Greenstone I was expecting any day now, and almost anything pertaining to Lance and thoughts about him that were not professional.

That was all of my thoughts, since nothing I thought about him was professional.

I focused on Nathan's wide, expectant and patient eyes. "Yeah, Mr. Lance and his friends are all around to make sure you stay here with your momma where you belong," I said. "They're really nice people who think you're awesome and want you to be happy always."

Nathan reached up to play with a strand of my hair. It was a punch to my heart. He'd done that with his chubby baby fists ever since he was born, and he still did it now.

I hoped with all my soul that my little boy would still look at me exactly like he was now—like I had all the answers in the world—and grab a hold of my hair like this.

I knew my time was very limited, as gazing up in wonder at your mom and touching her was not something boys did for very long.

"I am happy though, Momma," he said, smiling to prove his point. "And I'm really happy that Captain is here to come to school with me and have pancakes on Sundays."

Fuck. Another thing that I hadn't prepared for. How in the heck I was going to tell my son that his favorite superhero wasn't a permanent fixture in his life?

"I'm so glad that you're happy, baby," I told him, trying to make sure my voice didn't break or my own smile didn't crack. "But Captain is a superhero, right?"

He nodded seriously.

"Well, you know that superheroes don't just help one family. They've got a whole world of people to look after."

Another serious nod.

If there was anything my five-year-old didn't fuck around with, it was superheroes.

"So that means, at some point soon, Mr. Lance is going to have to go off and help other people. He won't be able to come to school with you and have pancakes," I said gently.

Nathan's smile disappeared.

My own wavered but I made an effort to keep it firmly in place. Nathan didn't need to get more upset by seeing his mother's sadness at the prospect of his hero leaving. My little boy was an empath. He felt deep, he felt for himself, and for me, if I let any kind of sadness show. Which was why I perfected the 'mom smile' the smile a parent gave their child when they didn't want them to know their suffering and take it on as their own.

"But I like Captain," he said, his voice as close to a whine as it ever had been before. As almost perfect as my boy was, he was still a kid. "He likes us."

"I know, sweet boy," I said, brushing his hair from his face. "He isn't a dummy, so of course he likes the most awesome kid on the planet." I tried to keep my tone light and teasing, so my son's developing little brain didn't hear the tightness in it. The fear.

"But you're the most awesome mom on the planet," he countered.

I rolled my eyes dramatically. "Well, of course I am."

"And he likes you."

Wow. No way did I see that observation coming from Nathan's mouth sounding far too wise and knowing for my liking. And my son noticing the fact that the robot badass had any feelings toward me was way too perceptive for my liking. Maybe I needed to have him exorcised. Maybe had the spirit of some old monk rattling around amongst action heroes and dreams about sugar.

I recovered quickly. "Of course he does," I said with a grin. "But just because he likes us, that doesn't mean he can stop being a superhero, do you understand that."

Nathan's bottom lip jerked out and he nodded slowly, defeated.

"Hey, honeybear," I said. "You want people to be helped, happy, right?"

Another sad nod.

"So it would be pretty unfair of us to want Lance to stay and not help other people, right?"

Nathan's brows furrowed. "I guess."

"My honeybun, he's not gonna forget about you, promise."

I knew he wouldn't. My kid was unforgettable.

Me, on the other hand, I thought Lance was using all his energy to forget before he even left.

I was doing the same.

Or trying to.

CHAPTER TWELVE

I SPOONED the peanut butter into my mouth, staring aimlessly into our back yard. I loved this time of day, that last glow of light bathing the garden in just enough darkness so I couldn't see our crappy fence that I kept meaning to get around to repairing. I couldn't see the trash heap that our back yard neighbors continued to add to as if they were trying to make a record for height width and stench. I could almost pretend that it stretched farther than it did, that there was nothing but nature beyond our home.

I'd always dreamed of living on a property with acres. So I could have chickens. Other animals. Definitely at least one dog. Maybe a goat. As long as the goat and the dog could become friends. Natural predators became friends all the time, right? Or was that just wishful thinking on the account of the predator that was currently in my living room, doing something to the security system.

Hence me hiding in the kitchen with my peanut butter thinking about my fantasy life, building more to it. This was a habitual daydream.

I'd grow all my own vegetables.

Nathan could explore.

He could breathe in the coolness of nature, instead of the trash from the neighbors in our close city air that seemed just a little too thick.

Maybe one day if I got a better job, figured out a way to save enough for a house deposit on a place like that, found a way to support us both living so isolated.

A dark shape in the corner of my vision punctured the low light and the daydream.

His eyes focused on the jar in my hands then the spoon that had just been hanging from my mouth. My stomach dipped with his cold blank stare on my mouth. There was nothing sexual about the way he looked at me. Nothing. I was a job to him. A task.

So why was I responding the way I was?

Well, obviously because I had two eyes and hadn't got laid in recent memory.

But it was more than horny single mother syndrome.

It was a thing, apparently.

Dangerous too, as Marie, my only other single mom friend, explained. You could find yourself desperate enough to jump the balding and overweight cable guy like some bad porno and then have to extract yourself from the situation when he wants to date you and for you to meet his mother.

This obviously didn't happen to me.

We didn't have a cable guy.

Luckily.

The only guys I came into contact with on a regular basis were Bobby, our line cook. Beautiful, chocolate skinned, bald-headed, muscled and oh so very gay. Logan, who had gone gray and worked it, was tall, barrel-chested and married to a woman I loved and respected and would kill anyone who looked at her husband. Then the busboys who hadn't even graduated high school.

And then my son.

So not really laden with options.

But it wasn't just the lack of male stimuli in my environment.

It was *him*.

There was something magnetic about him that yanked me in. Something very frickin' dangerous. You'd think I learned my lesson with dangerous after everything that had happened. You'd think after my marriage and my upbringing, I'd want a safe, normal and boring type of guy.

But that was not me.

I did not come from the trailer park with dreams of a 'normal life.' No, I wanted a life as abnormal, unique, and my own as possible. I wanted to bring Nathan up to understand that normal was a construct made to cage people into one way of thinking. I wanted him to think however he wished, dreamed, no cages.

No normal man would cut it for me.

"Please tell me that's not your fuckin' dinner," was what the dark, attractive, dangerous abnormal man said. No, *demanded*.

I dropped the spoon from my mouth. "Peanut butter contains a lot of protein," I answered.

He folded his arms.

I struggled not to watch the way his veins moved as he did so.

"It also has sodium, which is important to muscle health," I continued.

He did not look convinced or impressed.

Like at all.

"I'm not hungry?" I tried.

That was kind of a lie. I was hungry. But it was payday tomorrow.

And I budgeted fiercely around payday. Not just to the dollar. But to the cent.

All of our bills were paid—well, except the one I'd owe Greenstone Security, but I guessed that would be paid off once Nathan made me a grandmother.

The rest of them, though, rent, power, gas, Nathan's school stuff, health insurance, all paid up.

Which meant the fridge had the fixings for Nathan's breakfast, lunch, and snacks were in there.

The cupboards had the bare essentials, flour, sugar, canned food, Nathan's mac and cheese, all of which I didn't really touch in times such as these. Payday was tomorrow. I could skip breakfast and grab something at work. They always fed me at work. I wasn't sure if it was out of pity or kindness. I didn't say no to either. I wasn't too proud to accept a meal. Or the leftovers they always made me take home.

Nathan loved cherry pie and I swear Bobby 'accidentally' made extra every two weeks. And on those other weeks he 'accidentally' made too much peanut butter chocolate, my ultimate weakness.

We dined with Karen and Eliza at least once a week, and they never let me bring anything but a vegetable dish which was nothing to make. Then they came over regularly too, which put a small dint in the food budget, but they always brought over bread, sides, and wine.

I never *really* went hungry.

The supplies currently in the cupboard were my rainy-day collection. Just in case a huge unexpected bill came that obliterated my checking account and meager savings, in case we found ourselves without the means to buy food for a week.

So Nathan wouldn't go hungry.

No way was I touching that stash.

But I wasn't telling Lance that.

"What do you care?" I asked, surprising myself at the confrontational tone.

I was not confrontational.

No way.

I found ways to avoid confrontation at all costs, and was always the first to back down to rude customers, to bitchy co-workers, people that cut in line, or stole my parking spot.

The one exception was anything to do with Nathan.

Everything else, I shied away from conflict. I knew it was because of my past, and all of my negative associations with conflict and relating it to violence. I'd done a lot of inner work on that, meditated, tried to explore the trauma not hide from it.

But with Lance, it seemed I wasn't afraid of it.

When he was definitely the one person I needed to be afraid to engage with, not the overweight customer who told me his eggs were too hot and coffee too strong.

His eyebrow twitched but otherwise he didn't react to my tone. "What's your favorite food?" he asked.

I blinked. I hadn't expected the question. "Peanut butter?" I shot back.

Something in his face moved and I swear it was close to amusement.

But then it was gone, replaced by the scary blankness with a tinge of impatience that was his default around me.

I wanted to have a proverbial stare off with him, refuse to answer a question with such a harsh and almost confrontational tone. I wanted him to think I was the woman who could stand up to him. Because I assumed that's the woman that would end up with a man like Lance. A woman like Rosie. Strong. Able to take care of herself and take on men like Lance. Able to beat them in most circumstances.

But that wasn't me.

I was painfully aware of that.

If it was, Lance wouldn't even be here in the first place.

"Steak, rare, fries and broccoli," I relented. "A full-bodied red.

And if it was really my last meal, like on death row or something, plus a whole packet of Oreos for dessert."

I definitely didn't think it was possible to surprise Lance, who seemed like he was prepared for anything and everything, but he blinked once, slow and long at my response.

"Steak?" he repeated.

I nodded, almost salivating at the mere thought of it. The last time I'd had steak, Eliza and Karen had taken me out for dinner on my birthday. Logan and Esther had taken care of Nathan. They'd plied me with red wine beforehand so I was agreeable when we pulled up to one of the nicest restaurants in town and announced they were paying.

Then, when we got inside, they hadn't even let me look at the menu, Karen declaring that she knew I'd just order the cheapest thing on the menu and not what I actually wanted. Because she knew me so well, she knew what I actually wanted and ordered it for me.

I dreamed about that steak for a week straight after that. Promised myself one day I'd be able to take my friends back to that restaurant, order them a steak, wine and be able to pay for it without even blinking.

My birthday was in two months.

So I hadn't eaten steak in ten.

"Would've thought you'd be more of a quinoa person," Lance responded, causing me to curl up my nose in disgust.

"What would make you think something like that?" I asked, mad that the thought of quinoa chased out the taste of perfectly cooked, grass-fed beef from my tongue.

Lance didn't say anything, obviously back to his mute, badass routine. He merely looked around the room, pointedly pausing on crystals, and a book on the moon cycle, open on the counter.

I rolled my eyes. "That's so very cliché of you, Lance. To take me at face value. I thought you would've been able to read people better than that," I teased.

Lance made it clear that he did not appreciate me teasing him. He did that by narrowing his eyebrows, treating me to a glare that chilled my bones and turning on his heel and walking out.

Without a freaking word.

I blinked at the door for a couple of minutes before resuming with the peanut butter and trying to get my breathing under control.

He returned an hour later.

By this point, the peanut butter had all but evaporated from my stomach and I was trying to distract myself from my hunger by cleaning the house.

I was on my hands and knees, trying to reach under the TV cabinet for one of Nathan's toys when the door opened and closed.

Thinking it was Eliza or Karen, I didn't move from my compromising position, merely turned my head over my shoulder, in preparation to say hello.

It wasn't Eliza or Karen.

It was Lance. Standing frozen in my living room, bags in his arms, eyes focused squarely on my ass, which was all but hanging out of my shorts thanks to the angle.

I didn't do the sensible thing and scramble up and out of this position and try to snatch onto dignity. No, I stayed exactly where I was.

Because Lance was giving me a look that did not chill my bones. It charred them.

My panties too.

There was heat, hunger in his gaze. So naked that I almost leaped from my position and pounced on him there and then, hunger that I didn't think I was capable of due to my past all but possessing me.

But reason returned, and quickly, when Lance wiped that look off his face, replaced by indifference edged with contempt. Then he moved, away from me in the direction of my kitchen.

Hearing him place the bags down on the counter, I realized that I was still on my living room floor on my hands and knees. I scrambled up, hitting my knee on the coffee table in my haste.

My eyes watered as I bit my lip and clutched my knee, determined not to make a sound that would cause Lance to come running, expecting a threat or bullet wound, not a wuss who couldn't handle whacking her shin on the coffee table.

Because of this, I took longer to make it to the kitchen than I would have if I was a normal human being, capable of interaction with a hot guy like Lance without acting like an idiot or injuring herself.

I must have taken longer than I realized, because Lance had unpacked everything in the bags I'd seen him with and was chopping up broccoli.

I blinked at this.

The hot guy in my tiny kitchen, using my shitty kitchen knives and Sponge Bob cutting board. Then I blinked at the things around him. Potatoes, a slab of meat. A box of Oreos.

I had to bite my lip again to stop myself from crying once I realized what this was.

I was usually able to control my tears, being a mother made it compulsory. Being married to an abusive asshole also made it compulsory. Robert liked it when I cried. I guess it made him feel powerful. Like repeatedly hitting me, controlling what I wore, what I ate, where I went and who I was 'friends' with wasn't enough.

It was one my one little rebellion until I found the courage for my big one—not crying. No matter how much pain I was in, no matter what ugly, vile things he spat at me, no matter what he did, I managed to find some kind of control over my tears.

But right now, I was struggling. Because Lance had demanded, rather brusquely, what my favorite meal was, scowled at me, walked out and bought it without a word.

It was a kind of kindness that wasn't normal. But it *was* kind. I knew that.

It had been a long time since a man had done something like this for me.

Well, I was pretty sure a man had never done this for me. Except Bobby, of course. Or Nathan, pouring half a box of cereal onto the floor, the other half into a bowl and spilling milk all over the dining room table when he was making me 'breakfast.'

Lance had obviously known I entered the room, because he was Lance. But he'd continued chopping the vegetables, not acknowledging me. Likely because he was waiting for me to act like a regular human being, comment on what he was doing, thank him, offer him help.

I did none of that. Just stared at him and tried not to cry.

"Lance," I whispered, my voice thick and on the edge of breaking.

His gaze darted up to meet mine. It was hard, and it didn't match up with the gesture of this moment.

I guessed that was kind of the point.

"There're potatoes there, you wanna chop them into slices thin enough so they'll bake in the oven, since I'm guessin' you don't have a deep fryer."

It wasn't a question. I wasn't sure if he'd come to the conclusion I didn't own one because I couldn't afford one—true—or because I was not a mother that gave her child deep-fried food on a regular basis—also true.

But it didn't really matter, because beyond that not being a question, it was also an order, one that my body automatically listened to. Maybe because it was something to do other than stand in the middle of the kitchen crying in front of a relative stranger.

So I got the potatoes.

I chopped them.

Put them on a tray, oiled and seasoned them.

And put them in the oven.

"Bottle of wine over there." Lance nodded his head to the table since he was still busy. I knew he was busy, because after I'd put the potatoes in the oven, I was not. Usually, I hated to be idle, especially when I was idle in my own kitchen while someone else was cooking.

But I was okay with idle since it meant I could give Lance my full attention. Or more specifically Lance's biceps and forearms my attention. Because they were sinewy. Pure muscle. Pure power. I could take an educated guess and say they were used to inflict violence. That should have scared me, all things considered. But it made me feel safe. Especially since those powerful, dangerous arms were currently being used for the domestic task of cooking in my frickin' kitchen.

"Elena."

My name caused my eyes to jerk up and find Lance's. Shit. Caught. I swallowed roughly. "Wine." He nodded his head again. "Wanna open it?"

I looked from him to the table where there was an indeed a bottle of wine, the offending thirty-dollar wine that was delicious.

Again, I automatically obeyed the question that was actually a command.

It wasn't until I had my corkscrew in hand and was staring at the elegant and simple label did I regain proper brain function.

So instead of opening the wine, I turned to look at Lance's back. Tried not to get distracted by how wide it was, how I could see the sculpted ridges of his shoulders underneath his tee.

I obviously failed at that.

"We need to talk about the wine," I said, remembering the party, my anger, and the ensuing chaos that distracted me from talking to Lance about this earlier.

His shoulders stopped moving.

"We don't," he said without turning.

All fond feelings I had toward him for buying this food, for cooking it, for having great shoulders and forearms, they all went out the window with the cold voice that thought it could order me around.

"I know you're used to deciding things and them being so because you're..." I trailed off trying to think of the appropriate adjective. "You," I finished lamely. "But it's not gonna fly with me. So even though you've made this sweet and very kind gesture of cooking for me and buying the food and the expensive wine, it's not gonna negate me being able to speak up about something that bothers me." I was very proud of the fact I said that and my voice was sharp and strong.

Lance paused a beat after I'd finished speaking, then he turned.

"Straight up, Elena, thirty bucks isn't expensive for a bottle of wine," he said.

Wrong thing to say.

I gritted my teeth and put my hand on my hip in a gesture that I was sure even a badass like Lance might be able to take as a warning. "It is to me," I said through my gritted teeth. "And yeah, I get that a thirty-dollar bottle of wine is nothing to a lot of people. Maybe most people. Definitely people who work for fancy security firms in the city, drive nice vehicles and wear kickass clothes," I hissed, hating that I was complimenting him when I was trying to tell him off. "But to this person" —I pointed at my chest— "the single mom who has a kid to raise, to clothe, to feed, to fund his college tuition, to pay for whatever sport he decides to play, and to start building a savings fund for my house in the country with my chickens, dogs and goats—only if I can make the dog and the goat friends—then yes, thirty bucks for a bottle of wine that I don't need is a lot of money." I narrowed my eyes at Lance as his jaw ticked ever so slightly in an expression that might have passed for amusement. And as great as it was that the robot was capable of being amused, I didn't want it to be right now.

"*I* decide I don't want to spend thirty bucks on wine, that's *my* decision," I continued, voice sharper and firmer than before, bolstered by a need to scrounge up some pride. "My decision as an adult, and as a mother. Despite this, despite the shit that I have to keep up with in my life, the son I have to provide for, I also want to provide for my friends. To repay people that do shit for me. Do shit like save my kid. That treat me with kindness. That go above and beyond the call of duty for us." I gave a pointed look at the food behind him. "You took that away from me at the supermarket," I said, voice quieter. "The ability to do that. I know you were trying to help in your badass, 'I take control of everything' kind of way, and sure, I dig it. But not when it comes to stuff like that."

I let out a breath, tried not to search Lance's attractive face for a reaction. "In saying that, it's pretty much a crime to eat steak without red wine," I continued, picking up the corkscrew again. "So I'm going to open this. And I'm going to get two glasses."

He stiffened at this, as I assumed he might. "Yes, I know you're on the job, you need all your faculties just in case a plane falls from the sky and you have to save the neighborhood, but you can have a glass of red and not even dull the edges, I'm pretty sure about that." I didn't wait for him to reply, I walked over to the kick-ass cabinet I'd restored, with glass doors that showed my mixed collection of wine glasses and funky bowls and plates.

I took my two biggest ones.

"Furthermore," I said, after opening the wine and waiting for it to breathe. "I'm paying you back for the car repairs. Because that's the same as the groceries. That's the car I drive my kid to school in. That's my responsibility. It's one I want. And that's all there is to it."

I didn't look at him, instead, I poured the wine into two glasses. I took great care in doing this, like I was a heart surgeon, because I was a coward and didn't want to look at Lance, considering he hadn't said a word since I'd said my piece. I didn't regret speaking up. I'd spent far too long biting my tongue, not standing up for myself when a man thought he could control me. I had a voice. I'd use it.

But still, the way Lance was controlling me was nothing like Robert had. He was helping me pay for groceries and buying me wine I couldn't afford. Because Lance was a guy who I assumed liked control. Not in what I wore, ate, said and my basic human rights. But different things. Harsh, infuriating things that I was starting to figure was his version of sweet.

Sweet or not, I was not letting that fly.

I didn't need to think about it being sweet. That was a whole other story. A dangerous one. One that most definitely didn't have a happy ending.

When I didn't have much choice but to walk over to where he was still staring at me silently, I did so, hand outstretched with his wine.

For a humiliating half a second, I didn't think he'd take it, I thought he might just continue to stare at me, unravel me. That he might turn away and resume cooking without a word. Or, worst of all, he'd just walk out the door and away from the complicated, slightly crazy woman who talked about goats and dogs in between telling him off.

But he took the wine.

I exhaled.

But I relaxed too soon.

Far too friggin' soon.

CHAPTER THIRTEEN

Lance

HE DIDN'T WANT to take the glass. Fuck no.

He wanted to snatch both of them out of her hand, smash them on the floor, rip her clothes off and fuck her on the dining room table.

Shit, his fucking *finger twitched* with the force of that carnal reaction. That need. A feeling that was foreign, in all his life he'd never needed anything that bad as he needed her in that moment.

That's what his life was about, had been about for the past decade, controlling his baser instincts until they served his goals. Not his needs.

She was too good for him. That was the surface of it. Fuck she was too good for him in every way, and fuck if it tore at his fucking soul hearing her talk about herself, stand up for herself and hear the shake in her voice, hearing the shame at her talking about people like 'him'—who she thought he was at least—and people like her.

She considered herself *lesser*.

Because she couldn't afford fucking wine.

He wanted to shake her. Fuck sense into her. Kiss her.

Not necessarily in that order.

And then she kept talking. About fucking goats and dogs and farms. About the life she was giving her son. The life she was giving him without help. That she wanted to continue giving him. At first glance, it was her tits, face, eyes, ass, and fucking hair that drew Lance to her. He may have been a severely broken one, but he was still a man. And Elena Phoenix was a woman all men and women who swung that way stopped and looked at. Wanted.

But there was more. There was her standing there, scared of him—he knew that, since everyone was—but still standing up for herself, still determined. After everything that had happened in her life to give her good reason to be afraid to stand up to a man, she did it anyway.

Tits, ass, no matter how magnificent—and they were—meant shit compared to that.

Hence the finger twitch. The near loss of control.

It was a mistake not leaving this afternoon, after what he said. That much was clear. He'd told himself that he could lock it down. That this was just a job.

And he'd fucking lied to himself. It became clear the second he walked in here, seeing that sweet mouth wrapped around a spoonful of peanut butter. All that sweet turned bitter when he realized that was her *dinner* because she'd go hungry so her son could always be full.

Irrationally, in that moment, he'd decided both of them would always be full, in every way possible. He'd make it that way.

Somehow.

Which was why he'd been a stupid fuck, gone out got the steak, the shit to go with it, came back to cook it for her. Fill her up in the one way he could, because he knew that an empty man like him could never fill up a woman like Elena.

Still, he took the glass.

The way her entire body sagged, like her life had depended on him taking that glass, hit him somewhere.

That's why he spoke.

"Respect you," he said, taking care not to squeeze the stem of the wine glass so hard it would smash. It looked nice. Kick ass. Unique, not something he could run to the store and replace. All of her shit was like that. Despite the fact she couldn't spend thirty bucks on wine, her house managed to look like a million bucks. In her own, hippy, weird way. But it worked.

In a big way.

Everything about her worked in a big way.

That was the goddamn problem.

"Don't say that to a lot of people, mostly 'cause majority of people aren't worth respecting, or else I don't say that kinda shit," he continued, not having full control over his voice, that softening of Elena's features was puppeting him. "But with you, feels like it needs to be said, 'cause I don't think people tell you enough. You're a good mom. Good person."

Good, keep remembering that. Too good for you.

"Past ten years, haven't had a chance to do good shit for a good person," he continued. "Most of the stuff I do is the worst shit for good people, or sometimes for equally worse people. Until Greenstone. Still doin' bad shit, though. Shit that puts marks against my soul. So was bein' selfish buyin' you wine, fixing your car. Giving myself a few marks for the other side. Not doin' that shit 'cause I think you're a charity case, Elena. Doin' it 'cause I am. Need all the good I can take."

She blinked at him, her mouth opening slightly, full lips teasing him with what it would be like to claim them, have them on his skin. On his cock.

The cock that was always at least half-hard when he was around her, when she wasn't with the kid. Big reason why he focused on the kid. Or that's what he told himself. Not because he liked the kid. 'Cause the kid made it easier to breathe around the constant pain in his chest.

Christ, he was a stupid fuck for being here.

For still standing here, holding a wine glass, while she was inches away from him, close enough for him to know she smelled like honeysuckle.

He braced for it. Once what he'd said sunk in. He'd said more words in a handful of seconds to her than he'd said to... anyone in the past ten years. And it just came out, without him even meaning it to. Normally, it took great fucking effort, great fucking pain to speak to people. Luckily the Greenstone guys got that shit. Even their crazy fuckin' wives who treated words like they got a prize for every one spoke, even *they* got it.

Rest of the world didn't get it, which was why he separated himself from it the best he could.

Elena wouldn't get it. Because she was Elena. She was also a woman. Women hear shit like that spouted, women who were interested—and fuck if he knew she was interested, she couldn't hide shit on her beautiful face and it was torture—they reacted. Reacted by wanting more words, more feelings, all that kind of crap. And he'd have to be cruel to Elena to get her to stop.

He didn't want to be cruel.

But had to be cruel to be kind and all that shit. His life, he was cruel to be cruel, and he didn't give a fuck. Most people he dealt with deserved cruel. Others didn't, but that was life.

With Elena, he wished he knew how to be kind without being cruel. The old him, dead and buried and decayed might have known one day.

But that man was dead, and it was this man standing in front of a beautiful, soft woman he was gonna have to be hard for.

So he braced.

As Elena tended to do, she shocked the shit out of him by taking a sip of her wine. No, he'd call it a gulp, like a kid drinking Kool-Aid and it was cute as fuck. She took that gulp, lowered her glass, looked behind him. "Should I make a salad while you grill the steaks?"

It was Lance's turn to blink.

"Should I make a salad while you grill the steaks?"

Yeah, she just said that.

He'd thought it wasn't possible for her to get under his skin anymore. But that, right there, that did it.

Not trusting himself to speak, he took his own gulp of wine, shit he hated but he'd drink because she'd poured it for him. The corner of Elena's mouth turned up slightly and her eye twinkled but otherwise, she didn't remark on his action.

He nodded once against the burn at his throat that had nothing to do with wine.

"Yeah." He could only get one word out, it was thick and uncomfortable.

Not trusting himself not to do something stupid, he turned his attention to the steak, made short work of getting out of the fucking kitchen so he could grill them.

The air was muggy, fresh, but it didn't do anything to whisk away the smell of honeysuckle and Elena. Neither did the scent of charring steaks.

Nothing would.

He'd be smelling that shit on his deathbed.

Elena

I didn't have an excuse for what I did.

Not a logical one at least.

I did have reasons for what I did.

Many of them.

Like a thirty-dollar bottle of wine. Like steaks cooked to perfection. Like a car with working AC. Like a son asleep in his room, home, safe and sound. Like the words he'd spoken to me, right in my kitchen, showing me something deeper about him. Something damaged. Something beautiful. Something I wanted. Needed.

That was why I reacted the way I did. That's why I didn't press him for more when that was all I wanted... more. I wanted to jump on him. Kiss him. Have him fuck me on my kitchen counter.

But I had a son who sometimes wandered into the aforementioned kitchen for a glass of water or a snack at all hours and I really didn't want to scar him for life.

I also sensed something about Lance, about how rare those snippets of information were, how precious those collections of sentences were. They were meant to be handled with care. He was meant to be, no matter how unbreakable he seemed.

So I made the salad.

Drained my entire glass of wine in the time it took to make it, get out the rest of the fixings to go with the steak, set the table and put out appropriate condiments.

Then I poured another one as he came in with the most delicious smelling steaks I'd smelled in my life. I refilled his glass too, as it was empty.

All this without words.

All of the food was put on our plates without words too. Eaten that same way. Well, there may have been an embarrassing groan of ecstasy that came from me with my first bite of steak. I couldn't help it. It was pure heaven. Cooked to perfection. Melt in my mouth. Even better than that seventy dollar one from the fancy place. Maybe that was because Lance had bought it for me, cooked it for me, and his words had served as an appetizer.

Because the rest of the meal was just as mouthwatering.

You'd think it'd be awkward, eating an entire meal with someone you were borderline obsessed with and crazy attracted to in complete silence.

Somehow it wasn't.

It was a strange gift for me, that silence to contemplate my thoughts, to savor my food. To savor the company. Never did I get to sit down and eat a meal in silence. Heck, I barely ever sat down and ate a meal, period. Breakfast was usually coffee, a bite of whatever Nathan had. Lunch was standing up in the kitchen at work. Dinner was snatched bites in between getting Nathan ready for bed, or while cleaning up after he'd gone to bed.

And the sit-down meals we had semi-regularly with Eliza and Karen were far from silent.

So yeah, a quiet meal with Lance was little more than heaven. For once, the quiet didn't bring with it all of my problems that I had to dwell on, panic about. I didn't think about Robert, about money, about my son's safety, because it was all taken care of by Lance. For this moment at least.

I read somewhere that a moment was exactly ninety seconds, well, not exactly since the length of a solar hour depends on the solar day which varies with the season, but ballpark.

With Lance, a moment was for however long that silence lasted.

It lasted the meal, the cleanup and the rest of the bottle of wine.

Another reason I did what I did.

The reason a lot of previously logical people did very stupid things.

Alcohol.

I'd gone past my two drinks rule because I needed the wine, it tasted so great and because I needed *something*.

Which meant I was tipsy.

I didn't stumble or anything as I walked Lance to the door after he spoke the first words since the infamous ones.

"Better go, it's late, you've got an early morning."

I had nodded to this. It was all true.

"Thank you, for dinner," I said, my voice little more than a whisper.

He gave me a long, not at all blank look. "Dinner was for me, dinner was selfish."

That was a punch to the ovaries. But like a good one. A really good one.

I didn't say anything as we walked through my living room, though I did start to panic at my magical moment being over. Obviously it had to be over. He couldn't stay.

Could he?

So that was when I did the stupid thing, right as we got to the front door. Something, more than wine, something animal took over me. When he turned to presumably say goodbye, bark at me to lock the door behind him and set the alarm as he always did, I pounced on him.

My hands fisted his tee, pulling at the thin fabric and yanking him toward me. Now, Lance wasn't exactly a man that could actually be manhandled by a woman like me, so I knew that this had to be consensual. I was a woman, I knew by the way he looked at me that this was most definitely consensual. In my wine addled brain, I knew that despite what his looks, his words told me, he wasn't going to be making the first move. Maybe any move. He thought of himself as bad, maybe he was. But right now, I wanted bad. More than anything.

Which was why I grabbed him the way I did and crashed our lips together. Lance didn't react at all, at first. The man who I imagined dodging bullets better than Neo in *The Matrix,* being able to react to anything and everything, seemed shocked still by me kissing him without warning.

That didn't last for long.

Pretty much until my tongue teased at the seam of his lips.

Then he reacted.

He did that my grabbing my ass, palming it rough enough that I knew I'd have bruises I'd savor tomorrow, the other hand tore through my hair and he yanked at me so my body slammed into his. My hands were still at his chest, trapped there so I couldn't do anything. It should have panicked me, the fact I was all but trapped.

Because I was kind of distracted by the fact the Lance was kissing the shit out of me.

All of that emotion, all of that heat that had been absent, only hinted at since I'd met him, it all flooded into that kiss. Flooded into me with enough force that my knees were close to giving way. My heart crashed against my ribcage. Every nerve ending in my body responded.

He wasn't tender or patient with me. Not like any other man who knew my history might have been. Another man might have thought I needed to be treated with care. Tenderness. Maybe I did.

But not at this moment.

Holy shit, not at this moment.

I moaned into his mouth as he yanked at my hair, beautiful pain erupting in my scalp.

Immediately the kiss stopped.

Not just stopped, Lance was no longer touching me but totally out of touching distance.

Out of pouncing distance.

Everything was blurry, red-tinged with my passion, with the fire. I lifted a shaking hand to my swollen lips, blinking rapidly so Lance came into focus.

And when I focused on him, I sobered.

Instantly.

The moment was over.

Well and truly.

The moment was destroyed.

I'd done that.

He proved it by looking at me for a beat longer then striding out the door. It slammed behind me. It took a long time for me to realize I hadn't heard his boots thumping down our walk, or his SUV start up.

He was waiting on the stoop for me to lock up.

A weird part of me wondered if he'd stay there all night if he didn't hear me. A big part of me hoped for that.

But then the logical part of me took over. I walked over to the door. It took three tries to slide the new locks home. To set the alarm.

The beeping of the new system echoed through my ringing ears.

I waited at the door for Lance to leave, wishing he wouldn't. Wishing he'd storm back in here, finish that kiss.

Give me another moment.

But he didn't.

CHAPTER FOURTEEN

Lance

"WE CLEAR I'm taking point on this?" Rosie asked him, pulling a brown manila envelope out of her purse. She didn't wait for him to answer as he opened the door of the precinct for her. "Because we're in a police station, it's probably one of the worst places to commit murder," she said conversationally, her heels clicking on the floor. Only this bitch would wear heels on the job. Granted, today's job wasn't meant to get dicey, their location being the main factor in this.

Almost certainly why Keltan suggested that this be the place they make the drop.

The fuck.

He and everyone in the office had noticed the change in him. They were trained to notice threats, of course. Not that it was hard.

So they were here. With Rosie taking point. Another strategic choice from Keltan. If there were a match for Lance, sure every single man at Greenstone was equal to him, but Rosie was the only one who may be more fucked up than him.

And here she was, in heels, swinging her purse and wearing a miniskirt.

She popped a bubble between her pink glossed lips, leaning over the desk at the front of the station.

Jesus.

She was good. Every man in the area was in the palm of her hand and she hadn't even spoken.

"We're looking for Detective Hudson," she said, after sucking the gum back in her mouth and licking her lips.

The kid at the desk looked like he might blow his load right there.

"Um, he's the second desk on the right," the kid said, pointing his arm to the bullpen, trying to flex his bicep as he did so.

Fucking hell.

This would have gone a lot different if Rosie wasn't here.

Which was precisely why she was.

"Thanks." She winked at the kid.

He followed her when she turned on her heel and walked in the direction of the desks, like she wasn't committing murder on a weekly basis.

They made it to the desk.

The fuck was so distracted by Rosie's legs that he took ten whole seconds to recognize her. Five more to recognize Lance.

He went to get up, open his mouth, face smug and mouth curled into a satisfied grin once he realized where he was. There was still some of that cowardice around his eyes that had been there at his last visit. Lance was happy to see the cut on his eyebrow would scar and he still had a shadowing of bruising under his eye.

Elena's was only now almost completely healed.

After fucking *weeks.*

"Now, now, don't get your tightie-whities in a bunch," Rosie said conversationally. "We're just here to get your signature on a little piece of paper and then we'll be off on our merry way and you can go back to being a dirty cop and an overall piece of shit human being." She smiled sweetly, holding out the envelope.

Hudson didn't take it, his face reddening.

"Oh, and just before you decide to act like you actually have balls when we both know you don't, only real men have those." She winked. "And anyone that beats up their wife is not a real man. Plus, that shirt. Dude, don't be that guy. Where was I? Oh, before you say anything or do anything, I'd remember what we have on you and what we'd have to do if you decide to act like the douchebag everyone knows you are."

The fucker narrowed his eyes at Rosie, probably to try and hide the real fear in them. "Are you blackmailing a police officer, in a police station?" he asked, voice sharp.

She grinned wider, shaking the envelope. "That's exactly what I'm doing. How sweet of you to notice."

"I could have you arrested," he snarled.

Lance's fists were tight at his sides.

Rosie tilted her head, regarding him, like he was an amusing child. "Oh, if I'm going to be arrested, it's going to be for something much more interesting than blackmail. But if we're talking about getting arrested, let's have some fun. Throw words like kidnapping, domestic abuse, sexual assault around. How's that sound? Great, I didn't think so. Now sign this fucking thing before I lose my temper right here in front of all of your nice police buddies."

He stared at the paper. Back at Rosie.

Lance stopped being so pissed that Rosie was taking point in a place he couldn't pummel this fuck all over again. This was satisfying in a way pure violence couldn't be. Hudson was being controlled by a woman. Not just that, bested by one and talked to exactly how every woman on the planet should talk to him. Like he was worse than shit on a shoe.

The fuck was uncomfortable. It was satisfying, to say the least, to watch him squirm like an ant under a microscope. Though nothing would feel greater than to watch his lifeless body tumble into a shallow grave.

But Elena had her wishes.

And fuck, if he was keeping them.

Never in the time since he became who he was now had he taken any other human being's wishes into account. But here he was. Standing in front of a man every cell in his body called him to kill, and he was instead relishing in his discomfort.

For Elena.

For Nathan.

The kid who thought of him as a superhero and had no idea that he was looking up to the villain.

The kid who touched parts of him that weren't supposed to exist anymore.

Yeah, he wasn't too hot on killing that kid's father, no matter how much of a piece of shit he was.

Hudson had been staring at Rosie, then the manila envelope for a long time. Lance could see the cogs working in the fuck's mind. Though he was stupid in almost every way, he was a narcissist. Therefore, he wouldn't likely do something directly that would damage him, and he knew Rosie's threats weren't empty. That was why neither he nor his father had given Elena any more shit.

They were working up to it, of course. Fuckers like this were stupid enough to keep going until they won.

Because they thought they deserved to win.

The second this fuck laid his hand on Elena, he lost. Lance

planned to make sure he was there when he realized he'd lost and he left Elena and Nathan alone.

He ignored the strange pang he got with that thought. Though neither Elena or Nathan were something that he could ignore. But his focus moved when the man—who he planned to end, one day—looked at the envelope.

"Ah, so I see Neanderthals have some brains at least," Rosie remarked as he opened the envelope and began to read.

The entire fucker's form went tight as he understood what they were serving him. His beady, hateful eyes darted from Lance to Rosie.

"That cunt put you up to this."

With that sentence, Rosie lost all of her sweet façade. Everything about her changed. Her true nature moving toward the surface, in a way that disturbed even Lance. Seeing someone that beautiful, that unassuming transform into a pure threat, it was something to shake even the most experienced of men.

"I know we're in a police station," she said calmly. "But you talk about Elena like that one more time, I'll rip your cock up through your throat and make you give yourself the most unenjoyable blow job you've ever received."

Bitch was funny, threatening and sexy at the same time. Luke was a lucky man. But then again, the fucker was definitely going to go gray early with all the shit Rosie put him through. Their kid was already taking after her, so Luke was in for even more shit.

Hudson glared at Rosie, most likely thinking such a look would affect her in some way. Fucker was stupid if he thought someone like him could intimidate someone like Rosie. Rosie wasn't intimidated by anyone. Fuck, the bitch intimidated *him*.

"I haven't got all day," Rosie snapped. "I've got to get a manicure in like an hour and I want time to grab an iced matcha before that. So if you could stop pretending like you're gonna do anything but sign the papers to try and hold onto your nonexistent manhood, I'd *really* appreciate it."

"This isn't the end of it," Hudson seethed, snatching a pen from his desk.

Rosie rolled her eyes. "Let me just get you a hairless cat and a lair in the mountains to go with the B-Movie evil villain line."

Hudson didn't reply to this. Obviously. Seeing Rosie unaffected by threats he had practice in being one of the weapons at his disposal in battering what he considered the weaker sex. Lance was happy one of the strongest people he knew—*people*, not women—was giving him an education on who exactly was the weakest here.

He thrust the paper back at Rosie.

She went to grab it but he held onto it.

Lance stiffened, ready to step in, regardless of the location or the badge the fucker thought protected him from justice.

Real justice. Not the kind he doled out.

"She thinks she's got some new friends, it'll protect her. It won't. She knows who I am. Who my father is." His eyes darted up and down Rosie's body, then flickered to Lance. The fucker wasn't brave enough to hold eye contact, he was scared of him after the beating. As he should be. "You'll learn too."

Rosie still hadn't lost her cool. Then again, she could be gutting a rapist and be talking about her favorite show on Netflix. Lance knew that, because she'd done that last week.

"Oh, color me excited. I love watching assholes fall, especially when they think they're on top of everyone else. I also love teaching them just how low on the food chain they really are." She snatched the paper, glanced through it to make sure that he hadn't tried to fuck them.

That would be stupid.

Rosie folded the paper, satisfied. Lance relaxed. Only slightly. He would never relax completely. Because this fucker was still breathing. Because he was still stupid enough to think he could fight back.

Because this wasn't over for Elena.

His promise was keeping him from making sure it was truly over.

He'd broken a lot of things over the years, promises included.

But he wouldn't break one to Elena.

He just hoped he wouldn't regret that.

Elena

The next day, the one where I woke up with a splitting headache—because I was a lightweight and because sleep deprivation was really frickin' getting to me—there was no coffee on the coffee table when I stumbled in there, Nathan on my heels.

He didn't notice, nor did he notice his mother may or may not be dying from a red wine-induced headache. He was too busy telling me how marshmallows were trees in his dreams and how awesome would that be?

He didn't notice Lance wasn't there until I'd gotten him fed, myself caffeinated and both of us borderline ready for work and school. After I'd found a waffle iron in Nathan's backpack and told him he could not make waffles at recess.

Then, he was cranky.

Obviously I was cranky, having been used to the good coffee, Lance's presence and the absence of a wine hangover.

Nathan got worse when we got outside and did not see the SUV that was usually there.

He peppered me with questions the entire drive to school. Questions I could not answer, did not want to answer and could not concentrate on while driving.

So he was not happy when he got to school.

Neither was I.

The bad mood continued until the late afternoon when Karen called to say she had a free afternoon and could pick Nathan up and hang out, knowing I had a long shift today. She seemed to sense something in my voice because she also told me she was making her risotto.

I cheered up then.

Karen's risotto was the *shit*.

She'd done a semester in Italy while at college—how frickin' cool was that? My only experience of travel was driving across the country trying to escape Robert—and while there, she'd learned how to make this porcini mushroom, sage, and orange risotto that angels would sing about.

I had sung about it.

She saved it for special occasions, whenever one or all of us were craving excessive amounts of parmesan and carbohydrates.

My day continued to go up from there, as my headache went away and some sense returned. It also helped that Bobby made peanut butter cake. Chocolate, peanut butter and the knowledge of good friends and risotto were waiting for you at home were all I needed to get my head out of my ass.

I kissed Lance.

Maybe not my smartest moment, but not something I was going to regret.

Firstly, because it was epic.

The best kiss I'd ever had in my life.

The hottest.

Secondly, because I'd been torturing myself with Lance, my feelings for him. I made a move, for better or for worse, I'd done something so I wouldn't spend the rest of my life wondering when all this chaos was over and done with.

I would not regret the kiss.

Whether Lance came back or not.

Shit, I really wanted him to come back.

The kiss was better than peanut butter chocolate cake.

Better than Karen's risotto.

So, when I saw a familiar SUV parked outside my house when I pulled up, my heart skipped a beat. Then another twelve beats.

He got out of the car as soon as I parked and got out of my own.

I glanced over to Karen and Eliza's, waiting for Nathan to run out and jump on Lance. He did not do so, luckily.

Lance was wearing shades, so I couldn't gauge his expression. His jaw looked hard, his hair looked great.

That wasn't something that needed to be noticed right now. Or the way I could totally see the outline of his abs underneath the black tee he was wearing. I hated that almost every time he saw me, I was either wearing my work uniform, a towel—okay that was only once—or cut-offs and whatever tee was clean at the time. The only time he'd seen me borderline presentable was at church, even then, I didn't get to pull out the stops I normally did.

Granted, I hardly ever pulled out any stops apart from doing something cute with my hair and showering, but still, I liked dressing up, I liked looking nice, especially when confronted with a serious hot guy who looked beyond nice, all the frickin' time. But that was life, I was facing the hot guy while wearing a diner uniform that smelled of grease and coffee, with no makeup and questionably clean hair.

"Inside," I said the second he stopped in front of me, deciding to take charge of the situation, and maybe he'd be distracted by that and not notice the hair or the grease smell. "Nathan is next door and probably watching the street for you periodically and I think it would be better if we..." I trailed off. If we had a quickie on the sofa? Made out again. Got married?

"Inside," I said instead of all of that.

His sunglasses stayed focused on me for a long pause before he nodded once.

Right. So he wasn't even going to speak to me.

Fine.

Good.

I straightened my shoulders and walked purposefully to the house, waiting until we were inside and the door was closed before I spoke.

Lance was barely two steps in when I started on him.

"We need to talk," I said, my voice rushed and panicked.

Lance obviously picked this up in my tone, because he picked up everything. He did not react outwardly, nor did he say anything to the four words that men usually ran from. He just folded his arms and jutted his chin up slightly, which was his way of telling me I had his attention.

Well, that and the fact his eyes were searing into my skin.

"There is obviously something between us," I continued, somehow keeping eye contact and enough courage to bring up the thing that I'd been feeling sick about all day. "I know you're an intense guy and a big badass alpha male, so some of the smoldering looks and what people would call overprotectiveness can be explained away with that. But I'm also a woman. One has been out of the game for awhile, that's true. I haven't known a proper, healthy relationship with a good man, so my experience is rather lacking. But women know when something is going on with a man. Even a woman like me. Especially in this situation. Because this" —I waved my hands between us— "whatever this is, it's not normal. I've tried to ignore it, talk myself out of even having this conversation. I've tried to think of all the reasons why having this conversation, having you in my life is a very bad idea, but I'm still here. Talking."

I swallowed roughly and ignored my sweating palms and butt at Lance's intense, and silent gaze.

"I used to be afraid," I continued. "Of pretty much anything. I grew up with parents who I knew to fear before I learned to talk."

Lance's jaw went harder at the mention of my parents, his body wired. I wondered if he'd looked up my history. I didn't doubt Greenstone had the ability to find out my real name, and find my parents, if they were alive. I had no idea. After Robert had proposed, I moved straight out of the trailer park and in with him. He told me I should cut them off.

I thought it was because he cared for me, didn't want me connected to ugly, vile, abusive people. But no, he just wanted to replace them with more ugly and vile.

"I went straight from that life to one with Robert," I said, shaking myself out of thoughts about my parents. "First, I was afraid of screwing things up with him, because he was so perfect, because he was cultured, and I so wasn't. Even before he showed me what a monster he was, I still spent most days afraid I'd say something wrong at one of his father's parties, eat with the wrong fork when he took me to a fancy restaurant, be the wrong kind of person for him." I rolled my eyes remembering how large my problems had seen then. "It took me a long time to realize that he not only saw that fear, but he relished it. He made sure to create more. And when he couldn't in those ways, he moved onto more traditional, sure-fire ways to make a woman fear a man."

Lance's arms were no longer crossed against his chest. They were long against his sides, hands fisted, shaking.

A visible, visceral reaction to my words? The pain in them? Or just me saying out loud the ways that Robert had hurt me?

Probably a combination of all of it, and other things that I didn't know enough about him to think of. But another reason that showed me that this conversation was a good idea. This was beyond the reaction of a good, albeit scary intense alpha male who had only professional feelings toward the woman he was meant to be protecting.

So I had to keep going.

"Once I left, the fear didn't leave me," I continued, taking a breath. "It got so bad I could hardly breathe around it. Everywhere I looked, I saw him, coming to drag me back. Coming to kill me. To take my son from me. Then that fear, his fear, it slowly receded. It never really went away. I wish I was a strong enough woman to say that I stopped fearing him as I started to build my life. It wasn't that. I just got too busy to give myself the luxury of fearing a memory. I had different things to fear. Like losing my job. Like not getting enough shifts to cover bills. Fear of being a bad mother, not bringing my son up right. Not giving him the childhood he deserved." I smiled. I knew it was melancholy, because I was filled with it. "I'm coming to learn that being a mother is being in a constant state of fear. I would like to say that having this bitter emotion following me around from ever since I could remember makes me somehow numb to it. But that's not the case. I've never not known a state of fear. And when Nathan was taken from me, I was shown the highest peaks of terror. Then he walked through that door holding your hand." A tear trailed down my cheek with the memory of it.

Lance stayed where he was, hands fisted at his sides, eyes never leaving mine. Breathing evenly, face blank.

"Ever since then, ever since I've been around you, I don't feel afraid like I used to. I'm afraid of what I feel for you. It unsettles me. It terrifies me. Because of how powerful it is. A feeling that shouldn't be that powerful considering you barely speak to me. I don't know your favorite book, music. I don't know what kind of past you've had to make you the man you are." I paused. "I don't know your pain," I whispered. "I can feel it though, as stupid as it sounds. I feel it, and my own pain recognizes it. You make me feel less alone. Less afraid. And that's why I have to have this talk with you. I can't keep feeling like this, I can't get used to feeling like this if we're never going to be anything more. If you don't want more from this. From me." I looked out the window to the yard, then around the room at the toys strewn about.

"I have a little man that is relying on me to make better decisions on who's in his life than I have in the past," I said, regaining eye contact with Lance. "I already know that having you in his life is a good decision, though you might not teach him what he needs to know about proper vocabulary, you'll give him a proper kind of role model to look up to. But that's going way too far, considering we've only kissed. I'm probably making the hugest mistake even saying any of this," I said, contradicting myself because Lance wasn't interrupting me as I'd expected him to and now I was spiraling.

It was now I chose to purse my lips, fold my own arms and not say a word until Lance said something, anything, even if it was to totally shoot me down and send me low enough to bury myself in Reese's cereal and bad TV.

But he didn't say anything.

No, he just crossed the distance between us in two strides, snatched me by the face and kissed the ever-loving shit out of me.

I couldn't even fathom what was happening until after it was over, my whole body was electrified, my lips felt swollen and bruised, my panties were drenched and my body was crying out for more.

That was of course, when he stopped kissing me.

But he didn't move. Didn't let me go. That was a good thing, not just because of how awesome it was to have his hands on me. But because I was almost one hundred percent sure that if he let me go, I'd fall to the floor and that would be really frickin' embarrassing.

"We're both allowed one mistake," he murmured against my mouth.

And then he let go of me and walked away.

Luckily, I didn't fall over.

But I did just stand there, mouth half open, heart beating in overdrive, staring at the empty space that used to be occupied by a beautiful, harsh and insanely confusing man.

"WE'RE BOTH ALLOWED ONE MISTAKE?" Karen repeated, frowning at her wine glass. Not just because I bought the wine when I was across town and that meant it was my favorite 'Two Buck Chuck'. And not because I'd eaten the last of the risotto.

Eliza was at my place, putting Nathan to bed, sensing I needed some adult time.

She was frickin' right.

I'd just recounted the whole 'event'—that's what I was calling it, for lack of a better word—with Lance that had happened only a handful of hours ago. It seemed like seconds and a lifetime all at once.

I nodded after taking a sip from my wine. It may have been that I was beginning to rely far too much on my one to two glasses I was having a night. That was definitely a bad thing for a daughter of two alcoholics, but it was a problem for me to worry about when I was lying in bed worrying about a plethora of other things too, not now when I was recounting my crazy kiss with Lance with my girlfriend.

"He didn't say anything else?" Karen probed.

I raised my brow at her. "Yes, he then got down on one knee, presented me with a diamond large enough to sink the Titanic all over again, asked me to marry him and professed his undying love for me," I said dryly. "I just left that part out."

She poked her tongue out at me. "Okay, so do you think he

meant that kissing you was a mistake or that walking away was the mistake or was he just trying to be a badass and say something to drive you crazy and walk away?" she asked.

I rolled my eyes. "Those are the three-million-dollar questions. I don't know what's going on in his head."

"What if I'm a bad kisser and that's why he said it was a mistake?" I blurted the fear that had been bouncing around in my head.

"You're a good kisser," Karen said without pause. "Don't be stupid."

"We're not allowed to say stupid, you know that," I scolded her like I would Nathan when he used that word, which wasn't often.

I'd outlawed it like I had a curse word because I didn't like it on principle and because my parents had routinely called me that all my life. I didn't like the way it made people feel. I didn't want my son to make people feel that way. Nor did I want him to ever feel that way. Obviously Karen was not a kid and could say whatever she wanted but I tended to get into mom robot mode.

"Plus, you haven't kissed me, so you don't know whether I'm a good kisser or not," I added.

Karen didn't say anything, she merely put her glass on the coffee table, leaned forward, snatched the back of my neck and kissed me.

I was so shocked that I didn't even try to fight her.

"You're not a bad kisser," she said after she detached, grabbed her wine and leaned back on the couch. "And that comes from someone who's kissed a lot of chicks."

I blinked rapidly at her, trying to figure out what the heck just happened. Then I took a sip of wine, leaned back in my chair and thought on it. "Well, if I'm not a bad kisser then why did he walk away and act like nothing happened?"

She shrugged. "Lesbian." She pointed to her chest. "One of

the reasons I became one, other than I was born one, was so I didn't have to deal with men's bullshit games."

My brows furrowed. "You think he's playing games?"

She thought about it. Properly, because Karen was a good friend and she wasn't just sitting here sharing empty placations with me. She was Frenching me to make sure I knew I was a good kisser and thinking hard about what the heck was going on in my previously empty love life.

"No," she decided. "Granted, this is coming from a woman with little to no experience dating men, and I barely know the man in question. But I feel like I'm pretty good at reading people. Not as well as you do of course, with all of your *auras*."

She rolled her eyes. It was safe to say that Karen did not believe in auras, star signs, tarot, or the healing power of crystals.

"I'm a reasonable judge of character. He's damaged, that's obvious enough. He's hot as balls. That's even more obvious. He's dangerous." She tilted her head in thought. "I've seen the way he looks at you. How he is with Nathan. It's different. I can definitely get a better read on the men around him because they speak in actual sentences and do things like smile and converse. They're good men. The kind of men that would not let someone who played games spend so much time with a single mother and her kid. I think he's just really fucked up. He wants you, but he's also probably got it in his head that you don't need a damaged and complicated man in your life right now."

She sipped her wine. "I don't blame him for thinking that. Because I don't have to be heterosexual in order to tell that man is a world of trouble. That man is going to turn your entire fucking mind upside down. He's going to wreak havoc on your vagina, in a good way."

She winked. And my stomach dipped at the thought of what he would do to me, if two kisses had me feeling like this.

"But he's also going to bring a different kind of ruin to your emotions," she said quieter, more serious. "And honey, you've already had a man rip through your life and take over your brain, your body. Lance would never do it in a way that Robert did, with malice. I think he has the ability to hurt you more than Robert ever did. I see the way you look at him too. I know you've been on exactly two dates since I've known you, and that you've never let either of them passed first base. This one has made it to home with only a kiss. He's under your skin. And I want all of the best things for you. We both know I'm the romantic in my relationship."

That was the total truth. As much as it seemed like it would be the other way around, Eliza had a lot of demons in her past, trust issues that stemmed from parents who didn't support who she was.

"I had to work hard to get Eliza to trust me," Karen said, sipping her wine and making a face.

I rolled my eyes and sipped my own, more because I needed it with all the truth she was laying on me right now.

"I'm not going to sugarcoat what we were at the start," Karen continued. "It wasn't pretty. It wasn't easy. We didn't make each other happy. We made each other miserable. My family hated her, and not because she was a woman, which was why her family hated me. But because for the first year we were together, I was a mess. I'd call my mom crying, drunk, telling her about the latest fight, the latest breakup." She winced, because Karen was not a woman who cried.

"Real love, with real people, it's not pretty. We could've given up on each other. We tried, in fact. Because I convinced myself that love wasn't meant to hurt that bad. That love wasn't enough. But in the end, it was. I'm so happy that we fought for each other, that she opened up to me, that she trusted me enough to let me in. My family have almost forgiven her. Hers still haven't forgiven me and won't until I magically grow a penis."

She grinned. "If I could go back through all that hurt, all that misery, all those tears, sleepless nights, screaming matches, breakups—I would. In a heartbeat. But that's because I only had myself to worry about. I was luckily enough to have a relatively healthy history. A good family. An unscarred soul. So I could take all those hits."

She shrugged. "But that's a choice I would make for myself. But for someone I adore? For you? I'm not sure I want you to have to go through all of that agony, after everything you've already gone through. I want love for you. I want a man to adore you. Treasure you and Nathan. Make you smile. Lance *might* be that man. I have a feeling it won't be easy or simple to get there with him. It might very well be worth it, just like Eliza is."

He was. Some part of me knew that. Of course I didn't say it out loud because he was insane.

"You deserve a man that's simple," Karen continued. "That doesn't know the ugliness of life, that hasn't been crippled by it. But that same man might not be deep enough for you. To nurture you. To understand your pain. That's what love is. Someone who will understand your pain."

I wiped the tears from my cheeks that I'd shed for my friends. I knew that it hadn't been easy for them. We'd shared everything over the years. But I didn't hear it with quite as much naked emotion.

"That doesn't help me at all," I hissed after I pulled myself together.

She smiled sadly. "I know. I wish I could help you. But I don't think there's anything I can do to help. I will tell you, whatever happens, whatever you decide. We're here. We'll be here no matter what. You have a family that will wipe away your tears and let you cry as much as you need. That will hold you up when you need to break down. To celebrate the wins with you. To smile with you. That's going to be unchanging through all of this."

That helped. A whole lot.

But her words followed me home.

To bed.

Into my dreams.

"*I think he has the ability to hurt you more than Robert ever did.*"

CHAPTER FIFTEEN

I HADN'T SEEN LANCE.

Not since I did the very stupid thing. And then he did the other thing, that was not at all stupid.

Not since the kisses.

They were so much more than that. They were something that created a shift in my body. In my frickin' mind. The way he kissed me showed me that I was not another job to him. That those cold, blank, even cruel stares were a façade for something deeper. Darker. And he let me in. For the length of that moment we had last night.

Until whatever it was that stopped him, mid-kiss, when I was sure a frickin' tornado whipping through my living room wouldn't detach us.

But something did stop him.

The same something that made him come back, kiss me, then disappear.

Probably the deep, dark parts of him that I had no idea about and wanted to know more than anything.

I'd wanted him to rip all of my clothes off and fuck me. Both times. It would have been that. *Fucking*. It wouldn't be meaningful, tender lovemaking, the kind I'd been so sure I'd only ever want due to my history.

Lance proved me wrong on that score.

Proved me wrong with his absence, silence, with the lack of everything I'd come to expect.

It turned out that Greenstone Security hadn't given up on me for lack of payment. Duke came knocking on my door not long after Nathan and I got home to make sure we were okay and we knew how to work the security system. He was easy to smile, joke with me. He was just easy to be around. And he was attractive. Unnaturally so, like the rest of them. But it didn't make me uncomfortable like Lance's ungodly looks had.

I had a reaction to him. I wasn't dead.

He was great with Nathan too. Especially when I invited him in for dinner. I had decided to treat Nathan and me to our favorite jalapeno chicken recipe. He loved spicy. And this was hands down the easiest and most delicious meal ever. I made mac and cheese on the side. I even went all out and made it from scratch, not having it in me to serve up Duke boxed mac and cheese.

Plus, he kept Nathan busy, so I actually had the time to make it from scratch. He found two gloves and a ball and spent an entire hour out back with Nathan throwing the ball.

Then he stayed for dinner, making conversation, asking about me, asking about Nathan, finding out my interests, hobbies, likes. There was never silence at the table, brooding or otherwise. It gave me a glimpse into what life might be like with a man like Duke.

Or even Duke himself.

I might have been seriously rusty in the dating game, but I was also a woman. Women knew when men were interested in them. Women especially knew when men like Duke were interested in them. Because although he was softer, kinder than Lance, he was still alpha as all hell. He still had a kind of mastery over the whole 'sex god' thing, a look, the way he tilted his body toward me as he spoke. A man like Duke made sure a woman knew he was interested. And not in a pushy, creepy way. It was like an invitation, a gentle prodding toward something that would almost certainly be epic.

It would be nice.

Easy.

Full of laughter.

It might not be forever, but there was something I was learning about these Greenstone Security men, beyond them being hot as balls, muscly as all hell and more alpha than anything I thought existed in real life. They were decent men. I'd seen enough of that. They treated women with respect. With reverence. So I knew Duke wouldn't be extending such an invitation to me, me a single mom with a load of baggage and trauma if he didn't intend on it being something more than a fling.

It was a huge frickin' compliment.

It was tempting as all heck.

But something stopped me.

Someone stopped me.

Lance.

This was not a man I'd wished for.

This wasn't a man anyone wished for.

He was too broken, too hard, too cruel for anyone to find peace with.

But I wasn't looking for peace.

So I didn't take Duke up on his silent invitation.

I waited for chaos to come back in.

CHAOS CAME BACK IN.

In different ways.

In a person.

"I have a present for you," Rosie said, walking through the front door of my place like it was her own.

I was almost certain her own place was a lot nicer than this, considering the price of her outfit probably added up to about two month's rent.

She never made me feel like less than her. It would've been easy, since I was. I wasn't even talking about the financials. It was more about her confidence, radiating off her, like any situation was hers, like she could handle anything. The fact she was tough but also kind. Quick to help out a stranger, drop everything in her life to do so and then befriend said stranger even though she didn't have to.

That wasn't just her. That was Polly, who called me every morning at the crack of dawn, because she knew I'd be up and she was off about to teach a yoga class. She then told me that I'd become a lifetime member of 'The Problem with Peace,' one of the trendiest yoga studios in LA. So trendy, even I'd heard of it, because it wasn't pretentious at all, didn't cost the same amount as a security deposit on the house to join, and that the classes were the best in the state. She'd had all sorts of write-ups in magazines, magazines I read at the grocery store and then put back.

I used to love yoga. When Robert went to work in the morning, before I started with my chores for the day—he had a list for me—I would have a blissful hour of stretching, not thinking, of peace. Even when I was covered in bruises, when my entire body felt like an open wound, I would do some kind of stretches. Nathan was a great baby, so I managed it even after he was born.

As soon as he started walking, my pockets of peace were gone, chasing around a kid who woke with the sun and didn't stop until after it had gone down.

I didn't think I'd have the time, or the gas money to make it into the city to take a class that had a month-long waiting list to get into, but I thanked Polly and told her I'd try to make it all the same. She also promised her Ziggy and Skye would be out to visit soon and we'd have a yoga session here while the kids played.

Lucy kept in touch too, mostly by text. A mom with a full-time job that was a huge deal, I knew how precious her time was, so I appreciated it.

All of it.

They'd taken me under their wings, that was for sure, and it made me feel warm and good, because they were good people. You could never be surrounded by too many good people, especially when you had so much muscle memory from the bad ones.

And these people, Rosie included, didn't make me feel less than for my choices, for my shitty Walmart shoes, for my second-hand furniture, for the fact I was just a waitress.

None of it.

Which was why I liked Rosie walking into my home like it was hers, dressing like she should have been on a runway, grinning like the madwoman I was starting to realize she totally was.

Which was why I didn't even know what to expect from Rosie's version of a 'present.' It could be flowers, it could be a bubble bath, or it could be brass knuckles, pepper spray, detailed instructions on how to make a Molotov Cocktail—all things she told me she was going to make sure I had.

But the envelope she was holding in her hand didn't look like it could explode at any minute, so I took it.

"I'm going to open a bottle of champagne to celebrate," she said when I took it.

I opened my mouth to tell her I didn't have champagne, but she pulled a very fancy looking bottle out of her very fancy looking purse.

I then opened my mouth to tell her that I definitely did not have fancy glasses to go with that kind of wine that I decided not to think about the price tag of. Of course, I had some kick-ass wine glasses, but for red wine, since I didn't drink any other type, and I didn't really have the occasion to buy or drink champagne. Again, I didn't have time to verbalize this thought because another, equally glamorous woman walked through my front door, also without knocking.

Lucy didn't grin like Rosie did, because she didn't really smile like that. She had a sleek, mysterious, thing going. Every time I'd seen her, she was wearing head to toe black, her hair sleek and inky, eyeliner so perfect it looked photoshopped. That didn't mean she didn't smile, she did that often too, just smaller and more with her vibrant, almost violet eyes.

She was holding a wrapped box in her hands.

The pop of a wine bottle made me jerk in surprise.

"Perfect timing," Rosie said, taking the box from Lucy without spilling the freshly opened champagne. She looked at me. "This is another present, to go with that one." She nodded her head to the envelope I still hadn't opened. Her eyes then focused on the box in Lucy's hands. "Don't mind if I unwrap it for you, do you?"

She didn't wait for me to answer, she put the bottle and the box on my table and started ripping at gift wrapping so perfect, it hurt me a little to see it so quickly destroyed.

Lucy did not look at all perturbed by her best friend wreaking havoc on her gift wrapping, she moved in to kiss my cheek to say hello.

She smelled like expensive perfume I sprayed on tester sheets in department stores and put in my crappy purse to at least make it smell good.

"You didn't have to get me anything," I told her. I looked to Rosie, who was still unwrapping. "Either of you."

"My present is to go with Rosie's present," Lucy said in

response. "And Rosie's present is kind of a present to all of us." She paused. "Well, considering the fact that I don't have a child attached to me, or a deadline, or any drug lords after me—that I know of—it's definitely a present for me too." She winked.

I didn't have a kid with me either, Nathan had a playdate after school, which included dinner. It was the longest time I'd been away from him since everything happened, and I was definitely on the verge of driving over to his playdate and snatching him away and taking him home where I could watch him like a hawk.

But I couldn't do that. Part of being a mother—a big part— was the crippling fear of something happening to the little human that relied on you to keep them safe. Another part of being a mother, was making sure that fear didn't take over your life, didn't stop your child from experiencing life.

You couldn't protect your kid from everything. You had to be prepared to have them experience the bad in order for them to experience the good.

Initially, I thought that's why Rosie and Lucy were here, because they had their own, badass women superpowers and knew I was almost losing it and Eliza and Karen were both out in the city with meetings. Meetings they'd told me they would cancel if I needed them, because they knew me well enough to know that today would be hard.

I had told them not to be crazy and that I was fine.

I totally wasn't fine.

Which was why I was thankful for my new girlfriends coming to keep me company, distract me and just have some adult company. I didn't really have a lot of girlfriends. Karen and Eliza didn't count, since I considered them family. There were a few moms at school who weren't part of the Lululemon brigade, and we got on pretty well. But none that made me feel like these women. None that I would think would do what these women had already done for me. I felt like I could tell them anything and they wouldn't judge.

"Here you go," Rosie said, putting a long-stemmed champagne glass in my hand.

I gaped at the glass. Although my own glasses were kick-ass, unique and beautiful. They were not like this. And they did not come in a powder blue box that was currently sitting on my coffee table.

I gaped at Lucy. "Please tell the mother of a five-year-old child that makes a sport out of breaking things that you didn't get me Tiffany glasses that I will now be willing to protect with my life, they're that beautiful," I said, my voice a little thick. No one had given me anything this nice before.

I didn't even think I was into things like this, but seeing the box, feeling the glass, looking at the geometric shape that had a frosted bottom, I realized I was *totally* into things like this.

Lucy shrugged, taking a glass from Rosie. "Every girl deserves something from Tiffany, you more than most," she replied simply as if it were that simple. "And if something breaks, it breaks. That's life. Beautiful things break. But that doesn't mean we don't have pretty things. Some of the most beautiful things I've seen are those that have been broken."

My throat got even thicker, so much so, I didn't know how I was going to drink this extremely fancy champagne out of my new fabulous glass.

"Now, open the damn envelope," Rosie said before I could start crying.

I did as she said, because it seemed like a better thing to do than burst into tears. But then, once I opened it, read it, I burst into tears anyway.

"I also got you a pen," Lucy said, voice softer this time. "Because you have to use a Tiffany pen when signing the divorce papers that free you from that loathsome, weak, piece of shit."

I was blinking so rapidly the paper was blurry. But it wasn't too blurry to see Robert's scribbled signature at the bottom of each page. I'd all but accepted my fate of having to be legally connected to him for the rest of my life, because I would never risk serving him with divorce papers and potentially putting Nathan and I in danger. I'd never entertained the thought of marrying again, my main focus was always Nathan and keeping him safe. I put 'Ms.' on all official documents and considered Robert my ex-husband. I'd decided a long time ago that our vows were void the moment he laid his hands on me. I'd found peace in that thought.

But I'd never realized how important this piece of paper would be until I was holding it in shaking hands.

"How did you get him to sign this?" I choked out, still looking at the paper.

"I used my manners," Rosie answered. "The ones given to me by my biker club upbringing. The big, silent, murderous guy at my side might've helped too, but I like to think it was all me," she continued.

My breath hitched at that. "Lance was with you?" I asked, trying to sound casual about the man I'd kissed then hadn't seen or heard from in days.

She nodded. "Of course he was." There was a knowing look on her face, but an understanding too. She didn't ask any follow-up questions.

I was thankful for that. Then, with great effort, I pushed Lance out of my mind.

"This isn't a gift," I whispered to Rosie. "This is my life. My escape. You're giving me my life back."

All teasing left her eyes. "No, honey. *You* gave yourself your life back. You took it back. I'm just making it legal. First time I've actually made something legal, instead of doing something illegal. It's nice."

I choked out a half laugh, half sob.

Then I took a sip of two-hundred-dollar champagne. Then I used a Tiffany pen to rid myself of Robert in the eyes of the law.

I wasn't sure which tasted better.

No, I knew exactly what tasted better.

It was a shame that sweetness didn't last.

CHAPTER SIXTEEN

One Week Later

MY WEEK WAS NOT QUIET, or peaceful, regardless of Lance's absence and Duke's presence. Just like Duke had subtly come on to me with chivalry and respect, he took my subtle rejection the same. There was no bitterness, no aggression borne from damages to a fragile male ego.

He accepted it and treated me exactly the same, well, without as much of his sex appeal. He was obviously a natural flirt, as it became apparent the more time he spent with Nathan and I. He seemed to know the score without me having to spell it out. It was refreshing, being around males with a healthy sense of masculinity. I'd always had to tiptoe around Robert's. Anything I said that could be perceived as a rejection resulted in violence, name calling, anything he could do to make himself feel big.

People always wondered about victims of domestic abuse. Why they stayed so long. How they got themselves involved with such monsters. But the thing was, abusers were smart. Masters of deception. They didn't woo women with their fists, name calling, degradation. No, they were charming, kind, attractive, attentive. Robert had been. He'd gotten me to fall in love with a façade. I was especially vulnerable because I'd never known real love, real attention, real kindness. Therefore, I found it impossible to spot the false versions of it. I was desperate to matter to someone, to feel wanted, to feel worth something.

Plus, I was eighteen years old, about to graduate high school with no plans, shitty grades and no sense of who the heck I was. What I was, was the perfect mark.

There was also this thing with Robert, when his attention was focused on you, it was powerful. It could make you feel like the most beautiful, treasured person on the planet. Then it began to make me feel worthless, weak. There was such a power in that, I started to believe it. And I was still clinging to the times when he gave me love. Kindness. Because when he showed me that, he made me feel like I was worth something. Everything.

I deluded myself into thinking that it would get better.

But it didn't.

And I left.

To make a long story short.

It was only around decent men that I was beginning to believe that they were real, that they existed.

Duke's handling of rejection showed me.

I knew better than a lot of women how scary rejecting or breaking up with a man could be. Most men would never know that fear. If they broke up with a woman, they got tears, maybe some late-night drunken phone calls. But they more or less could go on with their lives without fear. If a woman broke up with a man, rejected one, she had to deal with the very real possibility that he could hit her, rape her, kill her.

Heck, the entire reason Duke was frickin' here was because of a man's reaction to a break-up.

I didn't forget that. No matter how well we got along. No

matter how good he treated Nathan. Even with Polly's calls, Rosie's texts, Lucy's emails. All received on my new phone, of course. Nathan had to teach me how to use it it was that fancy. Somehow my five-year-old knew more about technology than me.

I was still waiting for him to exhibit some behavior as a reaction to the kidnapping. For him to act out in some way, maybe even start wetting the bed, something that had thankfully he'd grown out of six months ago.

But his sheets stayed dry, and his smile stayed wide.

Until Nathan's teacher pulled me aside at school pickup. My stomach dropped at this, I got Nathan situated in the car with a book to keep him busy. I was yet to resort to shoving a screen in his face, in front of his still-developing brain. Not that I judged parents that did. Kids were hard, moms were constantly tired.

Once that was done, I faced Hannah with a smile and waited for her to tell me my son was biting kids, licking walls or bullying someone. It was my worst fear, that somehow nature would trump nurture and some sort of gene from Nathan's father would be passed onto him. It seemed impossible being around my kind, happy and well-behaved son. Most of the time I didn't even think about it. But fears crept in in the darkness, in my weakest points, in times like this.

"Is everything okay?" I asked Hannah, more than a little panic in my voice.

She must have sensed it because she reached forward to squeeze my hand. I was gonna be super sad when Nathan moved up a grade because I really liked Hannah and I knew good teachers at public schools were rare as all hell, even in a public school as good as this one. "Everything is fine," she reassured me. "I just wanted to have a quick chat with you about some of the things Nathan's been telling me and the kids."

Color drained from my face in a rush. I thought of all the stories Nathan could be telling kids about some random guy introducing himself as his dad whisking him away to an unfamiliar house, telling him he'd be living there, and then having more strange men come into that house and whisk him back to his mother in a strange office in the middle of LA.

Or how about the brooding hot guy that he became attached to and had been asking about all week? The last time he'd seen him, he'd smashed a phone. Or more aptly, dropped him off at school, never to be seen again. I was mad at Lance purely for that. For coming into my son's life, charming him with his lack of charm and abundance of bad assery and then disappearing without a word. One of the biggest reasons I didn't date, apart from not having time to and being too freaking scared. I didn't want men in and out of Nathan's life, upsetting him.

"He's a fan of Marvel, I assume?" Hannah asked, jerking me out of my spiral.

"Marvel?" I repeated.

She nodded. "Captain America, more specifically."

Shit.

Fucking Lance.

I grinned and hope it didn't look as forced as it felt. "Yeah, he loves that dude. Who wouldn't love Chris Evans?"

Her grin was not forced. "I'm more of a Hemsworth guy myself." She winked. "Nathan has a very active imagination. He's under the impression that Captain America came and brought him back from his dad's place, back to his mom's." She paused. "I'm wondering if this is connected to the new man on the pickup list and the firm word he had with me about not letting Nathan get in a car with a man calling himself his father."

Fuck.

My grin disappeared. How could I think this wasn't gonna come up? Lance didn't exactly blend in at pickup, and I'd had Lululemon moms who barely even blinked at me in the past come up and ask about him.

All of them had a mix of judgment and jealousy in their faces when they spoke to me. I did my best to brush them off while still being polite. I definitely didn't need to make enemies of the PTA moms. I knew they already judged me enough for my crappy car, my working-class job, the fact I was a single mother and that I didn't have time to do things like join the PTA. Or own two hundred dollar leggings.

I couldn't care less about what they thought of me, I had a couple of moms who were actually normal and whose kids were the same and ate things like gluten and dairy. That's who Nathan had playdates with. And as long as my son had friends, didn't get bullied and learned things, I didn't care what the uppity moms thought of me.

But I did care about what the teachers thought.

Because this was a good school. Evidenced by the Range Rovers and expensive cars sandwiching my crappy one. This was a *great* school, especially by public standards, because it was in the middle of an upscale area, which my neighborhood brushed enough to get me in the school district.

I wanted Nathan to remain here, get as good of an education as he possibly could. No way could I afford private school and the only other public one in the area was not great, to say the least.

I bit my lip and tried to figure out what a good mother would do in this situation. A good mother wouldn't lie. But then again, a good mother wouldn't have let it get to the point of her son being kidnapped by a violent ex. A good mother wouldn't have trouble putting food on the table, and a good mother definitely wouldn't have to rely on a hot and scary stranger to rescue her son, pay for her car to be fixed and pay for groceries.

But I wasn't going to lie.

"Things with Nathan's dad are... complicated," I began, which she already knew thanks to the scolding she got from Lance the first day back. "He hasn't been in the picture, and it's in Nathan's best interest that it stays that way. It's been, confusing for him, to say the least. But we have it under control now, his dad knows what's best for Nathan."

Hannah looked at me with understanding and kindness. Not even an inch of judgment.

"Okay, I just wanted to make sure you were okay," she said. "I know bringing up a little boy on your own must be hard." She glanced around. "Especially around here. If you ever need to talk, have a coffee or debate which Chris is hotter, I'm here."

The offer was surprising. But nice. It seemed that I may be a magnet for chaos, drama, violent men, but maybe my luck was turning. Maybe I was attracting good, decent people.

Or maybe more chaos, drama, and pain was right around the corner.

I WAS ON A BEACH.

My eyes were closed, and I was relaxed. When was the last time I felt relaxed? I couldn't remember.

The only thing I heard was the gentle hum of the waves against the sand.

I'd never heard a single isolated sound before. Not living with a five-year-old. There was music. Cartoons. Yelling 'mom' when he needed me to wipe his butt. The crash of him dropping something. The clanging of wooden spoons against pots while he 'played the drums'.

But there was none of that.

Just me, lying in a very comfortable sun lounger, the sun beating down on my bare skin.

Something tightened around my hip.

I looked down.

It was a hand.

A man was gripping my hip.

And I was not lying on a super comfortable sun lounger. I was lying on a man. A man corded in lean muscle, obviously dozing if his closed eyes and even breathing were anything to go by.

How he could sleep with someone splayed on top of him, I had no idea.

But when I focused on his features, I had an exact idea of why he could sleep. Because this was a dream, and impossible things happened in dreams. Like me having enough money, free time and childcare to just lay on a beautiful beach.

And me lying on Lance with his arms around me, like it was some normal everyday thing.

Something stung the back of my neck.

The sun.

It was no longer warm.

It was hot.

Like uncomfortably hot.

My chest suddenly constricted and my lungs seized as I choked out a cough. My entire body rattled with the force of it, but the man below me didn't move.

He was still in the dream.

I must have been too.

But why was I so damn hot.

And why couldn't I breathe?

My eyes snapped open, I wracked my body with the force of the cough that had woken me up.

My eyelids stung with the bitter acrid smoke that was filling the room.

Something bright flickered outside my door.

Fire.

Oh my god.

The house was on fire.

My throat was closed up, eyes were swelling, I felt like acid was filling my stomach, but I moved.

I sprinted to Nathan's room, trying to cover my mouth the best I could.

The visibility in the house was decaying quickly, but I could see a small form on his bed. I scooped him up, blankets and all, trying to cover his little mouth and nose the best I could while still giving him the opportunity to breathe. Oh my god, was he still breathing? How long had I been dreaming on a fucking beach while my son was inhaling the smoke from our house burning down?

I couldn't think about that.

He was breathing because he had to be. I'd keep him breathing by getting us out.

It was a blur of smoke and flames, running the short distance from Nathan's room to my front door. It seemed like it took a year, with tears running out of my stinging eyes, flames seeming to scorch layers of skin off my face.

I couldn't breathe.

The heat was unbearable.

I could smell my hair burning. Maybe even my flesh.

I took no notice.

I got us to the front door, unlocked it with fumbling hands. Smoke alarms screeched, crazy beeping was coming from the security alarm. That could mean someone knew what was happening, someone was coming to save us.

If we waited, it would be too late. Something in me knew that. If I waited for someone to come and save my son and me, we'd die.

I would not die.

I covered my hand with Nathan's blanket to turn the handle.

Nothing.

I tried again.

It wouldn't budge.

I put my entire weight behind it and it moved a little, but something was jammed into it.

Heat licked at my back and I could feel the thin cotton of my tank burning off me.

I had to find another way out.

The back door off the kitchen was out of the question, since most of the kitchen was currently in flames.

My eyes went to the windows, my only options.

Most of them were small, we could fit through if I smashed them, because Luke and Keltan had put security locks on them so we couldn't open them farther than a crack. If I smashed them, there would be a high chance of both Nathan and me getting cut. The one behind the sofa was larger and went straight into the flowerbed in our front yard.

I didn't hesitate. I moved, jostling Nathan in my arms, finding my bowl of crystals and smashing the window by throwing the bowl and the crystals at it. Considering the bowl was fake marble, it did the job.

The sofa, which by some miracle was not on fire, so I managed to use it as a boost up to the window and out into the cool air that was rushing in and feeding the fire that was licking at my heels. I used my free arm to brush more glass away but didn't waste time in making it a safe exit.

I jumped out, sharp pain erupting from my foot and arm.

It didn't matter.

I landed on cool soil, my lungs seemed to be coated in blood, my throat thick in ash, my eyes soaked with acid, every blink agony.

I kept going until Nathan and I were safely out of the flames.

It was then I opened the bundle I was holding.

The bundle that had been unmoving throughout the entire ordeal.

My heart skipped and then continued its thundering rhythm as Nathan blinked his eyes open, widening on me, illuminated by the flames.

Small amounts of black covered his cheeks, but he was unhurt.

I laid him down and explored every inch of him. He was unharmed, coughing, but not hacking or suffocating as I was.

He must have been mostly protected in the cocoon of blankets I'd fastened around him.

"Momma," he said, voice raspy. Never had there between a sweeter sound.

Tears, not from the fire but from my soul leaked out of my eyes and I clutched him to my chest. "Baby," I rasped, rocking back and forward.

He started beating on my back in panic. I immediately let him go, searching for some hurt I'd missed. His eyes were wide on the flames eating at our house.

Our home.

"Feebo is in there, Momma!" he screamed, trying to fight me. "He can't burn!"

I struggled to contain him.

Shit.

It was then that two figures came running.

One had a phone to her ear.

Karen crouched down, worry painting her face. She was in her pajamas. They had bananas on them. I had the urge to laugh hysterically.

But the terror on her face stopped me.

She put her hand on Nathan's head.

"Oh my god, Elena! Are you okay?"

I couldn't answer, because Nathan was still struggling, screaming for Feebo. Real pain saturated his voice.

I made a split-second decision that turned out to be very stupid.

I thrust my son into Karen's arms and went sprinting back into a burning building for my son's soft toy.

The last thing I remember was clutching a stuffed bunny by the ear and telling myself I had to get it back to my son.

I DID NOT WAKE up gently or peacefully.

I woke up painfully.

With someone yelling in my ear.

The world was shaking.

Or someone was shaking me.

Someone who was gripping my shoulders to the point of pain.

But pain was pretty relevant since it blanketed my entire body, inside and outside.

"Wake the fuck up!" a voice growled.

Not gentle.

Or kind.

No, *furious*.

"Stop shaking her like that," someone else, someone decidedly more feminine snapped. Someone who sounded concerned but sharp.

Karen.

The grip only intensified and the shaking did not stop. "Elena, I swear to fuck, if you don't open your eyes and breathe—"

I sucked a painful and deep gulp of air through my lungs as I realized that in all the time I'd been noting these voices and the emotion in them, I hadn't been breathing.

The grip on my shoulders relaxed a smidgeon as I coughed

and spluttered the oxygen I'd been greedily trying to suck up seconds prior.

My lungs didn't seem to work properly.

My throat was scraped and cut open to the bone.

Or at least that's what it felt like.

Memories and comprehension flooded back to me. Flames. Burning. Smoke. Carrying my little boy through a house fire.

Our house fire.

I struggled to sit up, my eyes blinking furiously, filled with grit or dirt or something that made them itch and sting and made the world around me blurry and tinged in black.

The arms at my shoulders where tighter than before, not being used to shake me but now to hold me down. I struggled harder, still not able to see, not able to lay my eyes on my kid, the last time I'd seen him he'd been in his Avenger PJs outside a *burning fucking building.*

Nothing mattered at this point. Not the fact I was still coughing, lungs tight and unable to produce a healthy breath, not my raw throat, or my painful near blindness.

Nathan was all that mattered.

I struggled harder, the iron grip on my body loosening some against the wild, animal movement of my body. Pure adrenaline and motherly fear had me fighting against one of the strongest people I'd encountered.

"Let me go!" I screamed. Well, I intended on it being a scream, but it came out as a bare, fractured whisper. Still, I did not stop fighting. "Nathan!" I screamed again, my voice managing to get a decibel higher.

"Stop." The words were uttered with force, just like the grip on me. I had thought it was firm before, I had thought Lance was using his full strength to contain me.

I was wrong.

Because I couldn't move now.

I figured I'd probably be in pain if it wasn't for the agony in my chest at not having eyes or hands on my boy.

"Nathan is fine," Lance said, coming into vision as I continued to blink smoke and soot from my eyelids. Every blink seemed to move broken glass across my eyeballs but I didn't stop because I needed to see.

"Where is he?" I demanded, my voice sadly not sounding as strong or as furious as I intended. In fact, it sounded utterly weak, broken.

Lance's jaw was a hard line. He had black marks on his cheeks. "He's next door. We decided that him seeing his unconscious mother outside his fucking burning home would not be okay for him. Eliza's with him."

My body sagged. Only slightly. As much as I trusted Lance not to lie to me about such things, as much as I knew that Eliza would not let harm come to my son, I couldn't physically relax or breathe properly until he was in my arms, until he was in front of me.

"I need to see him," I croaked.

"You need a hospital," Lance countered.

All the grit and smoke that had previously obscured my vision of the situation around us, or maybe that was at least a little mental because my mind was trying to protect me from seeing the home I'd made for my son reduced to ash. Whatever it was, it cleared. It did that so I could sufficiently glare at Lance.

"Take. Me. To. My. Son."

It was then, right then, amidst desperation, fear and severe smoke inhalation that I found what it took to out badass Lance.

CHAPTER SEVENTEEN

NATHAN WAS MERCIFULLY FINE, having been checked out by the paramedics. The paramedics who I refused to even have look at me until they'd completely cleared my pale, confused and brave son.

The cut on my foot wasn't that deep and didn't require stitches, it just required me to keep most of my weight off it for the next few days, something that was another kick in the ovaries, since my job consisted of doing nothing but being on my feet. It was something I'd figure out tomorrow.

I'd figure out once I'd processed this, nowhere near a sterile and expensive hospital.

Hence the confrontation with his hard, clear and cold voice. My own was raspy, uneven and little more than a whisper. But I made sure it was strong.

Not just because there was no way I was leaving my son, nor was I scaring him even more and having him watch his mother be put in a hospital.

There was also the fact that there was no way I was going to pay for a night in the hospital and the ambulance ride there. I wouldn't have hesitated if this was something serious that had the possibility of taking Nathan's mother away from him. But the paramedics had told me it was more a precaution than anything.

"You're going to the fucking hospital," Lance hissed at me after we'd been discussing the matter for a couple of minutes.

I glared at him. "I'm not going *anywhere*, you saying it in that tone and adding cussing to the mix isn't going to make it so," I hissed, resisting the urge to clutch my raw throat as I did so.

It was about then that numerous SUVs screeched up to the street, interrupting the confrontation and distracting Lance enough for me to win. Though the pure fury on his face told me it wasn't over.

We weren't over.

"WE'LL BE BACK TOMORROW," Rosie promised, leaning in to kiss my cheek. I was sure that I'd have a lipstick mark on that cheek since she was wearing lipstick.

At almost four-thirty in the morning.

She'd arrived an hour ago.

Wearing full makeup.

And six-inch heels.

Messy bun but the kind that would take any other about an hour of fussing to make the perfect thrown together look.

Frickin' *leather pants*.

On my best day, I wouldn't look that good.

Granted, this wasn't my best day, I was wearing some oversized sweats of Karen's and Lance's jacket. The one that managed to still smell like him despite the fact everything else reeked of acrid smoke.

I tried to subtly smell it the entire night.

I did not want to know what my hair looked like. I didn't know how much of it I had left.

Rosie smelled like expensive perfume, it stayed in the air after she leaned back from the kiss.

"I'll bring the essentials," she continued. "Foundation, concealer, lipstick, setting powder, contour, of course, mascara, highlighter, setting spray. And clothes." She was listing things off on her red-tipped fingers. "Starting from the bottom, La Perla." Her kohl-rimmed eyes went to my chest area, which was covered by Lance's jacket. "I'm thinking a 36D?"

I blinked at her. Did she just guess my bra size over top of a man's jacket at four in the morning?

"And panties, of course. I'll bring you a variety... you know, just in case." She winked and her eyes went behind me. My eyes did not follow her gaze because I knew exactly who she was looking at, the fact she even knew to look at him while talking about panties made my neck heat. And nothing to do with the minor burns I was suffering from all over my body.

"I'm thinking you and me are almost the same size, but I'll go shopping anyway," she added on a grin.

My stomach dipped at the thought of her going out and spending money on me. By the look of everything she wore, I would not be able to afford to pay her back if she went shopping for me. Not for one pair of underwear. Plus, she'd already driven all the way out here, along with her husband and sleeping child, and almost all of the Greenstone Security crew. They arrived as the paramedics and fire trucks were leaving. The men were standing around my front lawn, in some kind of badass circle, talking about whatever men like that talked about at four in the morning. Waterboarding. How to disarm bombs. Whatever.

Lance was there too, staring at me. I knew this because every time I tried to sneak a glance at him, I was caught by his piercing gaze.

So yeah, Greenstone Security had already done enough for me, getting out of their beds in their no doubt kick-ass houses in LA, leaving their families to come here to make sure we were okay. Rosie was not going shopping for me. No matter how much my now nonexistent wardrobe would thank her.

"Rosie, you don't need to—" I started to protest, my voice still weak and scratchy.

She held up her finger. "Nope, you do not get to try and make an excuse to stop me from shopping," she snapped. Her eyes narrowed. "And you also do not get to try the staunch woman alone shit. I get it. I respect it. But it's not happening. Your house *burned the fuck down*. You smashed through a window, holding your kid to get out of it. Then you ran back in to get your kid's toy —granted that was a little silly, but I'm a mom, I get it." Her voice turned soft now. "You're a hero. How about you let us take up some of the slack?"

I opened my mouth to tell her they'd already done too much for me.

She smiled. "Oh, and that totally isn't a question. We're taking the slack. We're helping. That means new clothes. Makeup. That means shit for Nathan. That means cocktails. Food. That means anything you need. 'Cause that's what we do, sweetie. We help our girlfriends out. We do it whether they like it or not, whether they ask or not and mostly often, we do it while they protest loudly." Her eyes went behind me again. "Those men behind us may be some of the most stubborn asses on earth, but they're not even a match for me and the rest of the girls. You're strong. You could maybe take me on. But the whole group? Forget about it. So just let us help." She gave me another wink and walked away before I could say anything else.

Her heels didn't even sink into the grass as she met her husband at the door of their car.

The door which he opened for her and gave her a slap on her ass as she climbed in.

She was right. I wasn't going to win against any of them.

That became apparent about ten minutes later when the badass circle had broken, Keltan had come to check on me, as well as Duke, who gave me a hug and a kiss on the forehead. Something I notice Lance reacted to.

He was the only one that stayed. All of them promised to be back tomorrow to help. Help with what, I didn't know. This was kind of beyond what they were here for. The firemen wouldn't be able to pinpoint the source of the fire until later, but I was almost sure it was something I'd done. I had a lot of candles lit last night. I was religious about blowing them all out before I went to bed, terrified of something just like this happening. But I was tired. Beyond tired, the entire month catching up to me. My thoughts were occupied. By the man currently staring daggers into Duke's well-toned back.

The firefighters would discover that I caused the fire. That I ruined my home. Almost killed my son. I probably wouldn't get insurance then, knowing that there would likely be some catch in my cheap plan to fuck me over.

The thought made me so sick I almost lost the contents of my stomach on Eliza and Karen's front lawn.

"Let's get you inside, honey," Karen said from beside me. "You need to get some sleep. Nathan's in our bed, why don't you snuggle up beside him, we'll take the sofa."

I blinked at my friend. "No. We can't push you out of your bed."

She raised her brow as if I were crazy for fighting about something like that considering the circumstances—and I was.

"Um, normally I'd say yes, but you almost *died* tonight. You're taking our bed and we're having no discussion about that.

We're also having no discussion about Eliza getting the office situated for you and Nathan."

Eliza and Karen had a two-bedroom, around the same size as mine, but they'd done a lot more work to it, and it looked way nicer than mine. Well, considering half of mine was a smoking mess, it totally looked better, but before that, it was almost embarrassing. Since they owned, they did things like knock out walls to make open plan living/dining areas. None of their walls had scratches or marker stains from kids trying to make 'art.' They had a huge deck out the back, along with kick-ass wicker patio furniture. All of their furniture was crazy nice. Elegant. Classy.

And their office was just like that, full of expensive computers, solid wood desks, rugs, art. Things that would take all day to 'clear out.'

"No," I said, though it was becoming clear that we didn't really have another option. The house was unlivable, the firefighter was able to tell us that much. Logan and Esther would take us into their house without question, but I couldn't put that on them either. They also had nice things, things they earned. And a five-year-old, even one with good manners like Nathan would rip through that place eventually.

I couldn't afford to have us in a motel for more than a handful of nights.

But still, the thought of having Eliza and Karen do all that, disrupt their lives invade their homes... it went against everything in me.

"We can't do that to you guys, you don't have the room—"

Karen's eyes narrowed. "It wasn't a question. You're staying with us."

"They're stayin' with me."

On this, we both moved to the voice and the man who we hadn't realized was eavesdropping our conversation.

His face was pretty much the same as it had been all night, tight expression, simmering fury.

"What?" I choked out.

His eyes bore into me. "We've got that place down the street. It ain't much. But it's three bedrooms. You and Nathan will have space to yourselves. Someone from Greenstone will be there at all times, mostly me. You'll be safe. So shit like this doesn't happen again." His sentences were short. Clipped. Painful.

Karen looked from Lance to me.

"I know you consider yourselves to be one step up from a Hemsworth brother in an *Avengers* movie, and you kind of are, but Greenstone Security can't stop me from forgetting to blow out a candle," I told him in my raspy low voice.

Something moved in Lance's face, something that wasn't fury. I didn't quite catch it.

"Not a discussion," he said. "Makes more sense and you know it. So don't hurt your throat tryin' to argue with me. Right now, you need to go in, get some sleep, so when your boy wakes up to the sight of his house, you're gonna have at least an hour under your belt to deal with that."

I hated that he was saying things like that, ordering me around like that, like he had a right to. I also hated that he was making complete frickin' sense.

My throat did burn like a mother and the paramedic had specifically told me not to strain it too much by talking.

So instead of talking, I just glared at him, turned on my heel and did exactly as he said.

Despite the fact I somehow knew it would turn me into ashes, just like my burning house next to me.

ALTHOUGH I DIDN'T THINK I would be sleeping with the

remains of my house, Nathan's home, still hot and smoking right beside us, somehow I did.

Not for long, though.

Partly because I kept having dreams of burning alive in my own home with my son in my arms.

Mostly because my very alive son was lying on my chest, obscuring my breathing and yelling, "Mommy!"

He first wanted to know why we were having a sleepover at Karen and Eliza's, and then when I'd gently, in a raspy voice told him the truth, I'd hugged him tight while he blinked rapidly trying to understand that all of his toys, everything he knew and made him comfortable was gone.

When I let him go, expecting tears, his eyes were dry, though they were full of hurt.

"But you saved Feebo," he said quietly, snatching the rabbit that smelled of smoke and had a charred left ear and pulling it to his chest.

He used his other hand to brush my hair from my face in a gesture that was about forty years older than he was.

"You saved Feebo for me, Mommy. So we will build a new house. It will be okay."

I had never worked harder to stave off a complete mental breakdown in front of my son in my entire life.

Somehow, with a little chubby hand caressing my cheek, I managed it.

"Yeah, buddy, it will all be okay," I whispered.

I didn't know quite how it'd be okay, but I'd make it so.

I started making it so by getting up with my son, having breakfast with Karen and Eliza—who were already up and had made pancakes and coffee—then I continued doing so by having the courage to step outside to see the damage, my son's hand clasped in mine, giving me strength.

It was bad.

To say the least.

But it wasn't bad, not really, with Nathan beside me, clutching his soft toy talking about how he wanted his new room to be up in a tree instead of in the house.

THE DAY WAS LONG.

Really frickin' long.

Lance arrived as we were standing in the yard, talking about how Nathan could not have a treehouse for a bedroom.

"Captain!" Nathan yelled. "I'm having a treehouse for a bedroom."

Lance's first words to me were, "You're not meant to be on your foot, go inside."

I managed not to scream at him because I'd had coffee, pancakes and my kid was somehow smiling and I didn't want to scare him by shouting at his favorite hero.

"My house is not meant to look like *this* either," I snapped, waving my arm toward the blackened mess. "But that's life."

He narrowed his eyes, obviously not happy with my new found snarkiness, or maybe it was the rasp to my voice, edged with hysteria.

Maybe it was everything.

"You bought donuts!" Nathan all but screamed.

I hadn't looked down to what was in Lance's hands for the entire interaction, mostly because I was too focused on winning a stare-off with him. When I did move my gaze down, I saw he did indeed have a box of sugar covered crack in his hands.

"We've had pancakes already," I told him, feeling bitchy because I was exhausted, my throat was sore, my foot really did hurt like a bitch, and all I wanted to do was kiss Lance and let him take care of me.

Granted, the man was not looking at me like he wanted to take care of me, he looked like he wanted to murder—or at the very least, torture—me. But he pulled me out of a burning building. He stayed with me all night, he then arrived at seven in the morning with donuts and, looking at his other hand, coffee.

"Well, you can have pancakes and donuts," he clipped, leaning down so Nathan could snatch the box from him, despite being taught not to snatch. "How about you take those into your aunt's house, bud?" Lance said in a question that was actually an order, but in a slightly kinder tone than he used with me.

Nathan did not hesitate to heed that order.

I watched him run into the house before I turned to glare at Lance.

He was already glaring at me and spoke before I could scold him like I wanted to.

"Kid's standin' in front of his ruined house, he's havin' fuckin' pancakes and donuts, Elena," he said.

Shit.

He was an asshole who ordered me around and my son—who actually liked it—but he was right. Nathan was being remarkable, beyond remarkable considering what he'd gone through, he frickin' deserved copious amounts of sugar before eight in the morning. It put a smile on his face.

Lance didn't wait for me to respond. "He goin' to school?"

I shook my head. I'd wrestled with whether to make him go through a normal day and not disrupt his life anymore or keep him close, let him watch movies and play at Karen and Eliza's all day.

I'd decided on the latter. Right now.

"Good," Lance said. His eyes went up and down my body, I was still wearing the sweats and had morning hair and most likely, morning breath. "You're not goin' to work."

Again, not a question.

I folded my arms. "That's not your decision to make," I snapped, even though I totally wasn't going to work. I wasn't a total idiot. I couldn't speak properly, was limping and my freaking house burned down last night.

Having Lance think he could make that decision for me, after disappearing for a week had my hackles up.

He stepped forward, all the way forward so I could smell him, feel his heat pressed up against my clothes.

"It concerns you. Your wellbeing. So yeah, cupcake, it's my fuckin' decision to make," he murmured, breath all minty fresh and delightful.

Cupcake?

I pursed my lips. Not just because my breath was not minty fresh, or delightful.

Because his presence was doing all sorts of things to me, despite my lack of sleep, despite my smoke inhalation, the house behind me.

There was a challenge in his eyes. A dare. A hunger, mischief that hadn't been there a week ago.

Something had changed.

Really changed.

Before I could inspect this, say anything, or kiss him, morning breath and all, an SUV pulled up, and the Greenstone Security pulled up.

Shortly after that, my landlord arrived.

It was safe to say, he was not happy about the fire. He wasn't a bad landlord and I had been an excellent tenant, that was until I'd burned the house down.

But the second he started to speak to me with his bushy brows furrowed and splotched cheeks reddened, Lance was there. Duke was pulling me back, telling me that they'd take care of it.

I should have argued him on that. Told him that this was my

house, my life, I needed to take care of it. I needed to make an example for my son, myself.

But I didn't do that.

I let him lead me back into Karen and Eliza's, where I had two donuts, a shower, and when I came back out, my landlord was gone.

Logan, Esther, and Bobby were there instead, looking at my house in horror. Then they each looked at me in horror, each hugged me, demanded to know if I was okay, then to see Nathan. As predicted, Logan and Esther offered up their place for Nathan and me to stay for as long as we needed.

Of course, Lance interrupted this by telling them that Nathan and I were already "sorted."

Esther rose her brow at this, looking back and forth between us with a knowing gaze.

Bobby went murderous again. Logan was contemplative.

But again, there wasn't time for this interaction to continue, as this was the point my insurance agent arrived. Again, Lance took over talking to him. Or grunting at him. Peppering him with death threats. Again, I let him.

There were visitors, calls, barked orders for me to "get the fuck off my feet"—from Lance—for the rest of the day.

Nathan was a dream, excited about having a day off school, with adults everywhere, treats for every meal—Bobby brought half the diner with him at lunch—and movies that he was never allowed to watch in the daytime.

But then the time came.

The time of the day where Nathan was getting tired, I was beyond tired and we were both yearning for a home that didn't exist anymore.

It was at this point Lance walked in the door to Karen and Eliza's, narrowed his eyes to where I was cleaning dishes in the kitchen and declared it was "time to go."

I had already explained the temporary living arrangements with Nathan, to say he was excited was an understatement. He all but sprinted out the door once Lance had made his commands. First thanking Karen and Eliza for letting us have a sleepover.

My kid had some manners at least.

I did not sprint. Not just because I physically couldn't.

But because I'd been alternately dreading and looking forward to this moment all day.

An enclosed space.

With Lance.

The man I'd seen a week ago with his tongue inside my mouth, giving me the best kiss of my life, cementing his place under my skin, in my bones.

My mind should not have been consumed with that all day. It should have been consumed with my son's possible psychological trauma. The fact we didn't have a home or belongings. Wondering if my insurance would payout, even with Lance going full badass on them. Figuring out how we would rebuild, with the Greenstone Security bill still looming on the horizon. And then, of course, Robert.

So yeah, any one of those things would have been appropriate to settle on. Dwell on. Instead, it went to wondering how in the heck things would go with Lance, once we were alone.

And now, I wouldn't have to wonder.

CHAPTER EIGHTEEN

DESPITE NATHAN BEING SO EXCITED at the prospect of having "sleepovers with Captain" he crashed pretty darn fast. He would have gone headfirst into his Happy Meal—something saved for very special occasions or when I was too tired to cook—if I hadn't carried him to his new bedroom.

His new kick-ass bedroom.

Rosie had been to visit.

That much was obvious as soon as we walked in the door and there were seven bottles of wine on the dining room table.

'One for every day of the first week you have to co-habitate with the only caveman left from the ice age' was the accompanying note.

It did not stop there.

The fridge was stocked.

With everything you could think of. Snacks. Sodas—all diet, and I knew this was a woman because all women knew that sodas had to be diet, no matter how much sugar you consumed in other forms—fruit, fancy looking salad containers.

The pantry was the same.

There was a bowl of crystals on the coffee table. I knew this came from Polly.

When Lance showed me to 'my' room—*right frickin' beside his room*—there was a comforter that I knew he did not pick out. It was like my old one. But so much better. It was the deepest purple that it looked like you could dive into it. The fabric was so soft I was surprised it didn't melt under my fingertips. There were throw pillows.

Scented candles.

The bathroom off this room—I had the master, which I was sure was Lance's doing—was filled with products.

Glass containers of moisturizers that I had only gazed at longingly in department stores. Makeup I didn't even recognize. Perfume. It was like a counter at a department store.

The drawers in the bedroom weren't full, but they had things in them.

Beautiful silk things in the top drawer. Beautiful, sexy things I'd never owned.

Cashmere frickin' socks.

Sweats.

Lululemon leggings.

I'd cried. Right there, in front of the leggings, after the shower Lance insisted I take right after I'd put Nathan to bed.

Then, I'd called Rosie, sobbing, making no sense, babbling about Lululemon leggings.

"Babe, you're welcome, I'm guessing with all the crying and babble, it's a thank you," she interrupted somewhere. "But you don't need to thank me. That's the most fun I've had since I tortured human traffickers in Venezuela."

I couldn't decide whether she was joking or not, and she didn't give me time.

"I can tell by your tears, you're sober," she said. "Drink some of that wine and cry drunk tears instead. I'll call you in the morning." A pause. "Everything is gonna be okay."

On that, I made an embarrassing sob into the phone.

"My cue to go," she said, smile in her voice. "Wine, now."

I nodded and went to do what she said, wearing some of the most beautiful silk pajamas I had ever put on my body.

Lance was in the living room when I limped in.

His eyes went to me immediately.

And then all over the pajamas, that covered me head to toe, but his gaze melted them right off. My entire body responded.

We stared at each other.

For a long time.

Too long.

"You need to sit down," he said, his voice thick, not empty. Not by a long shot.

But it was still a command, despite the desire it was cloaked in.

So that was what made me straighten my spine and remember the events of the day. Of the week.

"I do not need to sit down," I snapped. "I need to get some things straight."

He stood, jaw hard, fists at his sides. "You've got a cut on your foot that you've barely rested all day," he clipped. "So yes, you need to *sit the fuck down.*"

The last sentence was a growl.

A growl.

It hit me right at the bottom of my stomach. Right in between my frickin' thighs.

But somehow, I managed not to let that show, let any one of it show.

"Firstly, I need to thank you," I said, my voice still a rough rasp. It hurt to speak. But then again, it hurt to breathe, so it wasn't like I could stop the pain. I focused on Lance. "You saved my life. Risked your own. So thank you."

He was gritting his teeth. I could see that by the way he was holding his jaw, it was something I was coming to recognize being connected to one of Lance's highest levels of fury. Gritting his teeth so tightly his entire chiseled jaw shook.

"Don't thank me," he ground out. "Just don't ever fuckin' do shit like that again. And *sit the fuck down*."

"I also need to tell you, that pulling that crap ever again won't go down with me," I continued, ignoring his words. "I get you're a dangerous badass who even Chuck Norris is afraid of, but I swear to every god that's worshipped on this planet, you try to keep me from my son when my last memory is of him coughing smoke from his lungs, I will fuck you up. In whatever way I can. You may have experience with some bad dudes, scary dudes, but you haven't dealt with a mother being kept from her son. So straight up, you pull that shit ever again, I'll end you."

Lance stared at me for the longest time, a complex cocktail of emotion that I didn't know if I had the emotional intelligence to decipher. It was jarring, seeing it all on the surface like this, when only a week ago, I could only guess at his depths.

"You went back into a burning building for a fucking *toy*," he said, voice quiet, barely audible. But the velvet threat in the tone shook the air.

"It was an important toy," I argued, voice small.

The eyes I'd been unable to stop staring at turned stormy.

In a blink, he was around the coffee table that had nothing on it but a bowl of crystals and right in front of me. Right there.

He gripped my shoulders. Still not gentle.

I didn't think he *knew* gentle.

"More important than your fucking *life?*" he roared in my face.

I flinched, but I didn't flinch back as I should've. I didn't run like I should've.

"Are you fucking dumb?" he hissed, still in a shout, still in my face. "You could've fucking *died!* You almost fucking did. You bled. For a *toy.*" He slung the words at me like punches, not pulling a single one because I was hurt, scared or physically, mentally, and spiritually exhausted.

No. He did not stop to spare my feelings. To treat me with care.

He kept going.

"You have a *son,*" he accused. "A son that almost lost his mother for a *toy.*" The single word was hurled at me like a weapon.

It hit true.

"It's not just a toy," I screamed. Or I tried to. My voice was still husky, raw, barely audible. Every word was agony. But I kept speaking, because anger, fury bubbled up in my veins. "That motherfucking toy is the only thing that has stayed constant in my son's life. He believes that toy protects him. That it will not let anyone take him away from his mother again. He's been taking that thing everywhere since..." I trailed off, partly because I needed a break from talking but mostly because I couldn't verbalize it. I didn't need to. "So yes, I risked my life for a toy. A toy that makes my little boy feel safe. Protected. And maybe it was fucking dumb. I was just trying to do the best I could for my *fucking child.* Now can you get out of my face because I just almost burned to death. My *son* almost burned to death." My voice broke on the end. Broke like a glass on marble. Shattered.

All bravado, anger, determination, or whatever had been holding me together gave way.

And the tears started. My body shook with the force of my first sob.

Lance's eyes flared. I waited for him to flinch away, to tell me to stop crying, stop being weak. Or to just leave me there to cry it out on my own. This wasn't his job after all, to console a hysterical woman.

He did none of those things. He did the thing that I would never expect him to do in a hundred years. He took me in his arms and let me sob into his chest.

He held me.

For a long time.

He was the one to finally break me apart.

But he kept me together too.

I WOKE up in an unfamiliar bed the next morning with no memory of how I got there.

My last memory was of Lance's smell. Of his arms around me. Of his tee, how it dried my tears and smelled like fresh laundry and safety.

I had no idea of how I got into the most exquisite sheets I'd ever lain my body in. If I had no memory, then I must have been carried here.

By Lance.

Lance held me in his arms as I cried.

Lance carried me to bed.

The thoughts hit me before the reality of my house—or lack thereof—set in. It showed me where my priorities lay. Or what rocked me to the core most, not the house fire I almost died in, but the cruel kindness of the man that pulled me out of it.

That epiphany was cut short when I blinked at the time on my phone.

It was nine-thirty in the morning.

I hadn't slept that late in... recorded memory.

Sleeping in is nothing but a fantasy as a single mother.

Nathan didn't let me sleep in.

I was looking forward to his teenage years, when I'd have to yank him out of bed by his ankles at noon. I'd been resigned to the fact I wouldn't get any kind of sleep-in for at least another ten years.

But it was almost ten.

I'd missed the shift at work Esther had forbidden me from turning up to.

Nathan was beyond late for school, and no way had I planned on giving him two days off in a row.

I'd planned on getting him back into a routine, to a semblance of normalcy. I could get him dressed because in addition to outfitting me with everything a woman could want, Rosie had made Nathan's dreams come true, right down to a Captain America comforter on his twin bed in the room down the hall.

No way was he in that bed.

The sounds of life coming from the kitchen had me jerking up. It was the smell of coffee that got me fully out of bed and limping down the unfamiliar hall that didn't have a single photo on the walls.

I expected Lance.

Nathan.

I got neither of two of my favorite men.

I got one of my favorite human beings instead.

She was in the kitchen, the one with a familiar setup to mine, but with no cool knick-knacks, or personality like mine had.

A pang hit my stomach.

Like mine *used* to have.

"What's up, sleepyhead?" Karen asked, grinning, handing me a coffee cup, leaning on the breakfast bar.

I took the cup without thinking. Then I looked around for my son.

"He's at school," Karen said the second panic started to rise in my throat.

I focused back on her. "Eliza arrived early this morning, planning on trying to stop him from pouncing on you and getting him ready so you could sleep," she explained, sipping at her own cup. "Lo and behold, he was up, eating oatmeal and barbeque sauce." She screwed up her nose. "Something that is super fucked up, by the way. He was dressed. Talking to Lance, who was grunting at the appropriate moments."

I gaped. "Lance got Nathan up, dressed and made him his crazy oatmeal?"

She nodded. "That he did. I want to hate that guy, I really fucking do. But then he keeps turning shit around."

"That he does," I murmured, wondering if I was mad that Lance got my kid up and ready and took him to school, without waking me or giving me a chance to say goodbye or smell his hair or anything.

"Nathan went in and kissed you goodbye," Karen said as if she could read my mind. "But you were sleeping like a zombie, or so he said. We really need to get that kid into the *Walking Dead*, educate him on the fact that zombies do not sleep."

I raised my brow at her. "Nathan is five years old, Karen," I reminded her. "A little young to watch the dead come back to life and eat the living."

She shrugged.

"He was okay?" I asked, sipping coffee and worrying about my little buddy.

Her eyes turned kind. "Yeah, babe. He was fine. Resilient kid. I dropped him plenty of times when he was younger, he got right back up."

I narrowed my eyes at her but couldn't help from grinning.

Karen regarded me with a raised brow, skepticism and worry mixing on her face. "How are you still holding it together?" she asked, her routinely strong voice cracking slightly. "With all of this happening, things that would bring down anyone, you're still..." She trailed off.

I smiled wider. "Still somewhat sane? Walking around?" I finished for her.

She nodded.

"I'm a mom," I said by response. "It's what we do. In times of crisis, we handle, we get through it, for our kids. And then, when it's all over, when everything is as close to okay as it's gonna be, I'm surely going to crumble." I thought fondly of that moment where this constant state of fear and adrenaline would stop keeping me going and I'd curl up in a ball in the bottom of a shower. "But not now, not when Nathan needs his mother. I'll get us through this."

Karen's eyes shimmered. "You're such a fucking badass," she whispered.

I shrugged, uncomfortable with the respect and admiration in her eyes. It definitely didn't feel deserved. "I'm a mom," I said by response. "It's what any mom would do."

She shook her head. "No, babe. Not any mom would do everything you do and continue to do for that kid. Not every mom would be strong or brave enough to walk out that door three years ago. To make a life for her kid with almost nothing. And not every mom would be strong enough to handle all the crap you've handled and still play, laugh with her son. You know that. I hate how well you know exactly what a bad parent would do in this situation, but you do. And instead of taking that trauma they put onto you, injected into you and resuming the cycle, you broke it."

Tears started to drip into my coffee, so I glared at Karen. "You're not allowed to make me break down yet," I scolded.

Karen gave me one more look that threatened to chip at my resolve before her expression changed into something more familiar and light. "Okay, but, you've got to promise that you'll call me when you have your breakdown. When this is all over."

I nodded. "So in about thirteen years?"

It was then she laughed.

And somehow, despite everything, I laughed right along with her.

Lance

"You need to rein your shit in."

Lance stared at Keltan, his boss, his friend, a man he respected. For those reasons, he didn't plow his fist through his face. And because that was against the rules.

He was trying to remind himself of those rules, as he had been all morning.

The morning that started with a small human being shaking him awake and asking him where his shield was.

"*I can't find it in the closet,*" Nathan said. "*Or under the bed.*" His eyes lit up with a kind of energy only kids could have at this time of the morning. "*Do you have a secret safe?*" he asked, voice lowering from the near shout it had been before. "*I promise I won't tell. Even my mom.*"

Lance moved upward in his bed, fully awake, pain radiating from an area in his chest. "Don't have a safe," he said. "Or a shield."

Nathan screwed up his face in confusion for a beat, but then it cleared and he nodded. "You don't need one," he said, like it was obvious.

"I do," Lance admitted.

Nathan continued to stare at him in that probing and uncomfortable way that kids had. Like they could see everything you were trying to hide from the rest of the world.

"*I'm hungry,*" he said finally.

Lance restrained a laugh.

"Do you know how to make oatmeal?" Nathan continued.

"Yeah," Lance said.

So he got up. Made the kid oatmeal. Even gave him the barbeque sauce to put on it, interested, impressed and disgusted at watching him eat the whole thing. Eliza arrived in the middle of it, seemingly surprised to see Lance feeding Nathan, but decidedly more shocked at what he was feeding him.

She offered to take over, take him to school, both of them not needing to say that they were letting Elena sleep.

"I got it," he said.

The woman looked at him, really fucking looked in a way that made him uncomfortable before she smiled, big and bright. "Yeah, you do," she agreed.

Then she left. He got Nathan ready for school.

Took him there, dropped him off, promised that he'd be there to pick him up, another punch to the gut with the look on the kid's face when he made him that promise.

He'd driven to Greenstone. After making sure someone was sitting outside the house. He didn't want to leave Elena. No fucking way. Not with what they knew about the fire.

But he trusted his team, even if he didn't like the way that fuck Duke looked at Elena.

He had shit to do.

People to kill.

Keltan sensed that. Saw that.

Hence his order.

"*Rein it in?*" Lance repeated. "First time I see her in a *week*, after a week of tryin' to scrape her off my bones, I'm seein' her unconscious in her burnin' house," he bit out.

He was pacing.

That was against the rules.

A clear sign of lack of control. A sign to the world, and most importantly, himself, that he could not keep his shit locked.

The fists clenched at his sides, another one. The edge of panic to his voice, the way it shook, the fact he was admitting to his fucking boss he had a connection to Elena that was beyond professional, yeah that was bad.

And he couldn't control it.

Because. Elena. Almost. Died.

His vision blurred with that thought.

He stopped pacing, looked into the clear and steady gaze of the man in front of him. "Saw the kid, cryin' in the middle of the yard, covered in smoke, tears, pointing at a house that was little more than inferno telling me to go and save his mother."

That memory shook him. The reality of the moment fucking broke him, took him back to another time, another life, where he couldn't save anyone.

Standing here, in the cool, air-conditioned offices at Greenstone, his skin was melting from his fucking bones. He was ready to tear it from them, his hold on his shit was that far gone. He was about to choke on it. All of it.

Then he calmed.

Instantly.

Most likely disturbing Keltan, the change from feral to empty. Lance sure as fuck felt disturbed at how instant the change was. How he hadn't even tried to do it. Fuck, he didn't think he could change back to what he was before.

But it was simple. He was thinking about how helpless he was in that other life. And he was remembering who he was now.

The man that was far from helpless.

"He's dead," he said, voice calm, familiar. Comfortable. "Don't give a fuck about what Elena says about this shit anymore. What her morals tell her. Straight up, I'm ending him, and you can fire me, try to stop me, though I really wouldn't consider the latter, since I respect you, like your wife, wouldn't want to offend her by fucking you up."

Keltan raised a skeptical brow at this but Lance kept going.

"You know me. Hired me 'cause of what you know I can do. I'm the best at the worst. And I'm pointin' all of my worst at that fucker. You're with me, against me, I don't give a fuck. Just don't get in my way."

KELTAN HADN'T STOPPED HIM.

He wasn't that stupid.

Likely he was making arrangements for some kind of damage control when Lance did what he said he was going to do.

Because Lance always did what he said he was going to do.

Especially when it pertained to killing.

Which was why he was sitting down the street from the fuck's house.

Watching.

Waiting.

He knew he was home.

Saw him pull in.

Stupid enough to still be at the place where Lance had beaten the shit out of him before.

Or arrogant enough.

He almost kills his ex-wife and son, and he comes home with his fucking dry cleaning, not a care in the world.

Soon he wouldn't have a care in the world.

Because he wouldn't exist in this world.

Wouldn't be able to harm Elena or Nathan again.

So why the fuck was he still in the car?

Because of the kid that woke him at six in the morning asking him where his superhero shield was.

Because of the woman who had cried herself to sleep in his arms last night.

Because she had felt so right in his arms when even breathing had felt wrong for the past ten years.

He knew, he fucking knew if he walked into that house, did what his blackened soul was urging him to do, he'd never feel that rightness again. He'd be crossing a line that he'd crossed many times before. But one that would make it sure that he could never have the thing he wanted.

The life he wanted.

He had a choice.

Kill the man who posed a threat to Elena and Nathan, kill the prospect of maybe having a life.

Or drive away. Leave it to chance. Leave a threat out there in the world so he could be selfish, have something he didn't deserve.

Life or death.

CHAPTER NINETEEN

Elena

Three Days Later

"WHAT'S THIS?" I asked when I walked into the living room, going to throw my keys on the side table and catching myself just before I threw them onto the floor as I had for the past three days straight.

I knew this wasn't my house.

I had to drive past my burned-out shell of a home in order to get here. The front door was different. There were no flowerpots outside it.

Nothing of mine or Nathan's decorated the walls.

In fact, *nothing* decorated the walls.

It was a stark and utter contrast to our cluttered, warm home that was charred wood and black ash.

Despite the fact that I had all this evidence that I wasn't

walking into the front door of my home, I still had to catch myself from throwing my keys on the side table I'd restored myself.

Lance watched me do this, because he was Lance and he watched me do everything. Before the fire, I thought it was just his intense way, something he did with everyone. I could almost believe myself when I thought it. But after the fire, it was unmistakable that it was something he only did with me. And Nathan. But it was different with Nathan.

Every time we were in the same room I felt it. That mixture of fire and ice in my bones. His stare that imprinted itself into my skin. It was like he expected me to burst into flames just like my house. He barely left mine and Nathan's side now, the week-long absence never mentioned. I itched to know the reasoning behind the absence. Why he left. Why he came back. But I was a coward. I was fragile. My first few layers burned off in that fire. I was exposed to the nerve. I didn't want him to tell me why he left or why he came back. I wasn't strong enough for answers I might not like. And I didn't want to tempt fate either. I didn't want to point out the obvious to him about him being well and truly back in our lives, scare him off.

Not that he seemed like he was going anywhere. He was always there with me to drop Nathan off at school. Pick him up with me. Have dinner with us, though he barely grunted responses to Nathan's chattering, not that he really noticed.

And he was there, in the room right next to mine, sleeping. Or I presumed he had to sleep at some point. Because even though my son thought he was some kind of superhero—and I was inclined to agree since he *pulled me out of a burning building* —he still needed some shut-eye. So did I. Because I was most definitely not a superhero.

Yet I snatched a mere few hours for the nights we had been here. Not because I was afraid I'd wake up in a burning house again. No, I didn't have fears with Lance under the same roof.

It was the fact that I was under the same roof as Lance, so close to him I could smell him in the air, *that* was the big reason I couldn't sleep. I tortured myself in the nights when the sheets felt too heavy, the air felt too stifling and my body was overcome with an animal kind of hunger. I managed to chase away that want, that need for Lance in the daylight. It was much easier in the daylight, when all the reasons why I couldn't give in were illuminated, stark, clear. But as the sun set, it obscured all those very good and very practical reasons.

And now, those very good and practical reasons were disappearing in the daylight too, walking into the house that wasn't my house and seeing my son wearing clothes I hadn't bought him and holding a fishing rod that was taller than he was.

Lance was wearing clothes I didn't recognize either, the man version of Nathan's little boy outfit.

Where Nathan's little pants, boots, and shirt were absolutely adorable, Lance's were straight up scorching.

I wasn't exactly familiar with most sportswear, but before this moment, I would've been confident to go in blindly and say that any kind of fishing attire would not be sexy.

Like at all.

Right now, I was being proved very, *very* wrong.

"We're goin' fishin'," Lance said in reply to my earlier question, the one I'd almost forgotten I'd uttered before I started taking all of this in.

"Lance is taking me to his church!" Nathan all but screamed at me, his grin threatening to split open his face it was that wide. "And he got me my very own rod and special fishing clothes."

I smiled back at him, his happiness infectious and welcome. This past week had been tough for my little man, to say the least. Heck, this *month*. Although Nathan was one of the best five-year-olds to ever exist, he was still a kid.

There was only so much he could handle.

So the smile hit my heart.

Reality hit it a second later.

"We're gonna go in a sec, but we have to go and find worms in the garden," Nathan declared.

I wrinkled my nose up at the thought of digging up slimy creatures and handling them. Though I definitely didn't mind getting my hands dirty in most ways—I was a mother and a waitress after all—worms and any kind of insects was where I drew the line.

"How about you go get started and I'll talk to Lance," I said to Nathan, my smile still in place, but a little more forced than before.

Nathan didn't need to be told twice. In his excitement to go and dig up worms, he forgot he was still holding the rod, and just let it go before running toward the back door. Luckily Lance's badass instincts extended to the aftermath of an overly excited five-year-old.

I waited until the sound of the back-door closing echoed through the small living room. Then I stepped forward, dropped my purse and keys on the sofa that had appeared yesterday.

Along with another bottle of wine and a note from Rosie:

Not as kick-ass as your previous one, but it'll do for now.

It was one hundred percent more kick-ass than my previous one, considering my previous one had been found at a flea market and restored with random patches of fabric. This was pure velvet, a deep purple, long and luxurious. And expensive. I knew that just by touching it. It was like you could sink into it. Sitting in it was like sitting in a cloud.

I couldn't even resist stroking it as I dumped my bag and keys.

"Didn't think you'd mind. Kid doesn't have shit on today, his homework is done. Figured you could have an afternoon where you can do whatever shit you want. Take a break. Read a book. Whatever."

Lance spoke before I could. It was an incredibly long sentence for him. I savored every word, even though they were uttered in that same deep, flat tone. That tone I felt everywhere in my body, more specifically right between my legs.

I took a deep breath and forced myself not to stare at the way his army green tee clung to his muscled biceps. Then I focused on the words, not just the tone, not just the fact that Lance offered up the first sentence as somewhat of an explanation.

He knew that Nathan had homework. That he'd finished it. He knew that he didn't have a playdate scheduled, or anything else.

And he wanted me to have time to myself, to maybe read the book that was sitting on the coffee table, the one that I'd only managed the first chapter of.

All of this hit me in different places than his masculine and commanding voice. Because though the words were spoken in a cold and indifferent tone, the words themselves were far from cold and indifferent.

The fishing rod, the fishing gear, my son's beautiful smile, all very, very far from cold and indifferent.

Which was the problem.

"You made Nathan smile," I said as response. His face stayed blank, but the hand holding the rod twitched. I noticed it because I was training myself to notice every tiny movement, change of expression, tightening of muscles. They were all Lance's almost invisible expressions.

They were what I clung to in the darkness.

And his overall hotness, obviously. But that was more for when I quietly put my hand into my panties late at night, imagining his body on mine, instead of in the bedroom next door.

The invisible expressions were used for much more dangerous fantasies, ones that the fishing rod and Nathan's smile were adding to.

"He looks up to you," I continued. "He thinks you're a hero. He's getting attached. He's getting used to your presence."

I paused, biting my lip, looking out the window that backed onto the yard, watching Nathan digging in the dirt with his hands.

"I think he's falling a little bit in love with you," I whispered, eyes still on the window because I was a coward. A coward who would never ever admit that *I* was falling a little bit in love with him too. I may not have protected myself against a man who hit me, bruised me and scarred me. But I had to protect myself against this man.

He'd hurt me worse than Robert ever had.

I knew that. I might have been willing to be brave and admit my feelings to Lance, or to creep into his room at night had it not been for the little boy with fists full of worms and a gentle soul.

I had to be brave in a different way. For my son. To protect him.

My eyes found Lance's. They were not hard. Indifferent. It took the breath from my lungs, that miniscule amount of emotion lurking in his irises.

"Nathan's been through so much," I said. "Too much. Far too much. I'm going to have to live with the fact that it's because of decisions I've made. It's because I didn't protect him as a mother should."

My breath hitched at the same time Lance's brows narrowed.

"I'll live with it," I continued before Lance could protest, and it looked like he was going to. "He smiles and it makes the world go away."

I smiled out the window again before I locked eyes with Lance. "And you've made him smile. *You*, his Captain America. The man who drops him off at school, the man who he's expecting to pick him up from school and who he's getting used to waking up in the same house as. The man who's gonna take him fishing." I sucked in a breath. "No matter what you say, I know that's not just you doing your job. That's something more than that. As much as I want that to continue, as much as I want my son to have someone who isn't afraid of worms and knows how to use a fishing rod take him on a boat and show him how to reel or hook or whatever, I can't have that. Not if he's going to expect you to take him next weekend and the weekend after."

I swallowed my want for that. My visceral want for my son to go fishing with Lance every weekend for the rest of forever.

"This is going to be over," I said. "I don't know when, but I know that somehow, it's going to be over. The job will be done and you will be gone. And my son won't have anyone to take him fishing and be there to show him how to replicate a badass glare. And it'll break his heart. I can't have anyone breaking my son's heart."

I swallowed the tears that were creeping up my throat, choking me. "I won't let *anyone* break my son's heart. I need to protect him. And not just from men who mean him harm, but from men, good men. Like you."

I let the words hang there in the air, heavy, horrible. I felt empty now I'd uttered them. No matter how necessary they were, I wanted to take them all back, swallow them all just so we could have more time with Lance.

But I had to be brave.

"There's another thing," I whispered. This time I wasn't strong enough to maintain eye contact, so I looked at my awesome new shoes that Rosie had bought me. "*I've* been getting used to you being here. To having another adult in the house, even if conversations are limited to a series of grunts and withering looks." I paused as my lame attempt at humor failed horribly. "I'm forgetting what you're here for. No, I'm not forgetting, I'm *pretending*, which is worse. I'm pretending you're here because this is more than your job, protecting Nathan and I. I'm pretending that we mean more to you than a mission, a paycheck, whatever. I'm pretending that you... care about us."

There it was. All of it. Spewed out onto the unfamiliar carpet in a foreign house. I wanted to empty my stomach onto this carpet, that's how sick I felt saying all of this.

I still didn't have the courage to look up at Lance, to see his face shutting down, body closing off in disgust at my delusions, at my obvious attachment to him.

So I kept staring at my feet, waiting for him to dismiss me, break my heart, or just walk right out of the house, never to be seen again.

The low thump of his boots against the carpet told me he was walking. I braced for the sound of the door, the emptiness of his exit.

But boots toed my shoes. A hand grasped my chin tightly. Almost painfully. It jerked upward, forcing my face to move, forcing my eyes to focus on Lance's face.

My stomach dropped at the intensity in his eyes. At his closeness. His touch. He hadn't been this close to me since the night I cried in his arms. Neither of us mentioned this. Or the two kisses we'd had before the fire.

Even then after those kisses, he hadn't looked at me the way he was gazing at me right now.

This was not an invisible reaction, the twitching of a finger, tightening of a jaw, the jerk of an eyebrow.

No, this was *everything*. This was Lance taking off his mask. Or at the very least, lifting it enough for me to see the man underneath.

"This is *not* pretend," he rasped, voice a razor, cutting at my emotional skin. "*We* are not pretend. I fuckin' wish it was pretend. Way I feel about you. That kid. The fact I want to rip my own skin off thinking of you hurt. Of you in danger. The fact that I can't go a fuckin' second without thinking about you when

I'm not with you. The fact I can't be without either of you for more than is absolutely necessary." The hand tightened. Expression deepened. "I wish to fuck, for your sake, that it's pretend. But it's not."

The words, the admission hit every bone in my body with the force of a bus crashing into me. There was an ugliness to it all that punctured me. Hurt me. Worse than Robert ever did. And it made me feel warm and wanted in a way that Robert never had, even in his most charming of episodes.

Lance's hand jerked, moving my face closer to his, making it so my body pressed into his. His lips were inches from mine, breath hot and minty on my face. My knees wobbled with my body's visceral reaction. As if he sensed I was about to collapse merely from his closeness, knowing that he favored minty toothpaste and that he felt something for me was a combination ruthless and beautiful enough to make me fall, his other hand fastened on my hip.

The area burned. Ached in a place to the right and south. My body wasn't just waking up from a coma. It was being resurrected from the dead, and he hadn't even frickin' kissed me yet.

He was going to kiss me. I knew that, I felt it, the thickness, the sex in the air.

Lance wasn't going to ask for permission to kiss me again. This was not a man who asked for things like this. He knew that he already owned the right to them.

Just as his lips brushed mine and my inner thighs clenched, the back door crashed open.

"I've got the worms!" a voice declared.

I jerked my head back and tried to scuttle away from Lance. He didn't let me. He let go of my chin, but his hand stayed firmly on my hip, holding me in place.

I scowled at him, the best I could through the haze I'd been put under. No matter how powerful his sexual prowess was, or how intoxicating his touch was, it wasn't going to distract me from the fact that Nathan seeing Lance and me in this position would complicate things even more.

But short of physically fighting myself away from his grip, that would likely confuse and scar Nathan even more, I couldn't move.

Nathan, to his credit, didn't even notice. To be fair, his attention was on the two fistfuls of dirt he was holding up at us, things squirming amidst the brown stuff that was dropping all over the carpet.

"I got worms," he repeated, grinning.

"I see you," Lance said, still not letting go of me even as I tried harder to move so I could stop my son from dropping dirt all over a floor that wasn't ours.

"Good work, buddy," I told Nathan, smiling. "Let me go," I hissed at Lance under my breath. "He's dropping dirt all over the floor."

"Yeah, and I'll clean it up," he murmured. "Just wanted to hold you for a second longer."

Then he leaned into me, took a long inhale, frickin' *sniffing me*, and stepped away so he could retrieve a plastic container for Nathan to drop his fistfuls of dirt and worms into.

I didn't even have it in me to be grossed out witnessing all of this, I was too shocked and turned on at the fact that Lance had full-on smelled me and then his eyes had darkened with pure sexual hunger afterward.

Then he left.

Got a container for the worms.

Cleaned up the dirt.

Took my son fishing.

And I spent the entire afternoon trying to recover from what just happened.

Spent the entire afternoon coming to the conclusion that I'd never recover from Lance.

NATHAN CAUGHT A FISH.

I knew this, because he brought it 'home' in a brown paper bag, along with the biggest grin I'd seen on my son's face in recorded memory.

It was safe to say he liked Lance's version of church.

I liked it too, especially when Lance ordered me to "sit my ass down and keep reading" while he cooked up the fish.

It was the most delicious thing I'd ever tasted.

And I only half tasted it, since I spent most of the meal sneaking glances at Lance, sensing the change in the air. In us. He was here to stay.

He was taking my son fishing and cooking us dinners.

He was here to stay.

It scared me.

Excited me.

Enough so my hands were shaking as I read Nathan his story that night.

They continued shaking as I put the book away in his new shelf full of books donated, gifted, and handed down from our family and friends.

Lance was waiting for me in the living room.

He was standing in the middle of it.

Not sitting, relaxing, with a bottle of wine open and Barry Manilow playing, ready to seduce me.

He'd already seduced me.

In a complicated, cruel and intense way.

"I've got to go," he said before I could speak.

I blinked. "You've got to go," I repeated.

He nodded once. "Got a job. Urgent. Wouldn't take anything less than that. Wouldn't leave you if it wasn't only me that could do it. But I've got to." He paused, jaw tight as he looked out the window. "Duke's outside. He's gonna hang out. Crash if it takes all night."

"All night?" I repeated, obviously turning into a braindead parrot.

Another nod.

"Is it, are you..." I trailed off, trying to process. "Are you going to be in danger?"

This was Lance's turn to blink, obviously not expecting this response. "Be safer than I am standing right here," he growled.

Growled.

And then he crossed the room, grabbed me by the back of the neck.

Kissed me.

Then he left.

CHAPTER TWENTY

LANCE WAS RIGHT.

He was gone all night.

Duke slept on the sofa.

He was still there when Nathan and I got up in the morning. Lance was there too.

But we couldn't exactly have any kind of interaction with a five-year-old boy and a thirty-year-old badass sitting at the breakfast table with us.

Lance was dropping Nathan off at school. Duke was trailing me to work.

That had been decided at some point before I woke up.

That pissed me right off.

Of course, I didn't say anything, just glared at Lance and did my level best to go out of my way to be super sweet to Duke.

It was safe to say that Lance did not like that.

At all.

I should have felt a sick satisfaction at this, for the emotional wringer he'd put me through since last night, since the moment I met him.

I didn't.

The only satisfaction I'd feel was with Lance's lips on mine and his cock inside me.

That was for certain.

And I was definitely sick.

LANCE WAS at the house when I got home from work.

Mowing the lawn.

Shirtless.

I almost walked into the front door gawking at him.

It was embarrassing.

So I hid in the small room at the back of the house, doing laundry, folding and washing until the mower turned off, the front door opened and closed and the shower turned on. Then I had to lock myself in my bedroom so I didn't barge into the bathroom and assault a naked and wet Lance.

Why did Nathan choose to play little kid's football? Why did it exist? And why did Marie insist on taking him back to her place after practice, so I could have 'a break?'

This was not a break.

This was torture.

I waited until the shower turned off and enough time had passed for Lance to be dressed and decent and then I walked into the living room.

He looked up from his phone the second I entered.

"We need to talk," Lance said, voice tight.

I nodded. "You bet your tight ass we do."

Lance leaned back ever so slightly blinking slowly once. This was his version of surprise. It was subtle but I promised myself that I'd tried my hardest to make him look this way as often as possible.

Granted, I just made that promise at this very moment, but whatever.

I took the small pause and worked it to my advantage. "You disappeared for a *week*," I snapped, though it was kind of late to make accusations like this, I was sick of all of this dancing around.

"After that kiss." My entire body did an internal shudder. "Then, last night, you kissed me again, and *just left*."

Something happened with Lance with the mention of the kiss. His entire body tightened, as did his expression. He was closing off, his shields going up, he was using all his badass weapons to tell me to back off without saying a word.

The skin at the back of my neck prickled, almost all of my survival instincts telling me to take heed of the nonverbal warning.

"The kiss was a mistake," he all but growled when it became apparent he wasn't scaring me away with his usual badass weapons.

I jutted up my chin in defiance to the cold words, maybe to hide a little of the hurt that came from them. "No, it wasn't," I gritted out.

"You're too young."

I laughed. He was grasping at straws now, which boded well for me. And the fact he was still standing here. Lance was not a man who stayed somewhere he didn't want to be to preserve someone's feelings. This was a man who protected me, my son, who protected people's lives on a daily basis, but he didn't protect people's feelings.

Not even mine.

"You find me a woman who is forced to be a single mother, at any age, you make her bring up a kid, try to make sure they're fed, clothed and housed. Also trying to make sure they are the same. This life with Nathan has given me so many things. But one thing it's taken is any youth. No mother is young." My words were a challenge. A dare, for him to try to argue with me.

I knew he was older. It was kind of obvious, not just with the years, the lifetime behind his eyes. But the small wrinkles at the edges of his eyes that were not from smiling. The small sprinkling of salt at the edges of his pepper hair.

I would've guessed mid-thirties.

He at least had a good ten years on me. But it didn't matter. Because I was right. I didn't feel young. I felt ancient. And no way would a man my age be able to handle all the baggage I came with.

"I have shitty taste in men, or I used to," I said when he didn't speak. "But not now." I narrowed my eyes at Lance.

"I know you've got a past. A dark one. That you think ugly things about yourself. Ugly things that have you shutting out most of the world. That had you walking away after the kiss. But you came back. You pulled me out of a frickin' burning building. You saved my life. Do not fuck with me with all your 'it's for your own good, I'm a tortured badass' stuff right now. Straight up, it's not gonna work."

Again, Lance did that shock blink thing.

I was kind of impressed with myself.

"You disappeared. That's not happening again," I declared. "Whatever happens from here on out, you don't disappear without a word. Not because it hurt me, which it did. But it confused my kid. Hurt him too."

Lance flinched.

I held fast. "I'm a nice person, forgiving, I don't forgive people that hurt my kid. But the only reason I'm forgiving you is because I'm almost certain you thought you were doing him a favor just like you thought you were doing me a favor by walking away." I didn't let him speak because I was on a roll and I needed to get this all out before I choked on it. "Our home is a shambles right now. My life is. I don't need to complicate it more. But I like you."

Biggest understatement of the year.

"I feel safe with you," I continued. "*Nathan* feels safe with you. You told me that the things you did for me were selfish. All I'm asking right now, is for you to be selfish again." I didn't lower my gaze, even though his was getting so intense it was getting hard for me to stay standing. "I'm asking you to stay." My voice was little more than a whisper now. "Stay because it's your job. Stay because of your conscience. Because you want to. Because I want you to. Because Nathan wants you to. Pick a reason, I don't care which one." That was a total lie. I wanted the last three reasons to be the reason. "But just stay."

Lance had started this conversation with his hands straight at his sides, which was mostly his default posture, that or the 'universal badass', which was arms crossed over impressive pecs, legs spread slightly wider than hips, chiseled chin jutted slightly up.

His hands were not across his chest. They were fisted at his sides. Another sign I had learned to recognize as a chink in his armor.

His eyes were swimming with all sorts of things. Things I wasn't smart enough to decipher. I hadn't studied him enough yet. But I planned on getting my frickin' Ph.D. in Lance if I could.

"Okay," he said.

"Okay?" I repeated.

He nodded, it was violent, jerky, like he was mad at his decision.

I was not mad at it.

He *wanted* to stay.

Cue interior happy dance.

Something moved in his eyes.

Something that stopped my interior happy dance and turned on an entire other area between my legs.

The air turned thick. My body hummed with expectation. Of another kiss. Then something that was a lot more than a kiss.

Then, of course, Duke bowled through the door. I didn't immediately move from my spot, inches away from Lance's mouth. He didn't move either. I only knew it was Duke who bowled through the door because he cleared his throat and said, "I interrupting somethin'?" in a harsh tone I'd never heard from the man before.

I jerked back, realizing what this looked like.

Lance didn't move, only to narrow his eyes slightly at me, then a lot more at Duke.

I didn't have time to figure out what the heck had just happened because Keltan walked through the door too.

He looked between Lance and I. Then between Duke and Lance.

Then he grinned.

Lance did not grin.

Neither did Duke.

I threw up my hands. "Can we stop with the male testosterone?" I demanded. "I know Nathan isn't here right now but I don't need him soaking it in through the air when he gets home. I *like* my smiling, chatting child."

Duke stopped glaring at my words.

Lance did not.

Keltan stopped smiling, looking to Lance. "You haven't told her yet?"

Lance's eyes narrowed more. "Told you, she doesn't need to know this shit," he ground out.

"What shit?" I asked immediately.

Lance focused on me. "Shit we got handled."

I glared at him, forgetting all the fond feelings I'd been having toward him. "Does this shit have anything to do with me?"

He weathered my stare for a beat then nodded once.

"Well, then, it's shit I need to know," I said slowly.

"It's about the fire," Keltan said, eyes on Lance, as if he were a lion he just let out of the zoo and wasn't sure if he'd attack or not. "We might not be able to pin it on Robert. His alibi is watertight, his father no doubt has something to do with it. But—"

"Wait," I interrupted, the small *but* uttered strongly enough to get the attention of the men in the room. "You think that *Robert* set the fire?"

Robert wouldn't be sick enough to try and kill his son. Me, maybe. But Nathan? No. *He couldn't.*

"The fire department hasn't even come to a conclusion on what started the fire yet. And when they do, it'll be me that caused this. I just forgot to blow out a candle." There was an edge of desperation to my voice now. I was willing these men to believe that it was an accident from me rather than malicious intent from the father of my child that caused the fire.

Keltan's look was even and kind. I appreciated it that he schooled it so it wasn't full of pity. I knew the pity was there. In everyone. Of course these people pitied the woman who had her son kidnapped by an abusive ex, the woman who waitressed to make ends meet. The woman who now had nowhere to live and was at the mercy of a silent badass who'd carried her out of the fire and kissed her.

"Duke's got experience with arson," he explained, voice patient. Soft.

I looked to Duke, and despite the situation, I raised my brow, face teasing. "You a firebug in high school?" I asked, smile in my voice, if at least there wasn't one on my face.

He smiled at me. "Somethin' like that, babydoll."

Lance stiffened behind him, I wasn't sure if it was my teasing tone, Duke's smile, or the 'babydoll', maybe a combination. Regardless, he had no right to be jealous if that's what this was.

I definitely didn't have a right to feel glad about his possible jealousy.

"Duke went in this morning, before the fire department came back," Keltan continued. "Fire started in the kitchen, you burn candles in there?"

I shook my head.

"Leave the oven on?" Keltan probed.

I shook my head again.

"Front door was jammed shut," Keltan continued. "Not obviously. Something that might've been missed."

Shit. I remembered it. Not being able to open the door. How could I forget that feeling of naked panic at not having an escape from the fire?

I simply hadn't thought on it.

Or I had forced myself not to think about it.

"Guessin' he did it himself, or hired someone," Keltan continued. "Wouldn't have gone in the house. Either he knows the security system is tight, or he didn't want the risk of bein' caught inside, evidence tying him here. He was stupid enough to think that the town fire department wouldn't look into it. But we are. He knows you've got people on you, 'cause we made sure he knew. We know he's a stupid fuck, 'cause he took a woman like you, a kid like Nathan—two things he should treasure beyond all else—and he fucked that over. That's beyond stupid. Then, he took your boy. Put his hands on you. More fuckin' stupid. Colossal. He got bested by us. Realized you're not as weak as he convinced himself you were. Realized you were stronger than him all along. We know someone started this on purpose. And unless you've got some secret life we don't know about—impossible 'cause we know everything—it was him."

There was a lot said in that moment. There was information.

A shitload of it. And there was respect. Keltan respected me. He was making that clear. In his badass, hot guy way. It wasn't mushy in the slightest, but I had to bite back tears regardless.

"My ex-husband tried to burn me alive," I whispered. "My ex-husband tried to *burn my son alive*," my voice fractured on the last words.

Lance stepped forward, death glaring Duke as he tried to do the same. "Elena," he said, voice as gentle as I'd ever heard it.

I ignored this. Because there was something else happening inside me. Something breaking. Something getting stronger, I wasn't sure which. Maybe both.

I looked to Keltan. "You got a number for him?"

Keltan blinked. "Elena, I'm not sure that's a good—"

"You got a number?" I repeated.

He nodded once.

"In your phone?"

Another nod.

I held out my hand, request clear enough so I didn't need to speak. Good God, I was spending so much time around Lance, I was turning into him, with all these nonverbal, hard-faced demands.

I didn't know what he'd gone through in his life, but it was sharp, puncturing, it had sanded him down so he was all sharp edges. Life had done enough to me so I might have been hard edges too, if it hadn't given me things to make me soft. If it hadn't given me Nathan. And my son almost frickin' died. Because of a man who had tormented and abused me.

I was nothing but a sharp edge at this moment.

"Elena," Lance said, now standing so close to me, the warmth of his body made my own flush. His scent assaulted me. Both of these things, in addition to that same harsh softness to his voice would have made soft Elena little more than his slave, but I was hard Elena so I was unfazed.

"As much as I appreciate the fact you stepping in and taking care of things your way or the proverbial highway being part of your DNA, being a mother is part of mine. My son almost died. So no one is taking care of shit right now that didn't go through thirty hours of labor and suffer a broken tailbone birthing him into the world," I hissed. "Give me the phone, Keltan."

He gave me the phone.

I didn't hesitate to press call on the contact aptly named, 'Piece of Shit.'

As I put the phone to my ear, Lance's entire body got even more wired than it had been before, and he'd been pretty darn tight faced previously.

Not my problem.

Not right now at least.

I had another problem.

One that answered the phone with far too much frickin' cheer for someone that had just tried to kill his son.

"You're done," I hissed in greeting.

A beat of silence on the phone.

"What?" I spat. "Surprised that I'm calling you on the phone and not charred remains in a morgue somewhere?"

Lance flinched.

"Or that your five-year-old child isn't lying on a metal slab beside me?" I continued.

Lance flinched again.

I kept going.

"Well, we survived, asshole," I continued against the silence on the other end of the line.

"I wish I knew enough ugly words to spew at you, to call you, to make it very fucking known what a piece of garbage you are, but I don't have enough time. I don't want to waste any more oxygen on you than I already have. I just want to let you know, that before, I wasn't out to destroy you. I just wanted you to leave me alone. Even though you beat me. Continuously. Even though you broke bones. Put me in the hospital. Made me lie about it. Made me think I deserved the shit beaten out of me. Somehow convinced me that it wasn't rape when you forced yourself on me."

Another flinch.

Not just Lance.

Every man in the room.

I noted this but didn't let it stop me. A freight train wouldn't stop me. This was a tirade that was seven years coming.

"Even though you did everything to show me you are rotten to the core and deserve every horrible thing that could happen to a human, I didn't want that for you," I said. "Don't get me wrong, I'd be happy to hear about you getting a fucking hangnail, but I didn't care to be the one that made your life hell. I was too focused on making a good life for Nathan. Your *son*. The one you kidnapped for whatever warped reason that had nothing to do with love and everything to do with power. Image. I know for a fact that you don't love that boy because monsters aren't capable of that. You are a monster. And because you showed me just how deep that runs, I'm going to make it my personal mission to take you down."

He laughed, cold and bitter down the phone, the first noise he'd made. "You can try, bitch."

I smiled, even though he couldn't see it through the phone, I was glad that I did it. Because the smile wasn't for him. This phone call wasn't even for him. This was all for me.

"Oh, I'm not going to try," I said, injecting the smile into the voice that held not an inch of fear. "I'm going to do it. Because though you don't, I love my son. I love him more than anything in this world. And you may have been able to do whatever you wished to me without consequences—in this life at least—but the second my son's safety was threatened, I'm done. I'm making sure the very dangerous, talented, badass men standing around me right at this moment do everything in their considerable power to help me take you down."

My eyes looked at the badass men, landing on one in particular.

"They have real power, unlike the power you think you have," I said into the phone, eyes on Lance. "Beating up women and trying to kill children isn't power. It's the ultimate kind of weakness. And I've just figured out that asking people like these muscly, badass types for help isn't weak. It's making sure I'm using every weapon at my disposal. Be warned, fuckstick, I'm arming up and I'm not stopping until you're history."

I didn't wait for whatever venom he was about to spit, I hung up.

I focused on Keltan, who had been glaring pretty much throughout the entire phone call but was now grinning.

I handed him back his phone. "Thank you." My voice was even now. Pleasant.

He took it, shaking his head slightly. "Muscly badass type?" he asked, tone teasing.

I shrugged feeling oddly calm. "I call it like I see it."

"That you do, babe."

"Out," the single word was snarled from Lance's mouth. With enough violence and danger that I jerked slightly and turned to look at him. He was not looking at me. He was scanning the room, obviously talking to the rest of the men.

Keltan didn't seem at all threatened by the scary tone to Lance's voice, in fact, his smile widened. Like way more.

Duke wasn't exactly smiling, he looked to me with uncertainty, worry. I tried to give him a reassuring smile, but I wasn't quite sure if his worry wasn't well founded.

"I need to repeat myself?" Lance asked, quietly. He focused on Duke now, even more of a threat in his quiet tone.

Duke's shoulders tightened and his face turned dangerous.

Shit.

I did not want a fight between these two. They would take out the whole block. Like frickin' Iron Man and Captain America taking each other on.

"It's okay," I said to Duke, moving slightly between them.

Duke didn't look to me immediately but instead held his stare with Lance, likely having some kind of nonverbal communication only badasses like the two of them could decipher.

"I'll be right outside," he said to me.

"No, you won't," Lance said.

Shit.

Something about that made my stomach drop with just the littlest bit of fear but the rest of me got turned the eff on.

Duke obviously wasn't feeling that kind of way because his face got even scarier and I thought we were about to have a Greenstone version of Marvel's *Civil War* right here in this unassuming living room.

But the moment passed without an epic battle as Duke stopped glaring and walked toward the door, not before stopping to squeeze my arm. "You need me, you let me know."

There was no more scary glare, just the soft look he always had with me. I knew the offer was not to taunt Lance but more because he meant it and was just a good man. The arm squeeze might have been a little bit to piss off Lance, though, and from what I saw from the corner of my eye, it definitely worked.

I smiled at him and he smiled back, easily and warmly. Something the man behind me, close enough to press into the side of my arm.

Duke squeezed my arm gently once more before he walked out.

I admired his bravery for giving Lance his back in the state he was in. Then again, Lance wasn't exactly someone that would strike someone when their back was turned. That was more of a Robert move.

Nothing happened after the door closed behind Duke. Not immediately.

My entire body wired, heart beating through my ribs, despite the fact it had been even as I was talking to the man who'd tried to kill me and my son.

I was having trouble trying to breathe evenly, despite the fact my breath had been steady minutes ago hearing Robert's laugh.

I couldn't stand here, feeling all that with Lance's heat pressing into my arm, his presence pressing into my frickin' soul.

So I turned. "Lance—"

I didn't get anything else out, because this was when Lance pounced.

His hands went to either side of my face and he didn't waste any time yanking my mouth to his. Immediately his tongue was inside, pillaging, taking control.

I didn't think I had the ability to process something like this quite as quickly, but I responded. Immediately. With just as much ferocity as Lance was giving me. With all of the ferocity I'd refused to give Robert.

Everything that had happened this month, everything that had been piling up like sticks of dynamite.

Lance was the flame.

Frick, he was the flame *and* the dynamite.

He let out a growl at the back of this throat and his teeth grazed my lips. I responded to that growl, that small slice of pain in my lip. I responded in every way possible for a human woman to respond to something like that. And then all the impossible ones. My legs went around Lance's hips without thought, only with pure carnal need. One of his hands went to my ass, pressing me against the hardness of his jeans.

This was my time to let out a growl of my own, that I was

sure didn't sound feminine or sexy. I didn't care. I didn't care that I'd just come from a shift at work, that my hair smelled like fries or that I couldn't remember if I'd shaved my legs today, I didn't care anything but creating the much-needed friction of my pussy against Lance's denim-covered cock.

I got it. Oh, did I get it. It was very apparent that he had sufficient equipment to make sure I could get my friction. So I could get an orgasm in the next frickin' twenty seconds if this kept going.

I was going to do everything in my power to make sure that this kept going, because I needed this. I needed *him*. It wasn't until right now, seconds away from coming with all of our clothes on, that I realized just how much I needed Lance.

He obviously needed me too, if the sounds in response to my frenzied grinding were anything to go by.

The friction changed, just as my body was coiling up, preparing to orgasm purely from over the clothes grinding.

Then again, this was Lance, I was sure if he looked at me the right way, my womb would explode—in the good way, of course.

He was walking us somewhere. The bedroom, presumably. That was too far away.

I yanked my head back, my eyes met his. "I need your cock inside me. Now." My voice was a husky rasp, unrecognizable.

Lance stopped walking immediately. His entire face turned. Eyes darkened until they were an abyss, welcoming me, owning me.

With only that second of beautiful hesitation, Lance moved. Not toward the bedroom, but down. My back hit the floor and I barely noticed it, because Lance immediately started undressing me. He did it fast. There was none of that kissing every part of my body that I read about countless heroes doing in romance novels I consumed sporadically.

Because Lance wasn't a hero right now.

He wasn't going to make love to me like a hero.

He was going to fuck like a villain.

I wanted the villain.

And that's what I got.

Me, completely naked, my clothes in ruins around me, Lance, almost completely fully dressed, surging into me as soon as his cock was free from his jeans.

I came the second he settled himself inside me.

He did not stop. Did not slow down as I screamed with pleasure that melted my bones. No. He kept moving inside me. Brutally. His forehead pressed to mine, eyes open, holding mine captive in a silent command to not look away. It was the single most erotic thing in my life, having an orgasm that I'd never even known existed while staring at the eyes of a man who was unlike anything I'd ever experienced.

He didn't say a word. Not through my first orgasm. Or my second.

Or his.

Not that I'd expected him to. This was a man who used silence as the most powerful weapon in his arsenal—well, one of them anyway—so it made complete sense he used it with sex too.

But I didn't long for words from him. I didn't need them. Not with him on top of me, inside me.

I didn't need them when I ripped off the rest of his clothes and rode him a few minutes later either.

We were saying everything that needed to be said without uttering a single word.

CHAPTER TWENTY-ONE

"SO, HOW WAS IT?" Karen demanded.

I blinked at her. "What?"

"The sex."

My body jerked in surprise. "What sex?"

She rolled her eyes. "The sex you've been having all night, by the looks of it." She raised her brow as I opened my mouth to lie—badly—some more. "Honey, I know what a well-fucked woman looks like."

She had me there.

"So," she probed. "How was the sex?"

I didn't talk about my sex life with Karen. Not because I was some kind of prude. But because, until this day, I had no sex life to speak of. Karen spoke plenty about her and Eliza. Enough to make up for my lack of sex talk.

I had planned on telling her about Lance, at some point. I'd only just stumbled out of the sex haze he'd put me in. No, that was a lie, I was still firmly in the sex haze, but I was now able to form words that weren't 'more,' 'harder' or various profanities that I didn't even know that I knew.

We had obviously stopped having sex on the living room floor yesterday, gotten dressed just in time for Nathan to come barreling through the door, talking about how football was his new favorite sport and he was going to be a football-playing superhero when he grew up.

I focused on Nathan for the rest of the evening. Or tried my very best. Because Lance tortured me the entire evening. The way he ran his finger over the bare skin of my shoulder as I was cooking us dinner. He kissed the back of my neck when Nathan was doing his homework.

His hand caressed my ass as I was doing the dishes.

Yeah, torture.

And the second Nathan was in bed, asleep, we were also in bed, definitely not asleep.

I didn't even remember falling asleep.

I definitely remembered waking up, because it had been with Lance's cock inside me.

Then, after cleaning me up—we hadn't so much as had the pill conversation, other than Lance telling me he knew I was on it and that he was taking me bare, I obliged—kissing me lightly on the forehead, he left my bedroom because he knew that Nathan most likely would be coming in to wake me up.

We did not speak.

Not all morning. But there had been more sly touches. Touches that were a promise.

I had the late shift. Lance was taking Nathan to school. He kissed me when Nathan was brushing his teeth.

He kissed me goodbye and hello all at the same time.

Then, I'd stumbled down the street.

Karen had only just poured me coffee and we hadn't even been in each other's presence for longer than ten minutes. I had planned to tell her once I was caffeinated and the events had sunken in a little more.

I sipped my coffee while I contemplated how to answer her question. How was the sex? Were there enough words to describe how the sex was? Did any words even exist to do so?

I was pretty sure there weren't, and I flunked English in high school, so I didn't have it in me to even try and articulate what Lance had done to me. What I'd, in turn, done to him.

"We had sex on the floor of the living room," I said.

Karen raised her brows and then waited.

"And?" she demanded after I took another sip of my coffee instead of expanding.

"Twice," I said. "We had sex on the floor *twice*."

She grinned knowingly. "How many orgasms?"

I grinned back. "More than two."

She whistled. "Not that I can say I'm surprised, despite how firmly I am in the lesbian camp, that there is a man who just looks like he can fuck."

I nodded in agreement. "Oh, he lives up to that. He fucks like a man just let out of prison."

That was as best description as I could give it. For one, it wasn't making love with Lance, any of the five times we did it. It was *fucking*. Carnal, wild, mind-blowing fucking. And I was totally okay with that. Thinking back to how much I'd been okay with that made tender parts of me ache for more.

"So," she said, interrupting me from my thoughts. "You decided he's worth the pain."

I thought about it. About everything with Lance. About his cruelty. His coldness. His demons. About the way he moved inside me. The way he touched me. Looked at me. Protected me. How he took my son fishing. Helped him with his homework. Drove him to school.

"Yeah," I said. "It's worth the pain."

"WHY DO YOU DO IT?" Lance asked.

I looked up from where I was stitching Nathan's costume for the school play. He was a tree. As lively, funny and intelligent as my kid was, he was a crappy actor. Hence him being a tree. Thankfully he was very excited about that, because he knew how important the trees were to the world.

"Do what?" I asked. "Sew his costume? Because I don't do anything else for the school, including bake sales where I used box cake mix that contains gluten and that makes me a villain in the eyes of everyone there. I've gotta save face somehow. Even if I'm really crappy at sewing." I frowned down at the mess of fabric in my lap.

Well, this would be a tree from the future, a mutant, ravaged by global warming or the radiation of a bomb dropped by some crazy dictator.

Something ticked in Lance's jaw, his version of a smile, as I was coming to understand. A warmth spread through me. At being able to recognize that. At the fact I was sitting on the sofa, sewing my son's costume and he was returning from doing the dishes—despite the fact he'd also cooked and refused to let me even look at the sink—beer in his hands, wearing only socks, jeans, and a tee. We were far from being figured out. From being anything resembling a normal couple.

I still didn't know a thing about his past, his guards were still way up with me, and there was the tiny issue of my ex-husband trying to burn my house down and getting away with it, but I decided to ignore all of this and just enjoy the simplicity of this moment. Of it feeling almost domestic, knowing what Lance's jaw tick meant. Knowing that he'd be going to bed with me tonight, giving me one of the most intense orgasms of my life and holding me in his arms until he woke me in the morning with yet another intense orgasm.

"No, though gluten is the shit and those bitches are crazy," he said blandly.

I grinned at him, despite him calling women 'bitches.' Though he wasn't wrong, the women who gave me judgmental brow raises and whispered to each other whenever I delivered my gluten-laden box brownies to the bake sale were total bitches.

"Church," he continued, not moving to sit by me on the sofa as I so longed him to, he leaned on the doorjamb.

"Your life has been one big example of why God doesn't exist," he said, eyes on me with an intensity that I would never get used to. I hope I got the chance to never get used to it. "You deserved a life of ease. No way would a god on this earth or another let that shit happen to one of the most beautiful people I've ever seen." His eyes went far away. "I've known the ugliest of shit in the world. Everything I've experienced has served as proof there is no higher being. Suffering that is needless and cruel. Most of which you've endured and yet you still put on a beautiful dress and take you and your son to church every Sunday." He paused. "Why?"

I put down the sewing, mostly because I was about to stab myself in the finger if I tried to keep going after Lance laid all that on me. "Okay, so I'm going to be totally lame and quote a line from *A Walk to Remember*," I said, trying to keep the tears out of my voice because everything he'd just said was beautiful.

"Even though that movie is not at all lame and actually totally beautiful." I raised my brow at Lance in challenge for him to tease. Of course, Lance didn't tease. "Without suffering, there is no compassion," I whispered, never taking my eyes from his. "It would be very easy to believe in a godless world after everything I've been through," I said, after a very long moment. "It would be so much more comforting to me to believe in nothing rather than believe in a higher power that let everything happen to me. To let innocent people suffer every single day. I don't *want* to believe in nothing. I'm not sure if I believe in the god they preach about in our church every Sunday. I don't think there are specific ways you should be in order for that god to love you. But I believe in what church teaches people."

I paused. "Well, some of it, at least," I corrected. "It promotes kindness, patience, generosity. I want to instill all of that into Nathan. I want him to have somewhere to go once a week where he is reminded of all the things that are important in life. I want that for myself too. When he's old enough to decide, I will give Nathan the choice whether he wants to continue going or not. To explore his faith. But I *never* want my son to lose faith. Because that's what's got me through. Knowing that somehow, I'm not alone. That there's a reason, a plan. That there's something tying everyone in the world together. That there's something after this."

I stopped speaking, feeling strangely vulnerable, naked. I didn't mean to share that much. Lance had a way about him, to make me naked, and not just by ripping my clothes off—though he was really frickin' good at that—but stripping me down to the bare nerve.

I shouldn't have felt so comfortable baring my soul to someone who was yet to do the same with me. But I did. I felt safe with Lance. In every way a person could. Despite my past, which should have given me pause in doing things like blindly trusting a man, I was doing it.

"Don't you?" I asked, my voice little more than a whisper. "Believe in something more than just suffering and ugliness? Don't you want to know that there is something in this world that is more powerful than us?"

He didn't answer.

So stupid, *stupid* me decided to keep on going. Because I wasn't done letting this silent, dangerous man into my life, into my heart.

"If anything, what's happened to me in my life has only made my belief stronger. Things have been bad. I don't think I deserved anything that happened to me either. But everything that happened to me in my life, what my parents did to me, made it possible for me to be vulnerable enough to a man like Robert."

I fiddled with the fabric beside me.

"I would like to think if I had a better, healthier upbringing and a family that gave a crap about me, I'd have seen right through Robert. But that's a far too dangerous of a game to play. I'm just going to say that I was given parents like I was in order to stay with a man like Robert long enough for him to give me a son. A child that I would go through insurmountable suffering for. I'd go through my life, the nightmare it was, over and over again in order to see my son smile. To smell his hair. To have him curl up against me at night when he's too stubborn to say he's tired. For the kid that loves Brussel sprouts but hates fries. He is the entire reason I believe in something bigger than myself."

Now, Lance was no longer leaning. There was no pile of sewing beside me. I wasn't even sitting on the sofa anymore. I was sitting on Lance. Straddling him, his hands on my hips, eyes on my soul.

"Who taught you how to love like that?" he asked, voice thick.

I jerked, not just because he spoke but because of the words. The gentle way they hit the air. I wasn't even sure that his mouth had been able to form anything but a rough growl.

"No one taught me how to love," I said, moving my hand to trace his jaw. It was smooth. As always. "No one needs to teach anyone how to love."

His brows furrowed, a fraction, barely visible. "You never got it, before this, how did you know how?"

I smiled, even though my insides were quaking like the San Andreas fault was rupturing. "You just do," I replied. "You don't have to be shown love to know how to give it. It's in us, all of us, even big scary badasses who talk in grunts and don't use verbs," I teased. "I think you just have to find something that's worth loving. Nature does the rest."

It was then that I figured out what nature had done for me. It had given me someone else to love.

I loved Lance.

And I was about to open my big, stupid mouth and say it, but he kissed me instead.

Then he fucked me. On the sofa.

Fucked. Not made love.

It's important to make that distinction.

"YOU NEED TO QUIT," Lance said from behind me.

I paused throwing all my crap into my purse. But I didn't look around. "Excuse me?"

Lance obviously didn't like that I wasn't making eye contact with him, or maybe he didn't like the cold bite in my tone. Whatever it was, he grabbed my hips and turned me so I was facing him.

We were in a fight.

Because I had to work. For the seventh day in a row. Lance, apparently, had counted since my foot was healed enough to walk around on all day.

I had too. But not for the same reason.

Esther and Logan were not forcing me to work seven days straight. In fact, they were arguing about it every single day I turned up. Esther did not send me home, though. Merely grumbled about stubborn women under her breath.

"Takes one to know one!" I shouted at her back.

She flipped me the bird.

I did not *want* to work seven days straight. I did not want to miss weekends with Nathan. Time with him. But I also did not want Nathan to live on the street.

The insurance was going through. Somehow they were covering almost everything. Somehow, the landlord was covering the difference. Lance had something to do with this, I was sure.

I didn't know how long insurance would take to come through. I also needed money, a lot of it, to pay Keltan, who continued to brush me off every time I mentioned starting a direct debit every time we spoke.

His receptionist even made excuses when I tried to do it through her.

I would do it.

Somehow.

Hence the seven days working.

Hence Lance and I being angry with each other.

He didn't want me working seven days straight. I didn't want him telling me when I should and shouldn't work.

So I'd gotten ready in a huff, ignoring him, until this moment where I'd been about to walk out the door and he'd informed me I needed to quit and then manhandled me so I would face him.

He let go of me so he could fold his arms over his chest, I supposed to intimidate me with his badass stance, or distract me with the way his muscles moved with the motion.

The latter worked for a second.

Until he spoke.

"That diner, you need to turn in your notice."

I straightened my spine and moved my eyes from his distracting and beautiful muscles. "You see, Lance. For all your ability to read people, to know things about people just by noticing a few tiny things, you didn't hear the warning in my tone that told you to rethink that statement."

His jaw twitched. "Oh, I heard it," he clipped. "Just don't

give a shit about it. 'Cause we both know that you're better than that place. You're worth so much more."

I skipped over the sweet part of that sentence because it was sandwiched between things that made me raging mad. And it was spoken in a cold and harsh tone, even for Lance.

"I'm better than a place that gave me a job without references or any waitressing experience?" I asked. "For the people who helped me get out of a shitty pay by the hour motel room I was renting with my infant son? A place that has made it possible for me to feed, clothe, and house that son? I don't care if you have a fancy shiny office or fancy shiny SUVs that you think add up to something more. But I'm not better than all of that. I'm not worth more than that. Because that diner, the people, what it gave me, it's fucking *priceless*," I hissed. "Furthermore, the very fact that you think you have the authority to do things like tell me to quit my job because it doesn't measure up to your standards, or maybe because you're too embarrassed to have a..." I trailed off, snatching the word 'girlfriend' off my tongue before I uttered it. Because it felt wrong. Presumptuous. Also lacking. "A whatever I am as a waitress, that's *your* problem. Not mine."

His eyes went scary dark at the last part, even with me being used to his glares and silent violence, I stepped back, just a little.

And then a lot more when he advanced on me.

My back hit the wall and he boxed me in with the arms I'd been admiring a handful of minutes ago.

"I am not embarrassed to call a woman of mine who worked her fuckin' ass off to provide for her son," he hissed, anger frightening and invigorating all at the same time.

"Who starved herself so her son could eat." His hand trailed down the side of my body, brushing my breast so I let out a rough gasp.

"Who deprived herself of the life she was meant to have so her son could have his," he continued, lips almost brushing mine.

"Who constantly smiled and laughed even though she had every fucking reason in the world to break down." He leaned back so my eyes met his. "No, Elena, I'm not ashamed to call you mine." He stroked my face, in a stark juxtaposition of the violence etched in the rest of his body.

"I don't give a fuck about what you do for a job. You'll always be so much more honest, so much cleaner than me with *everything* you do. Everything you *are*. Being mine doesn't define you. But it defines *me*. It's everything to me. You're my woman."

I was his woman.

His woman.

That was so much better than girlfriend. It was weightier. More substantial.

"You're talented as fuck with your furniture shit," Lance continued, not realizing it was the first time he'd really called me his. "I'm not just sayin' that. You've got talent. Everyone knows you do. Just like everyone knows you're wasting that talent servin' people." His eyes hardened. "So you're gonna quit. And you're gonna do your furniture stuff." His voice was firm. Commanding. Like all of this was a foregone conclusion.

I took a breath. A long, fractured, painful one. Full of Lance's scent, his words, both bitter and sweet. "Okay, a lot of what you just said was beautiful. Like, put it in a script, a novel, a song kind of beautiful," I told him, my voice breathy and dreamy to bring home my point. "So beautiful that I don't feel like I'm in reality right now kind of stuff. Stuff that makes me want to forget everything else you just said to piss me off, rip all your clothes off and do beautiful filthy things to you right here on the living room floor."

Lance's eyes darkened at my words and his body moved to press against mine to show me just how much he liked that idea.

My nipples hardened. Knees weakened. My entire body

started to betray me. But my mind somehow regained control and I blinked away the near animal desire I had for Lance.

"But the stuff you said pissed me off enough to not do that," I said, hardening my gaze. "And looking at you, remembering just how good you are at sex, shows that what you said to piss me off is really frickin' bad. It's all well and good for you to tell me I'm talented, that I'm better than being a waitress, but how do you propose I feed, clothe, and house my son in the months or years it takes for me to start a business?" I asked him. "How do you expect me to take a risk like that that has no promises of success? Of a steady paycheck. The words are pretty, Lance, no matter how manly your voice is when you say them, but I don't work in pretty. I work in reality. And reality is me having very limited choices to make sure I keep my son and me out of the gutter."

Lance's eyes flickered with his residual desire that the hardness at my stomach told me was not completely gone. But there was also a hardness to his jaw that he didn't like much of what I was saying and that I wasn't jiving with the whole 'my word is law' thing that I was sure he'd worked off in the past.

"You're mine," he clipped out by answer.

I stared at him. Counted to ten like I did when Nathan spilled paint on our hardwood floor. Then I breathed in and out. "I am aware that you're not fond of speaking in complete sentences, or speaking at all for that matter, but at this juncture of the conversation, you cannot just grunt out two words as an explanation," I snapped.

"You're mine," he repeated, his words tight like he was trying to control his temper. Like *he* was the one dealing with a rogue alpha male who was making decisions about his life without thinking that they weren't his decisions to make. "That means I take care of you and Nathan. That means I'm the one to make sure you're eatin'." His eyes flickered up and down my body, heat trailing in their wake despite the fact I was pissed at him. "Both of you are eatin'. That you're living good. Not just living pretty, but beautiful. I got more than enough money to make sure that happens. To give you the time you need to make what you need. I'll take care of you."

Tears crept into the backs of my eyes with his words. With the firmness in which he said them. Lance was not a man to make empty threats or promises. He was promising to take care of Nathan and me. In a way that made it seem like he intended on sticking around for the long haul.

It was beautiful.

It was write a song, a book, a movie about it kind of beautiful.

But my life wasn't a song, a book or a movie.

My life was trusting a man who made similar promises to a girl from the gutter. I gave all my power to a different man who made those promises.

So I jerked myself out of Lance's arms.

He let me, because he was Lance and sensed I needed it.

"You need to let me take care of myself. My son. First. Do it my way. You don't get to come in and decide to have it yours. So you figure out if you can live with that."

And then, I turned around and walked out, terrified I'd come home to the reality that no, Lance could not handle that.

But I didn't.

I came home to Lance and Nathan throwing a football in the front yard. Nathan sprinted up to me, screaming about the catches he's made and that Captain was the best coach ever.

Then, Captain, the best coach ever and my man came up to me. Kissed me. Right on the mouth. In front of Nathan. The whole street. The whole world—or what it felt like to me.

"I can live with this," he murmured against my mouth.

And that was that.

I wish.

CHAPTER TWENTY-TWO

WE HAD one week after the confrontation.

One week.

Of some kind of perfect.

That wasn't at all perfect.

Because this was Lance. He was so far from perfect that he was pure broken perfection. He was cold and hot. Hard and soft. The change in our relationship definitely didn't change that about him. He didn't open up to me about the demons that didn't just lurk under his skin, they were part of him. From skin to bone. I didn't expect a mere week to make him comfortable enough to open up. To let me in.

I expected it would take a lifetime for something like that to happen. And no matter how deluded, or stupid it was for me to even think something this early, I wanted a lifetime.

It was a quick change, sure, to have Lance sleep in bed with me and for Nathan to get used to him as he was. For Nathan to see that things had changed—and the little angel barely blinked at Lance kissing me, he merely commented, very calmly, that that was how you got cooties. Lance, very calmly, responded that he was okay with cooties if they came from me.

This, of course, made me burst out laughing.

When I was finished, Lance was staring at me, and Nathan had become distracted with something on TV.

Lance stroked the side of my face, his thumb brushing my lower lip. "You got a nice laugh, baby," he murmured.

I tried not to swoon at the term of endearment that he'd been using for the past week.

"Gonna have to make sure I figure out how to hear it every day," he continued, making not swooning impossible.

He might not be opening up, but he was calling me baby, touching me with tenderness, he was making me laugh, making Nathan laugh, cooking dinner, giving me orgasms that I hadn't thought actually existed in real life. I didn't give a crap of what seemed too soon.

And that was my mistake.

I didn't have the excuse of being naïve. Robert had ensured that naivety had been beaten out of me. Instead, it was because of something Robert hadn't ever managed to beat out of me.

Hope.

I hoped that I might be given this little bit of beauty amidst all this ugly. That Nathan had been given it.

I hoped that I was maybe giving something a little bit beautiful to Lance too. That Nathan was.

I hoped that Nathan and I were enough to quietly chip away at his walls. To show him that he could have a life with us.

Maybe that's why I slipped one day. Six days into our week, when I didn't know it was the second to last day I'd get with him. I was at home. Baking cupcakes. From scratch. No box or anything.

I'd sent Lance and Nathan out for more eggs.

Nathan went because he went everywhere Lance went.

It was halfway through frosting my first batch that I realized I also needed more frosting. I called Lance to tell him this.

"Need anythin' else?" he asked, even though I was almost certain he was pushing a very large cart full of everything I could want or imagine.

"No," I said, concentrating on the frosting.

"Wine?" he probed, something resembling teasing in his voice.

I grinned. "Only if it's the five-dollar kind."

"What my woman wants, she gets," he responded. "Except that I'll be getting the thirty-dollar wine."

I rolled my eyes. "Whatever. I'm plotting ways to get you back."

A pause. "I'm really lookin' forward to seeing what you come up with, cupcake."

My breath hitched at the sex in his tone. How could he sound like that, through a phone, at the grocery store?

It should be illegal.

I took so long to answer, Lance spoke again.

"Got to go, babe, see you at home for payback," Lance said.

I swallowed.

Home.

"Okay, see you soon, love you."

It was only after I hung up did I realize what I'd done.

What I'd said.

I'd freaked out for the next twenty minutes pacing the kitchen and screwing up cupcakes until the boys came home.

My boys.

Lance did not act different. He kissed me. Hard. Despite the numerous cootie warnings. He poured my wine.

He acted like I hadn't just declared my love for him over the phone, after a week of being his woman. Nor did he act like it had scared him off.

So I relaxed. The number of orgasms and creative use of frosting after Nathan had gone to bed helped. Falling asleep in his arms helped even more.

I hoped like anyone hoped, that some kind of fairy tale was coming true.

My mistake.

At least Lance only took a week to show me that fairy tales were bullshit.

I should have thanked him for that, really.

But he didn't give me the opportunity to thank him.

He didn't give me the opportunity to say a word, in fact. Not after he'd said a whole lot of words.

It was after a wonderful day. One of the best since the fire, once of the best in recent memory.

It was unremarkable.

A Saturday.

Rosie was over with Rogue.

We were sitting outside, drinking iced tea, talking, watching Nathan play with the toddler, watching Lance paint the shit out of the fence in the back yard.

I didn't ask him to paint the fence.

Just like I didn't ask him to paint the door.

Replace the mailbox.

Do small things that made this place more of a home. Do things that weren't small at all.

Things that I thought, meant that he was staying.

But it turned out, he was doing them because he planned on leaving.

That very night. On that beautiful, unremarkable day.

Rosie had left.

Nathan was in bed.

I was coming from his bedroom to see Lance standing in the living room.

There was a duffel bag beside him.

The sight of that seemingly unassuming duffel bag chilled my blood.

My bones.

"What is that?" I asked, voice calm, even, eyes focused on the bag and then on Lance when he didn't answer me.

"I can't stay here, I can't be with you two," he said, not looking me in the eye.

My breath hitched. Loud. Like someone had hit me. It felt like that. A physical blow.

"I can't give you calm, peace," Lance continued, still looking at a spot on the wall above my head.

I laughed. Through the pain. Through the panic.

I knew he definitely wasn't expecting that since his eyes snapped to mine. "Peace is something that is lost to me whether or not you're here," I told him, my voice still strangely calm.

"I have a child, a full-time job, full-time friends, and a mind that demands a constant state of crazy. Each of those scrapes a little bit of whatever peace would've been left from my childhood, my marriage. Add them up, it's all gone, only chaos remains."

I stepped forward to reach up and cup his face. He stiffened slightly at my touch, but not as much as he would have if anyone but me had tried this. Though, no one but me actually try such a thing. "I don't want peace," I said, my voice a whisper. "I can't live in it. The world has swallowed up all my peace, and I'm glad. I want all the chaos that remains, I want all that you can give me. Don't try and use what you think I need as a flimsy excuse. If you don't want to be with me," I paused, thinking about the little human sleeping down the hall. "If this is all too much for you, I want you to tell me straight up. I'm a big girl, I'm well aware that I'm not exactly uncomplicated. I'm a single mom who works at a diner and currently has a house that is half burned down." I swallowed as the weight of all those words settled on my shoulders. Although it felt like I couldn't handle any of it, I knew that I could. That I had to. That I would, no matter what.

I straightened my shoulders. "Don't do me any favors by trying to find the right version of the 'it's not you, it's me' speech," I continued. "The truth works best with me. I can handle it."

That was a total lie. No way could I actually handle the truth if he said I was either not enough for him or that my life was too much for him, but it was a lie all women found themselves telling men at some point in their lives.

"What if *I* can't handle the truth?" he murmured. "What if I can't fucking handle the knowledge that there are two people in this world who have the power to damage me when I thought there was nothing left of me to hurt?"

It was a rhetorical question, of course. Because that's when he kissed me on the head, picked up the duffel bag and left.

I didn't say anything.

Didn't tell him to stop.

Didn't chase him.

I just collapsed.

Right there in the middle of the living room.

My knees were pressing into my chest, arms around them, hands shaking. My entire body was shaking. Tears ran in rivers down my face and I couldn't stop them. Nor could I stop the loud pathetic sobs escaping from somewhere deep inside my chest. I wanted to be sick. I wanted to smash everything around me. I wanted mostly to chase after him and beg him to come back. But my body didn't let me. So I just continued sobbing until long after he was gone.

Lance

His decision to leave was not easy. It was the hardest and most painful thing he'd ever done. And it was prompted, by all people, Rosie.

Not because she didn't want him to have some kind of ending, but because she *did*.

He knew that on reflection.

The afternoon that had been perfect. It was carved into his memory, how unnatural such contentment felt. Knowing he was gonna go to sleep with Elena, after fucking her, after feeling her pussy contract around him, with her clinging to him like a fucking clam, whispering about nothing and everything at the same time.

He'd wake up with her.

Eat her pussy or fuck her depending on how he was feeling.

They'd get up. Listen to whatever crazy dream Nathan felt like telling them about, watch him eat whatever insane thing he'd decided would taste good.

Then they'd drive him to school, with not a fuckin' second of silence. Nathan would request Lance hold his hand as they walked into school. He'd say yes, because there was no other option.

Then he'd drive with Elena to the job she still hadn't quit. They'd talk. Or maybe they wouldn't. What was certain was his hand on her thigh, feeling her warmth, her goodness.

He might grab a coffee at the diner, sit, watch her. Or get other jobs done.

A week shouldn't have been long enough to become routine. But it had. And instead of it making him feel like crawling out of his skin, it made him feel like he finally fucking fit it.

That's what he was feeling, like his skin fit and that the sun was nice and he couldn't wait to fuck Elena when Rosie left.

The fence at this place sucked. The wood was rotting in places and it stained from the sun. He was replacing the pieces that needed to be replaced, painting the pieces that didn't. Nathan had been 'helping' him for an impressively long time for a five-year-old while Rogue napped. He hadn't complained. Not once. Lance didn't think he'd ever heard the kid complain. Or pitch a fit.

He looked like he might when his mother declared it was his bath time and he had to stop helping Captain.

The name was a sock in the gut every time it came outta the kid's mouth.

It was a name he didn't deserve, but one he never wanted to stop hearing.

The kid didn't pitch a fit having to go inside. Elena had given a knowing look he felt in his cock before she herded her son inside.

He watched her do so, or more specifically, he watched her ass do so until Nathan had gone inside and she followed, presumably to make sure he was actually going into the shower and not just run the water.

Then, and only then, did he turn his attention back to the fence.

It didn't stay there for long.

"Dude, you are literally painting a picket fence white right now," a voice said from behind him.

Rosie was the only bitch who could creep up on him like that. Fuck, she was better than most men at Greenstone. And not just at creeping up on people. All of them were man enough to admit that Rosie was more hardcore at almost everything.

Growing up in an outlaw biker club had a lot to do with it. The rest was just *Rosie*.

He respected Rosie. Even *liked* her.

Right now she was irritating the fuck out of him. Because

even though she'd surprised him, he knew exactly why she was here.

Therefore he didn't look up.

"You're in a back yard filled with flowerpots and kid's toys, in the 'burbs, painting a picket fence white," she continued, leaning on the portion of the fence that wasn't done. "Up is down, white is black, Adam Lambert is straight," she continued, grinning. He didn't need to look up to know that. It was in her voice, that smile, that smugness.

As much as he was pissed the fuck off with her right now, he was glad to hear that shit in her voice. Know she was smiling with real happiness in her eyes. It had taken her, and most of the team a while to get back to that. The war with Fernandez had been rough. The blood had seeped into all of them, even if they won against the notorious head of the flesh trade.

Wars against a man like that were never won easy, or without casualties. It had been messy. Painful. Even for him, someone who didn't really feel pain, didn't really have that attachment.

So yeah, part of him was glad Rosie was smiling and joking again, the rest of him was fucked off that it was at his expense.

He kept painting.

She didn't make a move to leave.

"Of all the people who I thought would be the one to jerk you outta your shit, I didn't think it'd be a single mom who liked to read tarot cards and a kid who is arguably one of the most awesome to exist," she said. "I mean, they're both fucking amazing human beings and I already adore the fuck out of them, but with your history, I would've thought they would be the last people to puncture that titanium outer."

This, of course, made Lance snap his head upward. As Rosie had planned. And this time, no matter how well practiced he was, he couldn't keep the surprise from his face.

He knew Rosie was good. He knew she was like a fucking

dog with a bone when she got it in her head to find out shit, or kill someone who was hurting innocents. But he didn't think, amidst everything going on in that bitch's life, that she'd trouble herself to look into him. And even if she did, he'd been certain that she wouldn't have been able to find shit.

This was Rosie.

It was on him for underestimating her.

When he met her eyes, they weren't dancing with that smug happiness that had been injected into her tone before. They were saturated with pain. A knowing. Not pity, Rosie was smart enough not to look at a man like Lance with pity. Furthermore, she'd been through horrors of her own, she knew that well-meaning pity could do more damage than vicious words.

But there was a knowing that told him she knew everything, he hadn't buried his shit deep enough.

"You tell anyone?" he barked at her.

She didn't flinch at his tone. "Of course I didn't tell anyone. Do I look new?"

He didn't answer her, just clenched his jaw and started to think of new plans he would have to make to move away from Greenstone.

There was a pang to that.

He had told himself it was just a job.

He'd never been good at lying to himself. So he knew it was more than that. It was as close to a family as someone like him could ever get.

Or so he'd thought.

Now, as Rosie pointed out, he was in a back yard painting a fucking picket fence white. And the thought of leaving it behind, leaving *them* behind filled his stomach with acid.

But he'd have to. He'd made a promise to himself that if shit ever even came close to the surface, he'd be gone before the rancid truth polluted his life.

Rosie seemed to sense something in his expression. "I know that I've got beautiful full lips, but my proverbial mouth is very *very* tiny. I've got some understanding of why shit needs to stay locked down." Her eyes shimmered. "Trust me."

And fuck if he did. Him, the man who'd also promised himself that he'd never trust anyone again.

"I'm not going to hold this over your head, use it as blackmail for you to buy me an almond milk matcha every morning, in fact, I'm never going to mention it again," Rosie continued. "You have my word on that. I'm only bringing it up right now because you're painting a fence. And I am certain that Elena and Nathan are now part of my family, regardless of what happens between you all. I'm cheering for it all to turn up roses. For yet another Greenstone Security man to bite the dust. For another good woman to find her version of an ever after. But I needed you to know I know your history. I know how deep that's cut you. Killed parts of you. Important parts. And as much as it pains me, and it does, there are no words for how sorry I am about what happened to you, I'm not going to insult you by trying to find them. I know it. So I know that people who've felt the kind of pain you have and survived, they're people that deserve something beautiful." She directed her gaze to the house.

Lance's chest clenched as Rosie's words sent the past hurtling into the present. Ruining it.

"And they're beautiful," she continued, moving her gaze back to him. "You deserve that. In a perfect world. But we both know this world is ugly and cruel and unfair. I've seen enough of that. I've also seen enough damaged men and women defy the odds to give me hope for you. As much as I'm a hopeful romantic, I'm also a realist. I know there's a possibility of this ending. I really frickin' hope it doesn't. I'm also here to tell you you need to figure out quick smart whether you're gonna be here to build a fence in the front. Mow the fucking lawn. Take these two out of this shitty suburb into a beautiful house that we both know you can afford."

Lance didn't say anything about her not so subtly telling him she'd checked out his finances. It wasn't invasive now he knew she'd ripped apart his past, showing it for the falsity it was and finding the real.

"You need to figure out if that's gonna happen or if you're gonna disappear like I'm sure you've already been planning on doing since the second I told you I knew your past," Rosie said. "I'm not going to judge you for that. I get it. I really frickin' get it. But I won't get it if you fuck around here. If you be the coward I know you're not and half-ass this shit, make them feel attached and then rip yourself out of their life. Make it end bad. Hurt them. Because as I said, they're my family now. And no one hurts my family. As much as I like you and your quiet ruthless vibe, as much as my heart bleeds for the absolute shit life has given you, it's not going to stop me from ripping your dick off if you needlessly hurt that woman or that little boy. Capisce?"

Lance knew that a lot of friends, fathers, brothers or children might give a version of 'if you hurt my blank, you'll be sorry.' He also knew that almost all of them didn't have it in them to follow through on the empty threat.

This was Rosie.

She had the follow-through.

She wasn't just being metaphorical.

Though Lance was confident he could take almost any man on, kill them without thinking or guilt, he wasn't sure he could do that with Rosie. Not just because she measured up about even with him in her skills to fight.

No, because he'd shared a beer with her husband. Watched her kid grow. Seen what she added to the good in the world and what she took away in the ugly.

He could hurt a lot of people without the trouble of his

conscience. But he wouldn't be able to do it with Rosie. Which meant she would be quite literally ripping his dick off if he hurt Elena and Nathan.

It didn't matter. If he truly ever hurt the two single most precious things that had come into his life when he thought it was all but over, he wouldn't be able to live with himself anyway.

Rosie was eyeing him as if she could read his thoughts. And though Lance didn't believe in any of that bullshit that Polly spouted on the daily, he was a little shaken by the power of the woman's gaze.

She was waiting for his affirmative, to make sure her words had sunk in, her threat had landed.

He nodded once.

She nodded back. Then the ruthless look dropped from her face quickly and seamlessly replaced by the beautiful smile that distracted most men.

It was jarring, chilling really. Because the warm smile and the threatening glint in her eyes were both genuine. She was able to be warm and kind and in the next breath snap your neck if she felt you deserved it.

Dangerous, that woman.

She reached over to squeeze his shoulder. He didn't flinch from her touch, recoil from it. Something in him felt calmed. Comforted.

She left it there for a beat and then turned away, back toward the house.

Yeah, dangerous woman.

His eyes found hazel ones, staring at him across the yard.

Another dangerous woman.

One who could ruin him in even ways Rosie couldn't.

So he ruined himself.

He ruined everything now, so he didn't destroy their lives later.

CHAPTER TWENTY-THREE

Elena

WHEN A WEEK PASSED OF NOTHING, I went to Keltan. I knew that Greenstone was renting the place that Nathan and I were calling home, and according to my insurance company, would be for quite some time. Lance had declared he would "take care of it" whenever I tried to bring it up. I'd obviously tried to argue. He'd silenced me by kissing me. Or touching me. Or by being Lance.

He was not here to do any of those things.

I was going to be the one to take care of things from now on.

Which was exactly what I told Keltan over the phone regarding taking over the rent.

He'd tried to argue. Of course he did.

"Keltan, I know you're trying to be nice here," I interrupted him as he made excuses. "You have been beyond nice to me and my son. You're also a super proud, strong, badass guy that can not only take care of himself and his family but has made a business of taking care of other people," I continued. "Now, it's apparent that I can't do that. You're the reason I still have a family. Not only that, you've given me some awesome new girlfriends, your wife included. So the things you've given me are almost endless and very definitely priceless. I'm not as strong as you are, but I still have some pride. Please don't damage it by not letting me pay my way in the house that my son sleeps in. You're a nice guy. I know you wouldn't do that."

There was a long pause on the other side of the phone. A muttered curse. "I'll send you the details," he muttered.

I sagged in relief. It was a small victory, but considering all the losses I'd had lately, it was a big one. "Thank you."

"Just wanna get something clear," he said. "You are strong. One of the strongest women I've met. I'm blessed to be married and to know some fuckin' strong women too. Don't you talk about yourself like that. Also, no matter what appearances say to the contrary, I'm not strong enough to protect my family from everything. Now, given the fact I almost lost my wife 'cause of that, you know I'll die makin' sure I protect them from everything in my power. Life has a way of happening so even the strongest of us can't protect the ones we love. Just happy to be in the position where I can help you with that."

I leaned against the kitchen counter so I didn't collapse on the floor—I was only allowed to do that once—and stared out at a white fence. It taunted me. Flayed me.

I fucking hated that white fence.

I hated that I couldn't hate Lance as much as I despised that fence.

"Thanks," I said to Keltan, once I'd regained my composure.

"You hold tight, okay?" Keltan said. "We're gonna keep you safe. Keep your boy safe."

He was right.

They'd done that.

Greenstone Security kept us safe.

Just not my heart.

But that was my job to protect.

And I didn't do it.

THE GREENSTONE WOMEN had rallied around me since Lance left, none of them saying a word about his absence.

Karen had plenty of words to say about it. As did Eliza. None of them good. Granted, Eliza was the one that found me crying on the living room floor when she'd walked in, originally to steal some pie I told her I had.

She bore the brunt of my breakdown.

Karen arrived at some point too. I didn't remember much about that night.

Just the pain.

Breathing through it.

The next morning, I was resolved not to be the woman collapsing on the ground under the weight of her sorrow. I would not let misery seep into this house that was only just turning into a home.

So I put on my brave face.

Lied to my son, for the very first time, told him Lance had to go on a trip to help someone and that he'd be back soon.

I didn't have the heart to say he'd never come back.

It was not great parenting, but it was the best I had.

Nathan had been distracted enough by his new obsession with football—though five-year-olds didn't play full contact, as if that was something I'd let happen if they could—with the constant visitors we had, and with Duke, helping where he could.

Nathan was currently distracted by chasing Rogue around the garden while Rosie and I talked inside.

It was about something important, I knew that. Especially since she'd poured me wine without even asking if I wanted any.

"I've found more," Rosie said, voice gentle, eyes the same.

I braced. Because Rosie was a lot of things, and though she was kind with one of the biggest hearts I'd ever experienced, she was not what anyone would call gentle.

So I braced. Because if Rosie, of all people, thought I needed gentle, then something hard and painful was coming.

"More what?" I asked, trying to sound strong, prepared.

I took a sip of my wine to help with that.

She reached over to squeeze my hand, the one not holding a glass of wine. "More women. More survivors of that roach I refuse to call a man."

I blinked, quickly, understanding exactly what Rosie meant. What she was saying. There hadn't been much more news about Robert, apart from he was visiting his father in Virginia and they couldn't pin the fire on him. We still had a full security detail.

I clenched the stem of my wine glass even harder. "You mean it wasn't just me?" I said, my voice breaking just a little.

"No, sweetie, it wasn't just you," Rosie replied.

A tear rolled down my cheek. A symbol of pain for those women. For myself. And another one came out of shame. Hearing Rosie say that I wasn't the only woman Robert did this to gave me a sort of comfort that I wasn't entitled to.

"I'm glad," I whispered, afraid to admit the ugliness out loud, but needing to get it out of my head. "I'm glad that I'm not the only one, that it wasn't because of me being wrong, or not good enough, or whatever. It was him." I looked up at her, fear swirling in my stomach like acid. I was terrified she'd be staring at me in disgust, in judgment. But her hand squeezed mine again and there was nothing but kindness on her beautiful face.

"Does that make me a horrible person?" I asked her, already

knowing that it did. "Being glad that all these other women suffered like I did, so I'm not so alone in this?"

A tear trailed down Rosie's cheek, I watched it in wonder. Not just because not an ounce of her considerable amount of makeup moved with the liquid. No, because of the tear itself. I didn't know Rosie well, hadn't spent a whole lot of time with her to establish what was 'normal' with her. I knew her well enough that there was no such thing as normal in her life.

I was also pretty sure that she was not a woman prone to tears.

"You are not alone," she said, voice firm and eyes narrowed. Her hand squeezed mine tighter, showing just how much strength such a tiny woman had. Then again, I didn't need all the bones in my hands bruised to know that the woman in front of me was strong.

"And you are not a horrible person," she continued, her voice steel. Sure. "There are many horrible people in this world. I know many of them personally. I've seen true evil in the flesh. Inside people. That means I know true kindness. Goodness. And I know that's super fucking rare in a world of selfish, violent and nasty people. With as much evil as I've seen and known, I'm blessed enough to call some truly good people family. And that counts you. You are not a bad person for wanting to have people to share your sorrow with. You're human. That fuckstick is the monster. And we're gonna get him. Not my way, which would be cutting off his cock, battering it, deep frying in and then making him eat it like a hot dog before we let him bleed out."

I stared at her, for how detailed this plan was, and how casually she said it.

"Though I'm very sad we can't do it that way," she said. "It's smarter, and worse for him in the long run if we do this a different way." She paused. "You know how popular a cop is in prison?" she asked conversationally. "Not just a cop, but a rapist?"

I shook my head slowly.

She grinned. "Well, prison has a system, a hierarchy, like anywhere else in this world. The politics might change in different places. Who's on top. But it doesn't really change who's on the bottom. That's monsters that fuck with kids, cops, and rapists. They do not get a fun time in their state-funded vacation. In fact, their lives could be described as a 'living hell.' Which I'm pretty sure measures up to what yours was."

I chewed my lip, thinking about that, what she was saying.

"We've got three women to testify," Rosie continued.

"Three?" I repeated. "He did this to *three* other women?"

All that gladness I felt disappeared thinking about three lives ruined. Three faceless women who will have to deal with what Robert had done to them for the rest of their lives, regardless of what happened.

Rosie shook her head. "No, that's just who's willing to testify. He did this to a lot more women. Some we couldn't find, others were too scared to testify. Others had been paid off, threatened and weren't willing to do it. I'm worried that some of the ones who've disappeared he went too far with. I've got my best guy on it. Trying to find them."

I blinked at her again. "You mean you think Robert *killed* them?"

She regarded me. "You don't think he's capable of that?"

I paused. Remembered the times when he kept hitting me so hard, so constantly, I was sure he wasn't going to stop. That empty, satisfied look in his eyes seared the back of my skull. It was evil.

"Yes," I said, my voice almost inaudible. "I do think he's capable of that."

"Take another sip," she ordered. "Wine is needed on almost every occasion, but it's medically necessary here."

I did as she commanded, because she was right. No way

could I handle all of this without the subtle softening of the edges that wine gave.

Rosie waited until I swallowed. "We've got one of the best lawyers in the country ready to roll," she continued. "They've got connections and balls that means she's not gonna be scared by whatever shit his father pulls to try and scare her off. Plus, I'm guessing like father like son, he'll be a coward. When he sees the extent of shit we have on Robert, he'll back off, try to save his own ass. I'm not going to lie to you, it's gonna suck. You're gonna have to face him in a courtroom. Recount everything he did to you. But you are going to see him locked away for life. You're going to be able to be the reason why he never gets to see daylight again. That he's raped by a man called 'Big Earl' on the daily." She grinned. "You're going to be able to fight back. Even better, you're going to be able to win."

I couldn't help but take on some of her smile. The prospect of being in court, of having to say out loud, to a room full of strangers, what he did to me, it filled my stomach with bile. But the prospect of showing him that he didn't break me, showing him that I was stronger than he thought, being part of the reason why he was punished for a multitude of sins, it was tempting.

But there were realities to think about. Realities that were rushing in.

"I can't afford a lawyer," I told her. "I'm already going to be spending the rest of my life paying off Keltan's fee, along with insurance premiums on the house." Just saying it all out loud filled me with bottomless panic.

Rosie's smile disappeared and she looked kind of scary. "Okay, that's something we've got to nip right in the bud. Keltan is rich as fuck. I know it's crass to say, but I'm sure that when people describe me, crass is somewhere in the top ten. He makes his living off rich assholes who think their spouse is cheating, who need security, or fucked off the wrong drug dealer. Beyond that, he has a super famous writer for a wife and they are in no way hurting for money. None of the Greenstone team is."

I knew that.

I knew that from the clothes they wore, vehicles they drove, the fact they all owned places in LA.

Rosie was still narrowing her eyes at me. "They didn't do this because they want anything to help a woman get her son back," she said, looking out the window. "We're doing this because you're a part of our family. I know you're fiercely independent, that you want to stand on your own two feet. And girl, I see that, I love it and I look up to that. You're a strong woman. But you're not a stupid one."

She raised her brow at me. "Understand what an insult it would be if you even think about trying to bring up paying Keltan for this. Any of it. We're here because we want to be. I'm here because I want my kid to learn off you." She winked at me. "You wanna pay us? Get that beautiful life of yours back together. Have more parties with that mac and cheese. Make guac for me. Give your boy the life you both deserve. It's not weak to accept help, Elena."

"Okay," I whispered, looking out the window. "Okay."

I took a breath, thinking about lawyers, court testifying.

Then I looked back to Rosie.

"It was rape," I whispered.

She didn't say anything, not even when my pause after that ugly word stretched on and on. She waited.

"I've never let myself think about what it was. What was *really* happening to me. Because it was easier to think of it as sex. Like Robert did. Like he assured me it was. And I don't think at that time, I could've handled admitting to myself that along with beating me, my husband was raping me."

Tears streamed down my face.

I was happy that they were finally being shed. That I was

being cleansed with saltwater and ugly admissions. I knew if I held onto this it would kill parts of me that I could never get back.

"Because me saying no. Me crying. The pain. That was all rape," I said. "It didn't matter he was my husband. The father of my child, or I'd 'let' him do it many times before, because that's what he said. That's what it was. But it doesn't define me. It defines him. In all the worst ways."

I regarded Rosie.

"I'm ready to do it. Anything I can to take him down."

And I was.

I would do it. As much as I could alone, but with help. Without Lance.

Two Months Later

A lot could happen in two months.

Especially when every day felt like a year. Every moment like a week.

Especially when you spent every moment expecting a phone call. An explanation. Expected a knock on the door. A large figure to be waiting outside your place of work. Your son's school.

When you woke up in the middle of the night reaching for someone who wasn't there. Someone who had only been *there* for a week. It didn't build up the right, the reason to have a reaction this big and dramatic to a man leaving me. I wasn't a dramatic person. Not by any stretch of the imagination. But it was safe to say my reaction to Lance leaving me with an explanation that was thinner than my heart right now.

Nathan's was just as bad. He was confused. He was hurt. He was a sensitive being, so he saw my hurt, despite how hard I tried to hide it. So that made it all worse. When I told him I didn't know when, or if Lance was coming back, he didn't cry. Which was bad. Which was agony. Because he *wanted* to cry, I could see the wobble in his lip, the glassiness to his beautiful eyes. But he fought it. Fought it hard enough for his little hands to ball into fists and his entire body to turn stiff.

I wanted to hate Lance right then. To figure out a way to contact him, to see him so I could punch him right in the mouth for making my little boy have that reaction. But even with all of my mother's fury, I couldn't hate Lance.

I knew why he wasn't crying. Because he was trying to be strong for me. He was trying to be like Lance, his hero, the man he looked up to, and the man he'd told me, not two days before, that he wanted to be when he grew up. Of course he'd made me promise not to tell the man himself that, because he wanted to keep his cool, and that had further filled me with warmth.

Now it was pure ice. Shards of my broken heart.

I'd done my best to make this new rental look like *ours*. Few of our possessions had survived the fire, something that should have absolutely devastated me, considering everything they represented, but I felt strong enough to deal with it. Especially with Lance by my side. Or I'd tricked myself into thinking he was.

Rosie had single-handedly not just restocked my closet but managed to make it bigger than it had ever been in the past. And because she was Rosie, she did it without me being able to stop her. The first night in the house was just her getting warmed up.

Everything that she brought over was *me*. Was a style that I hadn't even realized I had. A style I hadn't been able to afford to have. Hippy but a little bit trashy. I was still a trailer park girl, after all. I'd hated all the beige that Robert had made me wear. The tailoring of it all. No skin was shown. He "didn't want everyone thinking his wife was a slut."

I didn't want anyone thinking that either. I also didn't want a beating for arguing with him. So I'd worn it. It covered the bruises well at least.

Now I had no bruises to cover and autonomy over my own wardrobe and my life, I hadn't exactly utilized it, because I was mainly in my work uniform and didn't have time or resources to go shopping. I'd usually snatch a couple of things at Walmart while getting things for Nathan. Karen and I would hit the vintage stores.

My previous closet might've *hinted* at that, but Rosie was some kind of magician to somehow see that. She was my very own fairy godmother by the looks of the small closet in the master. Nor would she hear a word about me paying her back. And for once, I didn't argue. I just thanked her and then humored her demands by doing a 'fashion show' for her, Eliza, Karen, Polly, and Nathan with every single new thing I now owned. It took over an hour. And over two bottles of wine. Uncontrollable laughter.

In a house that was within viewing distance of the blackened remains of our home. In a time where I was being protected by a man who'd made it clear he wasn't going to leave Nathan and I alone. In the midst of another man leaving Nathan and I alone when that was the last thing either of us wanted.

It was a gift bigger than some kick-ass clothes—and shoes, purses, and jewelry—it was priceless.

I told Rosie as much, near tears and maybe the tiniest bit drunk.

"Don't cry because that will make me cry and I can't do that unless it's over a kid ruining one of my purses," she demanded, her voice hard but eyes soft. She reached over to squeeze my hand. "But you need to realize that you're giving about as good as you're getting. Maybe better. I need more mom friends. Lucy, Polly, and I are pretty new at this, and it's like the blind leading the blind. I don't have a mom to call." She screwed up her face. "I'm not really sure if I want to take Mia's advice on everything. 'Cause yeah, she raised a rock star and all around amazing human being, but those two new ones are a question mark." She squeezed my hand once more before letting go. "You're a good mom. You're the mom I hope that I'm gonna be. You've got a great kid. I want to learn from you. So I'm basically bribing you with a few clothes and accessories for a lifetime of mom advice and you picking up the phone at three in the morning to listen to my kid's cough and make sure it's not pneumonia."

I smiled. It was real. Not the tight, painful ones I'd been forcing lately for my son's sake. "I will take your call at any time, and give you any advice that I can. But I'm also not a doctor, and unable to diagnose pneumonia over the phone, I feel like I need to say that for legal reasons."

She laughed. "Okay, it's a deal." There was a pause. "You can also call me whenever. You know if you need someone to listen to all the ways you feel like killing Lance. I could give you some ideas."

I bit back tears. Not that that was a change.

"Men attached to Greenstone Security are different," she continued. "I'm sure you've noticed that. And I don't mean just by the fact they're all disturbingly good looking and have impossible physiques for the kind of food they consume." She grinned quickly and the grin disappeared just as quickly.

"But they're intense," she said, voice quieter. "They all have wounds. Different ones. Deep ones. Ones that won't ever heal. Ones that cause them to make stupid decisions like Lance walking away from you because they think they're doing the right thing."

She paused for the longest I'd ever seen Rosie pause in a sentence. This was not a woman who paused. But she did.

"These men will cut themselves deeper than they've ever known to protect the women they love from hurt," she said finally, eyes meeting mine. "But that doesn't mean they're not just maniacs with emotional knives, cutting all over the place because the world has warped their vision. Lance has many more scars than most. He's cut himself deep for you. I know you didn't want that. Trust me, I know. More because I've been the one holding the emotional knife in the past. *I* was the bastard that walked away. That let my wounds, let my fear make decisions for me."

Another pause.

"What I did wasn't right," she whispered, her eyes on me but far away at the same time. "I wasn't thinking about what was right for me. I was thinking about what was right for the person I loved more than most anything in this world. None of this makes it any easier, I know. But maybe it makes it easier to understand." She squinted. "Or maybe I'm just drunk and being too much of a girl. What I'm trying to say is I'm here. We're here. And we will be long after we nail that dickhead's nuts to the wall. The Greenstone Security men are all well and good for eye candy and orgasms. But the Greenstone women are where it's at. We won't go anywhere. We've got your back, in all the ways men getting in their own way don't."

There was a promise I had complete faith in trusting.

CHAPTER TWENTY-FOUR

JUST AS QUICKLY AND smoothly as he was gone, Lance returned.

It was so ordinary I would have laughed, if, you know, my heart wasn't shattered into a million pieces by the man waiting outside the house I was well toward making a home for Nathan and me.

But he had, broken my heart, that was.

After only one single week as... whatever we were.

But that wasn't true. We were something from the start. I knew that. I could torture myself trying to argue that fact, trying to convince myself it was all in my head and I was making it into something more than it was because of my past or the situation that I'd found myself in in the present.

I didn't do that.

I tried to tell the truth, whether it was ugly or not. To my son. To my friends. Family. Most importantly, to myself. It was something I promised myself to do about a year after I left Robert. A year of sorting through the mess of feelings and trauma that he'd left me with. Lying to people was bad. Depending on the lie, and the person you're telling it to, it could be soul destroying. Lying to yourself was worse. Ultimately, there was no one else in the world who could take care of you better than you. You had to tend to your garden, make it beautiful. Even if it was sometimes using ugly truths.

The truth of what Lance and I had been wasn't ugly at all. It wasn't beautiful. There was too much damage there, on both sides. There wasn't enough knowing. Wasn't enough sharing.

But it was special.

It *could've* been something beautiful.

Entertaining lies our relationship might have made it easier to get over, but I didn't want it to be easy to get over. It shouldn't be.

So, pulling into our new driveway, with Nathan chattering about the fact that yes, he did indeed like ketchup on hamburgers and a lot of other things, so he should give ketchup on oatmeal another shot, I wasn't even close to getting over Lance.

And there he was, standing at the front frickin' door. It was only then I noticed the SUV parked at the curb. I should have been more observant. Considering the circumstances. But I wasn't.

Hence me only noticing the SUV after Nathan screeched "Captain!" at the top of his lungs and I noticed the figure at the front door and the car at the curb.

The worst part was, my very first instinct was relief. Even joy. Every knot in my muscles released. Until my brain caught up, that was. Then they all tensed up tenfold.

"Mom! Captain is back from saving the world!" Nathan yelled, pointing helpfully at the man whose shades were focused on us pulling into the driveway.

The joy in my son's voice punched me, right in the gut. It was a kind of joy that had been absent for the past two months. A five-year-old's world is small. They are still collecting experiences, deepening the well of the best and worst things that can happen to them. Nathan's had been shallow in regards to the worst things that could happen, before Robert came back into our life. Even then, he didn't gauge it as particularly traumatic, more confusing than anything else. Because his life had been so short, he didn't dwell on things for a long time, his perception of time was different. That's why kids as a whole, didn't tend to hold onto a lot of things that happened to them. They got over tantrums quickly, skinned knees. But Nathan did not get over Lance's absence quickly.

Lance had created something very big in my son's small life. So when he left, he left a huge hole.

And because he was a kid, that hole was easily filled back up again, without question, without hesitation.

That broke my freaking heart. Because as much as I loved to hear happiness in my little boy's voice, I didn't know how long it would be before it was all sucked out. I didn't know why Lance was back, how long he'd stay for. I could not promise Nathan that he'd yet again have to figure a way to live around that hole, figure out a way to pave over it. And that wasn't okay.

I parked the car. Took a breath. Grabbed my phone from my purse, shot out a quick text. Turned in my seat to face my ecstatic kid. "Nathan, when I let you out of the car, walk down the street to Aunty Karen." I glanced down at my phone as it vibrated, thanking all the gods that my friends had their phones on them constantly and that they worked from home. "She's going to meet you halfway between here and their place. She's gonna make cookies with you."

The cookie thing did not have its desired effect.

Immediately Nathan's bottom lip jutted out and his eyes watered. "But Mom, I don't wanna see Aunty Karen. I want to say hello to Captain."

I swallowed at seeing the hurt in Nathan's face, telling myself that it was for the best. "I know you do. But your mommy is telling you to go and bake cookies with Aunty Karen, so that's what you're gonna do."

Tears began forming in Nathan's eyes. "But why?"

"Because I said so," I uttered, making sure my voice was firm and not full of my own tears. Then, before he could protest any more, I unbuckled my seatbelt, got out of the car and got Nathan out.

He was not a happy camper.

As in arms folded, feet splayed, grimace in place in a very familiar stance.

"Nathan," I warned in the mom voice I very rarely had to use with my well-behaved five-year-old.

He did not heed the mom voice that usually garnered immediate obedience since my kid also hated getting in trouble. I didn't even know where he got that from, since he'd never really been 'in trouble' apart from one time he used the only expensive lipstick I owned to 'paint me a picture' on the walls. Or the time he'd used the crazy fancy cleanser Eliza and Karen got me for Christmas to make a bubble bath.

Even then, as mad as I'd been, he'd been too cute, too sorry for him to get into any real trouble. I was sure he'd grow out of this adorable trait and start acting like a little asshole.

Or he'd just start taking after the big asshole that was standing on our front stoop after a long absence.

"Don't make me count to five," I said voice tight.

Nathan stared at me and didn't move.

I gritted my teeth, both annoyed and impressed.

"One."

He blinked, his resolve starting to fail, but he held fast.

"Two."

Nathan's bottom lip began to wiggle.

"Three," I ground out, making sure that my voice was threatening, even though I had no clue about what I was supposed to do after five, it was just something I'd saw other parents have success with.

I was doubting my technique when I had to say, "Four."

But then Nathan relented.

He did that by stomping his foot, scowling at me.

"You suck," he said.

I blinked at the little human who had never said two words with that much anger directed at me—or anyone—ever. My own lip threatened to wobble, but I swallowed my hurt. I'd have to have a lot thicker skin if I was going to bring up a well-mannered kid, and I needed that thick skin in about thirty seconds when I faced Lance.

"Well, you're not being that great right now at not sucking either," I told the light of my life. I then pointed down the street at the figure who I knew was Karen walking toward us. "Go," I ordered. "Before I text Karen and tell her that naughty boys don't get any cookies."

Nathan glared at me for a second longer, until I raised my brow at him and he let out an exaggerated sigh and stomped off.

I watched him storm all the way down the street until he made it to Karen, who waved. I waved back, thinking I needed to stop by Alice's and get them a thank you for putting up with the no doubt surly five-year-old walking back to their place with her. I stared longer than I needed to, telling myself in the current circumstances, it made sense to make sure that Nathan got in the house safely.

That was lying to myself. I watched them for longer than I should have because I was a coward and I didn't feel strong enough to face Lance.

Not that it mattered whether I was strong enough. Life happened no matter how weak you felt. I knew that better than anyone.

Plus, I couldn't very well stand on my new—and hopefully

temporary—driveway forever. Lance wouldn't wait patiently on the doorstep forever. He was here for a reason, and Lance wasn't really a man to be kept waiting.

Apparently I was a woman to be kept waiting though. Without a call. Text. Smoke signal.

His gaze was on me the second I turned around and started walking toward him. I guessed it had been on me the entire time, but I had made a point to focus on my unruly child and not the unruly alpha male.

My heart was in my throat as I made it up the walk. Lance didn't move from his position, blocking the door. I couldn't run into the house and lock him out, even if I wanted to, which I really did.

But he was Lance, he would have just picked the locks. Wait, he didn't even need to. He had a key.

"Hi," he said, the very first time I'd heard him utter the greeting. Which was insane, for as many interactions we'd had and I'd seen him have with people, there should have been dozens of instances when he said the universally accepted word when first encountering someone. But he hadn't.

Until now.

He was saying hi to me. For the first time ever. After he'd saved my son. After he'd pulled me out of a burning building. After he'd been inside me. After he'd made me fall in love with him.

After he left me, when he came back, the first word he had for me was 'hi.'

Rage curled at the bottom of my stomach, coaxing itself upward. I was so freaking tempted to let it out. To scream at him for saying such a bland and mundane thing to me after he'd tortured me first with his presence, then with his absence.

I clutched my purse so hard I bet I scratched the fake leather. What I didn't do was lose my temper and blast all the ugly things at Lance that baser parts of me wanted to. Because that wasn't me. People hurt me, I didn't make it my mission to hurt them back. Maybe that made me a pushover. Whatever. I couldn't hold onto anger for things other people did to me. That just meant they got to hurt me twice.

"Hi," I replied, no way I was going to be able to make my voice sound happy, but I was going for neutral.

My eyes ran over his body without my control. He looked good. Obviously. He was Lance, in all forms I'd seen him, he always looked good. His crisp white tee was without a wrinkle or sweat stain, despite the temperature in the middle of the afternoon was climbing toward the hundreds.

And he was wearing frickin' *jeans*. I was in my clothes from work and was roasting from standing outside for less than five minutes. I would have been a sweaty, disgusting mess if it weren't for the fact that my car was cool and comfortable with functioning air conditioning.

Another thing to be mad at him about, the fact I couldn't feel the cooling blast of air on my face without thinking of him.

In addition to not being sweaty, like at all, he seemed bigger. His biceps were straining the hems of the tee, muscles of his arms seeming sharper, more defined. And they had been plenty defined before.

It was his face that held the biggest change. His previous sharp, clean-shaven jaw was covered in a trimmed, short, dark beard. It made him look wild. It made him look sexy as all hell. Especially when paired with his dark shades and the fact his hair had grown out a little so it curved around his neck.

I itched to run my hands through it. To feel what it would be like to kiss him with that beard. But I didn't have the right to do that. To touch him. Kiss him. He made that clear.

His shades had run over me in much the same way. With a hunger that was visible, even with the sunglasses covering his eyes. It was etched in his body. In his tight stance. The way his hands were fisted at his sides.

I wasn't sure if it was because he liked what he saw or because he didn't. I wasn't exactly at my best. I'd been working all day. I hadn't slept well the night before because I hadn't been sleeping well for the past month. I knew there were dark circles under my eyes but they were nowhere near as bad as they were when I first woke up because Rosie had stocked not only my closet, but my makeup drawer too. With all sorts of magical, beautiful and luxurious products. But the concealer was epic. It made me look halfway normal, like I wasn't falling apart.

But I was.

It was a sad thing, that it was mostly because of Lance. I'd managed to take pretty good care of myself even in the midst of the worst with Robert, especially after I'd left him.

But Lance took something too big with him. Left a huge hole that I couldn't eat around, swallowing hurt too much, so I'd dropped weight. A worrying amount, I knew. Enough for Karen and Eliza to constantly invite me for dinner and do their level best to shove food down my throat.

The same thing happened at work, Bobby changed the specials especially so they were all my favorites.

I *wanted* to eat, I didn't want my clothes to hang off me, I didn't want my friends and family to be worried about me, I didn't want my physical health to be impacted by an emotional sickness, mostly I didn't want Nathan to see this. To his credit, he hadn't noticed. Because he was a kid, and because he was working through his own hole that Lance had left.

So the work uniform I was wearing was no longer snug on the thighs or ass. Even the chest area of my top was loose.

My hair was thankfully healthier than it had ever been, thanks to more of Rosie's products that made it impossibly shiny, even piled up in a bun on top of my head that I had no idea what it looked like because I'd done it in the car on the way home, securing it with one of Nathan's pencils as my hair tie broke.

My face, despite how gaunt it looked, actually looked good. Rosie, Lucy, and Polly had all been regular visitors the past month. Lucy bought all sorts of skincare that 'didn't work for her,' Rosie came with wine so we could do face masks, Polly came out either with the kids or alone and we did yoga in the back yard that was slowly becoming my favorite place to be. Mostly because Polly always brought plants with her. I even splurged on some, since the rent Keltan was charging was significantly less than the last place, which I knew wasn't right but it seemed like I'd won some kind of battle to let me pay the rent at all. I was determined to make it feel like home, considering what little progress had been achieved on our old place. So my weekends, days off and afternoons had been spent outside, my skin deepening even more in color because of this.

That combined with the awesome skincare and new makeup I had on made me look good. Not happy, no makeup was that good.

I wasn't sure if the hunger painted on Lance's bearded face was due to my current appearance. It was more than that.

Something was between us. That couldn't be ignored. The heat in the air that would top any kind of heatwave California could have. The way my body erupted in goosebumps despite that heat. The need that started between my legs and spread throughout every limb.

It was physical, yeah sure. I knew that the sex we had wasn't normal. Wasn't sex that many people got to experience. There was an attraction there. Beyond attraction. But there was something else. The something else that made it impossible to forget Lance in the months he'd been gone, and it would be impossible to for the foreseeable future, regardless of why he was here.

"You sent Nathan away," he said after we'd stared at each

other long enough to make it uncomfortable. No way was I going to speak first. He was here, for a purpose, I assumed, it was up to him to lead the conversation.

I nodded, moving my purse on my shoulder. "I didn't want to confuse him."

Lance's body tightened even further.

"Thinking you're back only for you to leave," I continued. "I'm not letting him go through again. I *can't* watch him go through that."

I can't go through that, was what I left unsaid. Because I was going to go through it whether I thought I could handle it or not.

Lance flinched at my words.

Actually *flinched*. Like I'd struck him physically. Me alluding the pain my son went through these past months was a blow to him.

I hated that simple flinch made me immediately soften toward him. Because what I hadn't seen, what I had missed when I was cataloging his new muscles, lack of sweat and sexy beard was a sadness. Lance had carried around a sadness before. Cloaked in his empty glares, his brooding silences. It was something I could feel, something I'd itched to explore the closer we got.

But there was more now. It was a *hurt*. It was much closer to the surface. An exposed nerve. I had an instant urge to protect him. To soothe that sadness. Because this was a man much more vulnerable than he seemed.

"He won't have to," he whispered. Yes, *whispered*. Gently. Barely audible, like he didn't have the power to speak louder.

Yeah, *way more* vulnerable than he seemed.

"You won't have to," he said, louder this time. Stronger.

My body reacted to that. What sounded like a promise. An oath. I didn't trust promises. I couldn't. Every promise ever made to me had been broken. I didn't know what a kept promise sounded like. But this sure seemed like what it was meant to feel like.

"I'm not gonna leave again," he continued when it became clear I wasn't going to say anything. I was far too busy trying to keep my shit together. He swallowed visibly and some of that vulnerability I'd been thinking about flickered on his face. "If you don't send me away, that is."

I should. That was the smart decision.

The safe one.

Greenstone Security would eventually be completely out of my life in the professional sense. The case was pending and it looked like Robert was going to be spending a long time in prison. As it was, I hadn't heard a peep from him since I'd laid him out in that phone call. To be fair, Rosie had been with me when I filed a restraining order. I presumed he'd been served with it, but I didn't know.

I should have felt peace with that silence, but it didn't feel peaceful. It felt like the sky's inhale before a storm, when everything was still, quiet. A quiet so loud you braced for the destruction it would bring.

I was trying to shake off that feeling, that I was in the eye of a tornado, but here was Lance, a man that was a storm himself. A hurricane.

A normal woman stepped away from a storm. A sane one wouldn't walk right back into one.

But I stayed right where I was, still not speaking, but that was answer enough for Lance.

His shoulders sagged, slightly, as if a tiny weight had been lifted from the pile he'd been carrying. It was then he pushed his shades to the top of his head. When his eyes met mine, it was a punch in the throat. In the heart. Everything hurt and everything healed with that look. There was a nakedness to it. An agony. An honesty.

"I wasn't going to come back," he said. "I promised myself I wouldn't. Because it was the best thing for you and Nathan."

"You don't get to decide what's best for my son and me without consulting me. That's how a relationship works." I paused. "If that's what we had."

Lance's jaw went hard. "It's not what we *had*."

Pain speared through my chest.

He moved forward, slightly, moving his hand to lightly trail down my bare arm. "It's what we *have*," another whisper. "It's what I need from you. I can't live the life I did before knowing what I left behind. What I did to you. And Nathan. I was certain I didn't deserve that, even now I know I don't deserve either of you, but I need you."

The words hit all the right marks. All slotting into the places I'd left open in my fantasies of this very moment. I wanted to lean into that touch that lifted huge weights that I'd been carrying.

But then I thought of the little boy stomping his foot with a wobbling lip. And I hesitated. I knew that Lance was sincere. Whether that was naïve or not, I knew that he didn't plan on leaving. That he wanted to give this, us, a go. But I didn't know his history. The truth behind his pain. I didn't know how far that would reach, if it wouldn't stop taunting him, enough to make him leave again.

Because he was Lance, he saw my hesitation. He felt it. So he removed his hand from my arm. The loss of his touch was painful. I breathed through it. I'd have to be able to breathe through the loss of him.

Inhaling, exhaling. It's simple. You can do it. Anyone can do it, regardless of pain. You've done it through childbirth, through broken ribs, through moments in your life so horrible that you don't let yourself remember them.

My chest rose and fell.

Lance watched me breathe like it was the most fascinating

thing in the world. Like he could watch it all day. Like he was committing it to memory in preparation for my rejection.

"It's really hot out here," I said instead of telling him to leave so I could protect my son's fragile heart. So I could try and stop my own from shattering further.

He blinked, obviously expecting me to tell him something different than to point out the sweltering obvious.

"Inside is cooler," I remarked, rifling through my purse for my keys. "And we have grape Kool-Aid in the fridge. I know it sounds lame, but it's actually heaven on a day like this and we don't have beer or anything because Nathan drank it all." I looked up when there was only familiar silence coming from Lance. His face was blank. "Joking," I added. "He prefers tequila."

The corner of Lance's mouth twerked slightly and warmth spread through my insides. I retrieved my keys and Lance stepped aside in order for me to unlock the door. It occurred to me that he could have done so if he wanted, this used to be where he stayed, first alone and then with me. He didn't let himself in because maybe he didn't expect to be let in at all.

The doorstep was not large. Lance was not small. His scent compounded my senses, and even more of those weights I'd been carrying toppled off. My body loosened with that familiar scent which had been the reason I hadn't washed my sheets for three weeks.

His body brushed up against mine that made me take two tries to get the key in the lock. My own body's muscle memory kicked in and everything in my brain and mostly my uterus urged me to forget everything but the fact he hadn't been inside me for almost two months.

I managed not to jump him as we walked into the house.

Barely.

Turning around and seeing the look on his face told me he

was having similar thoughts. I clenched my inner thighs against the pure desire on the face of a man who wasn't pure at all.

We stared at each other for a long time.

He broke that stare about two seconds before I crossed the distance between us and kissed him.

Probably a good thing, I told myself as he looked around the living room.

A lot had changed.

I had been determined to keep myself as busy as possible. And considering my version of normal *was* busy, I had had exactly no time alone with my thoughts. Which was the point. When I wasn't in the garden, working, throwing footballs with Nathan, hanging with the girls, I was combing antique stores, garage sales and online sale sites. I'd managed to get an old coffee table, side table, entertainment unit, rugs. I'd sanded them down, painted them white, going for a French Country meets boho chic, with colorful throws, candles, paintings a lot of which I'd found with my bargain hunting skills, the rest gifted from everyone who'd rallied around since the fire.

I wasn't sure what Lance thought about my mish-mash of decorating styles, because he didn't look at it.

He started speaking.

Not about the decorating style.

Not asking about the Kool-Aid I promised.

But about something else entirely.

Something that changed everything.

CHAPTER TWENTY-FIVE

"IT WAS CHRISTMAS EVE," he said, the first time either of us had spoken since we entered the house.

I thought the long, tense silence was Lance's way of telling me that he wasn't talking anymore. That I had to lead it. Maybe it was just him, the strongest man I knew, finding the strength to start talking.

I never thought of that, that silent sentinel types might not be mean or scary, just unable to find the strength to tell their story.

Or maybe waiting for the right person to tell it to.

Or maybe that was just wishful thinking.

I didn't get time to ponder this because Lance was far from done, and I was hanging on his every word.

"Though it's hard to believe now, I had a normal life," he said. His voice was flat. Cold. Which meant it was his way of protecting himself against what was to come.

He laughed. I struggled not to flinch, because I knew he was affected by that. But it was hard.

That laugh.

It was cold. Ugly.

"Whatever normal is," he continued. "But in society's view of it all, I landed pretty square in the middle. I married my childhood sweetheart straight out of college, bought a house we couldn't really afford and got a job that I despised. Grilled out on the weekends. Had beers with the other husbands now and again."

He paused, as if he sensed I needed time to wrap my head around all of this. That he had been *married*. Had a *wife*. There was not enough time in the world to wrap my head around it. Mostly because I knew this story was going someplace really frickin' ugly.

It had to be.

Because the man that Lance was describing was nowhere to be seen. Not an ounce of him.

Whatever he was about to tell me was going to be bad. Bad enough that it ripped through this life he was describing without mercy, without stopping until nothing was left.

"I'm not sure if I loved her," he said. "I cared about her a great deal. She made me laugh. She was kind. We had history. Were comfortable with each other. I don't know if that all adds up to love. Marriage just seemed the logical step after we both finished college and we were still together. So we got married."

He didn't pace. Didn't move. Didn't blink as he spoke this to me. He was just recounting it, standing in the middle of the living room, as still and cold as a statue.

But his chest was moving erratically.

He was having trouble breathing.

Through the pain.

I wanted to help him. So desperately. But you couldn't help someone breathe.

"We were happy," Lance said, voice still disturbingly cold. "In whatever way people can be happy when they're not living a life that they really want. She got pregnant."

Pregnant.

I started shaking before he got any further.

Because I knew. Right then I knew. Looks I couldn't quite understand directed at Nathan. The way he was with him. The pain in his eyes when Nathan held his hand, called him Captain.

It made sense.

I didn't want to hear any more.

As a mother, I couldn't.

But I had to.

Lance had been watching me, waiting for me to breathe. He spoke when my chest started moving more evenly.

"We both wanted kids, even though I knew I shouldn't bring them into a life that didn't feel quite permanent. Quite full enough." His stare burned into mine. He was filling that hole up. With his pain.

"I reasoned that might change it all. Make the life more substantial. And it did. My son made it all lighter. Easier. Even though he cried all the time and tired us both out. We fought more, of course, as lack of sleep and all of that made new parents crazy. But we made it through and Nick settled down when he got older. Was a good kid. The best. Of course every parent thinks that." He smiled at me.

Smiled.

I'd wished for his smile for so very long.

But now I hoped I'd never see this smile again.

"Nick really was the best," he said. Voice cracking. Only slightly. Hairline fracture.

But it was there.

I held it together.

For Lance.

Because he wasn't done.

"I was working," he continued, eyes not on me but out the window. He shook his head. "I was always working then. Mortgage was more than I could afford since we got a new house, bigger one, for the sisters and brothers we planned on givin' him."

I almost lost it right there, thinking of Lance's lost future, of that big empty house. But I held it together. Lance was, under something a lot more considerable than my imagining of a lost future, he was in a lost past.

"We were overextended, 'cause Sandra wanted to stay home with the baby. I wanted her to be happy, straight up. She wanted to go back to work, we would've made that fly too. But she wanted to be a mom. Full time. Hardest job in the world, she was one of the best at it I've seen." His eyes touched mine for less than a second and I bit my tongue until I tasted blood so I didn't break down.

"No matter how good she was at it, pay was shit." He paused. "Well, the rewards were fuckin' priceless, but they didn't help with utilities, car payments, diapers. Strollers. I was drowning under it all but not enough of a man to tell anyone. Even my fuckin' parents, who would've helped out in a second. Who wanted to. Fuck—" He cut himself off, the only inclination I got that the sudden pause was from emotion was the tiny change in tenor of the curse.

He took a breath. A visible one. "Didn't want to admit that I couldn't provide for my family, 'cause I was brainwashed like the rest of them. To think struggle was normal. Those nights you stay up unable to sleep 'cause you're thinkin' of bills, credit, shit like that. I was working on Christmas Eve. My parents were staying with us for the holidays. Helping with the baby. Keeping Sandra company. She enjoyed it. We both did. My parents were good people. The best."

He had good parents.

I should be happy about that.

Lance having people to love him. Teach him love.

But I wasn't.

Because I remembered the conversation we'd had on the sofa. Him asking me how I loved like I did, like such a concept was foreign. He loved his parents. His child. His wife. He had loved them. He had known how, in the past. But something had happened. So terrible, so horrible, that it erased it all. It killed it all.

"They had me late in life, didn't think they could conceive," Lance kept speaking. "They were getting up there. We knew it. They knew it. Didn't know how many grandchildren they'd see born or grow up."

Lance's mouth twitched, not that full-on, terrible grin from before, but something more genuine, something that might've been born from real happiness.

"I reasoned quite a few, since my father's diet of steak and cigars seemed to somehow be balanced by my mother's strict vegetarianism and yoga regime. Regardless, they didn't take life for granted, didn't take family for granted. So they were with Sandra, Christmas Eve."

He looked out the window again.

Back to me.

"She was driving. They were going to a cheap diner we went to every Christmas Eve. A tradition. I was meant to be home."

A pause.

A violent one.

He ran his hand through his hair in a gesture I'd never seen him make. A common gesture that most people made daily, out of frustration, habit, whatever. Lance didn't make gestures like that.

But he was right now.

"*Fuck*, I was supposed to be driving," he hissed, tearing his hand from his hair. "But shit came up at work that was more important. I said I'd meet them there."

He paused. A lost future loaded into the silence. A tragic past was a bullet that he was about to blast through my chest. "Sandra knew how to drive in the snow. She grew up in the Rockies, for fuck's sake. We both did."

Another thing I hadn't known about the man I loved. Apart from he had a wife, a son, a family.

He grew up in Colorado.

"Truck was good," he said. "Made sure of that. Was in crippling debt because I wanted my wife and son in the safest vehicle they could be in. I wasn't there enough. Always working. We'd fought about that earlier in the day. Over the phone. But she didn't even really fight me on it. She was too tired. Tired of this being the regular. I was too. But I didn't see a way out. She didn't understand. I was the one that didn't fucking understand. Didn't understand why they all weren't at our regular table when I arrived fifteen minutes late. Why they still hadn't arrived fifteen minutes after that."

My hands started to shake at this point.

I knew where this was going.

I knew and I couldn't stop the hurt. Because it was already done. Despite the fact his cuts were still bleeding, it was done.

"No one answered the phone," he said, voice no longer blank. "I made excuses about that as I drank shitty coffee and stared at the door covered in cheap decorations. The baby got sick. Needed a diaper change. Outfit change, whatever. That's something you learn with kids, they always fuck up best laid plans. You're never on time with them. I convinced myself of that right up until the two cops walked through the front door. They knew me. Small town. Which was why they knew to find me at that diner. Tell me that my wife, son, mother, and father had all died on the scene of a wreck ten minutes away."

"Lance," I choked out, unable to fathom what he'd gone through. Unable to fathom the fact he was still standing, recounting this story.

"Need to get this out, cupcake," he said, he whispered.

With great effort, I stayed where I was, his eyes were willing me not to go to him. Then I nodded. "Okay."

"I developed ways of coping," he said, not wasting a second of silence. "Of surviving, I guess. First way to survive was to kill the man I was before. Simple enough."

I swallowed glass.

Lance kept going.

"It's not like I knew anyone in my hometown who specialized in creating new identities, but a man is desperate enough, determined enough, he figures it out. I did. Quick. Also figured out that in order to truly kill the man I had been, I had to do things that were unrecognizable. That would disgust my wife, make my parents disappointed, my son hate me. I did all those things."

"Lance, they would never hate you," I said, unable to stay silent. "*Never.*"

His eyes were cruel and vulnerable at the same time. "You don't know what I've done."

I didn't break his gaze. "I don't need to know what you've done. I know who you are."

I wanted to go to him. Needed to. The last two months, my anger, hurt. It was nothing in the face of this. But I sensed a distance. He was still in the past.

I couldn't reach him there.

He had to keep going.

"There wasn't anyone to punish," he said, his voice a whisper. "I don't know if that's what set me over the edge. The fact that there was no one for me to blame for it all. No evil. Just life."

Just life.

Fuck.

"I was weak," he admitted, something I knew he had never said out loud before, something he told himself every day. "Worse things have happened to better people and they were able to pick up. Carry on with a life where they don't turn into monsters. But that wasn't me. *Isn't* me. I couldn't find anyone to punish for ruining my life, so I decided I'd punish people who did ruin others. Found out I excelled at it. Punishing people. Killing them."

He threw these words out like weapons. I knew he was trying to scare me off, show me how ugly he was.

I jutted my chin up, refusing to turn away from him as he was trying to get me to do.

"It wasn't for a noble cause, the killing," he continued with a glint in his eye. Maybe hope. "Like everything I do in my life, it was for selfish reasons. That's why I came back. Not because it would be better for you, Nathan. But because it would be better for *me*."

"Lance," I whispered.

"Still not done, Elena," he replied.

I waited. Braced.

"I can't stand snow," he said, looking out the window at the cloudless sky. "The look of it, the feel of it, the sight of it. Everything about it covers me in the fucking *memory* of that moment. That exact moment when the door opened in the diner with the men that were about to tell me my world was destroyed and I didn't even look up from *my fucking phone*." He sounded angry now. Furious. With himself.

I wanted to tell him it wasn't his fault. None of it.

But I couldn't. Because I was a mother. I knew that if anything happened to Nathan, I would find a way to blame myself. I had done that. Nothing that anyone could say would stop that. It was an ugly truth I despised with all my soul at this moment.

"I learned ways to cope. To survive," Lance said, no longer looking out the window. "A stockbroker descending into the underworld and learning everything about death and killing would be classified as the worst way to cope, wouldn't it?"

He didn't wait for me to answer the question.

"I surrounded myself with death in order to trick myself into thinking I understood it. That I had faced it. Fuck, if I delivered it, didn't it *mean something*?" He ran his hand through his hair again.

"Seeing someone take their last breath, bein' the reason for that, it doesn't bother me. But snow. Fucking s*now* unravels me. Hence the relocation to one of the few states where I'm never gonna have to feel the bite of the worst day of my life ever again." His eyes were even on me now. "Didn't tell you all this for your pity, Elena. Didn't do it for any other reason than so you knew everything about me. Everything that's wrong and there's a lot of wrong. Almost all of me. I'm doin' this 'cause I want you. I want Nathan. There is no way I can have you, truly have you like I want unless you know it all. Unless you make the decision to let me into your life, your son's life, despite what I am. I'm not gonna change. The cut is too deep. Too permanent. Fuck, if I could, I would. For you. For Nathan. That's why I walked away in the first place, 'cause I knew I wouldn't and I wasn't gonna ask you to let a monster into your life."

"Stop," I whispered, the word a plea and a command.

He blinked, and stopped talking, obviously hearing something in my voice.

"I know monsters," I said. "I came out of one. Was raised by two. Married another one. Made an angel with a monster. I'm sure this cruel, evil world has produced so many different kinds of monsters that there's no way to truly know what one is. To define one. Because the world turns us all into different kinds of monsters. It doesn't matter. Because the kind of monster you are, it's one I'm in love with. One my son is in love with. One I know that would cut himself to the bone before he saw either of us take a scratch."

Lance jerked like I struck him with that four-letter word that had been lead in my stomach the past months.

I wanted to kiss him now.

For his arms to circle my body.

His lips to explore every part of me.

But I couldn't.

Lance was laying out his ugly truth. I had to lay out mine. Right now. So I could breathe. So we had a chance.

He expected it.

I could tell that. Because his hands were at his sides, clenched into fists. He was shaking with the effort it took for him to stay standing there.

"I need to tell you how much I hurt for you before I say anything else," I whispered. "I'm not going to tell you I'm sorry because that feels so weak. It's not enough. I know there's nothing that I can say that's enough."

There it was. Another ugly truth.

It was time for more.

"I had a husband that hurt me," I said, my voice was flat. Blank. Dead. Like his had been. "He beat me until I passed out. Until my bones broke. He raped me."

Lance flinched at this, I kept going.

"He raped me so he could hurt me inside and out, so he could hurt me in every way it was possible for a man to hurt a woman." I paused. "You hurt me worse than anyone ever has, and in my life, with my history, that's saying something."

His eyes shimmered, his entire body shook with the force of my words, his pain, guilt. A single tear trailed down his cheek and I stared, shocked into feeling something more than the numbness that had overcome me since he left.

Lance didn't even give me a moment, a second to breathe through the pain his single tear brought on. No, he just surged forward to give me more.

"I hurt you more than anyone else, I can't change that," he said, gripping my neck and forcing my eyes to glue to his. "But I'm also gonna heal you more than anyone else. I hurt you because I thought it was better than hurtin' you worse down the road when we were more attached... more—"

"We already were more," I choked out.

His grip tightened and his face moved with misery. He rested his forehead against my own, leaning into me as if he couldn't hold his own strength.

It was a huge thing when a strong person relied on you to share the load.

He leaned back to give me his eyes, the eyes that had followed me into my dreams and my nightmares every night since he'd been gone.

I drank up his gaze like it was liquid.

"You taught me how to be... something more than I was," he murmured. "Something more than I thought I was capable of. I'm not worthy of you, of Nathan. But I'll protect you from hurt, from everything I can. And everything I can't protect you from, I'll be there." He paused, there was a lifetime in that pause. The promise of a lifetime.

Tears were trailing down my own cheeks now.

"You have to earn back my trust," I said.

"I will," he promised.

"More importantly, you have to earn back my son's trust," I continued, instantly trusting his promise.

Lance winced. He knew he'd hurt Nathan, I hadn't explained how much, he hadn't seen it, but he winced at the bare *idea* of hurting my son.

That was why I was giving him the opportunity to earn both mine and Nathan's trust back, because of that wince.

And, not to be outdone, because I loved him.

"First," I said. "You have to kiss me."

The words were barely out of my mouth before he did that. And more.

He made love to me on the living room floor.

NATHAN HAD NOT HAD any kind of heart to heart with Lance when I texted Karen the all clear to bring him home.

He hadn't even hesitated to run into his arms.

Lance didn't hesitate to not only catch Nathan, but lift him up, and hold him.

I could only imagine how much pain such a simple gesture was for him. What it felt like to hold a child that adored you, that wasn't yours. Knowing you'd never hold your child. Watch them grow.

I didn't cry, as much as I wanted to, watching that moment. Mostly because Nathan was babbling on about everything Captain had missed.

Also because Karen was staring at Lance like she might try to scalp him.

I didn't blame her.

She had seen my hurt. My pain.

She was a good friend.

Family.

But, while Nathan and Lance were 'catching up,' I managed to talk her down. She must have seen something in my eyes, because she didn't yell curses at Lance when he gave her a chin lift greeting.

Then again, with what Karen and Eliza had gone through, I guessed she knew that this was never simple.

But that first night was, somehow.

With all the complicated we'd laid out, it turned simple. It turned into making dinner together. Eating together. Watching some stupid movie Nathan was obsessed with. Putting him to bed.

Putting ourselves to bed, making slow, desperate love to each other.

Complicated crept in sometime after midnight.

We weren't sleeping.

I didn't want to. I needed to soak up Lance, this reality more than I needed any kind of dream.

He was idly tracing patterns on my back, my cheek on his chest.

"I abandoned normal a long time ago," he said, breaking the silence we'd adopted.

"It was the only fuckin' way I could survive. Normal had to die so I could live. The history of normal and the possibility of a future with it. Every choice I've made in the past ten years has been to make sure I'm not even close to normal. Normal is death to me."

He moved me so he could grasp my face with a roughness that was his version of soft. "Now, I've never wanted normal more in my fuckin' life. Normal with you. Wakin' up on a Saturday morning with you, eatin' your pussy for breakfast, getting up and makin' pancakes with Nathan while you sleep in 'cause you deserve it and 'cause you won't physically be able after what I do with you."

My stomach dipped. Like all the way down. Knees quivered. Pretty much all the clichés you could think of in regards to what a hot man's words could do to a woman.

And he wasn't done.

"Fuckin' grocery shoppin' with you, arguing with you about thirty buck bottles of wine, buyin' them for you because it's actually for me, since I'm the one that gets to fuck you tipsy after you've had two glasses. Then either going to church with you and Nathan on Sunday, or takin' you fishing because I believe he needs to see two versions of worship to become a man." He paused, laid his head against mine. "Fuck, I want to teach him to be a man. Show him how to treat a woman."

Another pause. "Or another man, if that's his choice. I want to watch him grow. I want him to understand and adore his mother. I want to be a part in makin' him into the remarkable fuckin' human I know he's gonna be. I wanna be his father. In every way I can be, 'cept blood. And if you're up for it, I wanna put my baby in your belly, not because I don't think of Nathan as mine, but because I wanna watch it all from the start. I wanna be there every step of the way. I want to grow our family. I want fuckin' dirty diapers, getting up in the middle of the night. And if you don't want that, I'm more than okay with what I've got right now."

I sucked in a strangled breath as I hadn't breathed in the whole time he'd been talking. I'd been treating his words like oxygen because that's surely what they felt like.

"I do have you," he said it like a statement, like he said everything, with a force, with a power that turned me on all the time, even when it pissed me off. But there was a question there, a question in his eyes, a tiny bit of vulnerability that was just mine too.

I moved so I was fully on top of him, our naked bodies brushing.

"You have me," I told him. "You have us," I whispered. "And I want everything you just said."

He laid his lips against mine, positioned me so I could feel the hardness of him pressing against the softness of me.

"Then I'll give it to you."

I put a restraining hand on his shoulder, right before he surged into me. "How about we give it to each other?" I murmured.

He paused. "Yeah, cupcake. That sounds perfect."

CHAPTER TWENTY-SIX

LANCE DROPPED me and Nathan off the next day.

Well, he didn't drop me off.

He came into the diner with.

And Bobby was the first to declare, "Oh fuck no." When he spotted Lance, holding a cleaver, of all things.

Lance, to his credit, didn't even flinch at the angry muscled man directing fury his way while holding a cleaver.

He stopped right in front of him. Then looked to Logan, who had rounded the corner to see this. Logan was not a violent man, but he'd seen me the past two months. They all had.

He totally looked like he could brandish a cleaver too.

"A word?" Lance said, voice even, calm.

Bobby gripped the cleaver for a second longer, Lance kept eye contact. Bobby put down the cleaver. "Better be some good fucking words," he muttered as he, Lance, and Logan disappeared into the office.

I didn't know what the words were, but they definitely must've been good, considering no one was bleeding or maimed when they walked out five minutes later.

Logan was grinning.

Bobby was not.

But he looked less like he was going to hack up the man I loved with a cleaver, so that rocked.

What rocked even more, was Lance walking up to me, grabbing my hip and kissing me full on the mouth. "Have breakfast with me?" he murmured against my lips.

"We already had breakfast," I reminded him. And we did. He'd gotten donuts while I was showering.

Nathan was happy about that.

I was too.

But it had nothing to do with the donuts.

Lance's hand clutched my hip. "You need another one, baby," he said. "It's on me, fact you're twenty pounds lighter than what's healthy for you. Black mark on me. Plannin' on rectifying that. Starting now. With a second breakfast. Like the hobbits."

I raised my brow and choked down a giggle. "The hobbits?" I repeated.

He nodded.

Holy shit. I loved this guy.

Needless to say, I had a second breakfast.

"HE'S in your life now, for good?" Esther asked me as I settled on the seat beside her.

Lance was going to pick Nathan up from school, do some guy stuff with him. I had no idea what that was, but I was sure Nathan would love it.

Esther hadn't said much on the Lance subject, but I knew she had something to say, because she was Esther. Hence me coming out the back on my break when I knew she was out smoking.

"I want him to be," I said without hesitation. "He makes me

happy. Makes Nathan happy." I thought of the change in my son. The change in Lance. Their bond. It was special. Sacred. Natural.

"But?" she probed, sensing the word before I spoke it.

"I'm scared," I admitted for the first time out loud. "After everything I've been through, happiness is scary. Because life has taught me something's coming after it. Something to take it all away."

"I've learned a lot of things in my life, sweetie," she said, taking a drag of her smoke, a chesty cough following her exhale. "Almost all the things I've learned, I've learned the hard way. Despite what Disney tells us, there's no easy way to learn the things in life worth knowing, to get the things worth having. Money can't be unspent. Words can't be unsaid. Wounds can't be perfectly healed. But money can be saved. Words can be swallowed. Punches can be pulled. It's a sad thing to realize life isn't permanent." She looked outward into the empty parking lot, as if she could see her own end in the haze of her cigarette smoke amidst the sounds of her coughing. The thought chilled me.

Her wrinkled and tanned hand squeezed my own.

"But there's a silver lining knowing that life is temporary. That means that most of our situations are too. Our hardships. And I know from experience 'cause I think I've been through some of the worst a human has to go through. And we're not through. Not really. But we've realized that happiness, even temporary, is worth holding onto. So, my beautiful girl, just hold on."

I SOON DISCOVERED THAT 'GUY STUFF' was not going to a sports game, shooting wild pigs or learning torture techniques, as I half expected it to be with Lance.

No, it turns out, it was going shopping.

For football gear that Nathan would grow out of in five seconds but he loved and wore to bed.

And also, for the box that Lance had set on the table beside the glass of wine I was finishing.

He didn't say anything. Didn't make a big show of the presentation, just placed it silently on the table.

"What is this, Lance?" I whispered, looking at the box with wide eyes. My stomach was twisting with something like excitement and nerves.

It couldn't be a ring.

It was much too soon. Despite this, I didn't feel completely sick and panicked at the idea of wearing his ring, bearing his name—I was totally old-fashioned like that—and having a husband who actually *loved* me, protected me and who didn't use me as a punching bag.

And more importantly, who treated my son like the little king he was. Who would teach him how to be a man. A good one.

But it was too soon.

Irresponsible.

And the box was far too big for a ring.

Even though I definitely wasn't a woman accustomed to the finer things in life and had never bought myself any kind of jewelry that didn't come from Walmart or an outlet store, I knew what a velvet box meant.

That something sparkly and really frickin' expensive was inside. Because the *box* was nicer than anything I'd ever owned—well, before Rosie.

I didn't expect Lance to be the kind of guy that would buy a woman jewelry. Then again, I didn't expect Lance.I didn't expect him to come back after he'd left.

But he did.

He did all of that.

I should probably learn not to expect anything from Lance and just welcome everything that he gave me.

Which just happened to include whatever was inside this velvet box.

Lance didn't answer me, because despite the fact that a lot of things had changed between us, almost everything, his penchant for silence hadn't. He was a big 'actions speak louder than words' kind of guy.

I definitely didn't complain about that, since a lot of his actions ended in me having an orgasm.

This action didn't involve an orgasm. It involved him moving forward so his hands fastened against my wrist, undoing the watch there and letting it fall to the floor.

I didn't say a word, because even now, I was still affected, struck dumb by his touch. I didn't think I'd ever get used to it, to him. Lance wasn't someone you got used to. He would always make me feel like this, uncomfortable, excited, content. For as long as he was here. I really hoped that was forever.

My eyes widened when he opened the velvet box, snatching what it contained and not hesitating to fasten it around my wrist. I gaped at my old watch, lying sadly on the floor, staring at me with that fake leather strap and the scratched face.

And then my eyes went to the watch that was expertly fastened by large, capable and sexy hands. The hands and the watch were cold against my skin, cold in a good way. In the best way. The metal at my wrist sparkled against the sunlight. Or was it the diamonds? I was pretty darn sure they were diamonds. Because watches that came in fancy velvet boxes weren't made with fake diamonds. On that note, it wasn't 'metal' either. It was almost certainly gold.

Like real, legit gold.

I knew just by looking at this that it was worth more than my car. You could feel that. Even my own body, unaccustomed to wealth or nice things, it knew what was wrapped around it. It should have felt weird. Unnatural.

"You're always runnin' late," he said, stroking the back of my hand. "Didn't get you this to change that. I do not want to change a single thing about you. But I know you never have your phone anywhere near you, maybe I do wanna change that."

There was a bite to his voice that I guessed might have scared the pants off someone else. It definitely made me want to take my pants off. But it also definitely didn't scare me. Because I knew this man with the quiet menace and coiled violence would never hurt me.

"You're always lookin' down at that old, scratched thing," Lance continued, looking at the watch at our feet. "Don't want you lookin' down at somethin' like that. I want you to look down at somethin' beautiful, somethin' worthy of you wearing on your body." He paused. "Maybe I'm selfish. I wanted to put something on you that you'd look down and see me."

A tear trailed down my face and landed on the watch. The watch that was worth so much more than metal and stone.

I looked up, to eyes that were so much more than a stony gaze. I moved my hand so I could cup Lance's stubbled cheeks. "I don't need to look down at a beautiful watch to see you," I whispered. "But I'm keeping this one anyway," I added with a small smile. He rewarded me with a lightening of his eyes.

"You remember that morning when Nathan asked me where my place of worship was?" Lance asked, voice thick and odd.

I made myself pause, pretend to think, as if I hadn't memorized every moment, every word, every silence I'd had with the man who'd brought my son back to me. The man who bought us donuts. Who grilled burgers in my back yard. Who held my son's hand. Who fixed my car without asking. Who made it his life to protect us. Who pulled me out of a burning building.

The man I was in love with. He hadn't said those four words yet, but I was wearing evidence of his love for me.

"Yeah, I remember," I whispered.

"I was lying," he said. "I don't have a place of worship, fuck I had nothing to worship. I had a pocket of peace on a lake in a shitty boat. A pocket of loneliness I pretended was peace. I had nothing to worship and everything to curse. Until you. Until Nathan. Your smile is the altar I worship at." His hand moved to brush my bottom lip. His eyes fastened on it and my knees wobbled. Then his hand moved to the column of my neck. Down to my chest, right between my breasts. "Your lungs, inhaling and exhaling is what I thank god for. You are my church, Elena."

I didn't know what to do with the words. The pure happiness they spread through the core of me. The terror that mingled with it.

But then I remembered Esther's words.

So I just held on.

Two Months Later

I don't know why he did it.

I guess I'll never know.

Terrible people don't have reasons for doing terrible things. Not reasons that make sense to anyone who isn't terrible at least. What was that expression, 'some people just wanted to watch the world burn'? Then there were people, people like Robert, who didn't just want to watch the whole world burn, just strike the match on people in it.

So he struck the match on me.

Because he wanted to hurt me.

For ruining his career, presumably.

Or for testifying against him in the upcoming court case that would almost certainly see him have life in prison ten times over for various crimes that were continually being added as Rosie found more victims.

That was something he didn't do to himself, it was things he did to innocent women.

The fancy lawyer that Greenstone Security had fought against bail. But it seemed his father—who now had his own charges pending against him—still had enough friends in high places to do the lowest of deeds.

To say Lance had been angry about Robert being out on bail would be an understatement.

He smashed a chair. One, he replaced later and felt very bad about breaking. I'd understood his anger. His fear. It was the latter that had him breaking the chair, I was sure. Fear for me. For Nathan.

For a repeat of his terrible Christmas Eve ten years ago.

I had plenty of fear too, but it didn't land like it used to. Didn't crawl into the core of me. Because we had Lance. Because we had the entire team at Greenstone. And that was not something I was fighting against anymore. I welcomed it.

Lance was beyond protective for the first couple of weeks Robert was out on bail. Neither I nor Nathan went anywhere alone. Lance sat at the diner for every one of my shifts. That was of course when he wasn't sitting outside of Nathan's school. Then Duke, or Heath, or Luke was at the diner. None of them complained. Especially since they got unlimited pie.

Nothing happened.

Rosie and I speculated that Robert had finally grown some brains. *"If he'd grown balls and a dick too, he'd be on his way to a South American country right now, to disappear into the jungle and be eaten by snakes. But he's never going to do that. He's still cocky, regardless of his lack of cock or balls. He still thinks he's somehow going to get out of this."*

She was right. I knew Robert. He was an entitled asshole,

among many other things. Seeing him smug at the bail hearing was enough to show me he was deluded as well as evil. He would think he'd get out of kidnapping, assault and rape charges with five women to testify against him.

It was so very Robert.

I reasoned he wouldn't come and cause trouble for me. He'd be waiting until he won the court case. Then, I was sure, he'd try again. But that would never happen.

After the two weeks, things calmed down. Slightly. Lance was still uber protective. I didn't expect anything less. There was no such thing as too protective with Nathan.

It turned out, there was no need for Lance to sit outside of Nathan's school, for him to make sure that my kid never went to a playdate alone.

It wasn't Nathan that Robert wanted.

Not that I knew that at the time.

I was pulling into the parking lot of the diner, thinking of Lance and I's latest conversation. I had begun converting the garage of the rental into a workspace for me to work on my furniture. Rosie had gotten in touch with friends and I already had a website.

'Chaos Interiors' was the name of my business. Rosie chose it. And designed the site. And of course, it was perfect. Simple, with a touch of boho, with edge. I updated it whenever I had new stuff, and somehow, people followed it. Bought stuff.

Lance had entered the discussion of me leaving the diner, more gently than he had last time. In other words, he no longer structured it as a command, but an actual conversation.

Just like the discussions about him paying the rent, utilities and groceries had eventually gone, he won. Because he was right, if I really wanted to do this—and I did—I couldn't half-ass it. He wouldn't stand for me tiring myself like I had been lately, working at the diner and then coming home and working on furniture for hours, sometimes after Nathan had gone to bed.

Something had to give.

I wanted this.

I wanted to be something more than a waitress.

Do something I loved.

Create things.

Make broken, discarded things beautiful, show the world that broken was beautiful.

I also wanted to teach Nathan that he could be more. If he was brave enough, dedicated enough. It would take bravery to quit a job that had given me a steady paycheck for years, that ensured, no matter how lean times got, they never got dire. Sure, Lance was here, bulldozing his way through everything and distracting me with sex and pretty words so we didn't argue about him taking over the bills.

But I didn't want Nathan to remember a mother that just let a man take care of her. I wanted him to remember me as something different. I wanted him to be proud of me.

So that's why I sat in my car in the parking lot of the diner for longer than I would have. That's why I was distracted when I got out of the car, thinking of ways I could approach Logan and Esther tell them I was handing in my notice.

That was why I didn't notice Robert until he was right in my space, clutching my arm, bruising my skin and yanking me into his body.

I also hadn't expected it. It was broad daylight, the street across from the parking lot was busy, there were busboys outside the employee entrance smoking and eyes glued to their phones. Although I hadn't expected Robert to come after me, if I had, I would have thought it would have been when I was more vulnerable.

It turns out it doesn't matter where I was, he knew my ultimate vulnerability.

"Don't say a fucking word or I make sure our son doesn't make it to his sixth birthday," he hissed, breath minty and fresh as always.

Of course, my first reaction was fear. Terror. But then, my second, irrational thought was, he knows how old our son is?

My third reaction was to do exactly as he said, to do anything to save my son.

Anything.

Even if it was getting in the car with him, knowing I had a high chance of never getting out.

Lance

He was ring shopping.

Nathan was with him.

Because he wanted to teach Nathan about being a man. Show him that sometimes that was going to a jewelry shop, buying fancy shit, not because it sparkled, but because it lasted. The expensive shit was not bought by real men to show off. It was bought because they wanted it on their woman's skin forever.

Also, because he wanted his kid's opinion on the ring he was planning to slide onto his mother's finger.

Nathan was his kid.

He considered his just like Elena was his.

Not as a replacement for Nick. Never. But as something different. Something as precious.

He was planning on getting the paperwork together as soon as the shit with Hudson was sorted. As soon as the fuck was behind bars and outta their fuckin' lives. That would be soon. Thank fuck.

He had been wild when he was put out on bail. Cursed

himself for not killing him when he should. But he had been quiet. Smart. Surprising for a stupid fuck.

They'd kept tabs on him. Close fucking tabs.

Made it known that was what was happening. Hence him holing up in the McMansion, doing nothing.

He relaxed slightly after the first couple of weeks.

He would never relax completely. Not ever. Not even when the fuck was out of the picture. Because monsters didn't need to be chasing Elena or Nathan to ruin everything. Life was big enough of a monster. A slippery road. Sickness. Accidents.

Hence him not wasting time.

"I like that one." Nathan pointed at the exact ring he'd spotted when they came in.

It was Elena. A little showy, without being obvious about it. Classy. Unique. One of a kind.

He ruffled Nathan's hair. "I like it too."

Nathan looked up at Lance. "You're marrying my mommy, does that make you my daddy?"

The punch went straight to the gut. It took him a second to handle his shit to answer. He bent down so he could be eye level with that. "Is that what you want?"

Nathan thought about it. Because that's what the kid did. Considered every question, didn't answer straight away. Then he nodded slowly. "Yeah, that is what I want."

Another gut punch.

Lance kept it together.

"Good. Me too."

Nathan smiled. Big.

Right about the same time his phone rang.

And his world imploded.

"WHAT ARE you gonna say to her?" Heath asked.

They were at the offices. He'd dropped Nathan off with Karen, the second he got the call, tried to act like nothing was wrong. But she caught it. Kid caught it.

Because he couldn't rein it in. Couldn't mask his panic when he'd excelled at masking everything for a decade.

He broke all traffic laws driving to the city, on the phone to Keltan, Wire—the Sons of Templar's resident computer kid—Luke, Rosie. All of whom had nothing. Nothing but Elena's car in the parking lot of the diner and not Elena.

Nothing but Hudson's house empty.

It took Lance a few seconds to understand the words, them having been spoken in such a calm, even tone. A calm even tone didn't exist around here. It was impossible to be spoken with the chaos that was hurtling around his head.

The fucking universe.

How could anyone even think about being calm when his whole world was falling apart?

Again.

But he forced himself to swallow that chaos, that pain, that panic. It would do nothing to let it leech onto the false façade of calm that he was battling to keep on his face.

So he focused on Heath's words.

On the man himself.

He respected him. He respected all of the men. But Heath had gone through shit with his wife. Some of the worst that even Lance had ever seen. And Polly was a woman that should never have even known that kind of ugliness existed, let alone have it carved on her soul.

It was carved on Heath's too.

In a different way. In the same way a kind of pain was on Lance's.

The man had suffered through what Lance was going

through right now. He found it hard to understand that someone else had experienced a pain this big, because he didn't think the world was large enough to contain more of this. But he knew better. Knew the world always accommodated more pain.

He didn't have to answer Heath for the man to know he'd gotten his attention.

"When you first lay eyes on her, once we get her back where she belongs, what you gonna say to her?" Heath asked, still in that same, calm, reasonable voice. Like it was a forgone conclusion that Elena was coming back. That she was just out getting the fucking groceries or something. Not that she was taken by her unhinged and violent ex with nothing left to lose.

His fists clenched at his sides. As he was about to lose it, he realized what Heath was doing. He was giving him something to hold onto. Something to focus on that wasn't the fact that Elena was fuck knows where with her abusive husband.

"I'm gonna tell her I love her," he said without hesitation.

Heath nodded. "Smart opening, man."

Lance's fists stayed clenched. "She's already said it to me," he continued, remembering the way the fucking air tasted after she'd put those words out there. "She didn't mean to say it. Elena always blurts out exactly whatever's in her fucking head at the time. I never have to wonder what she's thinking."

He almost smiled at the memory of that. Then he remembered that there was no reason to smile right now. That there might not be another reason to want to smile.

"It was offhand, natural," he continued, having no idea why the fuck he was blurting all this shit out. "She didn't realize that she said it until after." He paused. "I didn't say it back. Not because I didn't. Not because I don't. But I wanted to say it after. When all this shit was in our rearview. When she didn't have that fucking shadow behind her eyes." His vision blurred. "I waited. And now I fucking don't know if I'm gonna get to tell her."

Heath moved forward, despite knowing what a dangerous move that was when Lance was like this. His hand settled on Lance's shaking shoulder.

"You're gonna get to tell her, man," he said, making a promise that he had no way of being able to keep.

Lance gritted his teeth. "Yeah," he said, sounding more sure than he really was. "She told me once, to have faith that things were gonna work out for people that deserved it." He struggled to get himself to control his emotions, control the sudden need to smash Heath's face in. To rip this whole fucking room apart with his bare hands. To rip this entire fucking world apart until he found her, until he was covered in the blood of the man that took her from him.

CHAPTER TWENTY-SEVEN

"IS Mom gonna come home soon, Captain?" Nathan asked, eyes wide and voice wobbling just a bit.

It was a punch in the fucking gut, and Lance was surprised he was able to feel new blows, he was in that much pain. But the kid who stole his heart, just like his mother had given him new pain.

Because he was trying to keep his shit locked. His fear. Pain. Five fucking years old, and he was braver than Lance himself.

He didn't know what was going on, that his father was a fucking psychopath and had kidnapped his mother, but he wasn't stupid. Elena hadn't been at home, the home she'd made for all of them. She was a ghost already, her presence everywhere and fucking nowhere.

Lance didn't lie to him when he'd asked where his mom was. He did that because of Elena.

"I never lie to him," she whispered, trailing circles on his pec with her finger. *It was after the initial court hearing, when she'd told Nathan his daddy had to go to jail because he'd done some bad things to nice people. Nathan had taken it well. Very fucking well.*

Just nodded and saying, "Yeah, he didn't seem very nice when I had my visit with him."

"I always wonder if it makes me a bad mother," she continued, her voice smaller, more vulnerable. "Telling him the truth when a lie would be easier."

His arms tightened around her and he had to stop himself from squeezing hard enough to hurt. He had to do that a lot. Stop himself from hurting her because he couldn't fucking control how much he loved her. He was broken in that way, he knew. Life with Elena would always be beautiful, but it'd be a battle. Because he didn't know how to love her right, gentle. She knew that. And she loved him anyway.

"That's what makes you a good mother," he ground out. "The best. Because you'll never do what's easier, you'll always do what's right."

And that's why he didn't lie to Nathan.

"I don't know, buddy," he said honestly. "But I promise you I'm gonna find her. And you know that men never break their promises."

Nathan nodded. "I know, Captain."

He trusted him, that kid. He trusted Lance so completely, with a purity he didn't deserve. A dedication he didn't deserve. But he'd work to earn it. He'd keep his promise. He'd get Elena back, for the both of them.

He crouched down so he was eye to eye with Nathan, who was sitting on the same sofa his mom had been in waiting for him in the Greenstone Security offices. Fucking full circle.

Karen and Eliza had been against him coming here, telling him it would be better for him to be in his own surroundings.

It probably would be.

But Lance wanted him close.

To her credit, although her eyes narrowed, Eliza had

conceded, her and Karen in the kitchen preparing supper for Nathan.

"But she'll be back, right?" Nathan asked him.

"Yeah," Lance ground out. "She'll be back."

Nathan nodded. "Okay."

Lance got his strength then. From a five-year-old. From the woman he loved. The woman he would be getting back. Whatever it took.

Elena

Robert had lost it.

That much was very clear.

But I didn't think he ever had anything to lose. He was just excellent at pretending.

Pretending to be human.

"If you'd just let me have the kid, if you'd just come back and didn't act like a total cunt, then we wouldn't be here, I wouldn't be here," he hissed. "We'd be a family."

I glared at him. "We were *never* a family."

That got me another backhand.

The sting reverberated through my skull but it wasn't as effective as I knew Robert wanted it to be, because he was focusing on the road.

It was getting darker now.

That was a good thing.

It meant a lot of time had passed. I wasn't sure how long Robert had been driving around with me drugged in the seat beside him, or if he'd taken me somewhere. It had been light when he took me.

Nathan would be out of school. I wasn't there to pick him up. But Lance would have been. He would've known something happened. Logan and Esther would have called him as soon as I didn't turn up for my shift, with my car in the parking lot. He would pick up Nathan, keep him safe. Robert had used an easy lie to get me to go with him. But I was okay with that. I'd never be more okay with a lie in my life. Nathan was safe. He was safe.

I had to chant that.

Because it became clear that Robert didn't have Nathan when I got in the car. When he rattled on about "Greenstone Security fucks keeping me from my son." That was before he'd plunged a syringe into my neck, when I was still conscious.

It was then I got it. He'd used the weapon he knew would shatter me, without lifting a finger. He couldn't get to Nathan. We'd protected him. Lance protected him.

And Lance would find me. I would try to escape if I could, I would fight. But I was cuffed, still struggling with the aftereffects of whatever he'd injected into my body. I couldn't move my hands properly, or my legs. I guessed that was the point.

"You've changed," Robert said, slowing so he could pull into a parking lot. I couldn't move my head to see where we were. "That fucker has changed you. You're not going to be a good wife anymore. A good mother. I can't change you back. But I can get you back for what you did to me."

"What *I* did to *you*?" I laughed, it was weird and slurred but I got my point across. "You're insane."

He smiled, it was unnerving. This whole situation was unnerving. But the smile, it was empty, unhinged, the face of a man watching things burn.

"Remember our first date, honey?" he asked instead of lashing out with the insult that I expected him to. "You were trying so hard not to look like the white trash whore you were, we had a nice dinner, then we came out here where you let me put my hand up your cunt, showing me what a whore you were."

I did remember. I remembered not having anything nice enough to wear to the restaurant he took me to, so I wore a secondhand dress that was two sizes too small and didn't go with the décor. I remembered the compliments, the smiles. The nice guy. Then we came out to a wharf that was Robert's 'secret place' that somehow no one had ever found because it was in a strange spot, outside of the city and not worth most people's time.

We'd sat on a wharf we had to ourselves and watched the sunset.

And I had let him inside. Because he'd kissed me sweetly. Made all sorts of promises. Because I didn't know my worth, so I attached it to those kisses and promises.

"I thought this is the best place to take you," he said. "It's my secret place after all. The place where you became mine. Where you'll always be mine."

He turned off the truck then and got out. I willed my hands to move, despite the fact they were in cuffs. They were in front of me, I could see them, limp and red, blood trickling from where the skin scraped off against metal.

I could wiggle my toes. Slightly. Not enough.

The door opened and I fell, right onto the concrete, without my hands to break my fall, my head took most of the impact. The pain was blinding and immediate.

Warmth trickled down my face, obscuring my vision as a figure stood above me.

I couldn't see his face, but I knew what the expression would be, the same expression he always wore when he hurt me.

Then I was up, limp in his arms, though my brain was screaming at my limbs to work, to fight.

They did neither. So I was helpless as he walked us down the dock.

It was then I knew exactly what he was doing. What the purpose was here.

It was always going to be the endgame with Robert. He

wasn't done with me. No, not with the white trash whore who'd bested him. He was done when I stopped breathing.

"They're going to find you," I said, desperate to use whatever I could to stall him. Until Lance came.

Even though we were in a place that no one knew about. Even though Robert hadn't used a cell phone that I saw, even though this car was most likely stolen and not traceable.

He'd find a way.

He was a superhero after all.

"You're not going to get away with this, whatever happens to me," I hissed as the end of the dock approached.

"I know," Robert said, surprising me with his lack of delusions of victory. "But that's okay, I'll be okay knowing I'm breathing and you're not."

We stopped.

At the end of the wharf.

I knew the water wasn't that deep. Robert and I had gone swimming here before. He'd dunked me playfully, but had kept me under for too long, so I panicked and almost passed out.

That should have been a sign.

But you could dive down to touch the bottom.

"Almost impossible to drown in," Robert had joked after he'd almost drowned me.

But nothing was impossible.

Especially when you were handcuffed and none of your limbs worked.

Fear clutched my throat at how helpless I was. Robert had my life in his hands.

"And you know the last thing you're gonna taste before you die?" he asked, squeezing me tight and moving me so my face was by the shadow of his. "Me," he snarled.

Then he kissed me, brutal, sloppy, invading. His tongue

slipped in and I didn't hesitate to sink my teeth in, biting as hard as I could.

His body jerked and he let out a moan of pain, ripping his lips from mine. I tasted his blood in my mouth, happy that my fight would be the last thing I tasted, if this was really the end.

"Cunt!" he screamed, voice garbled and wet.

Then he threw me.

No ceremony. No long monologue like the villains did in the movies to give the heroes time to get there to save the day.

Nothing.

The water hit me fast and cold.

Though I hadn't been expecting it, I managed to hold my breath just before I made impact. I sank, immediately, all the way to the bottom. I tried to kick my legs, flail my body, nothing moved.

But I should come back to the surface, shouldn't I? Humans were buoyant.

I did begin to float up just a little, enough to spark hope. But I stopped somewhere in the water, I had no idea how far I was from the top. But it didn't matter how close or far I was. I wasn't there. My limbs didn't work. My lungs were burning.

But I could see. Everything. Most importantly, I could trace the face of my watch, sparkling above the handcuff at my wrist.

I knew I shouldn't be able to see this clearly. I knew that I most likely wasn't seeing this clearly, this was probably some kind of hallucination that my brain conjured to distract me from the fact I was dying.

I didn't care.

I just stared at the glittering metal, reflecting in the water, and I let it distract me from the burning in my lungs, from the panic in my soul and the breaking of my heart.

The hands were still moving, counting down the moments I

had left. Real moments. Not the ones that Lance gave me. The endless moments.

This would end soon.

I would end soon.

Lance

He was on the freeway, driving when they got it.

He'd been driving everywhere. To every location they could think of. He was driving because he couldn't sit in that fucking office idle.

Keltan called him. Told him what they needed. What he needed.

They got the intel on where she was.

Wire got it.

No fucking clue how. Fucker probably hacked into a satellite for all he knew. Lance didn't care how they got the intel, just that they had it.

The second he heard the location, his blood froze. Snow covered him. It coursed through his blood. For a moment, he wasn't on the freeway in the sunshine, he was driving mountain roads on Christmas Eve, seeing flashing lights and a crushed vehicle.

"Lance?" Keltan's voice on the other end of the phone snapped him back.

His fists tightened around the steering wheel and he forced his focus here, in the present, where Elena needed him.

"I'm closest," he clipped.

He wasn't, but putting his foot flat on the gas, he would be.

Then he hung up the phone.

His mind didn't go anywhere on the drive. Not one single place. Not the past, not the future, the one where he didn't get there in time, nothing. Just on driving as fast as he could.

That's where his mind was, nowhere, when he pulled into the parking lot, where he kept the lights on to illuminate the figure at the end of the dock. He reached to his glove compartment, snatching the high-powered flashlight he always kept there. His other hand held his gun. He was still thinking of nothing while he ran down that dock, plugged two rounds into each leg of the man watching the water. He was screaming, the man, until Lance lifted him by the shoulder and cold-cocked him with the butt of his gun.

He wasn't going to waste time securing him, knowing Heath was seconds behind him, he'd gotten a text to say as much.

So he was still thinking of nothing right up until he shone the torch around the dock looking for her, and right until the light illuminated the water, and showed a couple of bubbles. He didn't hesitate then. He dove into the water.

He couldn't see shit, but he saw enough. He saw her.

She wasn't moving.

She didn't move when he got to her. Not when he clutched her body to his and swam to the surface.

Not when Heath, standing on the edge of the wharf, hauled her out of his arms and started CPR on her.

She was still unmoving, apart from the limp jerk to her body from Heath's compressions, when he got up on the dock.

Heath let him take over. Because he had to take over. Because she had to breathe. She had to.

His lips fastened over hers.

They were cold.

Her chest wasn't moving.

"Breathe, baby," he pleaded with her pale, still face.

Footsteps thundered down the dock.

Someone cursed.

Another person, Duke, sank to his knees beside him.

He didn't take notice.

He kept with compressions. He kept breathing for Elena. She couldn't do it right now. But that's okay, he'd do it for her, just until she could do it on her own.

And she would do it on her own.

"Anyone can breathe through any kind of pain. That's why I told myself. Breathing isn't hard. It's just sometimes you have to remind yourself that. As long as you remember, breathing is easy."

"Breathing is easy, baby, remember?" he told her, hands on her chest. "Remember, cupcake? You just have to remind yourself to breathe," he whispered, right before he fastened his lips over hers.

Then he kept going.

For how long, he didn't know.

"Lance." Heath's voice was tight. Knowing. Hand on his shoulder was firm as if he was preparing to pull him away. Restrain him. "She's..."

"Get your hand off me," he snarled, not stopping and not moving his eyes from Elena's face. "She's going to breathe. She's just forgotten that it's easy."

The hand left his shoulder.

He kept going.

He kept breathing life into Elena.

Until she did it for herself.

Until she remembered.

CHAPTER TWENTY-EIGHT

Elena

I DIDN'T COME awake slowly, there was no smooth, easy transition from unconsciousness, or death—I was sure I'd been pretty close to it—to wakefulness.

No, I came awake just like those people in movies who jerk up in their bed with a gasp. Except I couldn't sit up. I tried, my entire body was being held down by cement blocks.

My eyes shot open, not seeing anything covering my body but a thin, hospital issue blanket.

I choked on the air I was gulping hungrily, desperately, in my dream, my nightmare, my death—whatever it had been that came before this—had stolen a lot of air from my lungs. All I could remember was needing to breathe, to inhale and exhale against the pain, but not being able to.

I didn't care about the choking, the fact I may or may not be coming back from the dead, or that I couldn't move my body. There was one thought, one terrifying thought that bounced around my head and clutched my thundering heart.

I needed to yell, I needed to call to him but I couldn't say anything around my hacking.

There was pressure at my wrist. A lot of it. To the point of pain. But I liked that. I needed it. A focus point. An anchor.

I knew who was giving me that gift of pain, and I relaxed, only slightly but enough so my coughing started to calm down.

Lance leaned forward, bringing my hand up to his mouth and laying his lips on it for half a second before his eyes met mine.

"Nathan is fine," he said, knowing me, knowing exactly what I was trying to say. What my soul was screaming silently.

Everything in me relaxed, my heart began to slow down, I stopped gulping for air so desperately. Lance would not lie to me. If he said Nathan was fine, then there wasn't a thing wrong with my little boy. He was safe.

My son is safe.

I chanted that for the entire time it took to get my breathing under control.

Lance watched me the whole time I did so, never breaking eye contact, never relieving the pressure on my wrist.

When I was done, breathing easily, he spoke again.

"I'm buyin' you a ranch, goats and fuckin' dogs," Lance declared, forehead against mine. "And you're not arguin' about shit."

I blinked. Multiple times. From the words underneath his words. The pain, the joy, the panic, the fear in his tone. "That's a really weird thing to say to someone immediately after they become conscious," I responded, my voice raspy and thick, like it had been after the fire.

He didn't reply to that. "And you're marrying me."

I blinked again. My stomach dropped while my heart soared.

"I'm not having an argument about that either. We can have any kind of wedding you want, don't give a fuck where it is, how many people come, if it's officiated by a shaman—as long as the state of California recognizes that—all I care is that you're marrying me." He paused, not long enough for me to breathe through all the beauty he was giving me after some of the ugliest experiences of my life. "I'm adopting Nathan. As long as he wants that. As long as you want that. You want to wait, make sure I'm serious, give me time to prove I'm gonna stay, then we can do that." He stroked my face. "I'll prove to you, and Nathan, that you're getting nothing less than forever with me. But at some point, I want that boy to be mine. I already consider him that. Love him. But I want it to be official. So it's up to you, both of you when that happens. But it's gonna happen. And we're getting the ranch." He paused, eyes shimmering. "You're getting your dream, baby. No more nightmares."

Then he kissed me.

Long, slow, tender. So unlike Lance. But at the same time, it belonged to this new, tender, vulnerable part of him.

I was not at all happy when he stopped kissing me, but I did realize that I was in a hospital bed, after almost drowning. I probably shouldn't be making out with my boyfriend—I guess fiancé now, queue interior excited girly scream—in my hospital bed.

He didn't move all the way back from me, just far enough so I could see his eyes, take in the face I'd been so sure I'd never see again. Emotions struggled for dominance in my body, the need to sob uncontrollably with happiness was probably going to win. I needed to hold it together, because Lance was looking at me expectantly, like he wanted some kind of response to some of the beautiful words any human being had spoken, like ever, even if they were spoken in his hard, 'this is a forgone conclusion' kind of way.

What did I say to that?

To the man who not only wanted to give me my dream, but was making it clear I was getting it, whether I liked it or not.

What did I say to him proposing marriage to me? To him

wanting to make me his? More importantly, wanting to make my son his?

"Okay," I whispered, my voice choked with tears.

He blinked. "Okay?" he repeated.

I nodded, because I didn't trust myself to speak right now.

"To what?" he asked.

"All of it," I said. "The dream." I moved my hand upward to cup his face. "To you."

He blinked again. Then a single tear trailed down his cheek. He pressed his forehead to mine once more. "Never been more afraid in my life, Elena," he murmured, voice fractured. His strong man façade was falling. Cracking. I understood that he most likely had it firmly in place the entire time I'd been missing. He would have been purposeful, scary, badass.

But now, he was breaking apart. And he was doing it with me.

So I let him.

"It's okay," I whispered. "You saved me. Like I knew you would."

His eyes shimmered. "I almost didn't," he choked out. "I was almost too late, Elena. If I had been—"

"You weren't," I interrupted him, not needing him to torture himself with a false future. "You weren't too late."

His jaw was hard and he continued to stare at me, watching me breathe, as if he needed to do that in order to remind himself that he wasn't too late.

I didn't speak. I gave him what he needed.

It took a few minutes. No, it didn't. It took a moment. A beautiful, Lance moment. I basked in it. A moment I didn't think I'd ever have. My gaze went down to my wrist that Lance wasn't holding, panicked that it wouldn't be there, the thing that measured minutes, not moments.

It was there.

I let out a relieved exhale. I would never take breathing for granted again. No matter how bad my pain was, still being able to breathe was a gift. But looking from the man in front of me to the watch at my wrist, I knew that I wouldn't have to breathe through pain again.

Lance's large hand moved so his fingers could trace the smooth face. "I put it back on you once the doctors finished. Wanted something of mine on you." His fingers moved to my fourth finger. "Will make sure you've always got somethin' of mine on you."

"I can't take any more of your sweet, it might just kill me, and I already escaped death once," I told him, my voice a whisper.

His gaze darted up, eyes sharp. "We don't joke about you almost dyin', Elena," he clipped.

I smiled. "Ah, there's my badass asshole."

He glared at me, but then kissed me.

"Nathan," I whispered once he was done. As much as I wanted to continue kissing Lance, have his hands on my skin and his promises in my heart, I needed to see my son.

Lance got this, most likely better than most parents, because he didn't get to do that with Nick. He would never. Feeling the fear I had felt for Nathan when I thought Robert had him, I couldn't fathom how Lance was able to do things like walk around and breathe without his son.

Then again, human beings had the ability to breathe through the most unimaginable kinds of pain.

He was living proof.

"He's outside," he said, moving from my bed to stand. "With Karen, Eliza, Rosie, Polly, Lucy, Bobby, Esther, Logan, the whole team. Didn't think you'd want him in here until you woke up. Didn't want to scare him anymore. Kid's bein' brave, and got enough distractions, but he's worried about his mom."

My heart clenched. My sensitive little boy would definitely

be putting on a brave face, especially around the men he considered heroes. But this was a lot for him. When he'd already gone through too much. I suddenly had an overwhelming urge to hold my boy in my arms, never let him go, never let him experience anything hard or painful ever again.

But that wasn't how it worked.

Lance leaned in to kiss my head and then turned to leave the room.

He paused, about halfway to the door. Turned. Eyes found mine, as always.

"I love you," he said, the words floating across the room and hitting me square in the chest. The words took over my whole body. My soul.

I knew that he loved me, of course. A man like Lance didn't do the things he did for me and Nathan if he didn't love us. He showed us every day. He showed me by leaving—even though I didn't realize that at the time. He showed me by coming back.

Showed me with the watch at my wrist.

By taking Nathan fishing.

By coming to church.

And a thousand and one other ways, he showed me his love. Some of them sweet, some of them not. Because Lance wasn't sweet. Tender. Life had taken that away from him. The ability to love tender.

He loved me with a cruelty that shouldn't exist. A kind of cruel he wore like a second skin. But I would take his cruel love over any other man's sweet infatuation. I would suffer with him before I'd smile with anyone else.

He didn't wait for me to respond, just turned and walked out the door, taking half of my heart with him. He soon returned, with the rest of my heart standing right beside him, holding his hand.

Nathan didn't let go of his hand for the entire walk to my

bed. His eyes were wide, taking me in, lip wobbling slightly, brows furrowed. Lance was right, my boy was trying his hardest to be strong. He approached the bed tentatively, not jumping on it like he did in the mornings, not worrying about a limb or organ he was squashing. He climbed up very slowly, with Lance's help. He crawled up to my head so his little hand could cradle my cheek.

"You feel better now, Momma?" he asked, voice quiet.

I had to breathe through a lot of pain at that moment. The pain at what had been done to my child, what I could never take back. The pain at thinking I was almost taken away from him.

But I wasn't.

So I could breathe.

Because of the little hand on my cheek. Because of the man standing beside the bed, his large hand on Nathan's small back. Because of all the people in the waiting room.

Because my nightmare had finally ended.

It was time for the dream to begin.

"Yeah, baby," I whispered. "Momma feels so much better."

THEY LET me out of the hospital later the next day. I'd been unconscious for a few hours after they admitted me, and since Lance had already done the job of saving my life, I was physically okay, apart from being told to 'take it easy,' as if that were something possible in my chaotic life.

It started with all the people in the waiting room, all of whom refused to leave until they saw me. Lance was like a frickin' prison guard, monitoring the number of people in the room at one time and barking at them when their 'time was up.'

Though of course Rosie didn't listen to that bark, merely grinned at him and blew him a kiss.

"You're officially in the club now," she said.

"What club?"

"The Greenstone Security Old Lady club. It's practically required to like almost die or be kidnapped or whatever to get in. We're very exclusive, you know." She winked at me, her words light and teasing. But there was a darkness behind her eyes too. A pain.

Someone else breathing through it all.

She squeezed my hand, kissed my head and promised to be back once I was able to walk and drink.

Lucy and Polly were there too, Polly giving me a Rhodochrosite stone, for healing. I clutched the cool, smooth stone in my hands the entire way home.

Eliza and Karen didn't listen to Lance's commands either. Both were pale, shocked and tearful.

"I'm okay," I told them.

Eliza raised her brow, but then she looked to where Nathan was dutifully reading his picture book, to Lance, standing in his badass stance right beside him, then back to me. "Yeah, you are," she said.

Logan and Esther looked pale also. I knew their hatred for hospitals, the sterile smell and long hallways too much of a reminder of what they'd lost. But they came anyway. Because they were family.

So back at home, with my boys, the smaller one fast asleep in his bed, the bigger one I was using for a pillow.

A naked one.

Lance had just made slow, tender, beautiful love to me. Every touch, every kiss was worship. I was filled with reverence, covered in evidence that the world had not killed all his gentle.

We hadn't spoken in a long time.

We didn't need to.

"I didn't kill him," he said, breaking the silence.

I knew exactly who he was talking about, the man I hadn't even mentioned since I'd woken up. Sure a lot of people would need to know immediately what happened to the ex-husband that kidnapped and tried to drown them. But I wasn't a lot of people. Robert didn't matter to me. Not in the moments I had with Lance, with my son, the rest of my friends and family. He didn't get that. Didn't get to pollute that.

"Why?" I asked, surprised at the sentence, surprised this was the first time I'd even thought about Robert breathing in the world at all. He had taken me in order to make sure I didn't forget him, that he was the last thing I thought of before I took my last breath. He was wrong on that score. And after I took my first breath, it wasn't him I thought of either.

Now I thought of him. Now, I was surprised he was still breathing.

I realized that I had expected Lance to kill him. Despite what he'd promised me in the Greenstone Security offices in another lifetime.

It didn't bother me, that single broken promise. Because I knew that Lance would keep every other promise he'd made to me.

I understand Lance now. As much as anyone could understand a man like that. As much as a human could understand another human being. I knew that he needed to eliminate every threat to his sanity that he could eliminate. Nathan and I were his sanity now. I got that. Because he was part of mine. Part of Nathan's. Lance had lost his whole family in the past. Due to factors he couldn't control. Factors no human, no matter how badass, could control. Robert was a factor he could control. A *threat* he could control. He didn't eliminate him before all this, because he was respecting my wishes. Respecting me. Nathan.

All that changed when Robert almost killed me. When

Robert gave Lance a taste of the horror that no human being should have to go through once, let alone twice.

So in my eyes, his life was forfeit.

The promise was forfeit.

Except that it wasn't.

Lance had never broken a promise to me, and he never would.

EPILOGUE

Twenty Years Later

WHEN WE WALKED into the small room, Nathan nodded at Lance with a side smirk on his face. My heart clenched with that look. Because it was one he'd learned from his father.

Not the man currently serving a life sentence in a prison three states away.

No, the man standing beside me, holding me by my waist because he likely knew that I couldn't stand up in front of by my own power.

In front of my firstborn mimicking his true father with a smile that we'd managed to tease from him. He was as handsome as Lance was when he did it too. My Nathan had grown into a man sometime when I wasn't paying attention. Sometime when I was trying to wrangle twin girls and grow my business. Then move my whole family to our home on a ranch two hours outside of LA.

My life had not slowed down in the past twenty years.

Not a single bit.

It had started moving so fast, it would all be a blur if it weren't for the man at my side, holding my hip, keeping me grounded. The man who bought me my ranch. Gave me my daughters. Gave our son that smirk on his face.

"Captain," Nathan said, his deep husky voice thicker than normal.

I leaned on Lance even more and his grip tightened.

Nathan may have changed a lot since he was five years old. Grown at least a head taller than his mom. Gained some pretty impressive muscles to rival his father, shown that he was the best big brother and man I could have ever hoped to raise. Played in the NFL and moved to New England into some big fancy mansion with his girlfriend—soon to be wife—Samantha.

He'd changed so much that it took me a second to realize that this beautiful, talented man was my son.

He had never stopped calling Lance Captain. Not when he was going through—a thankfully very short—rebellious teenage stage when it might have been very uncool to refer to your father as a Marvel hero. Not when he graduated high school, or college.

Lance was always his Captain.

Today was no different.

"Son," Lance said, his own low voice much thicker than usual.

Lance hadn't changed a lot over the past twenty years. His hair was now grayed at the edges. He'd grown a mustache that he somehow pulled off in a big way. His face tanned with the work he did on the ranch, lined with the worry he always had about his teenage girls and the smiles they gave him. His muscles were still there, due to the fact he worked out every day.

He still didn't say much to people that weren't his wife or his children. Didn't smile at those people either. But he was softer. He was no longer a hard edge. He smirked. He made dry jokes. He even laughed.

And he cried. On three occasions. Our wedding day. The day our daughters were born. And the day Nathan spoke about him in his college graduation speech. About his father, his Captain being his hero.

He didn't mention Nick. Sandra. His parents. Not since he told me about them. But every Christmas Eve, we went to a diner in town, had a family dinner, and we lit a special candle we put out every year for that reason.

Rosie was right, that would always be a wound.

But there were no longer any fresh cuts.

"Proud of you," Lance continued talking to the man in the tux, our son. Our son that was about to get married to his high school sweetheart. Money, fame and the fast life had not changed the way he loved Samantha or the way he treated her.

Lance taught him many of the things that made him treat her that way. I taught him others. I knew that my son would love that girl with everything in him. I knew he'd fight for her, protect her and work as hard as he could to make the marriage work.

My hopes were so very high for them. And I still had the ability to do that. Hope.

"We're *both* so very proud of you," Lance continued. "Know your mom isn't speakin' right now because she doesn't have the ability since she's runnin' through your entire life in her head and is likely two seconds away from burstin' into tears. Then she'll yell at me for lettin' her cry 'cause she promised me to stop her from doing that 'cause she'd ruin her makeup."

I glared at him. "Which I'm doing right now," I hissed.

He only smiled and kissed my head, which made me cry more.

"I'll take over for a sec, Captain," my son said.

I felt myself being passed between the two most important men in my life. Nathan's lips pressed into my hair, that also had silver in it, artfully covered by my amazing stylist. "Proud of you, Mom," he murmured into my head.

I tried to hold myself together and not sob into my son's nice tux.

"You gave me this life," he whispered. "You gave me the ability for all of this. I know you saved both of our lives. Not just that day you carried me out of a burning building, but the day you walked away with nothing but me. You were *my age*. I don't know if I'd be brave enough to do what you did."

I didn't give a fuck about my makeup now. Lucy was somewhere in the house, and she was a magician with the stuff, she'd fix me before the ceremony.

"Yes you would," I whispered, stroking my son's smooth face. "We raised a beautiful, kind, strong kid, your dad and I. You would do exactly what I did and more. You will do more. I'm not talking about scoring more touchdowns or whatever."

Nathan rolled his eyes. "Your son plays for one of the most famous teams in the NFL and still you know nothing about the sport."

I grinned through my tears. "You know I'm very excited about all your successes. But I'm not talking about money or trophies. I'm meaning being a good husband. A father, when you're ready." I narrowed my eyes. My son was young to be getting married, but I supported that on the proviso he still lived some more of his carefree life before kids. That, and I was too young to be a grandmother. "You're the best son I could ever ask for. You're the one that saved my life."

"Mine too," Lance added, his voice that special, rare kind of soft. He laid his hand on Nathan's shoulder. "Didn't think I had a life to save, buddy. But you and your mom proved me wrong."

Nathan bit his lip in a gesture that was so like my little boy and nothing like the man he'd become. I very nearly lost it right there, but my men helped me keep it together.

I stepped back, straightening Nathan's tie and messing with his hair in a way that was little more than second nature to me. He didn't flinch away from me as he usually did in adulthood, he stood there and dutifully let me do what I needed to do. And then, he broke my fucking heart by lifting his large hand and twirling some of my hair in his fingers just as he'd done when his hands were much tinier.

It wasn't for long, the hair twist, most likely because he knew I'd break down into a sobbing mess if he held our beautiful past in his fingers.

He let my hair go, I swallowed my tears.

Then I admired him. My boy.

My man.

"Alright, you ready for chaos?" I asked him. Because it's a way of life for us.

He grinned. "Yeah, Mom. All I've ever known is chaos, and it's all I'll ever want."

I bit my lip at this, to stop the tears. Nathan saw this, so he leaned in, kissed my head and murmured, "I'll see you out there. Love you, Mom."

Then he looked to Lance. "You'll take care of her?"

I was immediately in my husband's arms. "Always," he promised.

And like the last twenty years, he didn't break that promise.

ACKNOWLEDGMENTS

Ah, where do I start when I talk about this book?

I feel like I always talk about how hard my books were to write here. How they drove me crazy. Tore out my soul. Took my heart hostage.

This book did all those things.

But it wasn't *hard* to write.

Not at the start, at least.

The first half of this story poured out of me. My fingers could barely keep up. I hadn't even intended on writing about Lance yet. Duke was meant to be next.

But you know what they say about best laid plans.

Lance was demanding.

Even though the words came quickly, the story came slow. This is unusual for me. I don't really write slow burn. But it took me a while to learn who the characters were. To understand this story needed to be the monster it was.

I so hope you agree with me.

Now, let's get to the people I have to thank.

There's a lot of them.

I will always talk about how lucky I am in this part of my book. Because I am. I am so blessed to have a tribe of people around me who love me, support me, understand me. I know that not everyone has that. I know how rare it is.

Mum. You know the drill by this point. You are always here, right at the top. Because I would not be here, typing this, without you. You made me into the woman I am. You always support my good decisions. And you support my bad ones too. I know not everyone is as lucky as I am to have their mum as their best friend, and I count my blessings every day that I've got you. Thank you for always picking up the phone when I call. For understanding I get manic when I need to vent. For sending me chocolate from the other side of the world.

Dad. You can't read this, but I know you're somewhere, having a beer, watching over me. I miss you always.

Taylor. Life just continues to get better with you. We've been through what feels like a lifetime already. I'm so very grateful we found our way to each other. Thank you for being my best friend. For understanding that sometimes I have to watch makeup tutorials on YouTube to calm down. For knowing that *Breakfast at Tiffany's* is my movie when I'm feeling blue. Thank you for not judging how much chocolate I eat, or that I eat it for breakfast.

Your strength, kindness and passion inspires me every day.

Forever and then some, babe.

Jessica Gadziala. You have been my constant support through so many meltdowns and dark periods of my life. You read this book when I freaked out and thought people would hate it. I cannot say how much it means to me to have you in my corner. You're my #sisterqueen.

Michelle Clay. I don't even know what to say about you. You are one of the most special people in my life. You do so much for me and many other people without expecting anything in return. You support me, cheer for me and help me through so much. I am forever grateful that my words brought us together.

Annette Brignac. Another woman who is one of a kind. Thank you for being in my life. Thank you for reading my books. I am honoured to call you a friend. You are one of the best people I know. My life would not be the same without you. To the moon.

My girls, Polly & Emma. You're a whole world away from me and it breaks my heart. I miss you both every single day but I also know that no amount of time or distance will change our friendship. You two are my soulmates.

My betas, Sarah, Ginny, Amy and Caro. You ladies save me. Seriously. Thank you for reading my books when they are at their most raw. Thank you for helping turn them into what they end up being.

Ellie. Thank you for dealing with me. For editing this book. For not changing my voice. For being fucking amazing.

And you, the reader. Thank you. From the bottom of my heart, I thank you. You are why I'm still here, creating characters, writing stories. You've made my dreams come true.

ABOUT THE AUTHOR

ANNE MALCOM has been an avid reader since before she can remember, her mother responsible for her love of reading. It started with magical journeys into the world of Hogwarts and Middle Earth, then as she grew up her reading tastes grew with her. Her love of reading doesn't discriminate, she reads across many genres, although classics like Little Women and Gone with the Wind will hold special places in her heart. She also can't get enough romance, especially when some possessive alpha males throw their weight around.

One day, in a reading slump, Cade and Gwen's story came to her and started taking up space in her head until she put their story into words. Now that she has started, it doesn't look like she's going to stop anytime soon, with many more characters demanding their story be told as well.

Raised in small town New Zealand, Anne had a truly special childhood, growing up in one of the most beautiful countries in the world. She has backpacked across Europe, ridden camels in the Sahara and eaten her way through Italy, loving every moment. She's currently living London, loving life and traveling as much as humanly possible.

Want to get in touch with Anne? She loves to hear from her readers.

You can email her: annemalcomauthor@hotmail.com
Or join her reader group on Facebook.

ALSO BY ANNE MALCOM

The Sons of Templar Series

Making the Cut

Firestorm

Outside the Lines

Out of the Ashes

Beyond the Horizon

Dauntless

Battles of the Broken

Hollow Hearts

Deadline to Damnation

The Unquiet Mind Series

Echoes of Silence

Skeletons of Us

Broken Shelves

Mistake's Melody

Greenstone Security

Still Waters

Shield

The Problem With Peace

The Vein Chronicles

Fatal Harmony

Deathless

Faults in Fate

Eternity's Awakening

Standalones

Birds of Paradise

Doyenne

Made in the USA
Monee, IL
21 November 2024

70761440R00233